J.N. CHANEY
TERRY MAGGERT

VARIANT
PUBLICATIONS

LAS VEGAS, NV • PORTLAND, TN

CONNECT WITH J.N. CHANEY

Don't miss out on these exclusive perks:

- Instant access to free short stories from series like *The Messenger*, *Starcaster*, and more.
- Receive email updates for new releases and other news.
- Get notified when we run special deals on books and audiobooks.

So, what are you waiting for? Enter your email address at the link below to stay in the loop.

https://www.jnchaney.com/peacemaker-wars-subscribe

CONNECT WITH TERRY MAGGERT

Check out his website

http://terrymaggert.com/

Connect on Facebook

https://www.facebook.com/terrymaggertbooks/

Follow him on Amazon

https://www.amazon.com/Terry-Maggert/e/B00EKN8RHG/

JOIN THE CONVERSATION

Join the conversation and get updates on new and upcoming releases in the awesomely active **Facebook group**, "JN Chaney's Renegade Readers."

This is a hotspot where readers come together and share their lives and interests, discuss the series, and speak directly to J.N. Chaney and his co-authors.

facebook.com/groups/jnchaneyreaders

CONTENTS

1

Mark rolled the *Fafnir* forty-eight degrees to starboard and nosed down to match the escaping ship. It was small and disturbingly nimble for a freighter, which caused more problems than he had originally anticipated.

Their target's icon drifted right on his overlay, then veered violently left and up, moving almost completely out of view.

"Come on, Tudor. They're wheeling out of our targeting vector. Slippery little bastards, you know. Oh, and Valint is counting on us," Netty added. "I know you'll do your gosh-darned best."

"I'll take your message to heart. I sure do enjoy the sense of family," Mark said, casting an arch look at the controls.

"I saw that," Netty said.

Mark put a hand to his chest. "Saw what?"

"The tone."

Perry turned, beak open, laughing. "Tone? In a look? Very multidimensional of you."

Netty didn't hesitate. "Yes. He was smarmy."

Mark snorted. "Wait until you hear me use my soldier's voice."

"Heard it. Daily. For years, now. With that in mind, Valint is pouring on the power, too," Netty said.

The *Stormshadow* followed in their wake, burning hard, but both ships struggled to keep up with the freighter.

"How is this thing so unreasonably fast?" Valint asked, her voice cutting in through the cockpit speakers.

"It's heavily armored but undersized for a class ten," Perry said, reading off his screen. "Nothing much in terms of defense, but it's a rabbit—all drive and reactor. This thing is made to outrun danger."

Mark pushed the throttle forward again, his b-suit responding to the increasing g's. The *Stormshadow* fired lasers, but the smuggler ship rolled and accelerated again.

"We need to take out his drive. We can't match this rate, and he'll dust us," Valint said.

Mark rolled hard right and wrenched the stick up as their target abruptly changed vector and speed. "Damn, this guy isn't just fast, but squirrely."

"Smugglers have a tendency to get that way when you start shooting at them," Perry offered from his perch atop the co-pilot's seat.

"Netty, get a lock and fire. We're losing this race," Mark growled, ignoring the bird as the smuggler accelerated again. It was enough of a battle to keep the ship in sight, let alone try and close the gap.

"Working on it," Netty chimed in. "Firing."

The Invictus gun system hummed, emitting two rapid-fire bursts of energy. The first shots hit but missed the mark—the fleeing vessel's drive cone—while the second burst went wide right.

"Shit. I missed."

"Language, Netty. Language," Perry said. "You know that we're a paragon of culture and manners. And stuff."

"You try hitting a spot two meters square on a constantly moving target. And one that's speeding away from us at a rate of four thousand yards per minute. Mark, more speed."

"We're running as hot as we can," Mark replied, grimacing as he pushed for added thrust. The *Fafnir* rocketed forward, finally allowing them to close on the enemy ship. Something snapped on the ship's interior behind him, and he caught a whiff of chemicals.

"Anything serious?" Mark asked.

Perry raised a wingshoulder. "Not now. Or even later. Sally forth, young Tudor."

"Sallying. If that's even a verb."

"It is if you read the classics, farm boy," Perry countered.

They fired again, scoring hits on the armored ship's port side.

Mark scanned the data and made his call. "Netty, line up a shot but stage the laser left. Valint, on our signal, fire a missile and target that ship's belly."

"Why left?"

"I want to set this guy up. If we launch for his belly and starboard side, he's more likely to launch countermeasures and bank away from the shot. Correct?"

"Confirmed," Perry said. "Statistical analysis indicates that ninety percent of biological organisms will instinctively veer away on a flat plane rather than push vertical. It's one way to dictate what they do unless that ship's piloted by an AI, which would account for the erratic course changes. But, in general, your strategy is sound, Mark. I've got a bird ready to fly. Valint, are you ready?"

"We're prepped to fly."

"I was built ready," Netty chimed.

"Launch," Mark said, steering to keep the ship firmly in their sights.

Their Whisperwing flashed away, a smaller and slightly slower bird than Valint's Firewing. Their prey launched flares, and as Mark had hoped, rolled hard to port.

Netty fired three quick bursts, the first laser shots hitting the aft armor panel, but the second and third walked right into the drive cone. The smuggler's drive flashed brightly and gave a burp of dissipating plasma, then in a moment of triumph, their plume went dark.

"Score one for the good guys. Their drive is cooked," Netty crowed.

"Fine shooting, Netty. Take us in. Perry, you keep weapons trained on that thing. I don't like surprises, and I also don't like holes in me." When Perry made to speak, Mark held up a finger. "Unnatural holes in me."

"Excellent distinction," Perry said.

"Taking us in, boss. Speed?" Netty asked.

"Slow and slower. We're easing into this badger den. Don't like it, frankly," Mark admitted.

Netty navigated the *Fafnir* onward, circling the disabled freighter as Valint moved her own ship, tow grapple extended. The crippled ten spun on its long axis, the space around it filled with a whirling cloud of debris. Its aft radiator panels were cold, but the ship was venting plasma from its drive cone where their laser had scored the kill shot.

Mark watched his partner work, digesting the information as Netty worked to collect more data. The smuggler ship was a peculiar-looking vessel, beyond the obvious lack of weapons. It had no portholes or windows or openings to speak of. No forward comm node, hardly any vectoring thrusters, and more armor plating than any ship its size reasonably should.

"Looks more like a missile than a ship," Mark said.

"You're damned close to the truth," Netty replied. "Beyond the reactor, I'm struggling to pick up any thermal signatures on the inside. It might not even be pressurized."

"Meaning what? That it has no crew?"

"It's not unusual to use AIs to run ships," Perry said. "And without having to worry about injuring biological crew members, the ships can accelerate and change directions faster."

"Add the right stealth coating, and you'd have an ideal setup for a smuggler."

"That is, unless someone knows your route and schedule, then parks a couple lean, mean hunting machines in the way."

"It's easy to be a successful hunter when you know exactly where your prey will be and when. It won't always be this easy," Mark said as he unhooked from his harness. "Let's go see what the Daysun Collective was smuggling on this ship."

"Right behind you."

Mark suited up, and Perry stood ready as Valint circled, weapons up. They moved into the airlock, but he knew something was off as soon as the outer door opened. The hatch on the other ship hadn't just been welded shut but reinforced and braced with strips of armor plating.

"Well, that sucks. With all that bullshit on there, someone would have to cut the welds and pull it all off. Only then could you cycle the doors open," Perry said after examining the handiwork.

"Allow me to present an alternate tactic, bird," Mark said, drawing the Moonsword. He jammed the weapon right into the metal and cut down, then pulled it free and made three more cuts. When he finished, a perfect square—roughly three feet by three feet —fell in and rattled loud against the deck.

"Show-off," Perry stated.

"If you can do it—" Mark started.

"Then it ain't braggin', I gotcha," Perry finished, then turned, his eyes flashing amber readiness.

They stepped through and into the other airlock, Mark's b-suit lights turning on automatically in the dark. The inside door had been welded shut as well, and it had the same strips of armor plating.

He finished cutting through the second door, then stepped back, allowing Perry to hop through first. The bird's eyes burned with his charged stun attack. Along with the singed feathers from their siege on Chevix Station, he looked like a wild phoenix who was, frankly, sick and tired of everyone's nonsense.

He looked *dangerous*.

Revolver in hand, Mark kicked his leg through, ducked down, and pulled himself into the enemy ship. He stood on the other side and turned left. Something on the wall caught his attention, drawing him back to the airlock.

"Bird, look here," Mark said, shining his lights on the outer bulkhead.

The combat unit whistled low as he took in the ring of explosive packs secured in place around the doorway. The wiring ran down the far side, where it snaked into the airlock's control panel.

"It's rigged to blow as soon as someone tries to open the airlock, boss. If we'd taken the time to strip away that banding—"

"Boom," Mark finished for him, quietly. "And then a violent decompression of both ships. That's a bad day."

"The scoundrels," Perry muttered. "Although, they didn't foresee you cutting through with a sword. Another win for the blade. Their loss is our gain."

After turning right, Mark lifted the revolver and quickly swept back through the aft portion of the ship. But he immediately clocked there was no crew on board, nor was there room for any, as cargo had been stacked in every available space.

The galley and living areas were stripped out completely, leaving the interior of the armored ship bare. When they found their way forward again, Mark had to cut his way into the cockpit.

Stepping inside, Perry cursed with the skill of an aged stable hand. And then—he *repeated* it.

The interior was cold, tainted by the debris of burning insulation and scorched electronics. Despite the obvious damage, Mark could see no fire.

Perry circled a macabre scene—a Synth had been bolted into place where a pilot's seat would be. The artificial being's arms and legs had been removed, while a mess of cables and wires wound up and around its torso, before disappearing into an oversized harness affixed to the back of its head.

The Synth wasn't alive, in either the biological or the artificial sense. Its eyes were missing, the synthetic skin around them scorched black and melted. Scattered ashes surrounded the ship's former pilot, with white gas leaking from two canister-shaped devices wired to its chest.

"This is—Mark, this is—" Perry stared at the scene in open horror. He spread his wings, feathers rustling, before leaning in to examine the Synth more closely. After all, he was a professional.

"Evil? Vicious?" Mark prompted, but his tone was soft.

"Barbaric," Perry corrected. "They stripped it down and hard-wired it into the ship, giving it no choice but to fly their cargo. But they didn't stop there. They rigged it with overcharge canisters as a fail-safe. Just like the airlocks."

"But we didn't come through, at least not in the way they'd planned."

"No. But they likely programmed in proximity protocols, and as soon as we docked, the overcharge canisters went off and fried this poor bastard. Judging from the look and condition of the place, every system in this hulk is now worthless. And if we *had* come through the airlock, those charges would have decompressed both ships, killed you, cooked the Synth pilot, and scattered the cargo into space."

"Effective," Mark allowed, revulsion in every syllable.

Perry was nearly speechless. "I can't—this is just so—"

"Disgusting? Repulsive? Amoral?" Netty finished for him.

"All the above," Perry said, his voice fading to a hiss.

"Let's find out what was so sensitive that they were willing to fry their pilot and destroy their ship to keep it out of our hands."

Perry's wings snapped into place. "Let's."

Mark and Perry moved back out of the cockpit and stopped at the first stack of crates. He pulled one off the top, unlatched the lid, and lifted it free. The crate was stacked neatly with clear, molded packages, each holding a small blue device. He pulled one free and knelt down so Perry could see.

"Interesting."

"Meaning?" Mark asked, turning the package over. He found a label on the front, featuring two words in stylized print—*Cavu Lixil*.

"There are no records of any products, brands, legal or illegal drugs, licensed treatments, or approved therapies by that name. Which means this is. . . something else. Although the name has meaning. In three of the trade languages, a *Cavu Lixil* is a sepal structure that forms to protect a flower in its budding form. And, ah, that speaks for itself," Perry reasoned.

"Wait. A drug?" Mark asked, studying the device housed in the plastic shell. It didn't look like any drug delivery device he'd seen before... more like a breathing mask, but it also included formed goggles. "Sounds ominous, but looks like a mask. Could it be used for swimming underwater?"

"It would seem to fit the bill, but why would we find trace amounts of hallucinogens?" Perry asked. "I'm also detecting trace amounts of neuro-stims on the packaging. Boss, these are both type two controlled substances, not surprising, though. Inhalants seem to be the new fad amongst artificial stim producers. It's the most cost-effective delivery method, after all. Perhaps it's designed to induce a very specific and localized visual illusion—something only the wearer can see. Think of it as a personal, drug-induced escape."

"How do we know it isn't contraband goods stolen off a legitimate freighter somewhere? Maybe the individuals moving the crates had the compounds you detected on their hands."

"Could be," Perry said, pecking at the container nearby. "Sure as hell *feels* illegal considering it's stuffed onto an illicit fast boat, running dark and at breakneck speeds on a backwater transit route that doesn't get anywhere fast," Perry explained. "I see nothing about this type of thing on the Guild boards, so that is, for now, our best guess."

"Lucky us," Mark said, managing a look of sheer disgust. "But why that kind of packaging? These masks and branding look like the impulse trash they sell to tourists on all the transit stations."

"More information is required to answer any of these questions," Perry said, pausing for effect. "Look on the bright side. You're paid a bonus on drug and contraband seizures. That takes this contract from—ah, slim, if we're being charitable—to something a bit more robust. Might pay a bill or two with this one, boss."

"How long are you boys going to take over there? Were you planning on filling me in on any details?" Valint interjected.

"They appear to be drug runners," Mark said, dropping the package back into the crate. He reached up to scratch his nose but caught himself at the last moment, his hand bouncing against his visor. Even if the ship *had* lingering atmosphere, he needed to be on total alert—trace amounts of hallucinogens on the package did not bode well for contact with his skin. Or mind.

Or general state of existence.

"And?" Valint pressed into his moment of reverie.

"Perry thinks this particular ship is full of contraband, although we're unsure at this point. The ship was run by a Synth. They rigged the airlock to blow if boarded. Unfortunately, the pilot is… crispy."

"I can't imagine Perry is happy."

"The bird is decidedly *not* happy."

"I'm coming over. Don't touch anything until I get there. We need to catalog every item for the chain of custody. Striker will provide us cover from the *Stormshadow*. Do you mind if I come in through your auxiliary hatch? The *Fafnir* is currently tying up the airlock."

"Sure, please do."

"Tell her to wear clean boots. We're not mopping every time some barbarian comes aboard straight out of the field," Perry said.

"As if you mop."

"I'm more of a supervisor. It's my natural role," Perry said as Valint cut the connection with a sharp *click* in Mark's ear.

"What the hell are you doing?" Mark asked.

"We'll be fine. She *likes* me. You, she tolerates," Perry said.

"I should drag you behind the ship on a tow cable. Make you ride outside for a while."

"You wouldn't dare."

"Oh, wouldn't I…?"

"I'm a lethal instrument of war, sir. Take care who you threaten," Perry said, spreading his wings. He hopped toward Mark, his weight making the floor panel shift and pop back into place. "What the…?"

They both leaned forward, although Mark didn't notice anything off until he looked at Perry. A patch of shiny metal flashed in his b-suit lights—a scratch on the far edge of the next floor panel.

"What have we here?" Perry said, hooking his talons into the decking and lifting it clear.

Mark helped, and together they set the panel against the wall. They turned back, only to find a dark stretch of what looked like subfloor.

"What are *we* looking for, Perry?"

The bird shrugged. "It's a smuggler's ship. It could be nothing, or it could be something really juicy."

"Literally or figuratively?"

"Either. But if it's the former, give me a chance to step back so I don't get anything splattered on my feathers. You know what they say about cleanliness?"

"I do," Mark grunted and fished around inside the floor space. There were no recesses or hidden switches, just a span of unremarkable black metal.

"Didn't Valint say to not touch anything?" Perry asked.

"We're just *looking*," Mark reasoned and leaned back. A single pair of perfectly formed handprints shone in the angled light where the oil from someone or something's hands had transferred over.

Without hesitation, he leaned forward, put his hands on the prints, and pushed.

"Okay, Mark, that isn't *looking*. That is, in fact, *touching*."

The panel sagged half an inch under his weight, and something beneath the floor clicked. When he lifted his foot, the subfloor slid to the side and out of the way.

His light flooded into the newly opened space below and gleamed off several compartments of perfectly stacked, shiny bars.

"Look at all that platinum," Perry cooed. "You realize that

Peacemakers are allowed to claim a certain percentage of spoils as a bounty, right?"

"Claim what?"

They turned together and found Valint standing inside the airlock door, one leg still sticking through the cutout. Mark rose and moved out of the way as she pulled her leg through to stand. Then she joined them, her caramel eyes shining silver from the reflection.

"No," Valint said, starting to shake her head. "We don't claim a part of this as bounty. We're going to claim *all* of it."

"Did you hear that, Mark?" Perry said, beak dropped in a laugh. "It's time to go to the bank."

2

Outward—Procyon B

"THIS IS A BOON, a blessing, a gift from the War Father. A treasure with which we'll start our glorious rebellion," Drogo said, nodding on the screen. "I say we invest it in mercenaries, that we buy a whole fleet of Eniped cutters and take the fight to the Five Star League."

"One hundred and ten platinum bars," Mark said flatly. "We found one hundred and ten platinum bars under the floor, Drogo. We aren't going to buy a small fleet of workboats with that."

"Actually," Perry cut in, "considering that platinum's value is up per ounce right now, with the estimated weight in those bars, you could buy quite a few workboats. The issue is, we won't be able to convert that much weight to bonds without garnering attention."

Vosa moved, her image almost filling the screen. She blinked, slow and deliberate, and waited a moment before speaking.

"So, we stash it for now? What's our move beyond that?"

"Perry recommends a strong box. Most banks have a 'no questions asked' policy for those," Mark said.

"Striker has done business with the Quiet Room for many cycles now—" Valint started to say.

"I do not understand," Drogo cut in, "We know who our enemies are. Why are we so concerned about garnering attention? We should be soaking the skyways with their insides. That's the way we honor Len and Rustala's deaths, by slaughtering all involved."

Perry held up a wing. "We aren't ready to take this fight to Gyl-Mareth or Cai-Demond, let alone the Five Star League. How many ships do they have? Who is involved beyond them? There are still too many unanswered questions."

"Damn the questions. Damn this interminable inaction," Valint groused.

"What changes if we take the fight to them now and we all die out here in vacuum? Do you think anyone will even know what happened?" Vosa asked.

Drogo reluctantly shook his head but did not respond.

"If we rush this, we *will* have a fight on our hands. And it's one we are not ready to win. That much is true. We need to plan, to recruit, and most of all, to gain leverage," Valint reasoned.

"Recruit who? Peacemakers or outsiders?" Drogo countered.

"Yes to both," she said, leaning on Mark's chair. He couldn't deny the electricity of her presence, the strength and confidence. But it went beyond that, to something deeper.

"We know a few of the Masters are corrupt, but that doesn't mean *all* of the Guild is against us," Mark reasoned, picking up where Valint left off. "We need to be subtle and approach some of the senior Peacemakers we trust. That feels like a good start."

"Wealth is paramount to this endeavor," Striker added, his canine-shaped head populating another window on the screen. "Like the stash of platinum Mark and Valint found—liquid wealth, not bonds. Once we go to spend it, we'll find that it does not stretch as far as one might think. The nature of this wealth means we must use different channels and pay exorbitant prices, but that's the cost of war."

"Then we must amass large amounts of wealth," Vosa said, eyes glittering with interest. Vosa liked money.

"Yes," Striker agreed. "When it's time for me to invest, I like to keep a reasonable amount on hand, and a reasonable amount put away. That's why I recommended strong boxes and not bank accounts. If Gyl-Mareth or his cohorts grow wary, they may audit the banks and freeze any accounts they deem suspicious. Strong boxes can be registered to any name or shell company, which would allow us to safely store our procured platinum. It's all offline, as well, so it would afford us a certain measure of protection."

"Better than a hole in the ground," Perry said from behind them.

"He has something to add?" Vosa asked.

Mark stepped aside so Perry could move into frame.

"These drug runners are a special breed. This speedboat was piloted by a slaved Synth, mangled, and hardwired into the ship's navigation system. It was rigged to blow the airlock and fry the pilot, along with all connected systems."

Striker went rigid on screen while Rust appeared next to Vosa. Their disgust was evident, without them having to utter a single word.

"Those foul *organisms*," Drogo said, and Mark stifled a laugh.

Since their run-in with the Association of Peaceful Skies, the big alien had not only come to adopt the term for all bad guys but had also used it often.

"Sapient beings, mutilated, and slaved to pilot illicit cargo," Striker seethed, his anger growing with each word. "Who is responsible? Do we know more?"

"All we have is the information provided from the Guild contract for this particular ship. They believed it was a single, isolated shipment. But Perry isn't so sure."

"That's a nice way of putting it," Perry admitted. "I used much more definitive language than *isn't so sure*. The Guild, in their typical nearsighted ways, locked in on this ship only. The tip out of Spindrift said nothing beyond a questionable shipment; therefore, the Guild's interest stopped there. *Fools.* Normally, I would push the issue. After all, I do enjoy pointing out when people above us in the pecking order are wrong. This time . . . this time, we won't just let them bathe in their ignorance, but we'll benefit from it, as well."

"Explain," Drogo said, leaning in until his face blurred out the whole screen.

Mark shook his head. "Valint is the only Peacemaker listed on this contract, so she will tow the ship back to Anvil Dark for impound. Perry and I will make for the Quiet Room to quietly deposit our recently acquired cargo. After that, we'll check in with a few contacts. If Perry is right, these drug runners are operating with the support of a legitimate freight and salvage business. Regular business means regular shipments. And *that* means more speedboats."

"So, what, are we going to trace it back to whatever corporation is supporting them?" Vosa asked.

"No." Perry shook his head, his eyes glowing brighter. "We are going to track and hunt *every single ship* they send out into the black. We are going to build our army with their blood money."

"Like pirates plundering the Synth-abusing sleazeballs of the universe," Striker said, nodding approvingly. "Booty, bounty, loot."

"Exactly," Mark agreed.

"Call it what you will," Perry continued without missing a beat. "We want to create multiple caches, spread across several systems, to guarantee that we will have fast and reliable access to our money. In the event something was to happen."

"Then the Quiet Room feels like a natural place to start," Valint said.

"Agreed," Striker added. "I was one of their first customers."

"No doubt highlighting your naturally suspicious nature," Perry countered.

Striker chuckled. "I'm not suspicious as much as pragmatic, you feathered hooligan."

"Valint returns to Anvil Dark with the drug runner's ship, you create our first cache, and what of Drogo and me?" Vosa asked.

"We need to recruit others to our cause, but it's almost as important to convince Gyl-Mareth, and whoever else is watching, that it's business as usual," Valint replied.

"Perhaps that's easier said than done. As you pointed out, Mark has not one but *two* corrupt Masters trying to recruit him. What happens when he is forced to decide?"

"That's a good question, Drogo," Mark said, scratching his chin. He'd pondered that very question since twisting away from Anvil Dark, and he felt no closer to an answer.

"Make a decision or pick a side?" Valint asked, her left eyebrow raising.

"What if I don't pick a side? What if I play both angles?"

"That's a dangerous game...as you're assuming they aren't secretly working together," Valint countered.

"That's one risk, yes..." He trailed off, not knowing how to continue. Luckily, no one else pushed the issue either. They were sailing into uncharted, shark-infested waters now. Danger was everywhere.

Drogo hated any idea that wasn't open warfare but finally relented and agreed to the plan. Vosa was apprehensive, but Mark found that he had less reservations about her. Surprisingly timid for a Peacemaker, she stepped up when it counted, and most importantly, she was less likely to take rash, bold action.

They parted ways then, with Valint towing the speedboat back with her to Anvil Dark. Mark made himself something to eat, showered, and tried to sit in any one place for longer than five minutes at a time. He failed miserably and wound up pacing the hall between the galley and the cockpit.

"*Must* you do that?" Perry asked as he appeared in the cockpit and moved to turn around.

"I've got too much on my mind. We are stuck in a cold war with our corrupt guild, don't really know who our enemies are, and essentially agreed to become pirates."

"Yep. Sounds about right to me. So, where is the anxiety coming from?"

"All of the above."

"That's fine, but you're going to wear a rut in the deck if you keep that up. You'll grind your legs down to bloody nubs, and how useful will you be to our rebellion like that? Stop it. Please."

"Or...?"

"I'll stun you and lock your unconscious body in your room. And before you ask, no, Netty will not stop me."

"Netty, is this true?"

"No. You're *not* dragging me into this," she said innocently.

"Back home we call that 'pleading the fifth.'"

"Then I plead the fifth."

"Fine," Mark said and dropped into the pilot's chair.

They twisted to a hole-in-the-wall refueling depot that was an exoplanet beyond the gravity well of Luyten's Star. The *Fafnir*, with only two docking points, had to wait almost four and a half hours for its turn at the pump. Mark slept through most of the wait and woke up when the umbilical disconnected. Unfortunately, his sleep wasn't restful, and when he awoke, his anxiousness hadn't dissipated.

Their next jump took them to the fourth planet out from Procyon, specifically the larger of that planet's two moons. Beacons and markers filled the approach, cluttering the airwaves with proximity pings and automated messages.

"A corvette just matched our vector and is on an intercept. They're hailing us on all public channels," Netty said.

"Is that normal?"

"For the Quiet Room? Yes. You can't think of them as a bank in the Earth sense, Mark. Out here, they function more like a sovereign state. They have their own territorial boundaries, a fleet of ships, a military, a police force, and in a more recent turn, delegate representation with the treaty-holding systems."

"Do we tell them this is official Guild business, or something personal?"

"The personal route," Perry admitted. "Let's not give them reasons to doubt or look to confirm our veracity."

"Agreed. We don't like unnecessary questions. Netty, open a channel."

"It's open."

Mark's tactical overlay slid to the right, making space for a large comm screen. A well-lit bridge appeared, with a span of advanced holographic displays covering the back wall. The screen flickered once—just another reminder, beyond the occasionally malfunctioning lights and heaters, of their recent and violent encounter with powerful enemy ships.

"Greetings, Peacemaker. I am Glyn-Haard Jepson, Warrant-Adept of the Quiet Room Defense Corp. What brings you to our quiet corner of the system?"

Glyn-Haard was roughly humanoid, with a squat, flat nose, gray, almost charcoal-colored skin, and narrow blue eyes. He showcased many of the physical traits of the Ixtan natives, mixed with a few variations.

"You are well met, Gyl-Haard. My name is Mark Tudor. My partner and I are here on personal business."

"Understood," the Warrant-Adept said, then turned and spoke to someone off-screen. Mark's translator stopped working as his voice dropped in volume. The language both aliens spoke was peculiar—nasal and short, with clipped words and sharply punctuated consonants at the end.

The translator missed the first few words once the alien turned back to the screen.

"—Makers are welcome. Please continue in to pad seven for docking. Our Director, Jihan Milon, requests the honor of your presence. She will meet you in person. Once docked, proceed to lift four and down to executive level two hundred and seventeen."

"Understood. Thank you, Gyl-Haard."

The screen promptly closed, the system repopulating the space with his tactical overlay. Mark turned to Perry, only to find the combat unit perusing a large block of text at impressive speed.

"What?" he asked, without looking away.

"We're meeting the director of the Quiet Room."

"I know. I heard. But one correction. You've had that honor bestowed upon you, not me."

"I did say 'my partner and I,'" Mark countered.

Perry sighed, and the block of text finally stopped scrolling.

"Must I?"

"You must. I believe the Legal Eagle might come in handy."

"A mighty raptor's duty is never done."

They loaded the platinum bars into a rugged, hard-shell crate. Luckily, it had wheels, so Mark wouldn't have to carry it the whole way. Unfortunately, Perry added the stipulation that he would "ride" and not hop along with him.

"It's so much less dignified. A bird's place is in the sky, after all."

"Fine, but I'm riding the crate next time," Mark said, sliding back into the pilot's chair.

The moon shone gray in the system's yellow light, a seemingly featureless ball floating against the blue-green backdrop of the host planet. Ships, cargo haulers, and unmanned drones filled the sky as they approached, flitting by like insects on a warm Iowa afternoon.

"Is that it?" Mark asked as they drew closer. Towers and

branching structures were visible now, sprouting from the rocky terrain in large clumps.

"Those are all communication spires. The whole of this branch of Quiet Room is below the surface," Netty explained. "You'll see."

The *Fafnir* banked and closed, then descended toward a field of illuminated landing pads. The ground sunk below them as soon as they touched down, an invisible lift pulling the ship into a service shaft. A massive door irised shut above them, blanketing everything in darkness.

Marker lights flared to life a moment later, tracking the *Fafnir*'s progress until they emerged in a cavernous hangar. The ceiling was painted blue, like the sky, while a single intense light hovered on the far side, no doubt imitating the sun.

Mark stepped out, closed his eyes, and turned his face upward, the light splashing warm across his face. He might have stepped out of the farmhouse and not walked down the ramp of a spaceship, as when he opened his eyes, he found clouds and what looked strangely like birds flocking overhead.

"Really something, ain't it?" Perry asked, emphasizing "ain't" with an exaggerated southern accent.

"You know that's not how Iowans sound."

"I know, but you have to admit, once you hear it, it's so hard to let go."

"You aren't wrong," Mark chuckled, grabbing the case by the handle. "Come on, let's go find our hole in the ground."

3

THE UNDERGROUND HANGAR led to a grand entrance hall. Ornate chandeliers hung from the ceiling, but it was the large glass panels that provided the real light, as an artificial sun slowly crept from east to west.

Marble-wrapped columns broke up the space, the colorful stone battling the glossy floors for artistic dominance. Part of Mark felt guilty for walking on it, as every surface in the carefully cultivated and maintained space looked like art.

"This place smells like a million bucks," he said as they approached a wide counter on the back wall.

"Add some zeros to that and maybe you'll be closer," Perry countered.

"Greetings, and welcome to the Quiet Room," a Synth said as they approached. If the receptionists on Faux Linus were one end of the spectrum—inhibited from expression or developing personality or gender—the Quiet Room's hostess presented as the complete opposite.

Definitively a female, the Synth wore a beautifully tailored dress, the shimmering material hanging from one shoulder. Her glossy black hair was pulled up into a tight crown braid, while a single, bouncy strand hung purposefully over her left temple.

Given the right lens, Mark might never have known she was artificial…if it weren't for the eyes. They always gave it away—a little too perfect and keen, like flawlessly cut gems.

"Hello. My partner here…Commander Legal Eagle and I are looking to commission a strong box," Mark said, putting on what he hoped was a disarming smile.

"Of course, Peacemaker Mark Tudor. On behalf of the Quiet Room, allow me to extend the warmest greetings to you and your associate, Legal Eagle," the Synth said, flashing them a gleaming smile. "My name is Eve, and I will be the customer service representative for your visit today."

"Hello, Eve. It's a pleasure."

"Mutual," she said, her smile never wavering. "Please state your full name and Guild position, so I can create your biometric account."

Mark paused for a moment, looking between Eve and Perry.

"Clive Van Abel Tudor."

"Wait…Clive—?" Perry stammered.

"Very well, Clive. Please place your thumb firmly in the blue square to confirm biometric and biochemical information." She removed a small, rectangular device from…somewhere in her dress and held it out to him.

Mark followed her instructions and smashed his thumb onto the glowing screen. It flashed green and promptly went blank.

"Your name has a chin with dimples, by the way, handsome. And slick hair. Oh, does that name have slick hair," Perry oozed.

"Silence, bird, and comparing me to Clark Gable isn't the insult you imagine."

"Hmph. Ever see his ears?"

"Bird."

Perry sighed. "Got it."

Eve spoke, cheer in every word. "Great news, Clive. After running our proprietary financial, criminal, and social background checks, I can inform you that your account with the Quiet Room has officially been cleared and opened. Welcome, friends!"

"Social?" Mark muttered.

"Indeed," Eve said, beaming. "Here at the Quiet Room, we believe in embracing clients and partners that represent the highest standards across the systems. Now…"

"Please, call me Mark."

"Very well, Mark. You said you're looking for a strong box, correct? I would be more than happy to show you our full-service line of secure storage options."

"Who has access to your records? Who can see that I hold an account with the Quiet Room?"

"The Quiet Room believes in the privacy and anonymity of our client partners and thus withholds all private and confidential information from public disclosure. We also secure your data behind a state-of-the-art firewall and one-thousand-and-twenty-four-bit encryption protocol. We take pride in the fact that our data, your livelihood, has never been breached."

"Good," Mark said, looking at Perry.

The bird nodded, evidently pleased by the news.

"What additional protections do you offer beyond that?" he asked.

"A reasonable question," Eve said, her unwavering gaze sliding to Perry. "Added security measures are expected for agents of the law, such as yourselves. The Quiet Room offers a series of sensitivity protocols. For an additional fee, of course. With that, your accounts will be transferred to our unique digital vault. Isolated by a series of unbreakable, mechanical locks and managed by a quantum-level artificial intelligence, our vault is the most secure digital location in known space."

"Well, if that's the best you've got, it will have to do," Perry said, seemingly unimpressed by the information. He stopped short of yawning and looking away.

"Wonderful." The Synth held up her hand, a small port in her palm projecting a holographic screen before them. A series of products appeared—secure boxes, ranging in size from a six-by-six-inch pull-out drawer to a full walk-in vault. The prices appeared next to each in turn.

Mark considered the larger options and had to immediately rule those out. He could buy a workboat for less money.

"That should do it," he said, pointing to one of the medium options.

Perry shrugged, playing his part as the cold and detached partner. They'd agreed ahead of time that it might help them not attract unnecessary attention.

Eve smiled, and the screen changed, offering them a series of additional options. They selected what they needed, then read a scrolling mass of fine print, and at the very bottom he signed with his thumbprint. Once done, the holographic screen disappeared.

"All done. Now, I know you're excited to see your strong box, so follow me."

Perry said, "I don't know about excitement. More like…mildly satisfied."

Mark stifled a smile. "You don't get out much, do you?"

Mark and Perry followed Eve to the right and through a set of polished double doors, then into a large passageway. People of all makes and sizes moved about the space—coming in from over a dozen side doors and disappearing again.

The next room held a number of vestibules, each containing a lift. Eve led them into the third elevator, where she closed the doors with a wave of a hand. They immediately descended, the drop forcing Mark's stomach up into his throat.

Down they went, the floors whipping by the transparent shell around them. By the time they reached their destination, Mark was dizzy. He followed Perry and the Synth out into the hall, but it took several deep breaths to steady his stomach.

Their destination was a doorway unlike any he'd ever seen before. Roughly twenty feet high and twelve wide, with doors over four feet thick on either side. The space beyond stretched on and on, sprawling into eternity. Entrances lined both sides, each marked with a small glowing panel.

"Welcome to Vault Nine," Eve said, gesturing around. "It contains over twenty thousand secured chambers, with equal that in strong boxes, and over a quarter of a million hardened server racks."

"Vault Nine of…?"

"We have ten such vaults in this location alone, and the Quiet Room is proud to possess over fifty-five sites spread across the settled systems. All in the name of service to our client partners," Eve explained.

Mark whistled low as they headed down the impossibly long hall. Luckily, she stopped after only a few moments, as a door opened for them automatically on the right. The space beyond was spartan and bright, the only furniture a dark wood table nestled against the far wall.

"Ah, there it is. Right on time."

The ceiling opened up, and a robotic arm appeared on a track. It slowed, deposited a large, armored blue box onto the ground, and retracted back into the ceiling.

"This is your very own null chamber. It's insulated against sound, penetrating radio waves, X-ray, thermal imaging, and all other known forms of scanning and eavesdropping. The construction also features a protective metal matrix to prevent damaging electrical signals, such as EMPs, from degrading sensitive electronics. This card will allow you to access your strong box," Eve said, extending a hand toward Mark, palm up. "I'll secure the door behind you. When you're done, simply close the box, secure it with the card, and swipe the card at the door to leave."

Their Synth hostess showed them inside, then promptly stepped back out again. The door closed behind her, sliding shut with only a whisper of noise.

"This place is bizarre," Mark said as soon as she was gone. "What's wrong with my voice?"

"Beyond the obvious?" Perry turned his head, angled it down, and gave a single bark-like laugh. "Clive?"

"I'm glad you like it, bird."

"You have to admit, when you're used to calling someone something as inert as 'Mark,' their real name comes as a bit of a shock. My assertion is clear. Clive is a spicy name. It's got heft. Zest. It's a light-year beyond Mark."

"Get it out of your system," Mark said, waving him off. "I've gone by Mark my whole life, and I don't think now is the time to explain why."

"Clive," Perry breathed, "are you certain you won't change your mi—?"

"Mark."

"That's not on your birth certificate, I bet."

"No, but it was earned by my prowess with a rifle. As in—"

"You didn't miss the mark?"

"The bird wins a cracker," Mark said, waving grandly.

"Fine. Your name is—well, it's not nearly as good as your given, but it'll do. As to the technology—the nullifying kind, anyway—perhaps it's not only deadening anyone's attempts to pry into the chamber. Maybe it deadens or flattens sound waves inside, along with your arguably limited sense of humor."

"If that joke was your stage material, then *limited* is a term best reserved for you, bird," Mark answered with an affable shrug.

As Mark took a few steps toward their strong box, only to discover that even his boots sounded strange. The scuff and scrape of the soles against the ground was muffled and distant, as if the sound were disconnected from its source.

"I don't like this. Let's load up our secure box and move on," he said, swiping the card against its reader. The lid glowed green and promptly lifted free, revealing a spacious and clean interior.

Mark and Perry proceeded to transfer the platinum bars from the crate, working steadily and without comment. By the time they were done, the treasure consisted of a single layer laid across the bottom of the box, with a single row starting on the right.

"It looks so…" Mark started to say as he stepped back.

"Itty bitty? Teeny weeny?" Perry asked.

"Yeah," he admitted.

"You can't throw it in there and expect your money to reproduce and make you more, boss. Think about what all the wealth managers in the universe say. Make your money work for you with interest or dividends. In our case, we can't do that, so the work falls to us."

"We go hunting?"

"Yesss," Perry hissed. "But. I would very much like to research some options. Think of the invaluable intel we could gain if we found a way to prevent the deaths of those slaved Synths."

"How would we go about that…?" Mark started to ask, but the muffled, distant nature of his voice sparked an idea. He turned and looked around the room.

"Sometimes it feels like things fall into place."

"How would we make that work?"

"It's possible," Perry started to say but snapped his beak and turned back in the other direction. The bird seemed to mull over the issue for another long moment before speaking again. "Jamming technology is prohibited beyond military applications, but it might provide our answer."

"We would use a jammer to incapacitate the booby traps?"

"Allow me to think out loud for a moment," Perry said and started to pace. "The overcharge canisters are the threat to the

Synths. They're wired into the computer, which likely has trigger protocols programmed in for several scenarios. My thought is... perimeter detection for possible boarding as well as drive failure."

"So, to the drug runners, whatever precludes boarding?" Mark asked, his thoughts inexplicably flashing back to their pursuit of the speedboat. Had they killed the Synth pilot the moment Netty landed the kill shot on its drive? Or was it when they approached and tried to board? Neither thought sat particularly well.

"We are hampered by our lack of information. But I have a series of hypotheses," Perry said. "If we consider and negate each, we might find a plausible plan."

"Where do we start?"

"Oh. Isn't that the question? Namely, detection. As we saw with the first boat, they rabbited as soon as we appeared on their scans. That was the first domino leading up to our Synth pilot's death. The second was the shot that disabled their drive, and the third, our boarding. Naturally, there are many dominos filling the gaps between them, but those are what we know of right now."

"Why do I feel like this is leading us back to our brush with the *Radiant Sunrise*?"

"Give the human a cracker," Perry said, nodding. "Proper stealth would be a good start. But..."

"What?"

"Stealth only goes so far, and as we saw is negatively impacted by proximity. With modern shortwave scanners, even the best stealth tech is limited. But if we could replicate the technology they're using for these chambers, then it would be possible to project a nulling field around a ship—given enough projectors, mind you. If done properly, their sensors would simply read nothing beyond that point. Again, in theory."

"You say *enough* projectors. How many might that be?"

Perry shrugged. "It's hard to tell, as we're talking about encapsulating a moving three-dimensional object and speeding through space while having to account for the fourth dimension. Time. I'm running terabytes of calculations as we speak, but I'm missing more than a few necessary variables. We may need to bring in several engineers on this one."

"We're due for a visit with Armagost?"

"I said several, but yes, he would be a good place to start."

Mark and Perry secured the box, locking it with the card. Mark verified the lid wouldn't open and found that the gap between the body and the lid had somehow merged together.

"Huh," he breathed and stepped away. "That's some alien shit."

They carded out of the room and found Eve waiting patiently in the hall, her smile still firmly in place.

"All done?"

"Fini," Mark said.

"Ah. Très bien. Suis-moi s'il te plait," Eve replied, sliding effortlessly into French.

"Certainement."

The Synth turned to walk away, and Mark moved to follow, only to find Perry watching him closely.

"What?"

"I was making sure you weren't going to relapse."

"Relapse?"

"You only seem to speak French in your dreams, and judging

from your body language and what you say, bad things are happening. Color me concerned."

"I'm fine, Perry. Really."

"*Fine* is a woefully under-expressive term. But I'll relent for now. Let's see what Madame Eve has planned for us next."

The Synth led them back to the lifts, where they proceeded down to the executive levels. How far underground that was proved to be a mystery, although judging from the markings on the walls, Mark guessed it was between two and two hundred and fifty levels below the surface. The thought troubled him far less than it would have years before, when Valint first whisked him off that French battlefield, although the idea of so much rock and strata hanging over his head made his chest tighten a little.

The floor funneled them toward a single large office in the middle with a many-legged bot sitting at a desk. Three appendages sorted sheaves of what looked like black paper, while another pair prepared a mug of steaming liquid. A single eyestalk turned away from a series of holographic panels and settled on Eve.

"She is expecting them," came a voice from somewhere in the mass of limbs and circuitry.

Their Synth hostess led them through the door and into a wide and surprisingly airy office. The floor was polished wood, while several sandstone columns broke up the space. Mark noticed carved tablets inset on the pillars, each depicting a strange, stylized animal. As familiar as it was, everything present was decidedly alien, down to the swirling grain of the wood and the fearsome-looking, eight-legged creature.

A dark-haired woman sat at a desk, the wall behind her dominated by tall windows—a bright and sprawling landscape hovering beyond. Part of Mark's brain tried to convince him they were windows—thanks in no small part to the high-definition vista. That was the old him, the Iowa Mark. The new half, the one reforged by the intense pressure and cold of space, knew better.

"Thank you, Eve," the woman said, before pushing off from her desk and standing.

Mark was immediately surprised by her stature. Athletically built, she was his height, if not an inch taller, and when she extended an arm to greet him, her hand enveloped his.

"A strong handshake. Good," she said, nodding appreciatively. "Welcome to the Quiet Room. My name is Jihan Milon, and I'm the director of what you might call our local neighborhood," she said, before sitting down again.

"Mark Tudor, and this is my partner, Perry."

The bird said something quietly that sounded oddly like *Clive,* but Mark did his best to ignore him. Jihan gave Perry a friendly nod.

"You're human?" Mark asked.

"Indeed. Although my family hails from Helso, not Earth," she explained. She had high, strong cheekbones, expressive, gray eyes, and full lips. Like Valint, Jihan possessed the kind of raw beauty few inherited but all tried to replicate.

"I only ask because it's still a bit of a shock to encounter other humans away from Earth. Especially those that don't call it home."

"And understandably so. With your homeworld lagging so far behind in terms of industrial development, you must first expand your understanding of civilization from continents on your world to the span and breadth of hundreds of inhabited systems out here. Then and only then can the truth sink in—that our people have been seeded amongst the stars for generations beyond count."

The idea had been a lot to take in when he first heard it, and admittedly, it hadn't soaked in yet. Mark read too many science fiction pulps, the stories effectively establishing a baseline of all extraterrestrials being little green men with bulbous heads and dark, unblinking eyes. Well, in some rare cases, that description fit.

"You said you're from…Helso? What is it like?"

"It's a beautiful world, albeit somewhat smaller and a bit cooler than your home. We were known for our rich mines, but demand changed as financial institutions shifted away from the Palladium Standard. The move to Platinum favored some worlds over others, namely ours. We are also one of the galaxy's leading exporters of Helium-3. So, smaller, and more temperate, but resource rich. We also have some of the most scenic mountain ranges outside of the Eridani Federation. If you can spare the time, Helso is worth the trip."

"I think we will have to schedule a little vacation time, don't you think?" Mark asked, turning to Perry.

"I do love a good scenic mountain view, almost as much as a chugging, churning, and burning platinum mine. The power to extract, the alchemy to refine, and the wherewithal to market and distribute is truly a fascination," Perry said, finishing with a grandiose wave of one wing.

Mark ignored him and refocused on Jihan, who was certainly *worth* his focus.

"Truly," Jihan said. "And your work as a Peacemaker, you enjoy it?"

"I do." Mark kept the response simple. They had transitioned away from the exchange of pleasantries and into the threshold phase, where Jihan's true ambition would reveal itself. With Gyl-

Mareth and Cai-Demond's corruption, he had to proceed with caution. Besides, an institution the size of the Quiet Room was likely to have vested interests scattered across almost every revenue-generating industry, and as Mark was starting to learn, they didn't all have to be above board.

"You're probably wondering why I wanted to speak to you," she said after the silence stretched between them, fat and close. She didn't fidget or squirm, nor did she betray nerves—she just continued to project that façade of icy calm.

"It seems only natural to greet new partners," Perry said before Mark could speak. He sounded bright and chipper, but the response was calculated. Perry had purposely said "partners" instead of "clients."

Jihan smiled again, but the expression didn't extend above her cheeks.

"I wanted to speak to you on a personal level, beyond the potential complications of a Quiet Room Director and a Peacemaker."

Oh, here it comes, Perry said into Mark's ear bug.

Her heart rate just increased by twenty beats per minute, and I'm reading a five-degree spike in surface skin temperature. She might look cool and collected, Mark, but she's nervous, Netty agreed, using the limited scanning abilities of his wrist repeater.

This is a bank at its core, which has always felt like crime wrapped in paperwork, if you ask me, Perry said as Jihan took a breath to speak.

"As you may suspect, our business dealings are broad and varied. Although they're all legal and well within regulatory boundaries, some of our investors and client partners could be considered... unsavory, to those in the civilized world. In order to keep our other clients happy and content, the Quiet Room often commissions independent contractors to deal with the other half."

"Unsavory?" Mark asked.

Jihan nodded. "I know you Peacemakers see…oh, how do they put it? The worst of people on their worst days?"

"That sounds accurate," Perry deadpanned.

"Naturally, we are forced to commission certain groups for the dirtier sides of our financial business—namely, collections and contract enforcement. That's the unsavory part."

"You're looking to commission some collection work?" Mark guessed.

"Actually, no," Jihan said, leaning toward them. "I would like to commission you to *find* the man who does our collection work."

"He's missing? That doesn't bode well," Perry said.

"No, it doesn't, especially if you know him and his reputation."

Mark shifted in his seat, looking to his mechanical counterpart and then back to the Director. From what he knew about bounty hunters and contract collectors, they were a tough-nosed, rough and tumble lot who weren't afraid of anyone or anything. Considering what they were up against, this was a crowd he could recruit from.

"Tell me more," he said, leaning closer to her desk.

4

25 December 1925

"I DON'T KNOW how I feel about this," Perry said as the *Fafnir* climbed away from the Quiet Room, leaving the moon's almost nonexistent atmosphere behind.

"Which part? Us doing a favor for the Quiet Room, or having to track down a notorious bounty-hunter-turned-bank-collector who has gone missing?"

"Um, all of it? But I get it, really. The Quiet Room doesn't want to push this through the regular channels. Half the power of employing an intimidating collector is the idea that they might show up at your door without warning. If Jihan were to report him missing through the Guild, then naturally everyone would know, and that power would be gone."

"That's true," Mark said. "She is likely also limited as far as options within her own organization. Hence, she basically pulls us in off the street…so to speak. There's also built-in deniability if we were to say something and word got out."

"Bingo. And the human gets a cracker."

"One of these days you're going to actually have to cough up these crackers. I'm a fan. Kept my ass alive in the fields of France, more or less."

Perry began to laugh, then his eyes flashed as he sifted the reality of what Mark had known during the war—and beyond. "I…hadn't thought about that. Sorry, boss. As to the crackers, I know a guy."

"I'm sure you do. Netty, have you unpacked the data Jihan sent us about this missing collector?"

"I just finished. The encryption protocol was impressively robust. The Quiet Room does not play about with data protection. Sending it to your console now."

Mark's screen shifted as a stream of new data flowed in. A picture populated first, followed by a number of smaller text windows. The bio finished loading before a flashing red border appeared at the top, spelling *Withhold from Public Disclosure*.

Captain Niles Flint appeared to be an Eniped—a squat figure with leathery brown skin, small, dark eyes, and walrus-like whiskers. In the photo, he wore an armored beret and a vest. The left breast was covered in medals.

"Wait, is this a military record?" Mark asked.

"Not all of it, but part of it appears to be cut directly from his official Transcript of Service, so…yes," Netty confirmed.

Mark scrolled down through the sizable file. The first section was recognizable enough, despite not all of the letters translating correctly. It featured an enlistment date, initial training cycle, and then a series of dates. While some appeared to be anniversaries and drills, others listed only a date with a black line obscuring all other details.

"Why are they blacked out?"

"That data was likely redacted by the Eniped Naval Authority before it was handed over to the Quiet Room. As spacefaring races go, they *are* one of the most active militarily."

The military transcript ended with a single word before the data continued on the next page.

"Netty, what is this word? 'Args-graydun'," Mark asked.

"I believe it's a dialectal variant," she said. "I've been struggling to translate it."

"You *will* have difficulty finding a translation for it, regardless," Perry said, finally chiming in. "It's a word known by all and burned into their cultural subconscious but rarely uttered out loud. And for good reason."

"That sounds ominous," Mark replied. "Is it whispered?"

"Perhaps. You have to consider something. To the Eniped, war is an art form. It's studied, honored, and embraced, in the way of human painters and musicians. It, more than anything, is the foundation for their civilization. It's both an expectation and the greatest honor for young Eniped to serve in their military. Those that serve with distinction and honor are elevated within society forever afterward. That's where the honorific prefix 'Dal' comes from."

"So, if his name was Niles Dal-Flint, we would know that he served honorably? And since we know he served, do I take it to mean that he was dishonorably discharged from service?"

"Precisely," Perry confirmed. "To his people, he is Niles Args-Flint, a disgraced Eniped. Which likely explains how he ended up working as a bounty hunter first, and then running down collection targets for one of the largest financial firms in known space."

Mark nodded as he read, working his way through the list of Niles's accomplishments. Side windows popped up for each of the bounties the Eniped had tracked down, building a veritable who's who list.

"This guy's wrangled the worst of the worst—murderers, rapists, and thieves. He was essentially a privateer hitting pirates, then made the move into the financial sector. His list of enemies has to be *miles* long. I have to like him based off that information alone. Yet, he's a dishonored man."

"It's true," Perry agreed. "Dishonored Eniped, although allowed to return home, rarely do. They are somewhat like the Ronin of Earth's Samurai caste. Once dishonored, they wander, ever in search of ways to regain their honor."

"Maybe we play on that? If we can find this guy for the Quiet Room, perhaps we pitch him to help us rid the Guild of corruption? Perry, would his people look favorably upon that?"

The combat AI shrugged. "I could speculate, but that's all. Beyond that, it sounds like a good idea."

"Okay. It's not like we have to add it to our list of things to do, as we've already agreed to find him. But first, let's see Armagost, then locate our Treasure Island, to deposit the other half of our platinum bars, and after, start searching for our missing Eniped."

"Sounds like a plan, boss. Twist one coming up. To Armagost's exoplanet we go," Netty said with a touch of excitement in her voice.

The *Fafnir* arrived at their destination a few hours later. With the canyon hiding Armagost's base firmly on the night side of the world, they cut engines and lights, choosing to descend on thrusters alone. Without stealth, it was the best they could do.

The old Gajur met them on the landing pad, the scaly skin around his bulbous eyes creased with worry wrinkles.

"Are you here to check on your prisoner?" he asked. "Because you should know, I could only tolerate his meager attempts to manipulate me for a few hours before I sedated him and put him in a stasis module."

"You lasted a few hours?" Perry asked.

"In all honesty, the urge hit within moments of his arrival. I have equal patience for Ligurites and salesmen."

"You're better off," Mark agreed. He'd recommended a gag and a blindfold, but a stasis pod sounded like a better idea.

They decided to go for a short walk through the caverns in order to stretch their legs. The air was damp and still but a welcome change from the canned, recirculated stuff on the ship.

"So, you're escalating your battle on corruption to a full-scale rebellion now?" Armagost asked after they filled him in on recent events. "The Quiet Room has been a shadow player in many stellar conflicts over the years. No one knows it, but they financed the losing side of a failed Ixtan rebellion and used mercenaries to overthrow a tyrant government on Outward. Ironically, both of those events helped them take control of almost half the planet. They started construction on their bank there shortly after."

"Interesting," Mark said, thinking. "So, they're more active in military operations than they let on."

Armagost chuckled and nudged a rock with the toe of his boot.

"We had an old saying in the intelligence service: 'follow the money.' It always led to the *real* players. Mind you, sometimes it was indirect, but with enough work you could unwind the tapestry and find who was pulling the strings. I remember when I was a young analyst and civil war broke out between the Gyl and Cai. Our intelligence agency took interest, especially after several cloaked groups emerged. There were rumors the Quiet Room was providing the Gyl with anti-armor and ground-to-air weaponry, but we were never able to substantiate the claims. Ironically, the two sides are still warring today. Then again, you already know that much. As proxy wars go, it has become one of the worst kept secrets. Treaties rarely result in a true peace."

"Do you think they're part of the Guild's corruption?"

"The Quiet Room?" the old Gajur asked, already shaking his head.

"I doubt it. Their 'investments' have always seemed to be for short- and long-term gains—either the acquisition of territory or to help shift a territory's disposition to them. They have relied *heavily* on the Guild over the years, not only for policing but also for its regulatory assistance. A fractured, divided Guild would do them no good."

"That makes sense," Perry said. "If anything, the Quiet Room would probably seek to benefit more from a united, healthy Guild. One that doesn't necessarily have two presiding Masters from opposite ends of the same civil war."

"I have no arguments with that assertion."

Mark told him about Niles Flint next. Armagost digested the news and gave them a simple but well-considered response.

"All I'll say on that issue is this. Take care who you recruit. Yes, if he is still alive, a privateer like Niles would be a formidable ally, but it could come with some detriment, as well. Others might *not* join your cause if he is flying with you."

Perry and Mark both nodded, but neither found any reason to argue the point. It made sense. Lastly, they discussed the drug runner's ship and their conundrum with the slaved Synth pilots. Mark finished and gave the floor to Perry, who laid out his hypotheses, then closed his beak and waited for Armagost's response.

"Despicable. Synths have long been the victims of body part thieves and illicit pleasure dens. But to strip them down and force them to navigate ships carrying contraband? Well, that's a new low."

"We want to start hitting their shipments, but do it smart," Mark explained. "If we can find out what legitimate merchants and corporations are behind them, then maybe we can make some positive change."

"And potentially claim a fair bit of money and seized goods in the process?" Armagost guessed.

"Naturally," Perry said, unabashed.

"A null field is a good idea, but it doesn't answer all of your questions. What you need is a…" the Gajur said but bit off the words. He started to pace, before abruptly walking away.

Mark looked at Perry. The bird opened his beak, shrugged, and motioned to follow. They ran and flew, catching up to Armagost as he walked into his lab. The lights blinked on automatically, revealing the normally spotless and tidy space.

The old Gajur circled his tables, before settling down on a stool.

They hovered behind him but watched as he activated his digital drafting table and began sketching out some designs with a stylus. He stopped and started several times, before finally straightening and pushing away from the table.

"I don't think I can help you."

"That's all right," Mark said. "We didn't want to burden you with all of our problems. That doesn't feel fair."

Armagost spun on the bench, but there was no frown or disappointment on his face. Instead, the Gajur was practically beaming.

"Why apologize? I say that with great excitement, Mark Tudor. For the first time in a long span of solar cycles, I am finally faced with problems that I cannot easily answer. This is a good day. This is a day to live for."

"It is?" Perry asked.

"Oh, indeed it is, Mr. Bird. Indeed it is. Here is what I'll need."

Mark watched as Armagost wrote out a sizable list on his drafting table. When he was done, he flipped it toward them. The list of items flashed to life above his wrist repeater.

"If you have any problems with these components, Netty has a secondary list of alternatives that should work. Now, the one thing I'll need that isn't necessarily on that list—but that's as important—is a who and not a what."

"You need us to find someone for you?" Perry guessed, then mumbled so only Mark could hear. "This is starting to become a trend."

"Yes. I need you to recruit an engineer, specifically one adept at formulating and constructing high-density electromagnetic projectors. A second set of hands will not only help speed things along but is a necessity when it comes time to calibrate multiple sets of coils together. Find someone like that and bring them here, and, as long as I can work with them, we will build you exactly what you need. I'll present you with a few options, but it's been some time since I was out in the world. The people I know may have moved, retired, or simply passed away in that time."

"Noted. An engineer adept at building high-density electromagnetic projectors. Check," Perry said. "Anything else?"

"Well, now that you mention it. I have been subsisting on a diet consisting of pre-prepared, dehydrated meals for a long time now. I don't mind it, so please do not take this for a complaint, but something different would make for a nice change. Bring me some tasty treats, and I may be inclined to work a little faster. Netty knows what I like."

"Is that true?" Mark asked the repeater on his wrist.

"I have detailed files," she admitted.

Mark moved to leave but turned back, realizing that Perry hadn't moved.

"There's one more bit of unpleasantness about the Synth on that ship," Perry said as a compartment opened under his left wing. He reached out and removed something thin and long with his beak, then held it out for Armagost.

The Gajur bent with a groan and retrieved the item, then held it up to the light.

"A Synth memory module. One that appears to have been"—he pulled it closer to his face and gave it a sniff—"cooked well-done."

"Yes. It didn't feel right to leave and not take it with us. I tried to recover data, but the chips are too badly damaged for me to access. If you have the time, would you mind looking at it?"

"I'll do what I can, Mr. Bird, but in its current state, I can make no guarantees."

"I understand," Perry said, nodding.

Mark and Perry left Armagost's lab, but when they made it back to the hub that would lead them to the *Fafnir*, Perry jumped out in front of him. Armagost stopped behind them, as Netty's optical sensor appeared above Mark's wrist.

"There's something we need to address with you before we leave," Perry declared, spreading his wings to block the doorway.

"Not another mutiny," Mark breathed, and playfully reached for his revolver.

"Yes, Mark. This *has* to happen," Netty declared. "Do you know what the date is?"

"Of course, I do. It's…well, it's…" He paused and realized that he didn't, in fact, know the date. Time had a way of slipping away without notice out in the black.

"This is bad. It's currently the twenty-fifth of December, nineteen twenty-five."

"Yes. And tomorrow will be the twenty-sixth, and after that, the twenty-seven—" Mark said but bit off the words. "Wait, it is Christmas? Today is Christmas Day?"

"Most certainly," Perry said, "and we—meaning Netty, Armagost, and I—could not let this go on without rectification."

"Rectification? You make it sound like a circuit board in need of repair."

"Relate to it how you like, but we thought our human compatriot needed something familiar. Perhaps a bit of home. So, without dawdling or fuss, come with us."

Perry turned and led Mark back through the habitat, directly to the Gajur's kitchen. Judging from the pre-staged nature of the space, he guessed this had been in the works for a while.

"Sit, Mark," Netty demanded, her projected optical sensor morphing into an arrow. It pointed directly at a lone chair next to a table. Fearing Netty's wrath, Mark took a seat and held his hands up in surrender.

"I'm your prisoner."

"More like our guest," Armagost corrected. "Now, this was equal parts Perry and Netty, so I'm here as an extra set of hands. But I'll admit, once they told me about the religious meaning behind the holiday and the thematic overtones, I became intrigued. So, without further ado, we will pass this over to Mr. Bird."

"Thank you, Armagost," Perry said, bowing. Then hopped atop a pile of ingredients. Mark was so caught up with everything else that he didn't even read the containers. "We are going to make you...wait for it."

Netty promptly started to play a drumroll.

"Christmas dinner," the bird finally finished, picking up a can of blueberry pie filling in one clawed foot.

Mark gave an unbridled laugh and leaned forward as he scanned the room. "Feels a lot less like deep space."

"And more like home, we hope," Perry continued. "Once you've been forced to unbutton your pants from seconds and thirds, we will engage in the established tradition of gift-giving."

"But I didn't—"

"Nope," Netty interrupted. "This is our gift to you. So, sit back, relax, and prepare to be dazzled by our collective, ah, culinary skills."

Mark's smile was brilliant. "I'm ready."

Perry and Armagost jumped into action, pulling pans and dishes from cupboards, lining up mixing bowls, and firing up the huge, advanced reconstitutor. Mark slid forward to the edge of his seat and started reading the food parcels.

"Flour, sugar, baking powder, salt, dehydrated milk, cinnamon, and dried lemon extract," he said, reading through each in turn. "Where did you find all of this? I haven't seen anything beyond the brown labels of surplus food since before the war."

"Oh, it wasn't easy. Nor was it inexpensive," Perry said as Armagost opened up a chiller cabinet on the wall. He reached inside, removed one item, and set it onto the counter before Mark. It was butter, and not the horrid, simulated product he saw circulating the spaceport markets, but the honest to God, genuine article.

"You should know us by now, Mark. When Perry and I set out to complete a task, we don't stop until it's done," Netty offered.

"Nor until it's complete. Netty, will you do the honors? Play him the new one," Perry asked.

The AI's optical sensor projected above his wrist abruptly turned into a green tree, with sparkly flakes of snow falling all around it.

"This is 'Carol of the Bells,'" she said as a song started to play.

"This is—thank you," Mark managed. He was overwhelmed as the simple act of Christmas dinner made the gulf in his life seem that much closer to being…manageable.

Mark pushed out of the chair and joined them in their revelry, where together they prepared, or approximated, a Christmas meal. Naturally, the recipes were different, the turkey wasn't real, they couldn't find green beans, and it was all prepared in a reconstitutor, not an oven, but the end result tasted better than anything Mark had eaten in years. And he ate it amongst friends.

And true to Perry's prediction, he went back for seconds, and thirds. Almost an hour after finishing, Mark returned, enjoying a cup of real coffee, along with a generous serving of Perry's astonishingly good blueberry cobbler.

He'd barely finished his last bite and set down his bowl when Perry appeared from Armagost's exercise room, with a small, neatly wrapped package captured in his beak. The bird hopped up to him, dropped the gift in his lap, and after retreating a few steps, watched him expectantly.

"The gift is given. What happens next?" Armagost asked, his interest evident.

"I open it."

"Come on, Mark, the anticipation will overheat my circuits," Netty complained.

Mark hooked his fingers into the cover of the delicate paper and slowly pulled it back, revealing a pack of Bicycle brand playing cards. Besides some boxing on the edges, it appeared to be in flawless condition.

"How did you—?"

"How did I know?" Perry interrupted. "Bunn might have mentioned that when you first came aboard the *Stormshadow,* you said that you had played a few games in your time. There was also an explanation that you can 'read a face,' although I'm not sure what that means. It required much sneaking around and the trading of some memories, but I finally found these."

"This is a wonderful gift. Thank you, both of you," Mark said, pulling the pack open and letting the playing cards spill out into his palm. "But you know what this means, right?"

"Not the foggiest."

"Poker night on the *Fafnir* is now officially a thing."

"I hate to break it to you, Mark, but statistically and mathematically, you don't stand a chance against us," Netty said. "We're kind of supercomputers."

"With feathers," Perry added, eyes bright with smug satisfaction.

"Wrong, friends," Mark said, flexing and shuffling his new cards. "The art of card games isn't in the suits or numbers. For games like poker, it's in the deception and manipulation."

"I was constructed for these things," Perry said, giving him the side eye.

"We'll see."

They cleaned up and reluctantly left after that, bidding their Gajur host thanks and farewell. Leaving Armagost's home proved to be one of the hardest departures since Mark left Earth, a point not lost on him or Netty.

"We can come back whenever we like. As long as we're not busy...and we have fuel," she reasoned.

The Fafnir lifted off, and Netty navigated them out of the narrow ravine without flood or running lights. She had to, as Mark's overindulgence left him a little groggy, his lack of restful sleep notwithstanding. It didn't help that they were still on the night side of the small planetoid, although a stunning yellow glow cut the eastern horizon, with a wide swath of bright light behind it moving their way.

"Okay, stop one in the books, and I feel like it was a productive one. Armagost is working toward our goal of poaching these Synth drug runners, in order to find out who is behind them—"

"And take their loot. Plunder those Synth-mangling troglodytes for all they're worth, and when they're broken, desperate, starving, and penniless, we'll drag them into Anvil Dark and throw away the key. Or, we could toss them out an airlock and save the universe the burden of their continued existence," Perry interrupted.

"Touch dark, bird," Mark said.

"Not dark enough," Perry countered. He wasn't wrong, and he knew it.

"Netty, where to next?" Mark asked, changing his thoughts to action, not memory.

"We have options. The closest engineers Armagost highlighted are on Fulcrum. We need to fill this list of components, but I wasn't sure if you wanted to pay full price for them or go see Ja-Ra and claim your 'friends and family' discount."

"Well, when we are on Tau Regus, we are family." He chuckled.

"If I'm reading the room right, it sounds like Tau-Caius or Tau-Loka first, then Tau Regus, with a short stop at a food market for motivational snacks along the way. So, we can keep our Gajur mastermind well-fed. Then what? Aren't you supposed to check in with either of your new evil daddies soon?" Perry asked.

"Evil daddies?" Netty asked, the disgust clear in her voice.

"That sounds wrong on every level," Mark agreed.

"As intended," Perry whispered, his left eye abruptly going dark. "Steer us hard to port. I want full canvas on the mizzen mast. We make for pirate-friendly harbors with all speed. Argh. Prepare for a broadside…all cannons loaded and ready."

"I think we are watching the birth of something terrifying and new, Netty. A pirate bird of no renown."

"Not yet. But once they get a taste of my keen tactics and savage resolve, then songs will be sung. Toasts will be made. Argh."

"Shiver me timbers. Mad Mark and the Metal Chicken, space pirates to be feared," Netty laughed.

"Avast ye. The Plundering Peacemakers set sail."

5

NETTY TWISTED THREE TIMES, transiting over twelve light-years before reactivating their transponder. Then they set their sights on Fulcrum. A comm request buzzed in barely ten minutes into their flight. Once Mark saw who the sender was, his chest tightened.

The tactical overlay minimized as a new screen appeared, with Master Gyl-Mareth's face looming large and clear. His dark eyes, as usual, gleamed with an undeniable hunger.

"Mark, you are well?" The question felt disingenuous, considering the cold expression on the Master's face.

"We are, thank you. And you?"

The Master nodded—a simple, efficient, and emotion-free gesture. There was no flowery formality anymore, only plain and economical communication. "I don't see you operating under a contract right now. Are you available?"

Mark gave Perry a sidelong glance, but the bird was busy fighting to stay out of frame.

"I am, sir. What do you need?"

"I'm assigning you to an urgent contract—a class three warrant, to be exercised immediately and with the utmost prejudice. The target goes by the moniker *Glass* and should be considered supremely dangerous."

Netty's optical sensor flashed, and in response, a new data stream appeared on his screen. The contract downloaded and automatically populated a smaller window off to the side. Mark tapped it open and gave the details a quick, cursory glance.

"Should I call in backup for this one, sir? Doesn't Guild protocol require—"

"No," Gyl-Mareth said, cutting him off. "You have Perry, which should be all the backup you need. Besides, the *Fafnir* has proven herself a serious foe, and is already earning a reputation among the criminal populations. We have received intelligence that Glass *may* be transiting to Fulcrum, although we do not know the purpose of the trip. I want you to hit her en route. This is a war criminal, Mark, don't fool yourself. No matter what happens, she cannot end up in a prison mine somewhere."

"You want us to take her out?"

"Like I said, she is a war criminal with a body count too long to list. Read the contract, but don't wait too long. You'll see why *decisive action* is necessary. Message me as soon as it is done. Gyl-Mareth out."

The screen closed before Mark could respond. He turned to find Perry still staring at the screen.

"Were we just ordered to perform a hit?"

"It does sound that way," Perry confirmed. "Remember what you said about not being an assassin?"

"Mark, you should really read the contract," Netty said.

He turned back to the screen and swiped over, then maximized it to fill the space. Mark didn't have to read long to understand why.

"She bombarded a Cai stronghold on Outward and reduced it—"

"To glass, yes. Bombarded it from orbit with low-yield nukes and fused everything in a twenty-kilometer radius. That's undoubtedly where her nickname came from," Perry said.

"That bombardment killed thousands of Cai," Netty said.

Perry whistled.

"And now *Gyl*-Mareth is ordering her death. Why does my brain keep grinding over those facts? Was he the one that employed her to attack that stronghold in the first place?"

"That connection almost seems a little too obvious. A corrupt Guild Master who likes to collect favors and henchmen orders a hit on a wartime asset he used to kill thousands of his enemies," Perry said, "but we can't rule it out. What we *can* focus on is the fact that you're being ordered to bypass Guild protocol and violate someone's due process. As a Legal Eagle, I'm sticking hard on that fact."

"You mean, why are Peacemakers being ordered to kill on sight?" Mark clarified.

Perry nodded.

"I'm not, nor will I let someone like Gyl-Mareth turn me into an…" Mark started to say.

"An assassin, yes. I feel like you're starting to add a 'but' at the end," Perry said, sliding over on his perch. "If we ignore the contract, he will know something is up. Sound about right?"

Mark exhaled in disgust, sifting his options. "Perhaps we

approach this individual and warn them? Given context, we might even discover the truth behind the legend."

"It's possible, but we slide further up the risk index. We could try, but considering her reputation, she sounds like the type to shoot on sight, especially when confronted by a Peacemaker."

"And yet, we won't be the only law in Fulcrum airspace," Netty added. "At any given time, there could be two to six Peacemakers in-system, not to mention Fulcrum Planetary Defense Forces are no slouches. By my estimation, if this Glass is transiting into system, she is likely to cut and run rather than fight."

"Run, yes, but likely not until after lobbing explosive projectiles at us first," Perry returned.

"This is a rock-and-hard-place scenario," Mark admitted. "But my curiosity is piqued, so I naturally want to know what her connection is to Outward and the warring Gyl and Cai clans. Not to mention how the Quiet Room plays into all of this. There is risk, but it might be worth trying to talk with her, especially if it helps us start to unravel some of these threads."

"We could offer her protective custody. Fill another stasis pod at Armagost's retreat? Which, by the way, he is going to hate," Netty proposed.

"I hate it, too, Netty. I wish we didn't have to impose on him at all."

"But we do," Perry said, his voice louder and more decisive than Mark had heard for a while. "It sounds like we're adding another task to our ever-growing list. Recruit an engineer, buy stuff, find allies, locate a place to bury our spare platinum, and while we're at it, apprehend a potentially dangerous mass murderer. And yes, there's absolutely zero reason for concern with that last item on the list. Might I add, I still need some time in a repair shop. Damaged feathers will be falling off me soon."

"I love your grasp of sarcasm, Perry. It shows great nuance. Except for the repair shop time. Let's get you into the spa ASAP."

"Thanks, boss, can't wait to feel beautiful again. But we also forgot about our gig from the Quiet Room. How're we going to find time to track down Niles Flint? Truth be told, someone like that would be a valuable asset when confronting Glass."

"It isn't reasonable to believe that we could track down Niles before a confrontation ensues," Netty reasoned, "but we continue to operate under the delusion that we are alone in this. We have Valint, Drogo, and Vosa. It's time to divide and conquer. Vosa is a seasoned tracker and has successfully apprehended many hardened criminals on the run. Perhaps we reach out to her and see if she can find Flint?"

"Delegating responsibility isn't my forte," Mark said, swiping over to his comm screen, "but, Netty, you're right. If Vosa is a seasoned tracker, then she is probably the best fit for the job. Recruitment also takes a softer approach, which automatically rules Drogo out."

"He would likely agree," Perry chuckled.

Selecting Vosa's transponder icon, Mark opened a comms channel. His screen switched over a moment later, with Vosa's somewhat unnerving, opaque eyes clarifying first.

"Mark, you're all right? Has something happened?"

"No. Well, nothing bad, at least," he said, deciding not to burden her with details. "Are you currently under contract?"

"No. I just finished exercising a mass eviction on Sunward. That was a mess. I was going to take a few days off to recover, but I can help if needed."

"That sounds messy," Mark agreed. "I have been approached by the director of the Quiet Room and asked to track someone down—an Eniped contract enforcer named Niles Flint. We think he could be someone useful moving forward, especially if animosities increase. Gyl-Mareth ordered us to track down a war criminal they call Glass."

"By 'track down,' I take it he means that he wants you to do more than find this person," Vosa said, quietly.

Mark nodded, not comfortable saying it out loud even over an encrypted comms channel. His Mustilar counterpart turned and whispered quietly, where Rust likely sat offscreen.

"Rust has experience with this Captain Flint. We will look into his whereabouts and contact you as soon as we know something."

"Thank you, Vosa. You two be careful out there."

"And you as well," she said, throwing him a tight-lipped smile, and the comm channel abruptly went dark.

"Okay. That's one item we can scratch off our list," Perry muttered, stretching his wings. "Now we just have to tackle everything else."

"And we do that one step at a time," Netty said, spooling the twist drive. A few moments later, the *Fafnir* jumped and reemerged below the ecliptic in Tau Ceti space. It didn't make them invisible to prying eyes but less obvious, which felt like a good start.

"I want long distance scanner pings as often as you can manage them. We need to know the moment Glass emerges in-system," Mark said, pulling up his tactical overlay.

"Netty, bring us right eight degrees and up ten. I want to tap into one of these transit buoys. If it doesn't put up too much of a fight, I might be able to gain some network data," Perry said.

"Roger that," Netty confirmed, as the thrusters fired. A moment later, the ship slowed. "Okay. We're right on top of it. Work your magic."

Mark watched as Perry's screens flipped over and changed several times in rapid succession. A stream of data appeared in one window, only to have another flash to life, and then another.

"Done. I'm *in*," Perry whispered a moment later. "Not like it stood any chance against me."

Thrust kicked in again, propelling the *Fafnir* in-system. Fifteen minutes later, Perry stretched his wings and looked at Mark.

"I've sifted through all the data. They're tied together in sectors, so I was able to see a decent swath of Fulcrum's approach. I can say with about forty percent confidence that Glass is not in-system right now. They aren't exactly gambler's odds, but they're better than nothing."

"It's more accurate than we had only moments ago," Mark admitted.

"Netty, how do we handle this? I'd imagine if we cruise in with full sensors blaring, we're likely to put a whole lot of people on edge, right?"

"*On edge* is certainly a polite term for making a lot of people, as your species says, fighting mad. I cannot think of a *faster* way to get the Planetary Defense Force angry enough to attack, in fact. At this point, I'd like to recommend we play it slow and mosey on down to Fulcrum. We can keep sensors working in passive sweeps. The contract gave us a reasonable amount of data to work with, but according to reports, Glass flies with a hacked transponder, so she could appear as anyone."

"Great. First, people stranded to die out in the black, then corrupt Masters, stealthy battleships, and now war criminals with hacked transponders. On the other hand, I get to mosey, which plays into my desire to be a cowboy."

"Is that a common goal for young men on Earth?" Netty asked.

"Only about half the boys in my nation, and—yes, bird?"

Perry had a wing lifted in a rare gesture of politeness.

He pointed toward the screens. "I retract my previous statement. My confidence that she is *in* the system has been upgraded, and generously."

"In that case, I'm with the bird. We'll now do this the old-fashioned way— forge ahead and deal with things as they appear," Mark concluded.

The ride into Fulcrum was thankfully uneventful, with traffic control pinging them once they hit the outer planetary marker. Using Peacemaker credentials, the Fafnir was granted immediate permission to land. Their first target was the megacity Tau-Loka, and the first of Armagost's recommended engineering candidates.

Mark and Perry arrived on the seventy-third level of the colossal structure and were surprised to step out into the middle of a bustling commercial center.

Mark looked around, frowning. "I'd—I don't know—"

"Expected a festering sewer, but more space-ish?" Perry asked.

"That's it. This is remarkably free of looming danger."

That you know of, Netty sent. *Eyes out, boss.*

Eyes are out, so to speak. Thanks.

They walked in for several blocks, taking in the tall buildings and shopfronts, only to stop in front of a food market. The small business didn't only look out of place amidst the sea of glowing neon lights and hovering holographic advertisements, but it also looked wedged into place—a fragment of an older, dissociated world.

A shopkeeper appeared from the front door, a flat of strange, alien-looking fruit perched expertly on her right shoulder. She moved to a stand and started to refill the cubbies from the flat.

"Excuse me," Mark said, moving forward.

"Yes?" the shopkeeper asked, turning around. She looked to be a Mustilar, like Vosa, although she was a good half a head taller.

"We are looking for someone…" Mark started to say but watched as her eyes naturally moved down his uniform and settled onto the Galactic Knights insignia on his chest. At least half the color drained from her skin. "An old friend. They used to live in residential housing on this level. Are we simply in the wrong place?"

Her expression softened, and a bit of her color returned, but not all.

"An old friend?" she confirmed, turning back to finish restocking the stall. "They must truly be an old friend. They tore down the last of the housing blocks nearly six solar cycles ago. My shop is one of the last buildings left from the old neighborhood."

"Times have changed?" Perry asked.

"To say the least. Slow to fast, dark to bright, and from family to career-driven. I hardly recognize the place anymore. Luckily, people still need to eat, so I'm here. But even that…" The Mustilar shook her head, "I'll likely be closing up before too long. Synthesized protein shops have been popping up on almost every street corner. Most won't take the time with fresh goods like I sell. When all my customers are gone, I'll simply pack up and move on to the next place, wherever that may be."

Mark couldn't help but marvel at the woman's attitude. She'd been watching her way of life, livelihood, friends, and family slowly drift away and fade, and her response was simply to uproot and start again someplace new. Few had that level of resiliency.

He bought a meal and they strategized for a while, but it became clear that they would need to hop cities. Perry pulled up the list, and they perused the names. There were only half a dozen left, with a single individual, someone named Cal Tu'Tu, who evidently lived in Tau Regus, and ironically, not far from their Tunis friend, Ja-Ra.

"Makes sense. We need to see him anyway," Perry reasoned as they paid their docking fees and loaded back onto the *Fafnir*.

Mark took the helm as Netty navigated them onto the lowest transit lane. The flashing spires of comms antennae and transmitter hubs glowed beneath them, and yet, even with the altimeter reading five thousand feet, Mark couldn't help but feel like the belly of their ship would strike ground at any moment.

"It's different when you're not surrounded by nothing, isn't it?" Perry asked, seeing Mark's white knuckles on the stick.

"I'll be looking at the biplanes, ah, differently the next time I make it home," he confirmed. "Those boys are a bit more daring than I gave them credit for."

"Biplanes aren't even *planes*. They're glorified bed linens with wood frames and an engine that coughs more than a tuberculosis patient. No, boss, those boys aren't daring. They're dumb," Perry announced.

"Dumb—and swathed in glory," Netty said.

"Fair. I do like the scarves. Dashing, one might say. Unlike my b-suit, which gives me the air of a tall, lithe beetle with murderous intent," Mark said, waving down at his armor.

Netty laughed. "I don't think beetles can handle our weapon systems. Ah, there it is. Docking permission just came through for Tau Regus, Mark. My ship now?"

"The stick is yours," Mark said, sitting back.

Netty took over, parking the ship between two nondescript but impressively outfitted gunships. Neither ship flew Tau Ceti colors, and while they both showed ample signs of previous combat damage, their armor was impressively layered. They were heavy hitters, maybe class eleven or higher.

Mark didn't receive any attitude from the elevator attendant this time, as the bot recognized Perry and promptly straightened. It even bid him a good day as they stepped off on their destination floor.

"I think you scared that one straight," Mark said.

"Sometimes we need to be reminded."

"Reminded of what?"

"That there's always a bigger and meaner bird out there," Perry explained.

Mark nodded, his thoughts sliding back to the two gunships bracketing the *Fafnir*. That train of logic also extended to the *Radiant Sunrise*, the stealthy light cruiser that took out both Len and Rustala. It took a swarm of desperate Peacemakers to take down that predator. And, as Mark had learned the hard way in France, where there was one hunter, there were almost always more.

Tau Regus's twelfth level reminded Mark of the Irish district on the southside of Chicago. The megacity's ceiling was lower, the ambient lighting dimmer, and the buildings older and a bit grimier.

The place didn't look disheveled or dirty, but it wore its patina of age like a badge of pride.

With Perry leading, they found their destination, a large, gray housing block with little trouble. Thankfully, it was still there, although their lack of success left Mark with more than a little lingering doubt. Had too much time passed since Armagost secluded himself away from society? Had his extensive network dissipated into the ether?

Mark rang the doorbell and waited. Several moments passed, and he looked down at Perry. The combat AI was turned around, quietly studying the narrow passage between buildings. The space was cramped, with barely six feet spanning the gap between walls. Chairs, hammocks, and creative outdoor cooking pits filled the area making it look more like a camp nestled in the crook of a mountain than an alley in a megacity.

He reached down to ring the doorbell, only to have it click and slide open a few inches.

"Yes?" someone whispered from inside.

"Hello, my name is Mark, and this is Perry. We are looking for Cal Tu'Tu. Does he still live here?"

"Cal? No Cal here. Sorry, friend."

Mark could make out the speaker's outline, but their face was cloaked in shadow. Their eyes—large and perfectly round—shone in the light.

"Do you by chance know where he moved to? Or how long he has been gone? We're friends from way back and wanted to talk to him about a job."

The door crept open a bit more, and the light revealed the speaker. They were a head shorter than Mark, with a perfectly round face, wide shoulders, and narrow hips. Their arms were long and slender, ending in boney, six-fingered hands.

The narrowed eyes fell to Mark's chest, where he knew his Galactic Knights insignia stood out, then drifted over to Perry. The truth of their identity seemed to sink in.

"Sorry. No. I have—I've gotta go." And the door promptly slid shut.

Mark knocked and rang the bell again and again, but no one returned. After a gusty sigh, he wheeled and left.

Mark stopped at the end of the alley long enough for Perry to catch up, then turned and made for the lift. They passed the long ride up in silence. He was halfway to the *Fafnir's* docking slip before he realized they were being followed. A shadow hovered in an open service entrance behind them and to the left. When he turned to track it, the individual slipped back and out of sight.

"We leaving?" Perry asked, finally speaking. "I thought you wanted to stop in and have a Tunis family reunion?"

"I think we're being followed," Mark whispered, and subtly gestured the bird forward.

Perry nodded and followed. *Did you get a look at them?* he asked a moment later over the ear bug.

Mark stretched his shoulders, using the movement to shake his head. They passed into the hangar bay by the time Perry spoke again.

"I do believe it's our young friend from the housing block. He emerged two slips down from the *Fafnir* and is crouching behind that stack of crates."

"Can you get behind him? I'd like to talk to him again…without him fleeing."

"You got it, boss." Perry hopped forward, seemingly disinterested in everything around him, then abruptly launched himself up and into the air.

Mark continued toward the *Fafnir*, only to see the young alien appear from around the gunship next to them, with Perry prodding him along. In the light, he saw him for what he was—a Druzis Amalgam. Their people were well-known for constructing some of the highest quality computer systems in the known galaxies.

"If you had follow-up questions, you could have asked," Mark said, throwing the obviously young alien a disarming smile.

"You don't know what it's like for someone of my race living outside the Amalgam. If the law comes to talk to us, it's usually for one of two reasons, and neither of them are good."

"If it eases your concerns, we are not here to question or apprehend you."

"It does not, but please do not take offense," the Druzis said before looking around nervously.

"You knew Cal Tu'Tu? Or at least knew of him?" Perry guessed.

"Yes. Cal was my uncle, but he moved on to the next collective during the last solar cycle."

That means he died, Perry explained over the ear bug. *The Druzis Amalgam view life as two states of being—like matter. There's the active state, which is life, and then the potential state, which comes after.*

Mark nodded. It made sense.

"What did you want with my uncle?"

"We were here to offer him a job. We need a skilled engineer, and a mutual friend recommended him by name," Mark admitted.

"A job? Where? Here? Or up there?" the young alien said,

pointing toward the sky with a long, bony finger. His hands appeared even stranger in the light, as he had thumbs on both sides.

"Specifically, on that," Perry said, pointing at the Fafnir with a wing.

"Oh. Then I would very much like to help you with this job. Uncle Cal taught me everything he knew. I am your Druzis. Please, take me with you."

"He looks like he is barely past puberty. I don't know about this," Perry said.

Mark didn't know much about the Druzis, beyond their prowess with computers and electronics. He did struggle with the idea of taking on a young alien and potentially putting them in harm's way.

"I see your doubt. But please. Give me this chance. Give me a test, something difficult—impossible—and I'll prove myself. You'll see, Peacemaker."

Perry opened his beak to speak, closed it again, then turned to Mark.

"Why not? So far, we're not having much success. Wait here…"

The combat AI took flight and landed next to a ship further down the hangar. He picked around in a cluttered pile of components, flew back, and dropped a noticeably corroded cylinder at the young Druzis' feet.

"Install this sensor node in the secondary expansion port on our ship's bow relay. Configure it to scan in the infrared spectrum with a refresh rate no lower than five hundred and twelve hertz. If you can do that in…ten minutes, you pass."

The young alien bent over, scooped the component off the ground, and straightened again. "I can have that done in five," he said, turning to duck under *Fafnir*'s nose. He pulled tools from a small pouch on his belt, his fingers busy and dexterous. "By the way, my name is Tan. Tan Tu'Tu. If I *had* friends, I would have them call me 'T.'"

"T? Economical, in terms of letters. I approve," Perry said.

"Netty, are you tracking this?" Mark asked, speaking into his wrist repeater.

"Oh, yes, and with great interest," she acknowledged, a holographic countdown appearing over his wrist a moment later.

Mark watched as Tan disappeared into the *Fafnir*'s secondary access port, his legs dangling in the air.

"He's just a kid."

"A Druzis kid. Rumor is they're born with a circuit board in one hand and a flow iron in the other. If he can simply get that hunk of junk installed in five minutes, it will be a miracle, let alone get it to work, or recalibrate it to scan infr—"

"Done," Tan yelled, jumping down from above. He slapped the dirt from his hands, closed the bow access port, and stepped back. A wide smile formed on his round face.

"That was only three minutes and forty-five seconds," Perry said.

"Netty?"

"I'm booting up the sensor array now. And...new hardware detected. I've got good power feed and...how about that, infrared capabilities. It's flaky and short-ranged, but it works."

"Well, it *is* a RUJ-seventeen, what I would consider a sketchy node to begin with. Now, get me a twenty-one, and then you'd be in business."

"Me? Don't you mean us?" Mark asked.

"Wait. Are you saying—? Does that mean?" Tan asked.

"If you want it, the job is yours. Mind you, we don't know how soon we could get you home again."

"Never is too soon. I won't disappoint you. I promise," Tan said. "Can I gather my belongings? Do I have enough time?"

"Yes. We have someone else to see in the city. Grab your belongings and come back here. Netty will let you on board if we aren't back yet."

"Thank you, sir. Tan Tu'Tu will not disappoint you. I promise you that."

The Druzis shook his hand excitedly—the grip almost uncomfortably strong—and immediately sprinted for the lift beyond the hangar.

Mark turned to find Perry watching him.

"What?"

"Recruiting children to our cause now?"

"He's hardly a child, Perry. In Druzis Amalgam cycles, he is considered a young adult," Netty corrected.

"Young adult? That almost sounds worse."

"Armagost had a connection with his uncle. If that's the case, Tan might be the closest we come to finding someone on his list. And you saw for yourself, he's got talent," Mark reasoned.

"Talent installing old components on a ship, but will he have the know-how Armagost nee—?" the bird started to ask as a shout rang out.

Mark sprinted for the large doors and cleared the opening in time to see their new recruit get swarmed over by a host of men in dark, armored suits. He reached for the revolver and moved forward, only to have Perry land in front of him and block his path.

"Hold on, Mark. Those are Tau Regus Enforcers…the legitimate law here in the city."

They watched together as the armored men heaved Tan to his feet, slapped flexi-cuffs onto his wrists, and dragged him onto the lift. The young alien flashed him a desperate, pleading look, mouthed *help me*, and then sank out of sight.

"Missed it by that much," Perry said, his head sagging in defeat.

6

MARK MOVED around Perry and made it four steps closer to the lift before another commotion erupted further down the floor. Several drones buzzed in from above, while a crowd scattered.

"What's going on?" he breathed as one figure materialized from the throng, staggered to their feet, and sprinted toward them. They made it twenty feet before armored agents cut in from side passages and tackled them to the ground.

"If you listen to the friendly but tyrannical guards and soldiers and such, I think you'll know in a few seconds," Perry said.

"Your assessment of the situation is really—well, it's why I pay you the way I do."

"I don't get paid," Perry observed.

Mark turned and smiled. "Correct."

Perry managed to lift a single feather, beak open in a laugh.

"That's the spirit. We're a *team*."

Perry prepped for another comment, then looked up, where a

massive speaker thrummed to life atop a comm network pole. "Gotta save that one, boss. I'm guessing they'll make their announcement—"

"ALERT! This is an ALERT. You are under an official Tau Regus security notice. A city-wide lockdown is now in effect. All ports of entry are closed until further notice. Enforcers are exercising warrants in all sectors. Return to your habitations. We repeat, you are now under an official security lockdown…"

Mark watched the crowds scatter as people sprinted toward available exits. More drones circled from above. There were hundreds of them, their repulsion drives crackling and buzzing like a host of angry hornets. They flew down over the crowds, their lights flashing red as tasers glowed to life. Breathing slow and easy, Mark made himself relax, leaning against a building with his shoulders drawn inward.

"They mean business," Mark observed. "More than usual, anyway. Bit of an edge to this."

Perry's eyes flashed again as he continued to scan the scene. "This is—different. But why? Was it me? Was it something we said?"

"I don't think it was us. At least, not anything we did intentionally, although your usual charm might spawn the occasional civil conflict."

"Some people can bake. Some people can dance. Me? I inspire police actions," Perry said, beak dropping.

"Yet another gift. Step up here, bird. Let's get a feel for where this is going." He moved to the handrail and leaned over to look down, the impressive drop looming all the way to the lower floors.

Perry leapt up onto the handrail and with avian grace, launched himself into the air, and dove groundward at full speed.

Mark leaned out to watch—well, as far as his realistic fear of heights would allow. Similar flashing lights and scrambling crowds appeared to be covering the levels below them, suggesting the whole of the city was in chaos.

Two drones buzzed by, barely three feet on either side of him. Mark spun, shielding his face from the heat of their drives. They turned around and flanked him, the energy crackling from their extended taser probes.

"Disperse, citizen. You are under a security lockdown. Return to your habitation at once." The drones spoke together, their emitters projecting holographic faces into the air before them. Mark guessed it was to humanize the security robots and make them look less threatening. If anything, the artificially generated faces made the small bots look nefarious as their blocky eyes and frowning mouths twitched and reset.

"I'm Peacemaker Mark Tudor, here on official Guild business. Stand down," he said, pulling his identification and holding it before him.

The drone on the right moved in and scanned the badge. A moment later, the digital face shifted to a smile.

"Identity confirmed. Thank you, Peacemaker Mark Tudor. Have a nice day."

The two bots flipped and zoomed off to chase a few stragglers toward an exit, blasting him with a hot wave of repulsion exhaust in the process. Mark turned away, cursing, as Perry soared up from below. He spread his wings, coasted in a tight circle, and landed on the handrail.

"It's the entire city. I interfaced with a drone below and, using my credentials pulled a bit of data. All warrants and writs have been called in. *All* of them. This is bullshit, boss. No way this can stand—the system will crash. Hell, Anvil Dark's mainframe couldn't do this, let alone a single city AI with limited enforcers."

Mark watched through narrowed eyes as the city boiled to life. "A massive failure of the law."

"I think that's the point," Perry answered as a Nesit broke from behind a stack of crates and sprinted for a side passage. Three drones wheeled about and immediately hit the figure with tasers, crumpling him into a convulsing pile. Then they watched as the three drones cuffed and carried him off. "The order came down the security chain of command, but they're already scrambling and trying to verify it. Got a hunch here, boss. I do believe that Tau Regus was hacked."

"Hacked? You mean the *city* was hacked? Who would have the know-how and the gumption to hack a city's security agency?"

"That's the million-bond question right now"—Perry nodded—"but even more importantly, why?"

As if in answer, the repeater on Mark's wrist vibrated and glowed to life. Netty's optical sensor appeared a heartbeat before her voice filled his ear bug.

Mark, I'm receiving an urgent call from Valint. I'm going to transfer her through to the repeater.

"Do it," he said, watching as another figure was tased, immobilized, and carried off by drones. His ear bug crackled for a moment, before a familiar voice echoed in.

"Mark... Mark, can you hear me?" Valint's voice was strong and warm through the repeater, but she sounded out of breath. Was she fighting?

"What's wrong?" Mark asked, concern spiking.

"Where are you? Netty said you're on Fulcrum, is that right?"

"We're standing outside the top level in Tau Regus, but it's chaos —" he started to say.

"Let me guess," she said, cutting him off. "Security is swarming everywhere, rounding people up. That sum it up?"

"Yes. Wait. How do you know that?"

"The why is the less important part. Right now you need to listen. Time is of the essence. I've heard from one of my contacts in the city that a third party hacked the Protectorate's mainframe and initiated a warrant dump on all levels. They said someone or some group is using the chaos to round people up. We don't know who they're taking or why, but my contact did overhear that they're looking for several groups of individuals. One of them is a Tunis living on the lower levels. Does that sound familiar to you?"

"Ja-Ra," Mark drawled, looking at Perry.

"As good a guess as any," the bird confirmed.

"Then you'd better get to him quickly, and if you can, move him out of the city. But Mark, do it quickly and *quietly*. Whoever is behind this has some serious reach," Valint said.

"Hack into a city's security mainframe, call in all warrants, and generally throw the place into chaos? Back home, we'd say that individual has brass balls and a big stick," he said, undoing the strap on his revolver. "Headed there now. We met the nephew of one of Armagost's engineering candidates. You could say that he's beyond qualified. But the protectorate snatched him up right after leaving the hangar. I think we should try and grab him as well."

"I don't know. One is a coincidence, but two?" Valint said, before going quiet for a moment. "I'm starting to believe that trouble is drawn to you, Mark Tudor."

"Right place, right time. It's my motto."

"I'll accept that until it's no longer true," she said. "We're twisting to you right now. Be careful until I get there. We don't know who is behind this, or their strength. If it's the Five Star League, then I want you to cut losses and get out of there," Valint said.

"The city is on lockdown. How are you planning on gaining access to the docks? Do you want me to hack in for you?" Perry asked.

"No. There's no time. Get to Ja-Ra and the engineer. Striker has some nifty tricks up his sleeve. Getting in will be the easy part. Now getting back out…"

"If getting out is the sticking point, I've got a missile with a hangar door's name on it. Fly safe, and we'll see you soon," Mark said.

"You, too. Watch your back and don't blow yourself up."

The comm ended, and Perry managed to look sly and accusatory all at once.

"Ahhh. She cares about us."

Mark gave a slow nod. "You might be right. And your choice of words—you said 'us'—really shows personal growth. I'm tempted to hug you. A magical moment for me."

"You got me, Clive," Perry said, spreading his wings in a grandiose posture that Mark was coming to know as Perry at his most smug—and thus, fun—setting. "Deep down, beneath this crusty, cynical, belligerent exterior beats the mechanical heart of a romantic. You have stripped away my defensive veneer and exposed the *real* me."

"Really?" Mark asked, squinting. "I don't feel the romance."

Perry laughed and fluttered toward the lift. Mark joined him, where the operator bot was standing frozen, his normally blue eyes now dark.

"Down plea—"

"Don't waste your breath, Mark. It was disabled in the lockdown, but I have the master key." The combat unit hopped forward, flipped open a small access panel on the elevator's control column, and proceeded to jack in. The bird's eyes shifted from orange, to green, then blue, and the floor shuddered. A moment later, they were cruising down through the city's many levels.

"Where to first? Our Tunis friends, or the enthusiastic teenage wonder?"

Perry's eyes flickered, flashing like the read/write indicators on the *Fafnir's* comm panel. They passed a floor, and Mark caught sight of a large group—what looked to be twenty to thirty citizens, all bound, huddled together. A host of security drones buzzed around them, their tasers poised and ready.

"Okay. It let me in through the lockdown for a moment. They might be able to slow the bird, but they can't keep him out entirely."

"And the bird is referring to himself in the third person again."

"When you're this good, Mark, it's impossible not to." Perry said. "But in all seriousness. Tan is in a holding cell on level one hundred and seventeen. He is on the way down to Ja-Ra. I say we make a stop off."

Mark lurched into the handrail as the lift abruptly slowed and came to a stop. Two massive, concrete pillars framed in the entrance to the floor, Level 117 – Administration Only. A glowing, red security checkpoint barrier blocked their path ahead.

"Okay, bird. Let's prep for the real stuff. Weapons hot, eyes open."

"Roger that, boss," Perry said, a ripple passing through his feathers. His talons scraped against the ground as his eyes flashed from orange to crimson.

The combat bird stalked forward, his posture rigid and upright. The security barrier flickered as he approached, then promptly disappeared, and they passed through. Mark followed the bird well into the chaos of the administration floor before stopping at a wide interchange. Perry's posture changed, his wings relaxing before he scanned the long passage.

Armored agents moved past, a cuffed citizen suspended between them. They set the individual down against the wall, adding to an already long line of cuffed and immobilized aliens.

"How far will they let this go before someone starts asking the most important question?" Mark wondered.

"My circuits are filtering through a long list of those right now; would you care to identify *the* question being asked?"

Mark cleared his throat as he realized that almost all of the cuffed and immobilized citizens were looking expectantly at him, as Tan had when security was carting him off. It was…dread. Or hope. Or both.

"If you go high enough in any chain of command, there has to be someone that stops and asks, 'How did this happen without my go-ahead?'"

"Yes. That might be the case eventually, but I think we're still firmly in the, ah, *enthusiastic* phase of this fiasco."

"Let's make the chaos work for us, then. Bird, lead the way," Mark said.

Perry pushed forward as a pair of agitated Protectorate officers appeared through a door at the end of the hall. The ear bug filtered out every second or third word as the two Ixtan approached, casting a slurry of speech and grunts as they dragged a hapless Nesit—somewhere. They moved past without even noticing Perry or Mark, then loaded onto the lift and disappeared below, the Nesit's face a study in bewilderment.

"Netty, did you catch what they were saying?"

"Every word, Mark…in all its colorful glory. It appears the hack didn't only activate every warrant in the city, but it also triggered a number of Internal Matters investigations. While the Protectorate Officers are busy rounding up thousands of citizens, Internal Matter Agents are rounding up officers as well. That Nesit who was speaking—that was an officer. Or rather, used to be. They've got a world of shit coming down around them right now."

"I, for one, am not against the corrupt being hauled off in chains. But this is too much," Perry said.

And it was. And the scene wasn't grinding to a halt. If anything, a frenetic energy continued to build as more officers hurled their weight into the fray.

"Our engineer, our Tunis scavengers, and us. Wouldn't mind finding the source of this—whatever this is—but that's a stretch even on a good day. And this is most certainly *not* a good day. For a lot of people," Mark murmured as more officers appeared, hauling in five citizens in various states of disarray.

"I read you loud and clear, boss. We're moving," Perry said, before hopping forward and through the automatic doors.

The next passage was lined with more bound people as well, their bodies wedged so closely together that they were blocking the doorways. Clerks and city workers were actively trying to fight their way in and back out of their offices and had apparently stopped stifling their displeasure about it sometime before. Mark's ear bug struggled to translate the host of alien languages amidst all the obscenity. Someone wailed in pain, a scuffle went to a brawl, and two officers managed to stun each *other* with their weapons, both crumpling to the ground with a bray of pain.

"Yeah, this is bullshit," Perry said, capturing the spirit of the scene quite nicely.

By the time they reached the end of the passageway, Mark had to elbow his way through the crowd tucked against both walls to get through to the next chamber. A wide desk sat on the other side, manned by a booking officer that more than stood out from the throng.

The officer was—not human. And not alien, really, unless you consider jellyfish to be aliens.

The officer sat, translucent and damp, held upright by an odd skeletal system that ended at the base of fifteen tentacles sprawled all over the desk—and each appendage was hard at work on its own task, a feat that made Mark whistle in appreciation.

"Now *that* is police work," Mark said, frankly admiring.

A bowl-shaped apparatus covered the alien's upper body and head—if that truly was what it could be considered—and contained a foggy, green atmosphere piped in from above.

Perry hopped forward, undeterred by the alien's bizarre appearance, and fluttered up and onto the desk. Mark followed, fighting with where he was supposed to look. The alien, despite having what was clearly a face behind its breathing dome, didn't seem to possess eyes. At least none that Mark could immediately recognize.

"Take a number and get in line," the booking officer said, its watery voice echoing out of speakers on the desk. It didn't so much speak as it cleared its throat in a series of moist coughs that Mark found remarkably unpleasant.

"Sorry, but we don't have time for that—" Perry started.

"If you cannot tell, we are *more* than a little busy right now. Take a number and proceed to the end of the queue on the right. If you cannot wait, simply come back tomorrow. It matters not to me."

Perry and Mark looked back together, eyeing the people they'd elbowed through to gain entrance. He didn't notice the difference at the time, but the people on the right side of the passage weren't cuffed. They appeared to be waiting to recover an acquaintance or loved one from custody.

Perry cleared his throat and stretched his wings. It was a gesture Mark had seen before, when they were sitting in a particularly arrogant co-op manager's office on Faux Linus. The Legal Eagle was getting ready to take flight.

"Wait in line?" he murmured, before directing his voice to the ear bug so only Mark could hear. *I have an idea. Follow my lead.*

Mark nodded, the corner of his mouth pulling up as he fought to hide a smile. He was learning to enjoy the bird in action—his natural habitat.

"I wouldn't blame you for not recognizing my partner's b-suit, but his Galactic Knights Uniformed insignia should have given our identities away. We are Peacemakers here on Guild business. And the Guild does not wait in lines."

"The Guild…" the booking officer said, each syllable a clipped insult. The tentacles stopped moving for a moment before abruptly resuming their tasks.

The alien grumbled something quietly—its voice too low for the ear bug or its advanced translation program to pick up.

"I believe we started off on the wrong foot here," Perry said, throwing the alien what constituted a smile. "I'm Perry, and this is my biological partner, Clive. What is your name?"

The alien gurgled and rumbled for a moment. The translator labored before the word "Karan" formed.

"Good, Karan. We are well met."

"What is he?" Karan asked, pointing a moist digit at the nearest human—Mark Tudor. It was, Mark decided, a touch rude.

"This magnificent specimen is a human, variety *Iowan*. They're particularly hearty and prone to avoiding things like emotional outbursts or direct eye contact. They're almost all what we call *farm strong*—helps on, um, the farm—but I digress."

"I don't care," Karan burbled.

Perry didn't slow up. "Farms are, as I'm sure you know, are the cultural and *agri*cultural heart of the Earth economy. I know, I know —you're wondering when I'm going to talk about corn, and trust me, friend, I'm getting there. Suffice it to say, the Iowan is not merely a grain farmer—that's reductive, and to be fair, a touch culturally insensitive, sort of like pointing out they all wear black shoes and dress socks to church."

Karan looked between Perry and Mark, then back again, the strange, gelatinous face scrunching up in confusion. Then it hit him. Confusion was part of the bird's plan.

"Are you here to help with our predicament?" Karan asked, grabbing at any thread that would stop Perry from further gales of cultural description about Iowa. Or corn. Mark watched, still strug- gling to match the name to the bizarre-looking alien. Karan was—a lady you knew in town, not a being with enough digits to play an entire piano at once.

"That is still to be determined," Perry said archly, looking around. He switched instantly into a tone laden with authority, and did it without missing a beat. "We're here to exercise a warrant on a known felon. He is a flight risk, so his apprehension is top priority. Now, you mentioned us helping you. Perhaps we can. If you have this individual in custody, which we believe you do, then we will execute our warrant and take him off of your hands, or tentacles, in this case. That will be one less body you have to worry about during what is clearly a, ah—challenging hour for the people of your squad. And station."

Karan managed a damp huff. "I have neither the time nor this inclination for your—for whatever it is you're asking me. The warrant, if it's real, does not supersede our current crisis. Please come back tomorrow," Karan finished with the wheezing equivalent of a prim sniff.

Mark stepped closer, a warm smile on his face. "We don't mean to be a nuisance, but this is urgent. I—I don't want to report that Tau Regus is hindering the apprehension of a dangerous criminal. That's bad for *all* of us. Isn't it, Karan?"

"Dangerous?" Karan asked, then waved her tentacles all around. "If you haven't noticed, this place is now filled to the brim with *dangerous* individuals."

"Filled to the brim," Perry said, slowly sounding out each sylla- ble. "All we need is a signed release and you have one less dangerous individual to worry about."

The alien gurgled and moved again, then slammed one of her tentacles up and over the desk next to Perry, the end coiled by an electronic collar that pulsed with soft blue light. It was...a reader, Mark knew.

Which meant that Karan wanted to see the goods.

"Produce this warrant, and I'll see what I can do,"

Karan announced.

Perry clicked his beak, and a moment later, a holographic file icon appeared in the air before him. He flicked a wing, and the file zoomed into the collared tentacle, where it settled with a bright blue spark. Data appeared on the transparent visor of Karan's breathing apparatus and filtered down, streaming through strange symbols and one easily identifiable picture of their young engineer.

I hope this works, Mark sent.

It better. If not, I've been slimed for nothing. My feathers are not designed for this kind of mucosal insult.

Karan was still for a long time, save for one tentacle as it quietly slapped against the desk behind her. Then she started to jiggle and shift, her sounds existing in that spectrum somewhere between language and unintelligible noise. Either way, there appeared to be nothing for the ear bug to translate.

"This is abhorrent. Detestable," the alien hissed, her tentacles waving. One knocked a pile of folders off the desk while two rose up to wrap around the breathing apparatus. It looked like she was trying to hold her head.

"And now you see," Perry said. "We wouldn't have troubled you with this had it not been such a dire and urgent matter."

"Yes. Thank you. The *audacity*. The *disgusting* creature. I have no words," Karan spat, the tremors shaking her body growing in intensity. The effect was…hilarious.

But Mark and Perry both schooled their features into expressions of polite, professional respect.

With some effort, that is.

Mark backed away, as the alien looked like it may burst at any moment. Then she calmed, and the collared tentacle rose to hover before Perry. A holographic screen shone in the air—three boxes of text, surrounding a simple picture of Tan.

Perry lifted a wing and the screen flashed red before vanishing.

"Release authorized," Karan said. "Now please get it out of my holding cell. No, get it out of my city—off my planet. Disgusting creature. And to think it stood right here in my presence, and I almost—I'm a respectable being. The mere *proximity* of such a thing! Detestable. Horrific. Abominable."

"We stand before you ready to help, Karan. Point the way, and we will collect the vile wretch. This foul and lecherous cur!"

The alien lifted a single, shaking tentacle and pointed off to the right, at a stout-looking door.

"Follow me," Perry said and hopped off the desk.

Mark sighed, then flicked something damp from his hand. Space, he decided, was a lot like the farm.

But with *far* more tentacles.

7

Tau Regus, Fulcrum

THE SECURITY DOOR WHISKED OPEN, and Perry hopped through. Mark moved quickly to follow, then the portal slid shut with a mild *whoosh*. Holding cells lay on both sides of the hall ahead, although the lights were out in the first few spaces he passed.

"It's a sad thought that all these cells are filled with innocents," Mark said.

The clear walls on the next few stalls were heavily smudged, so he couldn't easily identify their inhabitants. A blur streaked toward him on the left, and a massive form struck the poly-glass, long arms and sharp claws slamming into the armored barrier in a staccato fury.

"Okay. So maybe some of them *should* be locked up," he corrected and ran to catch up to Perry. "What trick did you pull back there? Karan went from unhelpful to practically begging us to take Tan off her hands. Or, um, tentacles."

Perry snickered. "I used one of the oldest plays in the book. I'll tell you when the walls don't have ears."

They came to an intersection, only to find more passages of holding cells—one running left and the other, right. He'd never seen a temporary holding facility so large before. It made him wonder what Fulcrum's prisons looked like. Or, if Fulcrum even *had* prisons.

"The release forms say he's in cell Ghor-288, so it appears we have a bit of a walk," Perry said, nodding at the numbers listed above the cells. The halls were named like streets—Ghor ahead of them, Mong, behind, and Wetho, back and to their right. They were standing next to Ghor-11.

"Okay. A mere two hundred more cells to go," Mark grumbled.

"That's the spirit."

"Perry, I want you to stop calling me Clive," Mark said.

"Really? But it's such a refined name, a truly cosmopolitan moniker, that's both resplendent and—"

"Perry."

"Fine. But I want you to know that you're sucking all the joy out of my existence," Perry groused as they made their way down the long passage. "I'm a supercomputer *and* a lethal combat operative. Thus, there are few things I can't achieve. Are you following me?"

"Tragically, yes. You're about to say that annoying me is one of life's little pleasures, and denying you that makes me—what? A monster? A churlish lout?"

"*Churlish lout* is dangerously close to being British, and you know how we feel about them."

"In fact I do. We like them, but we don't want to be them. And while I've enjoyed this attempt to obfuscate my modification of your chosen language, I will remind you I'm a farmer. We can't be bored, or confused, or hustled," Mark said.

"I see that now. Had to try."

"A good effort. Now then, what are these?" Mark asked, waving at the nearest cells. They had no clear barriers, and he caught a whiff of something acrid as they passed, almost like residue from spent explosives. They found another pair of empty cells ahead, the lights inside flickering erratically. The ground was covered with shards of thick, clear material.

He turned to the next cell and found it filled with more than one inhabitant. In fact, it looked suspiciously like a family. His thoughts immediately went to Ja-Ra as he moved past, the collected aliens refusing to meet his gaze. Had his Tunis friends been rounded up, too? Were they somewhere in the warren of cells?

Those thoughts weighed him down until his boot sole caught on the ground and he staggered. Mark collected himself, but before he could continue, something…laughed. To his right. A sound so feral and primal the hair stood up on his neck in response.

Turning to track the noise, Mark didn't see the carnivorous monstrosity his subconscious expected, but a minute figure, so covered in overlapping scars and tattoos that he struggled to identify its race.

It was kind of adorable. In an awful way.

"Will you look at that? A Peacemaker struggling with a simple task like walking. Always knew your kind were—subpar."

"Do I know you?"

The small alien, although humanoid, was decidedly *not* human. He was roughly a meter tall, with feet that looked like cat's paws.

His arms were short and covered with weaving, complicated tattoos. And yet, it was his face that unnerved Mark so. He looked vaguely feline, with large, clear eyes and sharp, yellowed teeth. The branching network of tattoos, scars, and obvious burn marks gave him an aged, violent air. Mark understood what he was seeing.

It was a *warning*.

With a lazy laugh, the feline figure pushed away from the wall and started to pace before the clear barrier.

"What's the matter, lawman, is your precious order crumbling around you? Are you shaken, watching the beacon of civilization collapsing under its own weight?"

"I've seen some chaos today, sure," Mark admitted, looking from the alien's eyes back down the hall to the destroyed holding cells. "But I haven't seen anything that would lead me to believe society is dying. Assholes and opportunity? Sure. The end of all things? Bit premature there, whiskers."

"Oh, but it is, lawman. It *is*. You only hafta stop and listen... listen hard enough to it all unspooling. Delicious, really."

Mark paused and turned his head, as if listening, but all he heard was the metallic *click, click, click* of Perry's talons as he hopped toward him.

"I hear it wheezing. On the way out, says the signs—"

Perry laughed, interrupting the blowhard before turning his amber eyes on the being. "Vane? *The* Jarls Vane?" Perry said, settling in next to Mark, his eyes flashing. "Look at you, all tucked away and cozy in a holding cell. Last the Guild heard, you had gotten yourself blown up, smuggling stolen hydrogen fuel cells across the belt. Amateur shit, to be honest. I didn't buy the story, but—here you are."

"Well, if it isn't the Guild's songbird. Still twittering your bullshit for the odd memory or ride, I see. Hasn't anyone stripped you down for spare parts, yet?" Vane asked. His lip pulled up into a vicious snarl, teeth gleaming lethal in the uneven light.

"Oh, a few have tried, but I'm still here——"

"You see Glass yet? Seen her crews ripping open your precious city's soft underbelly?" Vane asked, interrupting. "She'll be the end of you all."

"As a matter of fact, no. Were we supposed to see her?" Perry asked, giving Mark a questioning look. "We saw some cells back there that looked like they were hit with breaching charges, but that's about it. Nothing I'd call apocalyptic."

"She is a reckoning."

"A reckoning?" Perry asked, cocking his head to the side. "Grandiose term for a filthy little jailbreak, whiskers."

Vane reached up and picked something out of his teeth, a bit of what looked like pulpy meat. He flicked it at them, the morsel hitting and sticking to the clear partition. There was hair in the meat. Mark was bored. He'd seen harder cases.

The lights flickered again, and a deep rumble shook through the structure below, carrying up Mark's legs and Perry's claws. Some distant, scarred portion of Mark's brain—that section that didn't come back whole from France—knew what it was: an explosion, and not a small one.

That was *ordnance*.

"Time to move," Mark ordered.

"Listen to your little human, Perry," Vane growled. "Your time's coming. Mark my words, bird. We will meet again, and *that* time, I'll pluck you clean, then hang your little fusion heart on a chain as a necklace for all to see."

"Probably not," Perry said, waving goodbye with a wing. "Except for the 'listen to Mark' part. He's one of the good ones, after all. If it was Glass that came through here to break people out, something made her decide to leave you locked up. Stew on that, you fuzzy little nightmare." Perry leaned back, taking another look at Vane's cell. "And do use your litter box, won't you? No one likes to see that kind of thing."

Vane ignored the barb, his eyes glittering with black hatred. "Soon enough. You don't know what's coming, but—"

"You do. Got it. End of days, et cetera. Okay, moving on," Perry said, ignoring Vane's spitting fury.

"Add him to our list of things you need to tell me about when we get out of here."

"I'd rather not," Perry said as they finally reached Ghor-288.

"We'll see about that, bird. Not the farm boy anymore."

"Fair. Watch that—that's not glass. It's synthetic. Cuts you once and you're done. Someone brought a wall down, boss. Building material that doubles as a weapon." Perry looked around again. "Step right. Good. Okay, let's move. And here we are."

The lights were off in Tan's cell, leaving the ambient glow filtering in from the hallway as the only source. The young engineer lay on the rigid cot, his back turned toward them, arms wrapped around his body in a piteous attempt at comfort.

"By the power of the almighty Transfer of Custody Form, I bid you open!" Perry said, approaching the cell. His eyes flashed, the cell's keypad responding immediately. The lock icon popped open, the screen turned blue, and a heartbeat later, the door slid up and into the ceiling.

Mark sighed, then moved inside, his b-suit lights coming on automatically. They flickered off and back on again repeatedly as the sensor malfunctioned. Tan stiffened as the lights pulsed, his entire body starting to shake.

"Not again. Please. I won't fight. Not again," he mewled, curling up into a tighter ball.

"Not here to hurt you, Tan," Perry said, but the Druzis youth didn't seem to hear.

Mark smacked the module on his armor and approached, the beam finally staying on. He cursed as the newfound light illuminated the truth. Tan's trembling legs and back were covered in bruises and taser burn marks.

"P-p-please…"

"Tan," Mark whispered, kneeling next to his cot. Then as gently as he could, he laid a hand on his arm.

The Druzis flinched at the contact and then went still, but only for a moment. Tan flailed and rolled onto his back, kicking and punching. Mark lunged forward, using the b-suit's augmented strength to fight for control, but the Druzis youth was stronger than he looked.

"No. Stop. I didn't do anything. Stop. Let me go," he wailed, breaking one arm loose as Mark secured the other.

He leaned forward, pinning the engineer's legs and arms to the cot in a desperate fury. But even then, Tan screamed and bit, his teeth gnashing the air. His wounds were even more evident on his head and face, as bruises and cuts covered his smooth skin. One eye

J.N. CHANEY & TERRY MAGGERT

was swollen shut, while the other spun wildly, unfocused and weeping.

"Tan, we aren't here to hurt you. *Tan!*" Mark shouted while fighting to secure the young Druzis.

"It hurts. Stop. The tasers…they *hurt*."

"Quiet him down or he's going to bring us the wrong kind of attention," Perry warned.

Mark wrestled his arms down again, but bit back his words as he was about to yell. He should have known better from the start. Tan wasn't only panicked and afraid; he'd been driven into an irrational quarter of his mind, a fight or flight response shielding his more sensitive, logical psyche. Yelling at someone like that was only going to drive him deeper in a fight response.

"Tan, this is Mark Tudor. Listen to my voice, Tan. Mark Tudor. We met a little while ago. I know your uncle Cal."

Tan struggled and gasped, his open eye swiveling back and forth, but he was no longer screaming or biting.

"Tan, you wired an infrared node into my ship, the *Fafnir*. I have a job for you. Do you remember? That job is still yours if you want it. All you have to do is calm down and look at me."

Tan gasped, grunted, and gave one final, half-hearted kick of his legs. His wild eye blinked once, twice, and then ever-so-slowly swung over to Mark's face. The blown pupil contracted, and he muttered something under his breath.

"Good, Tan. I'm going to let go of you now. Like I said, we are not here to hurt you. *We are here to help*. Please. Sit up. Breathe. Calm yourself."

Mark did as he promised, releasing his grip on the Druzis' wrists and pushed back. Tan flopped onto his side, kicked himself up into a seated position, and curled into a ball.

"H-help me? Mark Tu…Tudor?"

"Yes," Perry cooed, modulating his voice. "No one will hurt you now. All you have to do is stand up and follow us out of here. But you must remain calm. Can you do that?"

Tan sucked in a shuddering breath, looked at Perry, and nodded quickly.

"Leave. I very much want to leave. P-P-Please."

"Come with us," Mark said, holding out a hand.

Tan studied him for a long moment, then reached out and accepted help. A moment later, they were moving quickly down the passage, away from Karan, the chaos of Tau Regus booking, but more importantly, Jarls Vane and his poisonous gaze.

Netty guided them through the warren of holding cells, projecting a three-dimensional blueprint over the repeater. Although it almost proved to be more of a hindrance than an aid. There was simply too much city between them and the *Fafnir*, and the repeater was designed to be a low power relay.

Half an hour later, they stumbled onto a small, dingy service lift and punched the button for down. The old lift rattled and creaked but provided them a moment of calm and sheltered silence.

"You are the law, so you must know," Tan said quietly. "What is happening? What happened?"

"Someone with, as Mark put it, brass balls, hacked into the City Protectorate mainframe and activated all stored warrants. *Anyone* that has ever been *anyone* to the protectorate was immediately flagged for arrest, regardless of the crime, statute, or severity," Perry explained.

"Why would someone want to do that?"

"Because, my dear boy, in order for bad people to do bad things out in the open, they need an appropriate level of chaos. This is by design, like Mark's hair. It's intentional, despite being a disaster—"

"My hair is functional and convenient, bird."

Perry's beak dropped open. "If that's what you need to tell yourself, then yes, that's, ah, wonderful."

Mark inhaled, then spoke slowly, and with an even, mournful tone. "Sometimes, your tail feathers look like bakelite. Dirty bakelite a kid's been playing with. It's a bit beneath us, but I, as a good partner, keep that thought to myself." Mark leaned forward and pointed at Perry's tail, which was flared for dramatic effect. "That general area. A shame. You're usually so—crisp." He gave Perry an apologetic grin. "Now then, back to business, unless you wanted to discuss my hair again?"

"I'm good for now," Perry huffed.

"Thought so. Back to the original question—who are the bad people, and what bad things are they up to?" Mark proposed, although for their current company, he decided to play it vague. Vane's words bounced around in his head, along with the captured images of those blackened, empty holding cells.

Who did Glass spring from custody? And how far did her designs for Tau Regus extend—banks, chems, alcohol, food, or ships? If she had enough manpower and the gumption to take it, all those things were right there at her fingertips. Or was her gaze wider? Did it extend beyond Fulcrum?

"You mean to stop them? These bad people?" Tan asked as the lift abruptly jumped and the lights flickered.

"Well, ideally, yes. But not on our own," Perry exclaimed,

"Judging from the scope of this particular job, we would be woefully outgunned. Hopefully, the Tau Regus Protectorate can bring things back under order for now, as we have more important matters to attend to."

"Am I one of those matters?"

"Yes, and once we have secured our friend down on the lower levels, we'll be loading back onto the *Fafnir* and departing Fulcrum. If Glass has the power and the reach to hack a mega city's security agency, then she's got a lot more juice than Gyl-Mareth led me to believe," Mark said, cutting in.

Tan nodded, taking it all in, although he realistically knew little beyond that. He had a level of stoic resolve that surprised Mark, especially for someone so young. Then again, he had no idea what the young man had been through.

The lift stopped on level thirty-two, although it took them a little while to find their way out of the service corridors. Once they did, Mark found the streets and alleys...unruly. Crowds gathered in mobs, and while most looked to be rubberneckers, some had a potentially violent air about them. They'd grown brave after the Protectorate moved on, but he knew the danger still lay ahead, when the citizenry's anger outpaced their fear.

Obvious signs of the Protectorate were everywhere—glowing, red security barriers, broken flexicuffs littering the ground, and some fresh-looking scorch marks on the nearby columns. Evidently, the law had been met with some resistance. And force.

And, judging by the debris, raw violence.

"Helluva fight," Mark observed.

Perry bobbed his head looking around. "I wouldn't be surprised if there were corpses. This was more than a fight. This was almost a *battle*."

Mark scuffed his foot at a piece of uniform, scorched and torn. His eyes went vague as he bent to pick up the fabric. "A battle. Yes. It—it was that. Won't stay calm here, though. Crowds are going to form again, and they'll be pissed."

"They'll scatter again once the black suits return," Perry observed. "They're mad, not dumb. Well, not all of them, anyway."

Mark pulled Tan in close as a few people turned and noticed them. Their attention was a bit too focused to be only curiosity.

"Unless they've decided that enough is enough. I saw French peasants lash out at their German occupiers time and again. Didn't end well for anyone," Mark said, then leaned into Tan. "Stay close, but if I tell you to run or hide, don't hesitate. Understand?"

The Druzis nodded, turning a single, fear-filled eye toward the crowds around them. Mark read his expression easily enough. Even the known could look threatening if doused with enough doubt and anarchy.

They wove their way around the central markets, following Perry's lead. The bird flew up into the high girders, using his enhanced, spectral, and infrared modes to interpolate the crowd's composition and likely demeanor. Mark believed they were in the clear, until Perry abruptly routed them around a suspicious-looking mob.

"Did they see us? What were they doing?" Mark asked, after pulling Tan behind a noodle vendor's shack.

"No. No, I don't think they saw you. But their body temperature and excreted hormone level is vastly different than the other crowds," Perry called down.

"Body temperature? Hormones?"

"Trust me, Mark. You can tell much about a figure's demeanor based off key chemical and physiological markers. Think about it this way—the majority of the citizens gathering on this level have elevated body temperature and are excreting significant quantities of stress hormones. That's natural for the circumstances. These individuals are, how would you say it, cool as cucumbers? That's not natural. And before you ask, no, they're not Synths."

"In that case, good. Get some altitude if you need it."

"I can see what I need from here. Flying combat units aren't unusual," Perry assured him. "I mean, I'm magnificent, but not unusual. Do you need me to explain the distinction?"

"Is it like the difference between arrogance and pretentiousness?" Mark asked.

"No need to get mean, boss. Not when I'm covering you."

"True, eyes open, please, regardless of how amazing you are."

"Yes, sir. Wheeling north now," Perry reported.

They passed through an abandoned food market, at least half the produce stands and carts upended and smashed. The ground was slick with trampled food and smashed bottles. This was the spoor of a mob. This was violence, distilled.

Mark looped left and down a dark passage, then finally made the turn to Ja-Ra's hole in the wall. Remaining off the beaten path might have been a detriment to most shop owners, especially those looking to capitalize on foot traffic. But for those dealing in illicit or scavenged goods…well, their clientele was a different sort.

Hold on. Lookout ahead. Perry had gained altitude and switched to the ear bug.

"Are they armed?"

Excessively. I see body armor, a slugger, and a pulse rifle. This guy is definitely a merc.

"Can you take him out quietly?"

Take him out as in…neutralize? Perry asked, careful with his words.

"Subdue."

Without another word, Mark watched as a dark form streaked down from above and shot into a shadowy corner. A previously unseen figure grunted and toppled forward into the light. Perry hopped out a moment later, a satisfied look gleaming in his eyes.

"Mighta popped him a touch too—you know what, he'll be fine," Perry concluded.

Mark slipped forward and wrangled the unconscious alien's arms behind his back, then secured them with flexicuffs and did the same with his legs. Perry hadn't exaggerated his loadout. This particular merc looked ready for war.

"You need a permit for this, buddy." He picked up the discarded pulse rifle. Mark fished out four spare magazines from the merc's gear and stuffed them into his b-suit.

"That thing was constructed after 1920. Are you sure you'll know how to work it?" Perry asked.

"I figure they all work on the same principle—point the dangerous end at the bad guy and squeeze the trigger?"

"That about sums it up."

Leaving the unconscious lookout behind, Mark and Perry moved quietly down the dark hall, passing heavily stained wall panels and faded advertisements as they went. They passed two rusty shop doors on either side—both of which had been kicked in—but stopped right before the final turn. Quiet voices echoed ahead.

Mark leaned out around the corner and took a quick look. Six loaded mercs were standing around Ja-Ra's corroded, heavy door. A seventh figure—Synth, no doubt—was busy trying to cut through with a plasma torch.

He looked to Tan and gestured for the young Druzis to get back and find cover, then Mark lifted the pulse rifle, looked to Perry, and sent *Follow my lead.*

Gotcha, boss.

With his Peacemaker badge lifted in one hand, and the pulse rifle in the other, Mark swung around the corner.

8

"Peacemakers! Drop your weapons and put your hands in the air," Mark bellowed as Perry swung wide on his hip, eyes flashing with furious intent.

The mercenaries turned, pulled, and leveled their weapons with practiced fluidity. Perry spread his wings and jumped forward, his eyes flickering as his attack triggered. The mercs seemed to recognize what his eyes meant and backed away, some even shielding their eyes.

"Do it! Drop your weapons or we are authorized to use lethal force," Perry added.

The mercenaries looked at one another in turn, before one individual stepped forward from the shadows, his purple skin pulsing in the overhead light.

"I don't think we will—drop our weapons, that is," he said, his skin changing color as he spoke. His slit-shaped pupils elongated, until the entire orb was black. By the time he'd completed his second step, his complexion was as white as snow. "I think you should turn around and go find another alley to taint with your presence."

The other mercenaries, emboldened by their leader's strength, lifted their weapons once again and trained them almost singularly on Mark.

"There doesn't *have* to be violence," Mark growled, his grip tightening on the pulse rifle. The weapon responded, humming to life with a gentle whine. A glowing indicator appeared on the side of the receiver, showing that it was fully loaded. A separate indicator showed the pulse level was set at the lethal setting. Interesting, they'd skipped right over the notion of incapacitation and moved right to killing. Mark tapped the receiver, backing the intensity setting to less lethal.

"Unless you turn around, I don't see it ending any other way. You see, we aren't leaving without what we came for, and there's only one of you *Peacemakers*. So…"

"Ahem. There are two of us, thank you very much," Perry corrected.

"Make that four. Drop your weapons, before we have you brigands whipped from this city," came a cheery British accent from behind Mark's shoulder.

He half-turned and caught the familiar glint of shiny metal arms and legs in his peripheral vision. Striker pushed into the passage, four slug throwers leveled at the mercenaries. Valint slipped in right behind him, her scatter gun tucked tight against her shoulder.

"Got here as fast as we could," Valint said, moving to Mark's right. Although she kept a wide space between them. Lesson one and two of tactical encounters, never open yourself up for cheap shots or line up an easy two for one.

"Are you hard of hearing?" Striker asked, edging forward to stand next to Perry. The combat unit spread his arms, covering four of the mercenaries at once. "I said drop your weapons. Do it now, you ruffians."

"Very British of you," Mark told Striker.

"Thank you. There's no reason we can't be mannerly."

Mark watched as a wave of doubt passed through the mercs, although it lasted only a moment. Their leader, skin pale and eyes dark, stiffened and swung his weapon from Striker to Valint.

"That's where you're wrong, badge. Glass doesn't fear death, and neither do we," he snarled and fired.

Mark felt the pulse pass right by him and heard Valint grunt as Striker opened up with all four sluggers at once in a cavalcade of violence. The soft-nosed antipersonnel rounds hit center mass on all four targets, igniting each in a shower of sparks. Two staggered back from the impact, one fell, their weapon discharging wildly, and the last cried out, clutching at their belly as dark fluid began to shoot skyward in hot, looping arcs.

Perry screeched and streaked forward, hitting a merc on the left, while Mark, still aiming at the leader, squeezed the trigger. The pulse rifle barked, issuing forth a violent cone of directed energy. It hit the merc like a gale wind, blowing his arms out wide and knocking him back.

And then things got *really* interesting.

Valint recovered, fired her scatter gun, and cycled through three shots with practiced grace—more dance than fight, she was a ghost, or an avenging spirit. Perhaps both.

Another merc fell under the onslaught, but Mark watched as the others thrust their left arms forward, activating body-length riot shields that shimmered at the edge of normal light.

"Force is a force all its own," Mark said, his words even and factual. He snapped off two rounds in a blur as Valint and Striker fired together, their volley hitting the shields and deflecting off into the walls and ceiling. Mark fired again, only to watch the energy wave sweep his third round harmlessly aside. The mercs came together, forming a wall with their shields. They swung their weapons out and fired, the off-target shots hitting Striker with punishing frequency. Chips of concrete spalled away in stinging violence.

Mark jumped left and fired twice, trying to find an angle, but the mercenary leader turned to compensate. He was good. He was calm. More importantly, he was…competent. They weren't only well-equipped, but well-trained. It was a problem.

Valint dropped the barrel of her gun and moved behind Mark, then lifted it again and continued right. They moved and fired, working to create angles. Perry swooped in from above, talons leading, and hit the far-right mercenary. His shield flared with the impact, the force knocking him back. The discharge threw the bird into the air, where he spread his wings and whirled about in a blur.

The shields redirected energy and projectiles, but not without penalty. If he could hit it hard enough, the repulse might knock the merc off their feet, or if he was lucky, disable the shield altogether.

"Bird! Time for your dazzling personality!" Mark shouted, after firing twice.

"With pleasure."

The merc leader swung his weapon around his shield and fired as Perry dove forward, his wings spread and eyes flashing. Mark closed his eyes and felt the energy strike hit his chest a heartbeat later. The stun attack lit up the darkness behind his lids, the pain swirling in a cascade of riotous color.

The impact took his breath away, but not his wits. Mark dropped the pulse rifle, letting the weapon swing to his side on its sling as he pulled the Moonsword free. He lumbered forward, the color washing in and out in his vision, and swung at the merc leader in a violent overhead chop.

The Moonsword hit the riot shield with a bright flash of energy, jarring Mark's shoulders with the transferred force. He recovered and came in again, this time stepping into the swing, the blade flickering forward, faster than a rumor.

The sword went home.

Heat erupted, and then Mark was swinging again—all instinct, no thought, and a flawless strike that split the mercenary's shield in a crackling coruscation of light and heat.

In that moment, Mark was standing over the Tophin mercenary, the tip of the Moonsword hovering above his sternum.

Perry snickered. "Damocles, table for one."

"Weapons down. Do it now!" Mark bawled.

The mercenaries growled and whispered to one another in their glottal native tongue. They moved to regroup, but Mark lowered the sword point until it sank into the merc's ballistic plating, parting the metal with a whisper. Their leader squirmed, his eyes going wide as he watched the sword descend, unchecked and irresistible.

"So, you don't want to die after all," Mark said in a conversational tone, then looked to the others. "Weapons down. I won't say it again. I won't say *anything*."

They obeyed, sullen glances and silent threats filling the air around them.

Once the pulse rifles touched the ground, the combat AIs moved in and kicked them aside, then stripped their riot shield generators away.

"Over there," Mark ordered, waving his rifle toward the left wall.

Using his four arms, Striker wrangled their prisoners against the wall and cuffed their wrists behind their backs. Perry stood guard while Mark and Valint rounded up their dropped weapons and gear. He stooped down to pick up the leader's damaged riot shield and noticed that the door to Ja-Ra's shop was ajar. A crowd of small faces hovered in the gap, their eyes shining eerily in the light.

The door opened, and a swarm of small figures poured forth. They dragged the discarded plasma cutter and the fallen Synth back into the shop. One figure emerged from the throng that was a touch taller and older than the rest.

"You come!" Ja-Ra said, urging Mark to follow.

They moved into the Tunis' shop, Striker and Perry entering last, the knot of captured mercs huddled between them. Ja-Ra's family closed the heavy door behind them, the cut from the plasma torch having burned clean through half of the heavy portal.

"That door wasn't going to hold out much longer," he said as Valint approached.

She nodded, her expression tight.

"We need a solid exit strategy. I almost had to shoot my way into the hangar. If it was that difficult to get in, imagine how hard they could make it to get back out."

"You'll *never* leave here," the mercenary leader said, chuckling darkly. "Not as long as you have what *she* wants, and she *always* gets what is hers."

"And what is that? Exactly?" Valint asked, wheeling about.

The Tophin continued to chuckle, his eyes sliding away from Valint, before settling on Ja-Ra and his assembled clan.

"Why does she want them?" Mark asked, stepping forward. "Who did she break free from the holding cells on the admin level?"

"Want or need? Both or one. Does it even matter? Or is it simply that you do not possess them…?"

Mark followed the mercenary's dark gaze back to Ja-Ra. Valint went rigid, Perry cried out, and motion flashed in his peripheral vision. Mark barely got the pulse rifle halfway to his shoulder before Striker lifted all four sluggers and fired.

Valint cursed as the Tophin mercenaries slumped to the ground, the slugger rounds killing them instantly. The Tunis began to jump around, their frightened chatter droning all else away—until they froze as the lights flickered overhead, a distant shudder vibrating through the floor.

Mark stood in stunned silence, the pulse rifle hovering halfway to his shoulder. The mercenaries lay still at their feet, their pale skin turning a mottled assortment of colors as blood pooled around them in the hideous fact of combat. They were dead. All of them.

And Striker was their executioner.

"What did you…why did you do that?" Mark asked, finally lifting his gaze to Striker. The combat unit looked down to the bodies, then up to Valint. His eyes were like glowing red coals, gleaming from within his rigid, metallic face. There was no grief there, no guilt. No remorse. There was just the decision. Or the echo of it.

Striker paused, his joints clicking into place as he eased back. "Let us discuss the ugly truth, young Tudor," the combat unit said, his eyes finally switching back to their normal yellow glow. "These soldiers would not allow themselves to be taken into custody. They would never stop fighting us, nor would they abandon their mission. In this case, Glass would see them purée Ja-Ra and everyone he's ever loved and drink them through a straw."

"Grotesque, but…accurate, I think," Mark admitted.

"It is," Perry said, moving in next to the fallen mercenary leader. "Also, I'd like to note that justifying violence always sounds better in a British accent."

Mark watched as the bird clamped onto the Tophin's arm and rolled him over, revealing that the mercenary had somehow broken free from his restraints. A grenade rolled loose from his pale hand.

"Glass gets what Glass wants, and if she cannot, then no one else can possess it. They would have seen us all dead, themselves included. Her behavior, and those like her—it's known. I used it to analyze and predict a seventy-five percent chance that the mercenaries would make a suicide move," Striker said, holstering his sluggers.

"You couldn't warn us?" Mark asked.

"There was no time," Striker said, shaking his head. "I completed my analysis using biochemical and body language data inputs a tenth of a second before he decided to launch his ruinous plan. Unfortunately, in this scenario, I had but one choice available to me. The directives that govern Perry and me are quite clear."

"You did the right thing," Valint confirmed.

Mark nodded, struggling to digest the turn of events. But the further he got from the startling and violent action, the more his emotions changed. He felt less shocked at the AI's abrupt, execution-style shooting, and felt more disappointment? Glass was a brutal and terrifying unknown, and having prisoners to interrogate would have not only helped them unravel her motivations but also served to help them predict her ambitions.

Mark abruptly turned and moved toward Ja-Ra. The Tunis' animated chatter died away, and the small figures flowed back from him, moving like a flock of startled birds.

"Ja-Ra, why were they coming for *you*? Why does she consider you hers?"

"Ja?" the small alien said, shaking his head. "Don't know. We are not things, we are us."

"Exactly," Mark said. "But it appears this Glass, whoever she is, does not feel the same way. Why would she want you and your family dead?"

"You family. Us family."

Mark nodded, urging him on. He didn't push or yell, as the little aliens were obviously terrified. His time working with shell-shocked people in France had taught him that patience and a soft approach were much more effective than anything else.

"Was she a client? A customer?"

Ja-Ra nodded. "But not Glass back then. She was Mala Jin-Kincade. She was a soldier, indentured, fighting on contract to be free. That was many solar cycles ago, before Mark Tudor found Ja-Ra and his clan in Tau Regus."

"Indentured?" Valint asked. "Who was she fighting for, Ja-Ra?"

"She never said. No markings on armor or ships. Only told Ja-Ra that it was a matter of life or death that we never speak of her to anyone."

"Did she buy weapons from you?" Mark asked.

The lights flickered again before the Tunis could respond, another shudder passing through the floor. The whole of Tau Regus seemed to groan, like a wounded beast struggling for breath.

Ja-Ra's clan bunched together, clustering into a tightly packed crowd. They'd never looked more like strange, one-eyed alien bunny rabbits than in that moment.

"No weapons. Never weapons. She hired Ja-Ra to install security equipment and programming. She collected many things: components, controllers, computers, lasers, and scanners—all salvaged from dead military ships. Then we installed it on her fleet. We did not see her for a long while after that, until one day she returned, and not as Mala Jin-Kincade anymore, not as an indentured soldier. She had become Glass, and she took us to her base. We installed more security and defense systems there—many, many systems."

Mark turned to Valint, and they shared a look. The picture was clarifying in his mind—not only who Glass was but why she would want to keep Ja-Ra out of her enemy's hands. She'd been a revolutionary, fighting for freedom. The Tunis scavengers had likely played a key role in her preparations and battle strategy.

The lights went out, and the shop plunged into darkness. Mark held his breath and counted, the sound of his raging heart filling his ears. An explosion rocked the city somewhere beyond the shop, and a moment later, the emergency lights blinked on.

Striker bent low over the dead mercenaries, his four arms working quickly to strip away the bulk of their tactical armor and equipment.

"Bloody hell," he groaned, uncovering a small module sewn right into the Tophin's upper arm. A small red light flashed on the screen while a display showed a flat line. "They're tied together with biometric relays."

"Which means?" Mark asked.

"Glass knows the moment any of her people are killed. Well, it goes beyond that. A biometric feedback unit like this could tell her when her people are under duress, are injured, or are, say, sedated and captured. It's no coincidence that the power started to flicker right after Striker took her agents down. They likely escalated their attack on the city once those feeds went dead," Perry said.

"Literally and figuratively," Striker added.

"We need to get out of the city, to someplace off the beaten path to figure out what we're into," Valint reasoned.

"I think it's the same thing we stepped into before," Perry said, cutting in. "But yes. Step one, find someplace to lay low. I have detailed blueprints of this city. Given enough time, we could find our way back to the upper levels, but my intuition tells me that Ja-Ra might know a faster way to the *Fafnir*."

"You can get us back up to the ship?"

"Ja!" the Tunis said, and without warning, the clan swarmed around them, pushing them toward the back of the cluttered shop like a wave of one-eyed, hopping aliens.

Which they were.

9

MARK WATCHED as Ja-Ra's children and cousins unbolted a wall panel in the back of their shop and flowed into a small, dark space. He pursued, with Perry in front followed by Valint and Striker. The large, multi-limbed combat AI had to fold his arms into his body to fit.

His b-suit lights clicked on after a moment, revealing a heavily stained passage ahead. The path was so narrow, Mark's shoulders scraped against both sides.

They moved straight ahead for only a moment, before turning left and through a junction. He followed the Tunis around a right-hand turn, and the path opened into a wider, taller maintenance section. Mark swung the pulse rifle from left to right as they went, tracking sounds echoing in from the passages beyond. It sounded like a war zone, with panicked voices and muffled city announcements, all punctuated by explosions.

"They're tearing the city apart," Valint whispered.

"How much worse will it get once the Protectorate realizes what's going on?" he breathed, ducking low under a pipe.

"You mean, once a brazen attack turns into a small-scale war?"

"Yes. That," he said. Although, considering the size of Tau Regus's Protectorate force, Mark doubted the scale. He'd seen small skirmishes turn into ugly bloodbaths on the flip of a coin. If Glass had truly earned her nickname the way they claimed, this could sweep all of Fulcrum into the mix.

Ja-Ra led them out through a jaggedly cut hole in the inner wall and into a dark atrium. Service lights glowed above and below them, illuminating what appeared to be a wide service shaft. A steady breeze of damp, oil-tinged air blew up from below, carrying with it the noise of industry and machines.

They wound their way up and around the atrium, Mark and Valint fumbling their way over the small stairs in the dark. Ja-Ra and his clan, however, moved with practiced grace and stealth, their footsteps becoming lost to the rush of air and dripping humidity.

Mark became so engrossed in the climb that he almost didn't notice when the Tunis pushed off to the right and through another opening. It was darkness and grease-stained walls, more service shafts, and impossible lengths of cramped passages. He stepped through a cut in the wall and took almost a dozen steps before he realized that the ceiling loomed high overhead.

Mark straightened, stretching his back, and caught Valint doing the same. A quick glance around confirmed that they had emerged into the city, although where, he could not tell.

They started toward one of the large lifts, only to discover it was surrounded by glowing red barriers. He took a breath to speak, to get Ja-Ra's attention, but the Tunis took them right by without breaking stride. Two turns later and they pushed through a door to a side passage. Inside was a smaller lift, the doors battered and beaten from years of abuse.

"Up to the ship," Ja-Ra said, pointing toward the ceiling with an upraised finger.

They piled on and immediately started to rise, although with nowhere near the speed or comfort of anything more complex than an oxcart in frozen mud. Mark focused on his breathing while also making sure his knees weren't locked. The last thing he needed was to pass out and fall on his face. Perry would never let him live that down, and the ride continued to be—challenging.

The elevator banged and rattled, its noise growing more offensive with every floor climbed. Ja-Ra and his family clutched their hands over their overly large ears as the lift started to slow, the noise around them rising to an almost painful crescendo. Mark pushed through the crowd and out into the hall, only then realizing that the noise hadn't been the lift at all, but the sound of battle.

Flashes of light broke the gloom beyond the access passage door, with a sizzling, eardrum-rattling boom following right after. The ground shook, and dust rained in from above. If Ja-Ra knew the city as well as Mark hoped, then they were on the level with the hangar, but from the sounds of it, they would have to fight their way through to the *Fafnir*.

"Perry and Striker, you take the lead. Tan and Ja-Ra, stay here! Don't come out until we let you know it's safe," he said, his gaze never leaving Valint. The Druzis and Tunis nodded in his peripheral vision, then melted back into the dark passage.

"Regretting your decision to leave that French battlefield yet?" Valint asked, cycling her scatter gun.

Mark pushed the pulse rifle into his shoulder and canted it right, the charge indicator glowing in response. He'd only fired it several times below, so the mag-battery was still almost full.

"There's no place I'd rather be," he replied, reaching up and sliding the fire indicator from less lethal to lethal.

"Standing in a dark service passage, surrounded by violence, and solely responsible for the safety of these now-displaced refugees?"

"You're here with me, too. That accounts for *something*," Mark said, although he meant *everything*.

Valint did something to him when she was near—made his heart hammer in his chest and his fingers tingle. She also made him feel like he could take on the world, but also lose everything, all at the same time. It was a kinetic, almost uncontrollable sensation.

"If you two are quite done making eyes at one another, might we make for the ship and our freedom now? Before Glass and her people bring down the whole of the city on our heads? Or worse, reduce another site to glass?" Striker asked, his face hidden in shadow. All Mark could see were those glowing eyes, burning like intense, radiant coals.

"Let's do this together," he said, nodding at the door. "Two-and-two formation. AIs out to the wings, with Valint and me in the center."

Perry nodded, his eyes flickering from orange to red. Striker lifted the sluggers and turned, his servos and integrated hydraulic systems whining softly. Then, without preamble, hesitation, or fear, the two combat units pushed out and into the maelstrom.

Mark ducked out to shield Valint, his pulse rifle sweeping the scene. Striker had moved right, and Perry left, the bird unleashing a stun attack right into the faces of two mercenaries. The Yonnox, equipped similar to the Tophin from below, screeched and flailed, spinning in circles as they clawed at their eyes. Striker dropped one of the mercenaries while Mark caught the second with a pinpoint shot.

A squad of beleaguered Tau Regus Protectorate agents jumped up from their hiding spots and fired their blasters, and yet as soon as they appeared, Glass's mercenaries materialized from almost every shadow. Their weapons barked and cried, energy blasts, sonic rounds, and slugs singing through the air. One Protectorate agent fell immediately, another took a glancing blow, and the others dove for cover.

"Brigands!" Striker bellowed and fired two of his sluggers. The soft-cored projectiles ricocheted off the handrail, just missing the lead mercenary. The Yonnox swung his weapon around but couldn't fire before the AI let loose with the other two weapons.

The second volley hit the merc full in the armor, knocking him back and over the handrail. He screamed as he went, tumbling down and out of sight. Striker cried triumphantly and charged in, guns blazing.

Mark drew a bead on another mercenary and fired as Perry dove in from above, streaking like an arrow into another Yonnox. His talons hit first, tearing through armor and flesh, as they tumbled out of sight.

Valint moved ahead, her scatter gun popping off twice in quick succession. The shots hit a stack of crates, the first knocking one over, while the follow up blew two apart. A mercenary stumbled out from behind the ruined concealment, and Mark was ready. He tracked the running figure and fired three controlled shots.

Glass's forces shouted and pointed, firing an unorganized volley at Striker, Valint, and Mark, giving the Protectorate agents a moment of reprieve. In that instant, the city enforcement officers regained their feet and came together.

"Let's push them back together!" he yelled, waving the Tau Regus forces forward. Two of the black-clad agents fired, while the rest converged in the center.

"Forward!" Striker bellowed, with Perry matching his advance.

The mercenaries floundered, lobbing scattered and erratic shots their way, but Mark watched as they started to retreat. He made it a single step toward the hangar doors before glancing back and watching in horror as the Protectorate, the appointed defenders of the city, tucked tail and ran. Valint followed his gaze, caught sight of the fleeing soldiers, and cursed.

She turned to him a heartbeat later, a steely resolve returning to her caramel eyes.

"We don't need them," she said, dropping the mag from her scatter gun and slapping in a replacement in one efficient movement.

"We have done far more with far less," Mark agreed and checked the pulse rifle's charge indicator. It was down to half a charge already, the lethal pulse rounds having taken their toll on the battery mag. He had four fresh batteries and his trusty revolver beyond that. If things got personal, he would introduce Glass's thugs to the cutting edge of his Moonsword. The blade had a psychological effect on people that blasters and firearms couldn't match. As long as he was close enough, that is.

Valint and Mark moved forward, closing in behind Striker and Perry. The combat AIs had pushed the retreating mercenaries back to the hangar door, but the Tophin, Yonnox, and Nesit soldiers had regrouped and were using the large doors to great effect.

Both combat AIs stood before the large opening, waiting for targets of opportunity to present themselves. The mercenaries swung their weapons around the corners and fired wildly, the shots hitting the ground and ricocheting wildly into the air.

Mark crouched low over a fallen mercenary and pulled the riot shield generator off his left forearm. He tapped the small power icon, only to be rewarded with an almost body-length energy barrier. Valint staged behind him, and they moved forward together until they finally reached Striker.

"I suggest a stacked breach clearing," Striker said, his head swiveling around to face them. "Perry, then me, and you two in the rear. Agreed?"

"Do it," Valint said.

Perry leapt up into the air, flapping hard, but Striker was moving before the bird had even crossed the threshold. Slugs and blaster rounds skipped off the ground, a few hitting Striker's armored chassis and Mark's riot shield. Sparks and debris whined away in brilliant fury as the rounds sizzled past.

They pushed into the onslaught as the mercenaries opened up. Then Perry struck, his stun attack popping off in a flash of startling noise and light. Striker surged through the opening with a burst of speed in the next moment, his arms snapping out to either side. His sluggers opened up with instant savagery, raking the mercenaries stacked up on the other side.

Mark swung left and Valint right as they followed, adding their own fire to the mix. An ear-rattling moment later it was over, a fog from weapons fire hovering over two piles of dead mercs.

"I would normally recommend sifting through the aftermath to better understand the need for so much violence," Perry started, his eyes flickering back to orange, "but right about now, Glass is watching the biometric feeds of all these fighters go flatline. Let's load up our cargo and be gone before she decides to take her internal military strategy external."

"Meaning bombard the city from above?" Mark surmised.

"Exactly."

"If she takes direct military action against a megacity like Tau Regus, then I question the size and reach of her force," Striker said.

"It doesn't have to be big, only unafraid of conflict."

"That sounds like you're talking about pirates," the AI said.

Perry flew back and rounded up Tan and Ja-Ra's clan, then made for the *Fafnir*. They found the scorched remains of two beings not ten paces from the ship's bow access panel. A long, soot-stained burn mark stretched almost twenty feet on the ground behind them.

"I'm sorry for making a mess, Mark. These two tried to break into the ship right after I lost contact with you. I fired a warning shot with the laser, but they wouldn't stop, so I hit them on the low power setting. I didn't think it would do that to them," Netty said, her optical sensor appearing above his wrist.

"That was *low* power mode?" Mark asked, considering the remains. They looked more like scorched, dead trees than...Yonnox, or Tophin? He couldn't really tell what they had been before, other than alive and dumb enough to attack a warship.

"Serves them right," Perry said, circling overhead before landing on the ramp. "What kind of fool tries to break into a Peacemaker's ship? They're guaranteed to be armed and run by no-nonsense AIs."

"Those kinds of fools," Mark said, pointing to the scorch marks on the ground. He winced. "I'm not a fan of, ah, mass death, but I'm glad our policy is to shoot first and ask questions later."

"My life's motto. Well, that and don't trust a Yonnox. Based on the shape of those carbonized remains, both sayings work," Perry said.

"Efficient. You're practically a Midwesterner," Mark said.

"If I show up with a casserole and an apology then you'll know my transformation is complete."

"Noted, bird. And remember, no matter what the dish calls for, add cheese," Mark said, moving aside for Valint, who finished corralling the Tunis up the ramp and into the ship. She put a hand on Mark's shoulder and nudged him to follow. He cycled the airlock closed, but only after she'd cleared the bottom of the ramp and made for the *Stormshadow*.

"Netty, get us out of here," Mark ordered, pushing through the crowd as he tried to get to the cockpit.

"You got it, boss."

The ship lifted off, rocking him against the left bulkhead, then pitched back in the other direction. The Tunis, arms linked, swayed with the motion, chattering animatedly in their native tongue.

Thrust kicked in as Mark made it to the cockpit, only to find that Tan was already strapping himself into the co-pilot's seat. Perry was perched above the Druzis' head, his holo screen filling with data.

"Hold on!" Netty cried as the ship seemed to drop below him.

Mark floated for a moment as time slowed to a punishing trickle. Then he was on the ground, face down, with stars flashing before his eyes.

The *Fafnir* rocked hard from left to right, then rolled aggressively back in the other direction. Something exploded beyond the hull, and the Invictus laser fired a staccato of rapid beats. Mark caught his breath, rolled right, and scrabbled toward the oasis of his pilot's seat and its safety harness.

"Stay down, Mark. Give Netty and me a moment…" Perry said, then devolved into a series of grunts and curses.

He slid forward abruptly as the *Fafnir* nosed down, the thrusters firing again and again. Mark crawled back toward his chair and hooked an arm around its mount, then held on as the ship was flung into an aggressive barrel roll.

"Netty…what's…going on?" he asked as his guts turned to water.

"They had attack boats staged outside waiting for us," the AI explained. "Judging from the wreckage on the ground, we weren't the first targeted."

"I've got tonelock. Firing," Perry announced as a missile launched from beneath him. The ship rocked again, and the laser fired a searing bolt of punishment.

"That's a hit," Netty whooped. "Tango One is on fire. Mark, this might be your best chance to get off the floor."

Not wasting time, Mark pushed up to his knees, then crawled into the pilot's seat. He flung his arms into the harness straps and buckled them together before cinching it tight. It wasn't until he reached for his tactical overlay that he realized his right hand was covered in blood.

A quick search confirmed that it came from his head, although the exact location or severity of the wound he couldn't tell. He was still thinking and breathing, and in a fight, that was enough.

"Break it down for me. What did we fly into?"

"Same excrement as below," Perry said, "but it appears that Fulcrum Planetary Defenses were better prepared than Tau Regus. Glass has a…battlegroup."

"A battlegroup? You mean, like cruisers?"

"Perhaps even larger than that," Perry confirmed. "They have their hands full right now, as Fulcrum Planetary Defenses are no slouch. This could be our chance to slip away."

"Slip away? Shouldn't we stay and help?"

"Trust me, Mark. By now, you should know that I'm not one to shy away from a fight, but we do not want to be in the middle of this one. Not at this moment. Live to fight another day?"

"All right. Let's get our passengers to safety."

Mark zoomed out on his tactical overlay and tried to make sense of the mess before him. Red and green triangles moved over the changing map, with more being added by the moment. Despite her speed and proficiency, even Netty was struggling to identify all the moving pieces on the board and if they were friend or possible foe. The battle raged around them in silent fury, flaring their screens into shutdown.

When the images came back, there were fewer ships, but there was more chaos. Perry was right. They were in the middle of a storm.

And there was only one way out. *Through.*

10

"My stick, Netty," Mark said, taking control. He immediately nosed down and accelerated, pushing hard toward the ground.

The side of a massive comms antenna exploded to their left, the thousand-foot-tall spire tipping like an enormous, felled tree. Mark poured on more thrust to avoid the catastrophe as alarms and bells started going off.

It wasn't Netty but the *Fafnir* telling him that he was flying too low and too fast. The altimeter flashed 500 feet before he wrenched back on the stick. Thrusters kicked in, but the ship's limited aerodynamics worked against him, and they were barely 200 feet off the ground before he broke from the dive.

"You looking to scrape off some belly paint or just make sure we die extra fast?" Perry asked.

Rockets, missiles, and laser fire continued to pepper the ground and buildings around them as the mess of aerial combat engulfed Fulcrum.

"That's how we get out of here." Mark pitched right and then left to avoid a large gas processing plant. He didn't need to *see* the facility get hit, as the explosion reverberated through the entire ship.

"We fly lower and faster than any sane pilot or AI. Then once we're clear of the mess, we point our nose to the sky and get the hell out of here," Netty suggested.

Perry's eyes flared with concern. "If we don't become a smear on the landscape first—"

"I trust you, Mark. I've disabled my flight safety protocols. Push her as hard as you need," Netty interrupted.

Mark didn't respond as he poured every ounce of strength and focus into weaving the ship through Fulcrum's congested landscape. He rolled right, using the bow thrusters for extra push, then climbed up and over a long, tall complex. They cleared the other side, and a massive ship appeared as it unloaded its entire rocket battery in a single, blinding assault. The rockets hit a series of low, flat, bunker-like buildings and engulfed the entire space in billowing fire and dust.

"Well, now we know she's got at least one heavy cruiser. Holy hell!" Perry cursed.

"Throwing a lot of ordnance. That last round was about fifty thousand bonds," Netty informed them.

"I detest waste. It's the Iowan in me," Mark observed. "Ah. Here come the opportunists. Little bastards were an inevitability."

Several small Fulcrum fast attack boats swarmed around the larger craft, peppering its heavy armor with laser fire. They looked like gnats to the warship, nothing more.

One detail about the warship caught his attention, beyond its impressive ability to deal destruction and death. A large red skull had been painted on the aft armor panel, with a stylized bloody slash beneath it.

"Even *looks* like a damned pirate ship," Mark said.

"You think?" Perry agreed. "They're scanning us. Damn sakes, their sensors are good."

"Line these up. Two missile launches. Staggered launch, on my go."

Mark targeted the heavy cruiser's starboard rocket battery and fired, and their Whisperwing missile leapt forward.

"Next shot, now!"

Perry cycled the second missile as Mark wrenched back on the stick and crammed the throttle forward all the way. The *Fafnir* nosed up into an impressive and immediately painful climb, the engine screaming like an angry bird.

"Our first missile is dead. The second is tracking—and wandering, but still tracking, and…" Netty said, her voice fading out as Mark's vision and hearing tunneled. "Good hit. Some damage, but damn that's a big boat."

The g's stacked up on his chest and face, crushing him into the gel cushions. His vision closed in as blood rushed in his ears, but he fought to keep the stick back and the throttle forward.

"They launched at us. Missile in the air—forty thousand yards and closing fast," Netty said.

"We hit terminal velocity. Mark, stay with us. We're almost there. They only launched one," Perry said, his voice ebbing and flowing in his ear.

"The Invictus is tracking and firing. That's a miss. And another. This missile is smart. It's keeping the body of the *Fafnir* between us, like it knows where our only point-defense weapon is located."

"We have to operate under the assumption that they know everything about us——" Perry said.

"We broke the exosphere, and we're picking up speed. The missile is only four thousand yards out, closing fast. Perry, use the laser and blow it out of the——" Netty said.

"No. I want that missile as close to us as possible," Perry called.

"You want what?" Tan asked, speaking up for the first time.

"We're going to give this smart missile an aneurysm. Mark, once it hits one thousand yards, cut thrust. Netty, at the same time, fire the laser to get it to change its trajectory, and I'll launch counter-measures, flares, and our new static buoy. That should cook off its brain."

Mark nodded and forced the air out of his lungs. His vision was clearing, but slower than he'd like.

"We just got that static buoy. Mark paid good money for it," Netty argued.

"Well, this is a 'use it now or never' scenario. Two thousand yards. Mark, be ready to cut thrust."

"I'm gonna die, I'm gonna die," Tan muttered next to him, his hands pulled up to cover his eyes.

"We do this all the time, kid. Sit back and relax." Mark's knuckles were white against the throttle. He could say it, even if he didn't necessarily feel or believe it.

"Now!" Perry called.

Mark yanked back on the throttle, and the *Fafnir*'s engine immediately cut out. The Invictus fired, while the ship simultaneously launched a barrage of pulse flares, and one particularly loud static buoy.

"We broke lock. It's tracking on the static buoy now…"

An explosion rocked the ship then, the shock wave nearly throwing Perry from his perch. Several minutes passed, with a blessed calm falling over the ship. It confirmed two things: they were still alive, and according to the tactical overlay, well away from the fighting.

Thrust kicked back in as Netty navigated them out of the gravity well, but it was gentle this time, not the violent, suffocating weight that tried to suck his eyeballs out the back of his skull.

Mark took a deep breath, held it in for a moment, and slowly let it out. He reached up and rubbed his face, eyes, cheeks, and gums, which were sore from the hard-g push. *Alive.* Yes, they were alive, but as the old saying went, they'd gone from the frying pan straight into the fire.

Working his fingers up into his hair, Mark finally found the bleeding culprit—a laceration above his left ear. The cut was almost three inches long and still weeping, the hair around it stubbled and singed. In short, he'd taken a glancing round right off his dome. How had he come that close to dying and not known it?

Mark shook off the startling thought and turned to look at Tan. The Druzis was shaking visibly and still had his eyes covered.

"You made it," Mark said, unbuckling from the harness.

Tan slowly lowered his hands, his wide, unblinking eyes appearing. He looked around the cockpit, scanning everything in great detail, before locking in on the starscape beyond the windscreens. He took a breath and slowly let it out.

"Is this your first time off-world?" The question was straightforward, but Mark also wanted to break the tension.

Tan nodded, slowly turning to face him.

That fact felt weird to Mark, that he'd had more experience

traveling amongst the stars than a member of a race from a more advanced, spacefaring world.

"Enjoy it while it's, ah, fresh. Could've used less excitement, I'll say," Mark murmured.

"In space, exciting is bad," Perry added. "Or should I say overrated?"

"We don't have any followers, Mark. It looks like we are in the clear," Netty said, breaking in on the conversation.

"Valint?"

"She broke atmosphere one hundred miles north-northwest. She's burning hard for a twist point."

"Good," Mark said, melting back into his chair. He reached up and swiped at his tactical overlay to switch from sensor mode to the *Fafnir*'s exterior cameras. Fulcrum loomed large behind them, its megacities sprawling like mechanical continents. Flashes of light popped above the world. First one, then a dozen, and more—the unmistakable signs of conflict and war.

"Where to first? Armagost? How are we on fuel?"

"Low—below one third. We might want to refuel and refit first."

"Where's close…?" he started to ask, then remembered Ja-Ra and their Tunis passengers. "Oh, hell."

Mark tumbled out of his pilot's seat and turned left, only to come face-to-face with an odd sight. Ja-Ra and his clan had linked arms, forming a matrix of hooked appendages. Those on the outside were still clutching to pipes, handles, or whatever afforded the best grip. It kept the small aliens from tumbling back into the galley under their hard-g maneuvers.

"I'll be damned," Mark said.

Perry fluttered down to stand next to him.

"Ah, yes. Tunis. They're a resilient species."

"Safe? Alive?" Ja-Ra asked.

Mark nodded, and the Tunis web immediately began to unweave. The small aliens didn't disband like some might. No, they clustered even more tightly together, moving toward him, their eyes shining in the overhead light.

It struck Mark then—the full weight of his situation. It wasn't just him and Perry any longer. No, he had dependents relying on him, and judging from the open warfare engulfing Fulcrum, that crowd was likely to grow.

"Sit tight, Ja-Ra. We'll be twisting to a safe place soon. The galley is right down there, and it's packed with food. Some of it's even edible."

"Avoid the cheese," Perry bawled out.

Mark shook his head gravely. "Better listen to him on that one."

At the mention of food, the crowd of one-eyed aliens turned and immediately flowed down the passage and into the next space. Mark watched as they surged up and over the benches, some moving to stand on the table itself. Cupboards banged open as the space came alive with noise. He turned back to Perry.

"How does this change things?"

"You mean, with Glass committing herself to open warfare with Fulcrum? Or that your cupboards and food supply are about to go bye-bye?"

"The first one," Mark said, although he had to fight hard not to turn back to the galley. Judging from the noise, his supplies would be gone in moments.

"A lot depends on how Fulcrum responds. Tau Ceti is a powerful system, yes, but its military might is not centralized. The ruling worlds are bound by a complicated series of treaties and trade arrangements. There's no guarantee that they'll unite against a threat, especially if the threat only hits one of the system planets. There'll likely be posturing and angry words, perhaps some threats, but that's about it. Just a lot of air and not much ordnance."

"Will they reach out to the Guild?"

"Now *that* would be an interesting twist," Perry said with a snort. "Once the Galactic Knights Legion gets involved, things escalate. Tau Ceti, meaning the allied worlds, is not likely going to want a large, outside military force in-system…regardless of the reason or risk. They would likely view it as a long-term threat against their sovereignty."

"Mark, we're quickly approaching twist space," Netty said. "You want me to do the usual?" The usual being a series of confusing micro-jumps, followed by a longer twist to set them up, and then one final leap to Armagost's hidden base. The catch this time being that they needed to make a stop for fuel and provisions. Besides, Netty promised to bring their Gajur ally treats the next time they stopped.

"Do it. Send coordinates over to Valint through a secure link, and, if possible, make our provisions stop someplace off the beaten path. If you can manage it, maybe somewhere with open skies, fresh air, and some sunlight."

"You got it."

Mark returned to the cockpit, content to avoid the chaos filling his galley. Tan, he found, had not moved. Although the Druzis youth wasn't shaking nearly as much.

"I just unleashed a swarm of Tunis on my food stores. If you're hungry, I would suggest going now. Otherwise, you might not have another chance. A little something in your stomach might help steady your nerves."

Tan nodded absently, fumbling with the release for his harness before finally getting it to unlatch. He stood and wobbled for a moment, before disappearing around the corner.

"Okay, what's the plan, Netty?" Mark asked while sliding into his pilot's chair and tapping his overlay awake.

"Three short twists. One to the Tau Ceti outer marker, the second out of system, and the last to take us back in to Carson's Arch. I'm waiting for docking and fueling permissions in Greenway. Nope. There it is. We are now confirmed to dock in Banyon's Gulch. It's on the outskirts of Greenway."

"Beautiful. Let's go."

"Will do, but only if you let Perry take a look at that head wound," Netty said.

"Fine, but he's got to use more delicacy than a velvet hammer. The sumbitch was *rough* last time."

"A bald-faced lie. There was no last time, you crybaby. And as to my touch, I only have one kind. Fatal." Perry finished with a wink.

"I don't know what is more disconcerting, the wink, or the whole touching part in general. You must not have heard me the last time when you sutured the cut on my back. Were you listening, sawbones?"

"Hmmm," Perry said, turning to look away, "My auditory sensors must have failed at that exact moment. Better upgrade my drivers."

Mark gave Perry a gimlet eye, then the ship began to thrum.

The *Fafnir*'s twist drive spooled quickly, then jumped the drag-onet the short distance to the system's outer marker. Once there, they updated their logs, programmed in the next jump, and waited for the buoy to register them. Perry fetched their med kit, then cleaned and covered the cut on Mark's head. According to the bird, it wasn't life-threatening.

Their next twist took them two light-years out of system. This was the game—for anyone watching their travel habits, it would look as if they'd left Tau Ceti for Procyon. In reality, they would twist right back into system, jumping dark past the outer marker on their way to their true destination.

Carson's Arch was a busy world, an agricultural hub competing with Faux Linus for the title of food king. They jumped in beyond the gravity well and burned the rest of the way on low thrust, Mark's overlay updating with over one hundred vessels moving in and out. More appeared on his screen regularly. Ship traffic increased well before the planet became visible to the naked eye.

"Scans are showing no signs of hostile action," Netty reported as they passed between two enormous freighters. The news was welcome to the entire crew.

Tan returned to the cockpit as they were about to break atmosphere. He slid into the co-pilot's seat and strapped in, then turned to Mark, revealing a streak of what looked suspiciously like ketchup extending from the corner of his mouth.

"Feel better?" Mark asked.

"Yes, I do. Thank you. I ate something called a sausage, I think. It was very interesting—economical in its packaging, although I found the transparent layer difficult to remove."

"The 'transparent layer'?" Mark asked, then laughed. "That's a casing. You're meant to eat it all together."

"Truly?"

He nodded, stifling his laughter.

"The Tunis were dismantling them, so I followed suit. Next time, I'll try it as you suggest. Thank you, Mark Tudor."

"You're welcome."

They entered the atmosphere over Carson's Arch between the rings of two enormous, interconnected space elevators. Robotic ships dashed between them, weaving routes that brought them dangerously close to each other. Netty navigated them through the mess, and for good reason. Mark couldn't remember more congested skies, save for Prosperity.

The flight down was rough, as the thick atmosphere and strong sun made for excessive turbulence. Tan was green by the time the *Fafnir* smoothed out, although since he had gray skin to begin with, Mark wasn't necessarily sure if the color change meant that he felt sick. He'd shot a Wulgor in the shoulder, after all, his anatomical ignorance on full display.

"We will be landing in Greenway momentarily. The conditions, as the planet's climate engineers intend, are ideal. You'll enjoy clear skies, bright sunshine, and a temperature hovering below eighty degrees Fahrenheit in perfect humidity. Thank you for flying with us here at Netty Spaceways."

"You've got the voice and personality for radio, Netty," Mark said, throwing the AI a smile. He leaned to look out the port window. The landscape was green as far as he could see, the ground broken up into perfectly symmetrical plots of farmland. It was—

Like Iowa. But bigger, somehow.

"Yes. An absolute peach," Perry said as the retro thrusters kicked in. Their airspeed dropped, until the ship hovered, before slowly lowering onto their designated pad.

"What is it, bird?" Mark asked once Tan unhooked and disappeared around the corner. "You were practically giddy while tending my head wound. What changed?"

"Yes, but I was closing a head wound. I do so enjoy those. Now? Now the bird is stuck thinking about two things he hates most of all —one, when people chew their food with their mouth open, and two, chaos. Things are growing more chaotic by the cycle, and we are no closer to answers. If anything," he said with a derisive snort, "we are further away than ever."

"I disagree."

"Why?" Netty said before Perry could retort.

"We've rattled some cages and are starting to get a picture of who the players are. The Guild is hampered by at least two corrupt masters—"

"Cai-Demond and Gyl-Mareth, yes," Perry interjected.

"Gyl-Mareth was running a skimming operation with that Ligurite piece of filth. The Five Star league was invested in that scheme as well. Now we know that Glass is involved. And the fact that Gyl-Mareth wants her dead might be the most interesting development. That ties him and her back to the civil conflict still smoldering between the Gyl and Cai."

"Smoldering is actually a pretty good descriptor," Perry admitted. "Many claim the conflict is cold. Others, that it has been resolved, but those that know…well, they understand. What bothers me is that before these recent developments, we'd already gone toe to toe with one warship and barely survived. Now, Glass drops into Fulcrum airspace with a battlegroup in one of the boldest moves I've seen in years. Every time we turn around, this thing gets bigger and uglier. We're getting punch-drunk, boss."

"Things get worse before they can get better."

"But how bad can we allow it to become?" Perry asked. "Yes, I may be snarky and witty…the definition of streamlined elegance and lethal perfection, but I'm a being created around rules. If I see a thing malfunctioning, I fix it. If I see a scenario in violation of statute or law, I intervene. Again, how bad can we allow this to become?"

Mark unbuckled from his harness and pushed off to stand. He stretched his arms and shoulders, then his back. Everything ached, and for good reason. Part of him understood Perry's frustration. They walked around the corner, past Tan Tu'Tu and Ja-Ra's crowd. Mark intentionally did not look toward the galley as he cycled the airlock open. They moved through and stepped out into the bright sunshine.

Perry hopped down the ramp at his side, but they were almost twenty feet into the grass before either spoke.

"You can't look at this conflict as a whole," Mark said, turning his face to the sky and basking in the warmth. After weeks locked aboard a claustrophobic ship, their only reprieve had been Armagost's hidden base and the Quiet Room.

And both locations were underground. Tragically.

"What do you mean by whole?" Perry asked.

"When I first went to war, I struggled with the scale—so many countries were involved, cities destroyed, and thousands of miles of battlelines. But I couldn't *see* that from where I was standing, and that's where my mind froze. It wasn't the grind from field to field, or town to town. I couldn't move my thoughts beyond the bigger scale, and because I couldn't do that, I struggled to see an end. After a while, I lost track of the beginning, too, so there was only this massive cloud of violence—with no way out. It drove some guys crazy, and they either broke down or ran. Do you know what it's like to see a man come apart, in their head? Their mind, or whatever was left of it? It's—it's horrific. It's unnatural. I think seeing that might be as bad as the shells."

Perry chose his words with care. "I hear you when you dream, boss. That war took you to the edge of sanity. The memory of it pummels you to this day, but as this conflict grows, you somehow seem to get calmer and more poised. How?" Perry asked.

Mark opened his eyes and looked down at his friend.

Then he offered a small, helpless shrug.

"It's how I survived the war. I compartmentalized it, breaking it down into pieces that had a beginning and an end. First it was skirmishes, then it was days, and weeks. It helped. Although, I guess you could say Valint is the real reason I survived it all. Had I stayed on that battlefield, my life might have ended up very differently."

"I find that wise beyond your years, boss," Perry said, nodding. "And I'll do the same thing. I'll compartmentalize this conflict, and perhaps we will see the end of it together."

"I hope so, Perry."

They started walking, leaving the spongy grass behind and moving onto a paved path. Banyon's Gulch loomed ahead, a shiny collection of cylindrical and rectangular buildings. A thought jarred loose in his mind as Mark tried to form a to-do list.

"Perry, what did you put on Tan's warrant? What was so horrible that Karan practically turned herself inside out?"

The bird stopped, his talons clicking against the pavement.

"Oh, yeah, that," Perry said, laughing heartily.

11

"Karan is a Stygio. A race not only known for its unusual biological makeup but also"—Perry paused, devolving into laughter — "for the impressive memory of its members. With that memory comes a few…quirks. I played upon those quirks."

"How so?" Mark stopped walking. He waited for Perry's punchline, then waved a hand impatiently. "Spill it, bird."

"Nothing criminal. Heck, it isn't really much of anything, in reality. But for those that know the Stygio, it was perfectly played."

"Why don't you want to tell me?" Mark asked, letting his hands come to rest on his hips. He turned his head to the side, then refused to move.

"You might not appreciate my nuanced humor."

Mark leaned forward, eyes narrowed. "There's only one way to find out."

"Okay. The Stygio have perfect recall, which means they often become hyper-fixated on details. It also explains why individuals like

Karan are selected to serve in the role that she does. Stygio make good Peacemakers too, as their abilities allow for immediate and on-the-spot code and law recall. It also means that the Stygio have come to view data, both electronic and stored biological memories, as sacrosanct. In fact, it's the nucleus around which their culture and religions rotate. I know you're familiar with the Tsenjo and their bizarre, nomadic history."

"I am," Mark said, immediately reliving his second-ever job as a Peacemaker where he'd lugged shipment after shipment of tungsten crates between the stars. It hadn't been that long ago, but so much had happened since.

"So, understanding how strongly Karan feels about data, I simply logged into the GKU database through a backdoor and created a phony warrant for Tan. I doubled down on digital crimes, making our young engineer into a terrorist. His earliest crime, the one Karan was most likely to see first, was a high-profile digital heist, where he broke into several high-security data vaults. He didn't just *steal* information. He left behind a virus that opened—and distributed—thousands of private recordings from a…let's call it a library."

"A library?" Mark snorted. "Explain. Not buying it, bird."

"A library that saved, ah, carefully curated visual recordings of conjugal activity among the wealthy and elite."

Mark whistled as understanding dawned on his face. "Data is their religion. And Tan shared—"

"Broadcasted. Across multiple systems."

Mark snorted. "Oooo. Oh, boy. Tan didn't just steal *data*, which was sacrosanct—the crime included private moments of people who were, by nature, *private*. He really kicked the hornet's nest."

"Aptly put. It's no wonder Karan had blood in her eyes. Metaphorically speaking, of course."

Mark raised a finger. "If there was anything in her eyes, it was probably something damp. Or moist. Or both. She's a—well, I'm sure some people find her slimy state to be quite attractive."

"Not me, and I'm an AI," Perry said.

"Same, but not the AI part. So, quick question about your master plan—can you delete the warrant so Tan's life isn't ruined?"

Perry stopped laughing immediately and turned to face him.

"Of course," he snorted. "I mean. Yes. I should be able to—"

Mark cocked his head to the side and squinted, immediately eliciting a response from the bird.

"Don't squint at me, sir. Need I remind you? I'm a highly advanced combat AI who shares your dislike of mucosal bureaucrats."

"A highly advanced combat AI," Mark echoed.

"And I *should* be able to delete the warrant and all subsequent digital footprints from the Galactic Knights databases. It will be like it was never there."

"Should," Mark said, nodding his head. "Never there."

"That's what I said. Why are you doing that? Nodding your head and repeating everything I say?" Perry asked, his voice rising.

"I don't know—call it a hunch. I'm getting the feeling that you've never deleted a warrant out of the Galactic Knights database before."

"Well, why would I? I mean, beyond this scenario, that is."

Mark shook his head. "I'm staying guarded, that's all. I've seen your excellence on display before, so I shouldn't doubt, but…"

"There are no 'buts,' Clive. I will *show* you. Perry is not to be underestimated."

Without warning, the bird continued forward, with Mark walking behind him. They moved into Banyon's Gulch, ambling through an outer security perimeter. Their credentials allowed them to pass through without as much as a second glance.

Banyon's Gulch lay ahead of them, the canyon dropping off to the river far below. The markets sprawled out and over the drop off, with dozens of towers spanned by suspension cables to hold it all aloft. On the other side of the river spawned other hamlets, all the way up to Greenway itself, nestled at the base of the largest space elevator Mark had ever seen.

"This is your first time here?" Netty asked, the repeater on his wrist buzzing quietly.

Mark finished scanning the enormous markets, each more colorful and boisterous than the last. Shops with signs and flashing lights caught his eye, like futuristic versions of the roadside produce stands he found back in Iowa. Finally breaking free from the spectacle, he shook his head.

"I guess part of me expected it to look more like Faux Linus—a small industrialized town surrounded by farmland. This is so much more than that."

"At one point, Greenway *was* that small town, feeding most of the planet. Then came the elevators, providing affordable and regular food transport to space. You could say that was…the end, sort of," Netty explained.

"So, in another century or two, Faux Linus will look more like this?"

"Maybe, but not likely. The co-op despises Greenway, perhaps in the same way a jealous younger sibling views an older brother or sister. They've been fighting such advances for a long time, almost entirely out of spite."

"Interesting," Mark said as he walked across a wide suspension bridge and into the other market. "Do you have a list compiled of what we need?"

"Do I?" Netty chuckled, and a hologram appeared above his wrist repeater. It cycled downward, the text too small for him to read clearly.

"Is that all?"

"Through critical analysis I have formulated a shopping list based off your eating preferences, the *Fafnir*'s perishable needs, a few items Perry has requested, food-based gifts for Armagost, and last but certainly not least, food for Ja-Ra and his clan."

"Food for Ja-Ra and his..." Mark flicked his finger up until he reached the very bottom. An estimated total appeared, then a price. "Holy *shit*. How many Tunis will that feed? And do I have enough bonds to cover all of that?" The list was almost 350 items long.

"Don't let their size fool you, Mark. Tunis are ravenous eaters. They're also voracious scavengers and tinkerers, so you'll have to find someplace for them that isn't Armagost's refuge. He will most certainly not stand by while they disassemble and reassemble his home over and over again."

"Now you tell me."

"Sorry, Mark. I thought you knew."

"No. You're right. I was getting far too comfortable with the idea of stashing our important people with Armagost. I never stopped to consider how many guests he can or wants to entertain."

"Let's think of it like this: frozen Ligurites are okay, but ravenous

J.N. CHANEY & TERRY MAGGERT

Tunis that might scrap out his hidden base while he's in it, less okay," Perry said.

"Fine, Mr. Smart Bird, any ideas on where we can safely store an entire clan of helpful but potentially destructive Tunis scavengers?"

"No idea." Perry chuckled. "But my first guess would be Almost, based completely on my morbid curiosity of how long it would take them to dismantle that hellhole. Then again, you did say safe, so that rules Almost out all on its own. The betting side of me wants to agree with my morbid curiosity because Ja-Ra and his clan might actually finish construction on that place while they're there. It would be a feat completely unappreciated by the locals, I'm sure."

Mark crossed the bridge, pondering all the unanswered questions. He hadn't come up with any answers by the time he stepped off on the other side. None had come to him by the time he finished walking through the first market either, or the second. If anything, he seemed to come up with even more questions. It was maddening.

Mark stopped at a small corner shop and purchased a drink. It looked roughly like lemonade, although several chunks of unidentified fruit were suspended in the murky liquid. The first drink was tart, while the second was sweet. It was enjoyable, especially considering it seemed to cleanse his palate after every other sip.

An Ixtan in a dark blue suit watched him over the top of his data slate but lowered his eyes as soon as Mark noticed. He took another sip and turned to the south, toward Greenway, pretending not to notice.

After moving to the next merchant stall, Mark perused the news leaflets stuffed into the circulars. But as much as they looked like paper, the leaflets were so much more—the headlines scrolling and automatically cycling through different stories. He picked one up and turned, pretending to read as he tracked the curious Ixtan. The blue-suited figure had shifted his data slate pointing right at Mark and Perry.

"Do you see him watching us?"

Yes. I do believe he is recording us, Perry confirmed over the ear bug.

Without another word, Mark placed the news sheet back into the circular and moved off, playing up his oblivious façade.

And he is following us.

"Netty, what about you? Where should we take Ja-Ra and his clan?" Mark asked, moving right and through a crowd.

"Have you ever considered asking them?"

"I—actually no, I haven't," Mark admitted, immediately feeling the fool. He ducked left through a series of open stalls, weaving a complicated pattern of lefts and rights.

"They're smart, boss. Let's give them some credit and not get taken in by their, ah, cuteness. The Tunis are hardy survivors and didn't become some of the best scavengers around for no reason." Netty said it all matter-of-factly and without condescension or spite, just as she always did.

"Guilty as charged on that one," Mark admitted, turning to check out a rack of strange pineapple-like fruit. Despite his best efforts, their Ixtan shadow was standing at a merchant across the way, pretending to check produce for ripeness. If there were any doubts before, it was clear now. Only one question remained, who was he following them for?

"Even after watching them install our new laser and the ablative armor coating, I'm still suspicious. Nervous, even. I pay attention and in my heart, I'm still a farm boy who found himself out here, in the midst of—of whatever all this is." He sighed long and gusty. "As much as I'd like to think I have changed since leaving Earth, this tells me that I'm still set in some old ways."

"That's not a bad thing, Mark. In fact, a few of those old ways are what set you apart from the average spacefaring individual. Hold on to *some* of them because they make you who and what you are. Stay nimble and adaptive, and you'll be fine. I have faith in you."

"Speaking of nimble and adaptive," he whispered, turning and slipping between a horde of people.

Mark weaved his way through the growing crowd, slowly moving toward Greenway as he fought to lose their tail.

"Thanks for placing your faith in me, Netty. I—I'm glad you decided to come aboard. I don't know where I would be right now without you."

"You're going to make me blush." Her optical sensor glowed bright above his repeater, before dimming once again. "Not to kill the romance, but my sensors are indicating that you have *two* tails now."

"Confirmed," Perry added.

Mark let his gaze sweep out over Greenway's bustling commerce. He couldn't see their followers, but knowing they were there made the threat a little more real.

"This place is huge. How many unfriendly eyes are hiding in the crowds?"

"Too many," Perry said.

Mark nodded. In truth, the place was sensory overload, like a county fair or street market gone crazy. It was the perfect place for spies, a chaotic soup in which they could blend in.

"I think it would be a bad idea to show our faces in Greenway. In fact, we might have already gone too far, considering what happened in Tau Regus. We don't know who these unfriendly eyes belong to," Perry said.

"I hate the idea of not knowing," Mark admitted, looking around. How many people were harmed on Fulcrum when Glass said no one would be harmed? What if his presence on Carson's Arch prompted another attack?

"Netty, can you do our shopping for us? Purchase all the items on the list and have them delivered to the ship?"

"Done," she said after only a moment's pause. "Does this mean you're headed back?"

"Yep. Perry is right," he said, giving Banyon's Gulch and Greenway one last mournful look.

Perhaps once the conflict and corruption were sorted, he could return and sample all the delights Carson's Arch had to offer. A week wouldn't be enough. Maybe a month.

"A month at Carson's Arch sounds about right," he breathed and turned, waving Perry to follow.

"You couldn't handle a month of relaxation," Perry accused.

"Why?"

"You're a Midwesterner. It's in your blood. The need to work, that is," Perry reasoned, smug with his facts.

They made straight for the docks and the *Fafnir*, even ducking off the busiest streets to avoid the attention of the crowds. The ship felt smaller and more cramped than ever before, and it wasn't only the swarm of inhabitants now residing inside, but the idea of unfriendly eyes waiting around every corner. Ja-Ra's clan had begun dismantling certain systems, namely malfunctioning heaters, air circulators, and light panels.

He picked his way through the chaos, first moving toward the galley, then pushing on to the maintenance passage, and lastly, to the engine room. Mark found Ja-Ra inside, standing over a crowd of five other Tunis.

"Ja-Ra, what are you doing?"

"Broken ship. Lots broken. We are fixing for you, Mark Tudor."

"That's nice, but we still need to be able to fly. *Can* we fly?"

"Not yet. But soon. Then the ship will fly better than ever! Mark Tudor will see," Ja-Ra said.

"I'm right here, but I appreciate your passion. Speaking of flying. Ja-Ra, we need to figure out someplace safe for you and your clan. What about Almost? Would you be—" Mark started to ask, but the Tunis patron spun around, his colorless eye bulging in the socket.

"Ja! Not Almost. Too much Stillness there. Glass has a pact with them and the Dire Legion, Four Sun Skulls, and many others. We have a place. Trust Ja-Ra," the Tunis said in a remarkable piece of self-promotion.

"Good. Where?"

"It has no official name on charts. Tunis call it a, ah…Junkway. It's a secret scavenger hunting ground. Very special. We have a place there. Very secret. It will be safe for Ja-Ra's clan. Safe for Mark Tudor and his ship," Ja-Ra enthused.

"Perfect," Mark said, silently searching his memories. He'd never heard of a place by that name. "How do we get there?"

"Ja-Ra will show you the way. Need expansion tanks for the ship. Need more fuel. It is very long twists. A long journey," Ja-Ra said.

"I don't know if going that far away is a good idea."

"Very good idea. Safe place. Remember the warheads you took? There are more of them there. More weapons. Many more ships. You'll see. It is perfect." Ja-Ra finished with an enthusiastic wave of both hands that was almost a salute.

Mark nodded, then immediately turned and moved back out into the passage. He waved for Perry to follow and ducked into his quarters, then closed the door once the bird had hopped inside.

"You two catch that?"

"Every word. Naturally," Perry said.

"Thoughts?"

"I have no records of a place by that name," Netty admitted. "And I performed queries by all spellings, variations, hyphenations, and languages."

Mark turned to Perry.

"Nothing," the bird said, shaking his head, "but I'm highly intrigued."

"Highly intrigued. They want us to go someplace neither of you have heard of, and we'd need expansion fuel tanks just to get there. I've got bells ringing in my head."

"Well, naturally." Perry chuckled. "You are…cautious, boss. Let Netty and me study Ja-Ra's coordinates. We won't allow for a twist that will not leave us with enough fuel to jump back into colonized space. So, if that's your concern—"

"Do we have enough money for expansion tanks and the fuel to fill them?" Mark asked after Perry trailed off.

"In bonds? Yes. But you're sitting on the remainder of our platinum stash as well. It would be foolish to empty your account and leave none in reserve."

"I don't think now is the time for hoarding resources."

"True, but if Ja-Ra is right and there are military-grade ships there, think of the possibilities. If we could scrounge some truly formidable weapons, and we could pay someone to repair, install, and arm them. Come on, Mark, give me at least one PDC to work with, maybe two. If you want to survive an encounter with Glass and her battlegroup, you need to start arming us better. We aren't flying among friends any longer. The *Fafnir* is growing and evolving, but she needs sharper teeth and claws."

Mark turned and began pacing the room for a moment before Netty's voice broke through.

"Mark, I know you're weighing your options here, but I've got a priority communication coming in on a designated Anvil Dark frequency. It is Master Cai-Demond."

"I'll take it in my chair," he said, the hair on his arms and legs standing on end.

Perry gave him a barely perceptible nod.

Mark didn't register the walk to the cockpit, only the drop into the gel-pad cushions. He took a deep breath, ran a hand through his hair, and accepted the comm on his overlay. Master Cai-Demond's face immediately filled the screen, his eyes somehow darker than the last time they spoke.

"Master Cai-Demond, I hope you're well."

"I see you're under contract right now. A warrant for the criminal known as Glass?"

Mark registered the Master's lack of greeting, but also his expression. His face was tight, jaw set.

"Yes, sir. I haven't been able to—"

"Who assigned that contract to you? It doesn't show any meta data on our end. I need to know where it came from."

Mark set his jaw and returned the Master's gaze. He ran through that question several times, working to identify the angle. *Was Demond trying to root out my involvement, or was he suspicious of a connection to someone else? Perhaps Gyl-Mareth?* The silence stretched for a long moment before he decided on a skewed version of the truth.

"I was in transit when our dispatcher contacted me directly, sir. They said the warrant was of the highest priority."

"Was it from Gyl-Mareth? Why did they assign it to you? Did he say?"

Mark analyzed everything Cai-Demond said but also *how* he said it. It wasn't coincidence that the Master immediately asked about Gyl-Mareth.

"No, sir, my dispatcher only said that Glass is incredibly dangerous. I believe they sent it to me because we were the closest ship."

"Mark, our records indicate that Glass is dead. I want you to stand down on this warrant. Your time is far too important to spend it looking for dead soldiers. Do you understand?"

"Of course," he said, nodding.

Gyl-Mareth calls her a mercenary. Meanwhile, Cai-Demond refers to her as a 'soldier.' Interesting, Perry said over the ear bug.

"Good-good," Cai-Demond said, leaning back and visibly relaxing. "I've got a job I need you to do for me, something I trust in your hands only. I'll have it sent over shortly. It's a bit of a haul for you, so you might want to get moving."

The Master gave a clipped wave of his hand, and the comm terminated.

Mark let out a breath and stretched his neck, then looked up to Perry, where he was nestled in his usual perch.

"The plot thickens. One wants her dead, and the other wants us to think she already is. Interesting."

"Stranger still, there's no news of the attack on Fulcrum, and I deactivated our transponder the moment we landed," Netty said.

Mark's overlay updated, indicating that he had messages waiting. He swiped over, only to find that his warrant for Glass was gone. It wasn't completed or closed. The contract had disappeared. A new one sat in its place. Netty had details before he even tapped the icon.

"It's a low-priority investigation. Illegal boardings on a series of freight haulers. It's at the Algo Shipyards."

"Which are several systems away. Interesting, don't you think?" Perry asked. "That one Master wants Glass dead, and the other is sending you clear across the sector? And as he said, it would be a haul for us, so we'd better get going. The bird is…suspicious."

"If Cai-Demond knows we are here and our transponder is off, that tells us who those unfriendly eyes are reporting to," Mark surmised.

A message blinked into his comm panel. He swiped over and selected it, opening a single line of text.

`[Is it done? Is she dead?]`

No sooner had he opened it than the message flashed red and disappeared. A `[deleted]` icon appeared a moment before his comm screen emptied itself of all messages. A quick check confirmed that even his archived comms were just…gone.

"Netty, did you do that? Did you delete all the messages?"

"I did not."

Mark looked up to Perry, only to find the bird quietly shaking his head. They were in hostile waters, and a storm was building.

"Netty. Use the platinum and buy whatever we need to get to the Junkway. And do it as discreetly as possible. No names, no affiliations, and no IDs."

Netty's answer was immediate but gave Mark little solace. "I'm on it." Outside, the expanse of space felt a little more dangerous.

Because it was.

12

THAT AFTERNOON, Mark spent his time pacing the hallway and waiting for Ja-Ra and his clan to fix and reassemble the *Fafnir*'s twist drive and navigational systems. Then it was delivery after delivery, as small, automated carrier bots arrived at the docks, trundling about in an awkward symphony.

They filled the galley cupboards, then the storage closets, and finally started stacking crates in the service passage and the maintenance bays. Mark finished squeezing two crates out of the way. He straightened, stretched his back, and considered his work. The ship's maintenance spaces looked like the farm before he'd had a chance to go through his uncle's stuff.

"Cramped, but I think we can make it work."

"Definitely," Netty replied. "We've only got three more shipments coming."

"Three more?"

"Only three. We're almost done," Netty said, a hint of triumph in her tone.

The last shipment arrived while the larger of the system's two stars started to set. It was a bizarre phenomenon Mark had only seen a few times. The eastern sky darkened, sliding from amber to bronze in silent artistry. But as the skyline was darkening, the smaller of the two stars was rising in the south, hovering like an aggressive, haloed moon, plump above the mountains.

The landscape shifted from daytime's warm, yellow glow to the surprisingly bright silver night. It was under that sterling sky that Ja-Ra's clan installed the expansion tanks on the *Fafnir*. Perry flitted between trees, while Mark stood a quiet vigil.

The dock's automated fueling system took over once the installation was complete, adding to the ship's now bolstered reserves. Perry flitted down once the umbilical disconnected, but the only figure that approached through it all was the dock manager. He completed his post-fueling inspection, collected payment in equal parts platinum and bonds, then bid them a smooth voyage.

Mark and Perry were in the cockpit not five minutes later, the taller, more human of the two strapping in for takeoff. The *Fafnir* lifted off the docks, showcasing all the grace of a pregnant hippopotamus, then sluggishly burned hard toward the ecliptic.

"She flies, ah, a little *different*," Mark said as they finally broke atmosphere and slid out into the black.

"She should. Her extended range tanks put her securely into the class 6 category now. Congratulations!" Netty said.

"If we find those sharp teeth I was talking about, we might be creeping up on class 7 territory. That is, if her somewhat undersized heart can power it all," Perry offered.

"I don't want to know how much a reactor refit would cost."

"No," the bird agreed, "you most definitely do not."

With Tan manning the co-pilot's seat, they completed the first of a complicated series of twists.

"We are jumping all over the galaxy with our transponder turned off. Won't they be suspicious?" the Druzis asked.

Perry snorted. "That might be the *least* suspicious thing we've done in a while. But no. Netty and I have become quite good at covering our tracks. Thanks to a little worm I injected into the transit buoy system, anyone watching can see that we are clearly headed out toward the Algo Shipyards, and at a rather leisurely pace, I might add."

"Serves them right for being nosy," Netty added.

"Oh," Tan said, nodding. "But what happens if we run across the ships out there? Won't they flag us for running dark?"

"That's where I flash them with our Peacemaker credentials. You'd be surprised how fast most ships will stand down," Netty explained. "Peacemakers regularly run dark and quiet, especially when chasing dangerous warrants, so it isn't unusual for us. Think of the silence as our calling card. And a good one at that."

Perry laughed and chimed in, their conversation quickly descending into equal parts Legal Eagle and technobabble, mixed with quantum theory and other foreign scientific, legal, and geo-political concepts. Mark tuned them out while he cycled through his overlay.

First, he confirmed that he had no new messages. After that, he read the contract Cai-Demond had assigned him, confirming that it looked, felt, and smelled like a blow-off. There was nothing to indicate that it required anything more than what Netty defined as a 'warm body' to complete.

Lastly, he pulled up their upcoming twist calculations to better understand where they were going and how they would get there. The star map showed several long twists and one final jump, extending well-beyond an unlabeled dotted line.

"Netty, what's the dotted red line on our transit chart?"

"That's the terminator line, Mark."

"Terminator line? A termination of what, territory, a gravitational field?"

"No." She laughed. "That's the edge of the Milky Way galaxy."

He sat there for a quiet moment, zooming in and back out of the map, allowing that nugget of information to sink in.

"We're leaving the Milky Way galaxy?"

"Yep," she said before returning to her calculations. "More importantly, we're leaving known space. The place where we do business, so to speak."

"Ah, just out of curiosity, is that—normal? You know, leaving the galaxy?"

"No, not common, per se, although most try to stick to established transit routes. Those provide cleaner twists with less surprises. Those transiting the black beyond the galactic terminator are usually doing so because they want to avoid being noticed."

"That makes sense, but—" Mark said, zooming out on his map as he searched for their destination. He moved hand over hand for several moments, their twist path extending an almost impossible distance past the line. "Do I want to know how far out we are going?" Beneath him, he sensed an unknown gulf falling away, like he was floating. Or falling.

"Admittedly, it *is* an outrageous number. I think you may want to avoid thinking about it until after we make the trip," Netty said.

"Got it. Ignorance is bliss. Go ahead. Take us out when ready," Mark ordered, studiously avoiding the math he knew would reveal just *how* far he was from home.

Transiting via twist was a straightforward affair, so Mark tucked into his overlay for some research—

And then the symptoms started.

First, it was a mild ache behind his eyes, and reading the screens became—challenging. Mark focused as he reread the contract, starting at the beginning. By the time he finished the first sentence, he had no recollection of what he'd read. So, he started over.

Three times. Then four.

"Are you having any memory issues?" Mark asked, turning to Tan.

"You've asked me that at least five times now," the young Druzis said, laughing quietly. "I'd say more, but you're probably going to ask me again anyway."

Mark closed his eyes and leaned his head back, hoping a quiet moment would help lift his confusion. In that peaceful instance, he became aware of two things. One, his head felt strange, like his brain was wrapped in wool. And two, that the time spanning between heartbeats felt far longer than normal. Mark focused inward, counting between beats, and reached twenty.

"I feel strange," Mark announced.

"Yes. You've already said that several times, too," Tan confirmed.

"I'm sorry, Mark. I should have warned you. This transit is pushing the theoretical boundaries of the twist drive. Despite our work to streamline the power plant, it's producing far larger quantities of low frequency resonance. I didn't think of it, but considering your biology, it's likely to trigger you into a sleep-like state. Even if you stay awake, you're unlikely to retain much. Of anything, that is," Netty said.

Mark focused on her voice, fighting for comprehension, but the information started to evaporate from his mind as soon as she finished speaking. He looked to the screen and tried to read, but nothing would soak in. It skipped off him, a stone off the pond, so—

He considered relaxing. Sure, it went against his Midwestern work ethic, but still.

"Sit back and relax. Let us handle things for a while," Perry said.

"But, shouldn't I—?"

"No. Right now you have all the biological functionality of a potato. So sit there in your chair and do potato things," the bird instructed.

Mark nodded, melting back into the chair. Within a few moments, the fog claimed everything once again. He had no idea how much time passed, but the twist drive finally cut out moments later.

Netty and Perry started to talk, with Tan chiming in occasionally. As they did, Mark felt the fuzziness lift, and his headache faded. Fifteen minutes drained away before he fully felt like himself again.

"Did everything go all right?"

"There he is," Perry said, perking up on his perch. Tan turned sideways, and Netty's optical sensor flickered from purple to blue, then back again. It was, as he'd come to learn, how she mimicked a wink.

"Here I am? I've been sitting in this chair the whole time. And I expected a long twist to take more time. That was…short."

"Oh, the perception of time," Perry oozed, grinning. "Prepare to have your mind warped, Peacemaker Tudor. You only recently sat back down. In fact, you spent a good amount of time in the galley, ate several meals, talked with Ja-Ra, drifted aimlessly about the ship, shaved half of your face, then had to go back and finish the rest and had the same conversation with Tan almost a dozen times. It was thoroughly entertaining. Sort of like watching a deer that gets drunk on fermented apples and doesn't know what the hell is happening. Oh, but with fewer hooves..."

"I don't have *any* hooves, you miscreant. And there's no *way* I did all that. I've been right here the whole time," Mark argued, but when he reached down and patted his belly, it felt distended, like how it'd been when he'd partaken in seconds and thirds at Thanksgiving dinner. As if on cue, it gurgled loudly.

"Netty?"

"Everything the bird said. Our transit took almost eight full hours. I told you during, but with no short-term memory transfer, you can't remember. You appear to be incredibly sensitive to high-dose low-frequency waves."

"Eight hours?" Mark reached up to rub his face. He immediately found several patches of scraggly hair. "Did I hold the razor in my hand, or my toes? What the hell?"

"I'd pay good money to see that. Never thought of humans as prehensile, but then again, you *are* from Pony Hollow. Different breed of folks out there," Perry said, cheerfully.

"That sounds a lot like an insult. Luckily for you, I must investigate," Mark growled.

Pushing out of the chair, he moved to his quarters. His razor, brush, and soap were out, with the sink still a hairy, soapy mess.

Mark leaned into the mirror, inspecting one of the worst shaving jobs he'd ever seen.

He moved into the galley, then the maintenance passage, where Ja-Ra and his clan were huddled together in several groups. The closest Tunis had disassembled the computer module on his b-suit, while another was disassembling, cleaning, and polishing the light fixtures.

"Let me guess, I had an entire conversation with them about doing that?"

"Actually, it was your idea," Netty said. "And to be fair, your b-suit has needed attention for some time."

"Don't get me wrong. I love that they can repair almost anything, but it would be nice to remember the conversation."

"Let's talk to Armagost about it when we see him. He might have some ideas on how to block out the low frequency waves. Although, look on the bright side. To you, the travel time was much shorter than to everyone else."

"Shorter? Felt like minutes," Mark said, worrying over the streaks of unshaved hair on his face and neck. He locked himself in his quarters after that to shave and clean up his messes. Evidently, he'd rifled through his drawers and closet as well, although he couldn't determine what he'd been looking for. Perry opened the door with a command and watched him stand before the chaos of his quarters. Naturally, Perry was deeply satisfied to see Mark's confusion.

"I'm like a hog rooting for acorns," Mark mumbled.

"A hog that tried shaving," Perry added, helpful as always.

"Silence, bird. I think—"

"Mark, we're in visual range of the Junkway. You are *definitely* going to want to see this," Netty said through the overhead speaker.

He walked out of his quarters and turned right, only to find Tan standing at the fore windscreen, with Perry moving to perch on the panel next to him. Mark passed the two pilot seats, their projected overlays jumping and flickering erratically. A persistent hum of static echoed out of the speakers overhead.

The bow thrusters fired as he moved in between Perry and the young Druzis, Netty navigating the *Fafnir* around a massive, ice-covered chunk of space garbage. They cleared the ancient piece of debris, and Mark saw it clear—the Junkway, as Ja-Ra referred to it.

And yet, seeing it didn't necessarily translate to understanding. Space junk hung before them, scattered like floating pieces of a massive asteroid belt. A colossal helix sat at the cloud's epicenter, twisting like a dark serpent into space.

"What am I looking at?"

"Something I've never seen," Perry murmured with a touch of… awe. It was awe, and that got Mark's attention. "It's either a gravitational or magnetic phenomenon, slowly drawing all of this debris together."

"Both, I think," Netty chimed in. "I immediately registered a weak gravity well when we dropped out of twist, but there's a definitive electromagnetic field as well. It's playing hell with our scanners. And yet, I haven't been able to identify the source of either."

"Warm up the laser and missiles, just in case."

"Doing so now," Netty agreed.

They wove their way through the debris field, flying by chunks of magnetic ore and crumpled metal, but also what looked like entire sections of ships, whirling slowly in an eternal dance. They approached the Junkway's spiral-shaped core, only to reveal that it wasn't comprised of coalesced space junk; it appeared to be hollow.

"There's no way to confirm, unless we get in there and look," Netty admitted. "Sensors are almost worthless with this interference. In the end, it's your call, Mark, but taking the *Fafnir* inside is a huge risk, especially considering that we don't know what kind of tidal forces are at play. It might tear the ship apart."

"I'm with you. Let's play this safe," Mark said, nodding. "We need to get Ja-Ra up here." He turned toward the aft passage, only to find that the Tunis patron was standing behind him, his large eye locked on the windscreen.

"The Junkway," the small alien said, pointing.

"You weren't exaggerating. Now, where are we going? You said there's someplace for you out here?"

"Ja." Ja-Ra nodded and hopped forward. "The bell. The bell!"

"What does that mean, 'the bell?'"

"It's where we're going. Ja-Ra and his clan can stay aboard the bell. She always keeps us safe."

"So, you've been there before? Netty, does the name mean anything to you?"

"There are simply too many results that pop up in my archive, Mark. Unless there's some way to narrow it down."

"No need!" Ja-Ra said, crawling up into the co-pilot's seat. "I will show you." The Tunis zoomed out on the glitching map, then scrolled right, hand over hand, before zooming in once again and highlighting a small section in the helix. In total, it was the work of fifteen seconds, and he was done.

"Netty, can you get us there?"

"You doubt me?" she asked, blowing a raspberry.

"Never."

Thrust kicked in as the *Fafnir* pushed through the cloud, before turning to port and following the Junkway's helix-shaped body. They soared over the massive construct of space debris, the ship's spotlights illuminating its surface. Either by time or gravity, the junk appeared to have been fused together, forming an almost smooth matrix of different materials.

They passed whole sections of ancient-looking ships, their hulls covered in strange writing. Netty confirmed they were precursor languages, featuring elements of Cetan, Capian, and even Ixtan tongues. Gaps formed like massive caves in the Junkway's exterior, extending back beyond the limits of even the *Fafnir*'s strong lights.

"How long is the Junkway? How, ah, large? In volume?" Mark asked.

"Unknown," Netty said. "With interference playing hell on our scanners, there's no way to tell. It could be thousands of kilometers, or even millions."

"Millions," Mark murmured as the ship shuddered and seemed to drop. It smoothed out a moment later, but only after a few dozen warning lights flared to life. "*Millions.*"

"For the curious members of our crew, that was a gravity pocket. I'd strap in until we get to wherever we are going," Netty said.

Mark slid into his seat without comment, the ship rocking and pulling violently to the left. They hit more gravity pockets, but there didn't seem to be any rhyme or reason to their direction or strength of pull. The space around the Junkway seemed to be erratic, chaotic even, as if something had made the intergalactic medium—the fabric of space itself, unstable.

"Okay, coming up on the location Ja-Ra highlighted," Netty cautioned as the bow thrusters fired.

The *Fafnir* rolled left and followed the Junkway's ever-curving path, their velocity slowing considerably. A large arch-shaped shelf appeared, and Netty navigated them under and through, only to enter a fascinating series of wide tunnels and strange, looping formations.

No one spoke. Mark wasn't even sure he was *breathing*.

The bow thrusters fired again as they slid through another arch, only to come face-to-face with a massive shape ahead. Their aft end came around, the ship's belly thrusters firing as the flood and spotlights converged. There, perched in a wide, sheltered valley, sat a mountain-sized ship.

"That's—that's *enormous*," Mark rasped as the *Fafnir* slowly tracked up and over the behemoth.

With a bulbous hull, the ship was covered with domes, extruded out in varying lengths and widths that gave the monstrous ship a comical irregularity. The *Fafnir* reached the top, and the hull flattened out, revealing a long deck. Its walls and ceiling were transparent metal, Mark guessed—and inside stood tables, flat lounging chairs, and a pool.

"A pool?" Perry asked.

"Pretty tony for—well, it's fancy. Pools are like electric carpet cleaners. They're not for the unwashed masses," Mark stated.

As they began arcing past the deck area, Netty applied thrust, and the *Fafnir* dipped obediently toward the ship's nose.

Yawning across half their viewscreen, the curved hull gave way to a spherical snout. It extended forward in rings, the oversized sensor modules and docking hubs ancient but intact. Small pieces of debris glittered in the wan light, winking jewels declaring the hulk was large enough to have microgravity.

"Hell, if it was back home it'd have *weather*," Mark said.

"Like Lake Baikal. But a ship," Perry agreed.

Netty brought them to hover over the foremost docking ring, the ship's nose cone coming to a sharp but heavily scarred point. A name was written in large, blocky alien writing, with a slightly smaller designation printed below.

"That answers that question," Netty said.

"And what question is that?"

"Ja-Ra kept referencing 'the Bell.' The language on that ship is old, and practically speaking, extinct, but I have cobbled together a working translation. This ship is called the *Belle of Antrades*, and she's been missing for…some time."

"Care to be a bit more specific? 'Some time' could be almost anything," Mark said, jerking a thumb at the sprawling wreck.

Perry and Netty were quiet for a long moment, the silence spreading fat and awkward.

Tan broke the moment with an apologetic shrug, running a finger along the screen where a single line of data pulsed. "According to what I found, the *Belle* has been missing for—how many years are in your blocks of time?"

"A century? One hundred years," Mark answered.

Tan looked stunned. "Well then. That ship has been here, or missing, for nine of your centuries, and a few more years past that."

Mark whistled. "This isn't just a missing ship."

"What is it, then?" Perry asked.

Mark pointed outside, waving at the enormity of it all. "It's a grave."

13

Galactic Boundary + 212.5 LY

MARK STARED in awe at the ship, then a cagey look of doubt crept over his features. "She looks to be in remarkably good shape for something that old."

"Indeed," Perry agreed. "We do not understand anything about the Junkway. Perhaps the bizarre magnetic and gravitational forces have helped to preserve her. Or—" He paused and looked at Ja-Ra.

The Tunis was staring outside, his colorless eye locked on the enormous ship.

"Or our Tunis friends had something to do with it? Perhaps refurbished or reassembled it?" Mark surmised.

"Ja. We found the *Belle* a long time ago. We find it. We fix it. All the pieces—polished up and fixed, like new."

Netty accomplished a soft dock and, surprisingly, found that the ancient ship possessed an automated docking procedure that had activated. Somehow, it had power.

Perry followed the Tunis toward the inner hatch, his curiosity toward the ship and the strange aliens on public display.

Mark watched it all from the cockpit, with Tan moving in next to him. The inner hatch opened, and Ja-Ra stepped through. The Tunis patron cycled through into the larger ship first, followed by his clan in small groups. The last group moved through a short while later, leaving Perry, Mark, and Tan alone in the *Fafnir*.

"Now's our chance. We could detach and go."

Mark turned an accusing look at the bird.

"What?"

"And leave our small but mechanically inclined friends in that massive ship with no food? If it's true that they located and repaired this entire vessel, just think of what *else* they could do."

"I was going to say—you delivered them someplace safe, as you said you would."

"Let's go. I want to see this relic of a ship. And I know Tan does, too. He's gone from living his whole life on Tau Regus to flying in his very first starship, experiencing aerial combat, and then twisting out past a galactic boundary—all in the span of two days."

"Based on your measure of two days, four hours, three minutes, and fourteen seconds. No, fifteen, sixteen—" Tan said, not looking away from the airlock.

Perry cleared his throat, and the Druzis finally seemed to break free from his trance. He looked at Mark first, then the bird.

"What?" Tan asked, then took a startled breath. "Oh, sorry. I get locked in on numbers sometimes. What Mark said. A lot of firsts in a very short amount of time."

Mark chuckled as they stepped into the airlock together, the inner door cycling shut as soon as Perry hopped inside. The pressure equalized, his ears popped, and a moment later, the outer door hissed open.

Two things struck him immediately. First, a gust of relatively stale air, and second, a wave of unexpectedly yellow light. He stepped out into a foyer, with a large and ornate staircase sweeping up to the next floor. A substantial chandelier hung directly above, bathing the entire space in rich, incandescent light. The place smelled like his grandparents' house—leather, wood oil, and candle wax.

They moved forward, Perry's talons tapping on the glossy floor, the peculiar stone rich with veins of teal and green. Double doors sat ahead, leading to a long passage. Dark wood doors lined both sides, with curving light fixtures sticking out from the walls. One in six fixtures were lit, but it left them with more than enough light to see. He wasn't sure if he'd missed anything as much as the gentle yellowish glow of old-fashioned light bulbs. One bulb flickered in protest but returned to a steady glow after an indignant pop.

Mark moved slowly, reverently. "She looks like a pleasure craft. They called them steam liners on Earth. Of course, those chugged their way slowly across the oceans, not the vast black of space."

"Yes, different but probably closer in function than you realize," Netty said. "My records are old and fragmented, but the name *Belle of Antrades* appears in multiple records. The first is the contract of her construction to a shipyard called Bethel Gate, but like I said, the data is corrupted. There's no date or additional information. The second is a commission under a company that translates roughly to Silver Line. The *Belle* was to serve as a luxury liner, running an infinity route between stars with wealthy worlds that could support this kind of opulence. If the ancillary records are correct, the ship never stopped on its circuit, while a fleet of smaller vessels ferried guests, supplies, crew, and fuel back and forth. I'm sorry that I don't have more information about it. Its fleet, the race that built it, and even the shipyard where she was built were destroyed when Antares flared, scouring the entire system of life."

"They all died?" Tan asked, the skin pulling tight around his eyes.

"Yes," Netty confirmed. "My records indicate that an investigation was conducted by several groups and organizations, but they believed the cataclysm was absolute and all was lost. It appears that our history needs to be corrected."

"Not right away," Mark said, reaching over and opening the nearest door. It swung in smoothly, revealing a nicely appointed room. A bed sat against the left wall, with graceful, artistically carved chests straight ahead and to his right. "We can keep it a secret a little longer. If only to keep Ja-Ra and his family safe."

Mark moved to the door across the hall and pushed it open, then found a similar suite, and another one next to that. It was striking how familiar it all looked—the beds, rugs, chests…hell, even the light fixtures. If it wasn't an enormous starship, it wouldn't have looked out of place steaming its way across the Atlantic. Although—

"Let me do a little measuring," Mark announced. "Extrapolation, if you will, bird."

"Fancy word there, farm boy."

"Thanks, I've been trying this new thing called *reading*. Now hush and let me investigate. This is—this place is spookier than the iron bridge back home in Pony Hollow."

Mark moved into the room and stood next to the bed, staring with interest. Yes, similar, but larger than any bed he'd ever seen. It was substantially longer and wider. Even if he stretched out to his full height—well over six feet—he'd still feel like a child in his parent's bed.

It was then that he noticed the height of the ceilings, but also the doorways.

A wardrobe sat behind him and to his right, the doors yawning open. Mark hooked a finger inside and eased them open, revealing two bars groaning with clothing. It appeared to be uniforms of a rich, amber fabric. Mark pulled one jacket free and held it against his chest. It hung down past mid-thigh, confirming that whoever had lived in the room was crew, but also considerably taller than him.

Was it possible that this ship was crafted and operated by larger proto humans? If that were a thing.

Mark took a breath to ask Perry and Netty that very question when Ja-Ra appeared in the doorway, the fluffy tuft on his head swaying from side to side.

"You come and see," he said, then promptly disappeared again.

He hung the uniform jacket back in its place and closed the wardrobe, then moved out into the hall and followed the darting Tunis. The berths gave way to a large, circular hub lined with golden lifts. Clear transit tubes extended up and out of sight, yet only one of the elevators appeared to be working.

Mark and Tan stepped in last, with the lift rising smoothly as soon as the clear doors closed. They rose floor after floor, but the polished, well-lit veneer fell away. Darkness appeared, the floors and furniture covered by dust and decay. When the lift finally stopped rising, Mark stepped out into a relatively gloomy passage, the air heavy with the tang of neglect.

His b-suit lights clicked on smoothly, now free from the indecisive flicker that plagued them before. Dust motes hung like lazy snowflakes in the beams of light as they progressed forward, before finally moving through a wide, gilded doorway and into the goliath's bridge.

Spanning a hundred feet to his right and left, the ship's control center loomed all around. An elevated catwalk separated the space, with dozens of stations sitting in darkness below. He moved forward to follow Ja-Ra, then angled his lights down, revealing wide plotting tables covered in star charts. A radio and comms station sat beyond that, with what he thought was a multi-seat maintenance post.

But it was *nothing* like the *Fafnir*.

Everything was larger and far older, with hundreds of trouble lights and frequency selectors. Even the knobs and switches were gold and platinum, the bright metals having retained some of their luster.

A captain's chair rose above everything else in the middle of the bridge, giving it a clear line of sight forward to the large bank of observation windows, but also the rest of the room, and its substantial collection of workspaces.

"Never seen anything like this before," Mark said, his voice echoing out into the space.

"Are we talking scope or grandeur?" Perry asked. "Strictly speaking, larger vessels are in operation today, but they would be hard-pressed to match this ship's lavishness. Stone flooring is almost unheard of, due to its weight. And platinum knobs and dials? Well, few beyond the wealthiest federations would use finite resources like that."

Ja-Ra continued along the elevated path, before unexpectedly hopping and dropping out of sight.

"Ja-Ra!" Mark called, his breath catching. He broke into a run, thinking the Tunis had fallen through a rotten spot in the flooring. Perry leapt into the air and passed by in a blur.

And yet, Mark found no hole in the floor as he approached, only a step down onto another platform, and a curving stairwell leading to another space. The Tunis patron stood twenty steps down, his arm held out as he pointed to something below.

"See. Come see."

"Will you look at that." Mark chuckled. The winding staircase led down to a launch bay filled with no less than four small ships.

He followed Ja-Ra the rest of the way down, half of the bay's lights coming on automatically. Two of the four ships appeared to be short-range shuttles, their rounded, stylized hulls made to reflect the *Belle's* overall shape. They were covered with gold and platinum accents. The elegant ships gleamed in the light, reminding him of a trio of abandoned Rolls Royce Phantoms they'd discovered in a French barn.

And yet, it was the two smaller vessels that really caught Mark's eye. They were stubby, with narrow hulls in the rear, swelling toward the front, giving them a roughly insect-like appearance. Four extendable service arms hung from the front, with longer arms folded down the port and starboard sides. Mark guessed their use before Ja-Ra jumped up and swung the hatch open.

"Service pods. Perfect for scavenging! We will show you where the best relics are." The Tunis waved for him to follow, before disappearing inside.

"I think he means for you to crawl into that impossibly small craft with him so you can go for a ride together," Perry deadpanned.

"I didn't pick up on that. Thanks," Mark shot back.

He moved up to the service pod and stuck his head inside. Beyond the mass of technology covering the walls, it featured only two simple pilot's chairs and a single instrument pedestal. At least it didn't smell bad.

"I should make sure—"

"I'll oversee the transfer of the Tunis' food and supplies onto the *Belle*. You go with Ja-Ra and secure, ah, whatever it is he wants to show you. We need weapons first and foremost. Try to make sure they're from this century."

"Are you sure?"

"You know me. I don't say something unless I'm sure. Go. We need to divide and conquer if we are going to get everything done. Remember, you have two Guild Masters watching your every move, and my spoofing virus will only fool them for so long," Perry said while pushing Mark into the hatch with his head.

"Fine."

He stuffed himself inside the service pod, turned, and pulled the hatch closed.

"Ja-Ra, you sure this thing is safe?" he asked, but he barely had the lock secured before the ship rumbled to life around him.

Mark turned, only to find lights and gauges illuminating the walls and ceiling. The ship was noisy, with seemingly all of its archaic technology mounted on the inside.

"Ja. Safe. You will see," his Tunis friend said, the ship lurching beneath him.

Mark lumbered forward, smashing his frame through the gap between the open seat and wall. A perfectly round hatch opened ahead, with what appeared to be a powered rail system pushing the pod out and through. Judging from the steam leaking from the connected fittings, he guessed that the ancient-looking tech was still whole and operational.

"A steam-powered luxury liner. In space." He ran a finger along a brass-ringed gauge next to him.

After falling back into the seat next to Ja-Ra, Mark fumbled for the harness while the outer door slid open. He had just enough time to clip the buckle together and pull the strap tight before the pod was flung unceremoniously into space.

His Tunis friend nudged the pod left and rolled the tidy craft over with thrusters as he kicked in its small drive. It propelled forward smoothly, with surprisingly little lateral kick. Mark involuntarily reached for a control stick and throttle as the craft nosed down toward the Junkway. Ja-Ra expertly swung the small craft around, modulated thrust, and evened it to plane.

Mark chided himself for his lack of faith and hoped his Tunis friend hadn't noticed the dramatic flinch. But if he had seen it, Ja-Ra gave no indication.

They soared through the strange, spiraling caverns that housed the *Belle*, the craft's weak lights cast buttery circles that dispersed, leaving the ship—

Ghosts. This place is filled with ghosts, Mark mused, his eyes seeking anything of use or interest. Whether by time or pressure, the Junkway's bizarre gravitational properties drew the refuse together, then filled in the cracks with ice and ore, forming a tightly packed medium.

Mark sat back and rubbed his eyes, only then realizing they'd somehow already been flying over and through the massive construct for almost two hours. And in that time, he hadn't spotted a damned thing worth taking.

"How do you find anything here?" Mark asked, frustration in every word.

"Just wait. You will see," Ja-Ra said, his eye never moving away from the Junkway.

They flew on for a short while in silence, Mark's back cramping from the pod's small seat. It felt like a paradox—the enormous starship was seemingly manned by tall humanoids, yet their service craft appeared to be handmade for Tunis. Perhaps there was something to that? Ja-Ra and his clan somehow knew where the *Belle* was, after all, separated from colonized space by countless light-years.

"There!" Ja-Ra said suddenly and leaned forward. He raised a small arm and pointed ahead and to the left.

Mark tried to follow his finger to the spot, but the pod rolled and cut hard, diving toward the Junkway. Mark didn't see anything at first, until they were barely fifty yards above the surface. Then a dark, jagged hole materialized in the pod's lights, the edges scorched black from explosives.

"There was violence of some sort," Mark observed, then added, "War was here. War, and damned hot."

Ja-Ra made a sound of agreement, then nosed the pod down, and with a series of startled curses bottling up in Mark's throat, they dove into the opening. They transitioned from one shade of black to another, until the pod's lights shifted forward, and their world glowed to icy-blue life.

The pod soared down a tunnel and promptly exited into a soaring, icy cavern, the walls shining like glass. The bow thrusters fired, slowing the craft and jamming Mark forward against his lap belt.

"—Well, I'll be—" he stammered as the lights swiveled from left to right, illuminating at least a half dozen tunnel entrances.

Ja-Ra guided them into a spiraling loop as a red dot appeared on the small display set into the control pedestal.

"What's that?" Mark pointed.

They accelerated forward and into a passage leading down, the ice narrowing around them until they were practically scraping their way through. The red dot shifted to their right, before settling behind them. It started to move on the screen, closing in on the center. Mark knew enough to surmise what it meant.

Ja-Ra's large eye snapped from the passage to the screen and back again in time to follow a sharp, left-hand turn. It curved straight down, before opening into a large cavity. A hulking stalagmite loomed ahead. His Tunis counterpart reached up and flipped a platinum switch, the pod's lights instantly going dark.

Mark threw his arms out, more to confirm that the ship hadn't simply disappeared around him. He found the wall and the ceiling, his chest and throat tightening in smothering darkness.

The pod moved and turned, the momentum throwing Mark around like so much flotsam. But he couldn't see anything beyond the small craft, and his subconscious spun into a frenzy.

"Where *are* we?" Mark asked.

Thrusters fired, so much louder now that he was blind. The pod stalled, and their momentum shifted. They floated backward and finally seemed to come to rest.

A pinprick of light appeared in the darkness ahead—

As a ship slowly materialized, sliding into space. It struck him immediately how odd the craft looked, considering its marker lights were all different colors and shapes. But in seconds, Mark understood the truth. Whereas ships like the *Fafnir* utilized bits and pieces—weapons and modules from wrecks—this ship appeared to be made up entirely of salvage.

It possessed the sleek nose cone of a fast boat, with the mid-fuselage of a transport, riveted and welded to the aft end of what might have been a tug. His gaze crawled over the bizarre-looking craft as it slunk through the dark. It moved deliberately, like a predator stalking through the bush. And it had teeth—stubby wings and hardpoints, all outfitted with rockets, missiles, and slug-throwers.

"I've seen this thing before." Mark's eyes were locked on the hovering enemy.

Netty sounded dubious. "Really?"

Mark shrugged. "Well, not *exactly*. But the junkman in Pony Hollow had a car, if you can call it that—he had a car like this thing. It was made of…opportunities. But seeing this, I have questions."

"I get it. And I do too," Netty finished, watching the unusual ship moving about.

The predator ship floated down and over them, its marker lights illuminating their pod's surroundings. Ja-Ra had somehow navigated them into what looked like a cave, the tight space cleverly concealing them.

Darkness spilled in as the hunter disappeared overhead, but the reprieve lasted only a moment. It reappeared a moment later, sliding down right past their hiding spot, its marred, cobbled together hull barely paces from them.

Covered in scrapes and dings, bullet holes, and laser burns—*it* was the scarred predator now, not *him*. And separated from the *Fafnir* by thousands of kilometers and a mile of ice and metal, he didn't even have Netty to fall back on.

They were prey, and this was a hunting ground.

The ship slid past, its drive resonating enough to make Mark's teeth ache, but he said nothing, fear mounting as the predatory craft fired up a drive cone and turned into a tunnel leading away from the enormity of their surrounding chamber. Mark let out a pent-up breath and opened his hands, the knuckles cracking in response.

"One question, and I want an answer. *Who* was that?" Mark asked. His tone like iron.

Ja-Ra mumbled, the word too soft for Mark's ear bug to pick up. It was several moments before the Tunis spoke again.

"Jackals," he whispered. "Junkway has two kinds. Scavengers and jackals."

"Next time, we're bringing the *Fafnir*. Even if it won't fit into these tunnels, I want it to be close."

Ja-Ra nodded and quietly brought the pod back online. The interior lights glowed to life first, then the exterior floods cracked the darkness. They floated forward slowly from their hiding space, before confirming that the Jackals had gone. Nothing registered on their small locator screen, but Mark quietly wondered how accurate it was, surrounded on all sides by so much debris.

"What now?"

"We scavenge," Ja-Ra said simply, turning the pod 180 degrees.

Then Mark saw it clearly. Their pod hadn't been concealed in a cave, nor was the jutting shape separating the cavern an ice stalag-mite. They had been hiding inside a scorched fissure blown into the side of a long, slender ship. It hung down, the aft end of its fuselage encased in ice and rock.

Although he couldn't recognize the markings, Mark immediately recognized the craft as a warship, specifically the size of a heavily armored frigate.

The service arms extended from the front of the pod as Ja-Ra navigated them closer. He clamped them onto a bent and damaged service panel, the small craft laboring to pull it open. Mark's gaze instinctively snapped down to the sonar screen, although it showed no close contacts.

"All right, Ja-Ra, show me how to scavenge. And show me *fast*."

14

It took them almost two hours to reach the wreck—not including the time they hid from the Jackals—but once Ja-Ra went to work, Mark immediately understood how the Tunis had earned their reputation.

In twenty minutes, they'd searched the visible parts of the derelict ship, then isolated a portion still covered in ice, and planted several small sonic charges that began thrumming instantly. In seconds, the charges freed their target from the thick encasement, and Ja-Ra shifted the lights to reveal a stout-looking rotary cannon. Fifteen minutes later they'd finished removing that and moved on to find a damaged magazine filled with very old-looking rockets. After that it was sensor modules, marker lights, and anything else the Tunis could quickly disassemble and remove. They zoomed back up toward the surface barely an hour later, the heavily encumbered pod barely fitting through the tunnel.

They reached the surface as an enormous chunk of debris struck the Junkway barely a mile ahead. The impact sent a billowing plume of jetsam outward, with jagged fissures forming in the helix-shaped construct. Mark cursed and pointed as debris broke free from the ground. Chunks of ice, rock, and metal rocketed into the open, before hitting pockets of gravity and veering off erratically. Ja-Ra calmly rolled the pod right and accelerated to gain distance.

"It's normal," Ja-Ra said as the ground split below them. More ice fired up into the air as surface tension released, the clouds and shards scattering without rhyme or reason. The mess glittered in the pod's bright lights. It was awe-inspiring and beautiful yet terrifying at the same time. Mark hadn't seen anything so primordial and chaotic since trying to herd farm cats as a boy.

Unfazed, his Tunis guide navigated their groaning craft through the swirling debris—and to safety. By the time they docked with the *Belle* almost an hour and a half later, Mark was ready to retire from his fledgling career as a scavenger. In truth, he wanted to leave the bizarre chaos of the Junkway behind altogether. His nerves were frayed, his stomach was in a twist, and he smelled of sweat and fear.

Mark was also exhilarated.

He found Perry and Tan together on the bridge. The two appeared to be overseeing the Tunis, as the minuscule aliens rushed this way and that, carrying crates, wiping dust off of control surfaces, and tucking into repair jobs. And by "overseeing," he meant staying out of the way.

"You're still alive," Perry observed. "Good. Good."

"Two goods? Is my continued survival surprising?"

"Should I have gone with three?"

"No. But yes, I'm still here, although not for the universe's lack of trying. Or, should I say, the Junkway. This place is—different.

Unsettling." Mark stretched his back. He waved for Perry to follow, then once away from Tan and the others, filled the bird in on what had transpired.

"Jackals? That's what he called them?"

"It's how the ear bug translated it, anyway. Their ship wasn't like anything I've seen before. It appeared to be constructed entirely out of salvaged pieces of other vessels. They were well-armed, although I wonder how reliable their armaments would be, considering age and other factors."

"Other factors?"

"Who scavenged the systems and what condition they were in, how they have been maintained, and so on."

"Indeed, but underestimating *anyone* out here would be a mistake," Perry warned. "The kind that could prove fatal."

Mark nodded, understanding that point all too well. It was likely how the Five Star League hit squad felt right before engaging a Peacemaker in a relatively benign Class 5 dragonet.

"I would also say, don't judge a people by their ships, but certain actions allow for accurate behavioral prediction. Ja-Ra called them 'Jackals.' My memories are incomplete, but I do have several negative references to the animal that goes by that name on your world. They seem to be opportunistic predators. Perhaps that was the meaning behind the translation. Predators of opportunity are dangerous because their actions do not fall within predictable parameters."

"That makes sense," Mark agreed. "I know that I want the *Fafnir* close by next time. And...do we think the *Belle* is a safe place to leave our friends?"

Perry seemed to consider that question for a moment while

quietly watching Ja-Ra's clan work to prep, clean, and repair the giant ship.

"They have more knowledge and experience with this place than we do, and yet I think you're more concerned about their safety than they are. There must be something to that."

"Mark, if I may," Netty said after they quietly watched the Tunis for a moment.

"Go ahead."

"I have been passively listening in on the Tunis' conversations since they came on board at Tau Regus. They're an incredibly talk-ative lot, although I get the impression that trait does not extend beyond their familial circle. A word has popped up in scattered conversation many times since our arrival. I haven't had a reference to translate it until now, but it's the word Ja-Ra used to define the Jackals. It appears they have had dealings with these predators before, although I gather these exchanges were not necessarily by choice."

"Scavengers and predators coexisting in the same habitat," Mark muttered. "I don't like leaving them here alone, especially at the mercy of unpredictable, armed unknowns."

"*You* may not want to," Perry added, "but remember, our Tunis friends have survived out here for a long time before you met them. I know you're hardwired into the 'see a problem, fix a problem' model, Mark, but Ja-Ra and his clan might actually be better equipped to survive this place than we are."

"I know," Mark countered, "doesn't mean I have to like it."

They went to work setting up the *Belle* as best they could, but there were only so many things advanced AIs like Netty and Perry could do with such outdated technology. Perry rewrote many of the security procedures and lockout protocols, laughing to himself as he reworked the exterior hatches and door functions.

"You find coding to be hilarious?" Mark asked.

"Occasionally. You see, my humor is nuanced, much like the flavors of Iowan cuisine, which—"

"If you slander casseroles, there will be repercussions."

Perry snorted. "That's the trouble with being a comedic genius. I'm always ahead of the curve."

Netty scoured the primitive control program on the ship's computer, isolating the reactor, life-support, and power-management systems. After careful deliberation, she replaced them with watered-down copies of herself. The sub-minds, although based on her core code, were so simplistic they had to communicate through blocky text on the *Belle*'s old bridge screens.

"To call the software they used primitive would be an insult to primitives. And yet, despite its simple architecture, their hardware is surprisingly robust and cleverly constructed. If we could find a way to increase their memory, storage, and data transmission through-put, we could—"

"We could what?" Mark asked. "Get it flying again?"

Perry snorted. "The odds of that happening are infinitesimal. These infinity loop ships run low thrust ion drives. It's a miracle that Ja-Ra and his crew have kept this thing functioning for so long. It's doubtful that we could even source the right kind of fuel and reaction mass it needs."

"But if we could?" Mark pressed, and the bird cocked his head to the side, scrutinizing him closely.

"You're serious? This thing has been trapped here for hundreds of years. There's no telling how many structural instabilities she's hiding in her bones. Breaking it loose from the ice would only be the first of many labors. Why?"

"Labor doesn't concern me," he admitted, gesturing around to the seemingly tireless Tunis. They worked like ants, driven by an undeniable will to constantly deconstruct, fix, and build.

"You see the *Belle of Antares* as a potential way station? A haven amongst the stars?"

Mark nodded, not surprised by how fast Perry guessed his motivation.

"We know that Gyl-Mareth and Cai-Demond are corrupt, although their motivations beyond the Guild are still a mystery. The Five Star League is involved, but how? Glass engaged in open warfare against Tau Regus, on one of the most populated and well-organized planets in the Ceti system. Okay, why? We could use Almost as a base of operation if it wasn't filled with the worst sort of killers and criminals in all the galaxies, and let's not forget Jarls Vane," Mark said, letting the last point linger between them.

Perry clicked his beak, nodding slowly. "How could we? Jarls was a Peacemaker once. A *long* time ago. He backed up my partner Otto, an old Ixtan. Jarls was young and driven, and he performed well on that property seizure. Sometime later Otto retired, and I started to work on my own. Jarls petitioned me for a partnership. We worked together for only a short time, perhaps three or four contracts. He turned out to be the worst sort of Peacemaker: cruel toward those who needed protection, and indifferent toward those he should have cracked down on. I should have known better."

"How could you have known?" Mark asked.

Perry snorted with disgust. "You may not know, but Jarls is a Barundi, and in a bizarre fluke of evolution, they have come to branch, genetically and biologically along two paths at the onset of sexual maturity."

"Branch?"

"Yes. They'll essentially grow into one of two subspecies. The first is a docile, civil variety known as the Lòda, while the second is their surprisingly feral and unpredictable counterpart, the Mogúl. Vane didn't only lie upon his indoctrination to the Guild, identifying himself as Lòda, but he paid good credits to have a doctor falsify his records," Perry said, naming each offense with a growing tone of revulsion. He was *still* disgusted.

Mark spread his hands, inviting further explanation. "Okay, so, knowing all that—he hates you because why?"

"Jarls didn't just botch our last contract together, but he killed a person of interest in cold blood. I didn't just cease working with him after that, but I blacklisted him, effectively rendering him untouchable by all combat AI units. He didn't take it well. Then a few solar cycles later, he ended up smuggling. I took the contract, not knowing he was involved. You heard the rest. He was trafficking stolen hydrogen fuel cells, and in his attempt to escape, one came loose from its rack and broke open. It, ah, detonated."

"And Jarls Vane survived?"

"Somehow. And now that the sumbitch has seen me, his grudge is reignited."

Mark blew out a breath. "Quick note here, bird. I'm losing track of everyone who wants us dead. That's a bad thing, by the way."

"Agreed, and I've been working on that," Netty said.

A three-dimensional flow chart appeared. Two boxes sat at the top, displaying the names Gyl-Mareth and Cai-Demond. Glass was below them, connecting each with a dotted line. The Five Star

League was listed off to the right as well, with Jarls Vane off to the left. There were many more boxes displayed, some intersecting lines and others unconnected. Most were filled with question marks.

"It's nice to have as a visual reference, but all those open squares just remind me of how little we actually know," Mark said.

"More pieces are revealing themselves all the time," Netty answered as boxes formed, filling in with the text [Jackals] under the threat matrix, and [Tunis], designated as friendly. "As soon as you discovered Noka's connection to Gyl-Mareth, it revealed and threatened whatever network is in place. In a way, this was inevitable. We *have* to stay the course now."

"And by stay the course, you mean flip over all the rocks until we find all the slimy bastards involved?"

"There are likely dozens of intermediaries, brokers, syndicates, and militarized clandestine groups involved. This is likely going to get much, much worse before anything improves," Netty said. "As to their degree of slime, well, we shall see."

"We have an old saying," Perry declared. "Follow the money. And as I have learned over my tenure of service, loyalties will change as soon as the flow of Bonds is threatened."

"If you two are working to clarify the picture for me, you're only succeeding at clouding the waters," Mark said, waving a hand in frustration.

"Our unfortunate reality right now," Perry agreed. "Swimming in murky water while surrounded by predators."

A lull fell over their conversation as the Tunis worked quietly and diligently around them. Although, Mark hadn't seen Ja-Ra since they'd returned from their scavenger run.

"Mark, I hate to be the one to say it, but we really should get moving. Perry's spoof algorithm will only fool people for so long. Eventually it will look like we are flying in circles. Besides, Cai-Demond will want an update on the contract he assigned you, and you never did respond to Gyl-Mareth's cryptic message."

"I know," he said, silently hating the idea of leaving Ja-Ra and his clan so far from anything resembling civilization, especially considering their lack of tools to defend themselves. It felt wrong.

"Don't worry, we'll come back. And the sub-minds I installed in the ship come from my native code, so you know they aren't going to give up without a fight," Netty said, as if reading his thoughts.

Leaving the *Belle*'s massive control bridge behind, Mark and Perry moved down into the crew quarters. They cycled through the airlock, only to find Ja-Ra and two of his clan working in the cockpit.

"What's this?" Perry asked.

"They wanted it to be a surprise. And I might have stalled you a little to give them time," Netty admitted.

"Done-done," Ja-Ra said, slapping his three-fingered hands together and promptly closing the floor panel.

"Done with?"

Ja-Ra crawled up on the pilot's seat and pointed out the port windscreen. Mark followed, leaning out to look. The salvaged rotary cannon had been affixed to the hard point, midship. He followed the Tunis to the other side and discovered that the rocket pod had been installed there.

"That was fast. And they work? They aren't scrap like the stuff we brought you from those Peaceful Skies attack boats?"

"No. Those were damaged beyond repair. Cheap control boards, crappy wiring, and bad metal work. They were scrap before, even when they worked. These are old and heavy, but stout. Well-made tech, I like this very much indeed," Ja-Ra enthused.

To prove the point, Netty activated the rotary cannon. The barrels started to spin, then swung left, down, and up, as if tracking invisible targets. It was a formidable-looking weapon.

"You make it sound so simple," he said, considering his Guild bank account. They'd cleaned it out to get this far. The Tunis moved to leave, the strange, tuft-like hair on their heads swaying as they moved.

Mark followed, only catching up at the airlock. The door cycled open, and the little aliens bounced out.

"We'll return as soon as we can."

Ja-Ra shifted his weight from foot to foot, then awkwardly looked around. Something was bothering the small alien, that much was clear.

"What's wrong?"

"You mean to go after Mala?" the Tunis asked, refusing to use her nickname.

"Go after her, specifically?" Mark sighed. "No. Truthfully, our priority is to expose our corrupt Guild masters before more innocent people are hurt."

Ja-Ra nodded but did not speak for a long moment.

"And if *she* tries to stop you?"

"I won't back down, and I don't believe she will either." Mark left the rest unsaid because he could tell Ja-Ra had already drawn that conclusion. If what Perry said was true, Tunis formed a wider familial circle by adopting those they did business with and came to trust. That meant that Ja-Ra was faced with the prospect of two family members coming to blows—with only one walking or flying away in the end.

"She is smart, and her ships have thick armor. Your *Fafnir* is smaller and nimbler, but the reactor—it's no good."

"We'll get through," Mark said, pausing. It was the first time he'd heard the small alien reference his ship by its name.

"It is *no good*. No good for ship, and no good for Mark Tudor," Ja-Ra repeated. The Tunis removed something from a pouch on his belt—an ancient-looking dinged and dented data slate. He stared at it for a long moment, his three-fingered hand clutching it tightly, before finally holding it out to him.

"What is it?" Mark asked, accepting the device.

"How I can help," the Tunis said simply. Ja-Ra turned as the airlock started to cycle, the air equalizing loudly. "Look here, Mark Tudor. Coordinates for an abandoned missile platform. Its reactor would be a perfect fit for your ship. Take it to the Bone Yard. They'll know what to do."

Mark tapped the device awake, immediately taking note of four files saved to the home screen. By the time he looked up, Ja-Ra was already halfway out the airlock.

"Don't worry about Tunis. We will be okay. Trust Ja-Ra."

Then the door closed, and he was gone, leaving Mark with an unsettled, empty feeling in his gut. And it wasn't only because he was hungry.

He dropped heavily into the pilot's chair as the ship rocked away from the *Belle*, the ancient airlock releasing them with an audible clunk and hiss of vented atmosphere. Mark's overlay updated with telemetry and sensor data as Netty brought the reactor out of standby mode. Panel lights glowed to life, while the overheads dimmed for transit.

Thrusters fired, propelling them sideways as a blip appeared on the outer edge of passive scanner range. Mark froze as the icon solidified, his arm stuck halfway through the harness. A long moment passed as he waited for Netty to identify the contact as a threat or friendly.

"What is it?" he asked when the icon remained unchanged. "Was it not there before?"

"No. It didn't appear on passive scans, and I can't seem to—well, it doesn't fit any of the known ship dimensions and shapes. It's putting off a highly irregular heat signature, as well."

Mark eased his arm the rest of the way into the harness, looped his left arm through, and reached for the buckle. His thoughts came together, somewhat slower than he'd like—the Jackal ship was a composite of multiple components and sections of hull. It only made sense that Netty wouldn't be able to identify or categorize them based off shape. The heat signature was another issue, but considering the Jackal ships could be running any power plants, reactors, or thruster systems off scavenged hulks, it only made sense. If the welding and fabrication work was shoddy, the ship was likely bleeding heat and radiation.

"That's a Jackal ship. Has to be," Mark said, stowing the old data slate and moving to his overlay. "I think we should force a conversation—"

A separate, smaller icon appeared on the screen, followed by a second. Netty designated the missiles immediately, tracking their speed and course.

"They spoke first. I guess that answers the question of whether or not they're friendly," Perry said.

"Depends. Help me out, bird—are missiles friendly?"

"It might surprise you to learn they are, in fact, not. I'd say we have enemy assholes on the clock, boss."

Mark gave a single nod. "Then let's get at 'em."

Moving at a cognitive speed few biological beings could match, Netty flagged the Jackal ship red, then dropped the cockpit to tactical lighting, warmed up their laser unit and missile launcher, computed the distance to the enemy ship, and fired up their drive. She also updated his screen with the enemy contact's elevation above the surface, angle, and drift.

"Kill those missiles, Netty," Mark said as he fired thrusters, turning the *Fafnir* toward the threat. The Jackals were already moving, pushing a tight arc down and away.

"They're running," Perry offered.

"If they're a lookout for more Jackal ships, then we have to assume they know everything—specifically who we dropped off on the *Belle*. We cannot let them pass along that information," Mark growled, then took the stick, grabbed the throttle, and jammed it forward.

The ship responded in kind, smashing him back into the seat as the drive roared.

"They could all know already, but you're right. Go get 'em, Mark!" Perry said, taking control of the missile guidance system.

The Invictus fired a three-shot laser burst and the first incoming missile disappeared in a bright flash of plasma. The targeting reticle shifted before the weapon fired again. The shots missed the second target, as the missile appeared to jump right over them.

The laser fired once more as the *Fafnir* shuddered and rolled hard to starboard. Mark's neck popped as he flopped against the restraints, gravity abruptly shifting to the side and promptly back again. The ship jostled hard a second time, with warning lights flaring to life on the forward instrument panel.

"That was a gravity pocket. Sorry, there was no indication it was there," Netty said.

Mark rubbed a hot spot forming in his neck as the Invictus fired two more bursts. The missile was less than 400 yards away by the time it blinked off the overlay, the bright flash illuminating the vast canopy of black space ahead.

"Missile is locked. Firing," Perry crowed as the tri-fire cycled below them.

Their Whisperwing streaked straight at the fleeing Jackal ship. It closed, then abruptly curved down and into the Junkway, where it detonated in a shower of ice and debris.

"Was that a—?"

"A gravity pocket? Yes," Netty said as Mark rolled them hard to port, narrowly avoiding a large chunk of spinning debris. He watched the obstacle as they passed, the ice-covered fuselage looping in space as if orbiting around some invisible stellar body.

"Get us closer, and we'll flash their drive with the laser."

Mark poured on more thrust, and the Jackals slipped beyond the horizon ahead. Despite closing the distance at first, the enemy ship had displayed surprising speed and agility since.

"I know what you're thinking," Perry said, flipping between screens on his tactical overlay. "They know how to navigate this place, and we don't. All you need to do is get us close enough—preferably in one piece."

"Working on it," Mark grunted as gravity shifted yet again, this time to starboard. His neck was locked up, the muscles bound like steel cables. Pain radiated from his skull down to his middle back, making every direction change that much worse.

Fighting through the discomfort, Mark rolled again and eased the throttle forward a bit more, then pulled back on the stick for a bit of altitude. The Jackal ship finally appeared again, the odd craft speeding along right above the surface.

"I'm reading what might be a massive hollow cavity in the Junkway ahead. It could be tunnels," Netty warned. She updated the overlay, the gravimetric and surface density readings appearing in red. If they were tunnels, then the Jackal ship was speeding right for it. Considering how tight a fit it was for the service pod, if the Jackals made it inside, there was no way they would be able to follow.

He let his head sag back against the headrest and jammed the throttle hard. The Invictus fired twice and then a third time, but the shots didn't connect.

"They're almost to their hidey-hole. I'm firing!" Perry shouted and launched not one but two missiles.

Mark watched as the two weapons streaked ahead, the lead missile hitting a gravity pocket and correcting, the follower looping out wide to avoid it. He understood what the bird was doing. Perry was using the lead missile to identify gravitational and magnetic pockets.

The first Whisperwing hit a turbulent patch and spun out of control, veering right and then down, its warhead detonating barely fifty feet off the Junkway's frozen surface. But the second missile looped up and around that spot, then started closing quickly. The

Jackals were 1000 meters from the entrance to the caves, then 800—

Then 500.

The missile went home in a devastating flash. The enemy ship vanished in a blinding smear of plasma outside the tunnel mouth.

Perry managed to look smug and relieved, a feat for a being with a beak. "Splash one, boss. Knew it all along."

Mark relaxed. Sort of. But for the first time in a while, he smiled.

15

Mark brought the *Fafnir* about right over the mouth of the tunnel and fired the bow thrusters to bleed off the rest of their speed. He flipped through the overlay screens for a moment, but when he couldn't get the view he wanted, he unbuckled and moved to the forward windscreen.

A cloud of expanding debris hung in the air all around them, with one section of detritus spinning in crazy, looping circles. Mark leaned forward and looked down, only to find that a large portion of ice had been blown away from the tunnel mouth. His chest tightened as he analyzed the scene, and any sense of relaxation evaporated in an instant.

"Netty, shouldn't we be looking at intact sections of ship? Would one missile tear the whole thing apart?"

"Considering estimated mass, yes, a total loss debris field would be five to six times larger. Only a successful hull breach and reactor shot would have torn the whole ship apart. The Whisperwing warheads just don't have enough punch."

"Perry?"

"You think they survived a direct hit and crawled down into their hole?" the bird asked.

"Think it?" Mark asked, watching the debris. "Unfortunately, yes."

"The odds of surviving a direct missile strike are low, especially considering their orientation. It would have been rear quarter or drive cone. Both would have been crippling shots, if not enough to cause drive or reactor failure and overload. My analysis says they're dead."

"Analysis is well and good, but when gambling with other people's lives, I'd rather see a smoking wreck," Mark said, shaking his head.

His doubt deepening, he moved to the port side screens, then starboard, searching the endless black. Netty switched on the flood-lights, but with the debris expanding so quickly Mark couldn't tell what was metal from ice.

"Perry's right, Mark. According to data transmitted right before impact, our missile had a true lock. Mathematical analysis says that with a solid, drive-cone hit, the Jackals had single-digit odds of survival," Netty added.

He trusted both AIs with his life, but for the first time since working with them, Mark wasn't comfortable going strictly off the numbers. A jaded part of him wanted—no, needed—to see proof.

"Before you spiral too deeply into doubt, that tunnel narrows twenty-five meters down, so the *Fafnir* would not fit, Mark. Trust me," Perry said, "they're gone."

"When my uncle walked into the barn each morning, his lantern light would send the rats and mice scurrying for the shadows. This is no different. As soon as we leave, these parasites will creep out of their hiding spots."

"True, but it isn't our duty to rid the galaxies of all parasites and vermin, Mark. We're tasked with finding and maintaining a sustainable peace."

He knew Perry was right, but that didn't mean he had to like it. Nor did it mean that he had to sit by and do nothing. Mark vowed to return to the Junkway often, and the next time they encountered Jackals, he wouldn't settle for a theoretical kill.

They burned hard out of the Junkway's bizarre and unpredictable gravity well, before initiating the long twist back into the Milky Way. The transit seemed to take minutes, while in reality, they spent hours in twist space.

Mark found himself in the galley once his brain started to sort itself out, with Tan sitting across from him at the table.

"Was it the same? Did we have the same conversation five times?" Mark asked, rubbing his eyes. The sensation was strange, like he had cotton stuffed between his ears.

"I lost count," Tan said, chuckling. "What is the last thing you remember?"

Mark moved from rubbing his eyes to the aching spot in his neck for a moment. At first, he couldn't remember why it hurt, but after some deliberation, the memories started to trickle back in—chasing the Jackal ship, the missile strike, and then twisting away from the Junkway. How had eight hours passed since that time? It didn't feel possible.

"It's strange. When you first asked that question, the last thing I could remember was strapping in to chase the Jackals. But memories started to pop in after that, as if they were slowly loading into my mind. Then I hit the point where we twisted away, and everything is just—blank."

"I would find that highly unsettling. We Druzis have densely packed neurotransmitters and receivers in our brains, so naturally our memory is quite good. I could tell you the exact quantum signature I used to encode my very first processor board—all one thousand and thirty-two characters. Perhaps there's some way we could shield your mind from the low frequency waves. There's always genetic modification as well."

Mark shook the last option away. The thought of letting some unregulated medical pod fiddle with his genetic code felt wrong, regardless of the potential perks. Oh, sure, they could probably make him live longer, grow taller, and get stronger, and they could give him a deeper voice, improve his memory, or perhaps make his beard grow fuller and thicker. But the list of things that might go wrong was ten times longer than he was tall, and he'd seen enough bizarre aliens to fuel his imagination. With his luck, he would end up looking more like Karan, the bizarre jellyfish-like holding officer in Tau Regus.

Suppressing a shudder, Mark pushed out of the seat and rejoined Perry, the bird perched on the back of the co-pilot's chair.

"Is the mush in your skull back to its ordinary state of forgetfulness yet?"

"How very kind of you for asking, but yes, the porridge in my head is better. Thank you."

"You can call me many things—but not uncaring," Perry said,

slowly turning to Mark. He sat there, quiet and staring as the silence grew.

"You're truly a shining beacon of empathy," Mark deadpanned.

"Truly," the bird agreed, studiously ignoring his sarcasm. "Now that you have had a chance to cognitively recalibrate, we will make the first of a short series of twists. The first two will set us up for our jump right to Armagost's exoplanet. We will do a quick body shuffle to drop off Tan and the expensive goodies Netty insisted on purchasing. Then we will twist to a pre-designated buoy, activate our transponder, use my worm to manipulate our supposed travel path and time stamps, and jump to complete our contract."

"You make it all sound so easy."

"It's just a series of mathematical equations, Mark. And it just so happens that it's what AIs are made for. Strictly speaking, it isn't *all* we're made for, but I think you understand," Perry added.

"And typical Perry, glossing over the risk," Netty added. "What he didn't tell you is our fuel margin. We hypothesized three thousand four hundred and seventy-eight twists to find this combination. And all because of our dwindling fuel surplus. We should arrive at Algo Shipyards on proverbial empty."

"Even with the expansion tanks? I know the twist out to the Junkway was long, but we really used that much fuel to get out there and back?"

"Yes. That's why we decided that you should start your investigation at the Algo Shipyards. There are plenty of places to refuel. And according to Perry, there are also plenty of places where you could borrow, barter, beg, or steal bonds for fuel."

"From flush with bonds and platinum to once again living the life of a broke Peacemaker, struggling to fuel his ship. Things can change quickly out here in the black." Mark chuckled bitterly.

He settled into his chair and pulled up their contract. It read as unremarkable and tedious as the first time he had read it—a series of illegal boardings on freight haulers. The complainant was Selvo Cargo Lines, a shipping magnate based out of Brunus, a Daren-thal city on Ajax.

"Why does it show the complainant as Selvo but not specifically who filed it? There's no contact information, and the only meta data I see is a Guild reference number," Mark said.

"Perhaps boredom took them in the middle of typing something so mundane," Perry answered. "Kind of how I'm feeling *now* watching you gripe about paperwork."

Mark grinned. "Prepare for more thrills then, bird. I'm reading the entire document."

The second page of the contract detailed the location, times, and individual instances of each alleged event. Mark read through to the third page, which featured quotes by witnesses, detailing the perpetrators. They were described as disheveled, ratty, dirty, and erratic figures, all carrying bags. Ironically, three of the four adjectives popped up in all twelve of the eyewitness accounts. He flagged that detail and swiped back to the first page.

They twisted out then, making their small jumps to set themselves up for the trip to Armagost's hidden base. Mark tried to study the files on Ja-Ra's data slate, but the low frequency cognitive impairment reared its ugly head once again. According to Perry, Mark picked up and set down the device no less than eight times.

They offloaded Tan right away, with Netty giving them a visible countdown to their rushed departure. The Druzis looked both frightened and excited, the former to be disembarking from his very first starship, while the latter inspired by the fact that they were simply dumping him off with an unknown Gajur, in a hidden base, on an unregistered exoplanet twelve million miles from the nearest colonized world.

"Armagost is friendly and fair. Just don't create any messes, break anything, or," Mark said, hooking an arm around the Druzis' shoulder as they entered the workshop, "forget to put any of his tools back in their designated places. Bit feisty about that."

Tan looked out over the gleaming space. There wasn't a speck of dust in sight, and as Mark referenced, each and every tool hung neatly on a hook, the wall behind them painted to match its shape. There was neat and tidy, and then there was Armagost. Luckily, the old Gajur had never seen Mark's uncle's workshop. The disheveled, barely contained chaos of that space might have killed him on the spot.

They spent the next few minutes offloading crates—the surplus of goods Netty had carefully cultivated for her creator. Armagost inspected each one, seemingly measuring the boxes before finally opening them. He did so with almost obsessive care, carefully peeling open the lid so as not to tear or break the material. Mark's eye started to twitch twenty minutes into that routine, but he kept quiet and respectful.

"As long as the young man is everything you claim, we should have a working prototype in short order. You can return soon? A week's time is all we will need. Well, for the first item, at least," Armagost said after finishing with the last crate.

"Gladly." Mark shook the Gajur's hand. Although he silently wondered where he would source the money and fuel. The payout on his current contract would barely cover a refuel, and they had other needs beyond that as well.

"Thank you for all of your help, Mark Tudor," Tan said, returning his handshake. The Druzis' two opposable thumbs made the gesture feel *off*. "We will also work on the low-frequency issue. Trust me, your brain is in good hands. Well, I mean, it is still in your head, but you understand. Right?"

"I do. Thank you, Tan."

Netty spent a few minutes talking with her creator in private, while Mark and Perry loaded the empty crates into the *Fafnir* and prepared to leave.

"It's best we leave now," she said as he stacked the last crate into the galley closet and closed the door. "He's getting quite emotional and would not like for us to see."

"I understand," Mark said and moved to cycle the airlock closed.

Armagost stood at the base of the ramp and threw him an economical wave. He returned the parting gesture, passively inspecting the Gajur's face as the doors closed. There were no tears, color change, or tightness to denote sadness or grief. Mark reminded himself that he was perhaps the furthest thing from an expert on alien biology or behaviors. His time with Wyser the Wulgor and the horny fish ladies of the Hudonnec confirmed the point.

They twisted out of system and hid their tracks with a few short and economical jumps, then headed straight for the Algo Shipyards. The port was busy when they arrived, the outermost docking rings hosting dozens of massive cargo haulers. Smaller ships dominated the next ring in, with at least half a dozen military fast attack boats standing out from the crowd.

Docking control gave them their slip assignment and permission to dock an hour later, and Netty took them in.

"This place is like Trei-Seti's slightly less rusty bigger brother," he said as Perry hopped up behind him. "Still as damp, though. Is that a hint of mold I detect?"

"Piquant, isn't it?" Perry enthused. "I truly love sampling high culture."

The *Fafnir*'s outer hatch slid shut with a hiss before Netty's optical sensor appeared above his wrist.

"A touch *less* sketchy, yes, but not without its dangers. I scanned a departing ship while we were docking. It's been documented in several cases involving Salt Thieves."

"Great," Mark said. "Let's add a few more hostiles while we're at it."

"Let's not," Perry countered.

They moved through the docks, the space filled with crews, loader bots, and noise. Algo felt alive, in all the ways Chevix and Spindrift did not. He spotted hostels, saunas, a strange festival clogging up one passage, and so much more. Algo wasn't only a shipyard, it was a living, breathing community.

Netty guided them left and to one of the outer rings. They passed a checkpoint manned by a security Synth. Mark flashed his Peacemaker badge, and the Synth let them pass, dipping their head deferentially. A pressure door took them back to the industrial sector, where the atmosphere and energy changed instantly.

There were no festivals, food merchants, or hostels here, only the grinding wheels of industry. Maglev transporters zoomed by, carrying freight through the junction ahead, only to cut left and down the docks. More automated cars appeared, running at regular intervals, while loader bots and work crews tromped by.

They located docking pier C2 and turned left, following the significantly darker passage ahead. Almost eight hundred feet down the pier, Mark located slip CZ102. He double-checked the contract, confirming that it was the location of the most recent complaint. The airlock doors were large, scarred, and remarkably unremarkable.

"How was anyone here to witness someone sneaking aboard?" Mark asked, then scanned the ceiling. A security camera sat nestled against the far wall, but it appeared to be damaged and inoperable.

"There's no ship here now, but the passage could be busier during loading and unloading," Perry answered.

They searched the area for a few minutes, before moving on to the next spot, and the one after that.

"Big door," Perry observed when they reached the final spot listed.

"Cargo big. I like our chances, bird."

Mark cycled the portal open and moved into the space beyond —a cargo preparation bay. The massive room was large and mostly barren, with an automated conveyor carrying empty boxes in from above.

"Hello?" he called, as parcels flowed forth to fill the container. Once full, the conveyor whisked the full unit away and replaced it with another. It was seamless. It was fast.

"This place is moving at the speed of money," Mark said.

Perry launched himself into the air and circled the cavernous space but returned a moment later. His talons slipped and rattled on the floor, then he managed to go still, turning to eye Mark.

"It's…empty. No one here. Not even Synth laborers."

"I noticed," Mark said. "But is it always this empty, this automated? If so, how would there be witnesses to see anything happen?"

"If anything happened in the first place," Perry argued. "This contract smells fishy."

"Hudonnec fishy or questionable fishy?" Mark countered.

"Dunno. But we need witnesses. Let's kick over some rocks. Perhaps we aren't looking at it from the right angle."

"That we are looking at all is the problem. Glass engaged in open warfare with Tau-be damned-Regus, and there's likely other serious shit going on out there. Yet, we are here, following up on illegal boarding complaints. That's what, a Class 2 misdemeanor, punishable by fourteen days in holding and a five-hundred-bond fine? It's a chickenshit job no matter how you frame it. All I can conclude is that they want us out of the way," Mark said, finishing by glaring at all the inactivity around them.

"We're in agreement then?" Perry asked.

"We are."

"Let's ditch this loser of a contract and get back out there. We need to find out how Glass is connected to Cai-Demond and Gyl-Mareth. If we can do that, perhaps some of the other players on Netty's flowchart will reveal themselves."

"Yes. But let's run down a few of these witnesses listed on the contract first. Then we can drop it with clear consciences and move on. Deal?"

"My conscience is clear regardless. I'm pissed that we've been rerouted at all."

With Perry groaning and grumbling, Netty guided them back out of the docks and into the bustling crowds of the lower market.

"Okay, Netty. Where are we going? Who are we interviewing first?" Mark asked.

"This is strange," the AI replied. "I've cross-referenced our list of witnesses with Algo Shipyards' registry and have only come up with one match."

"One?"

"Yes. According to Algo's resident AI, only one of the people listed actually exists. Or, if more do, then they aren't registered as residents, workers, contractors, or legal transients."

"I didn't think it was possible. This situation smells even worse than before. It's practically rancid," Perry muttered.

"The one match, where are they?" Mark asked. "Got an address?"

"Yes. I'll lead you there," Netty offered and pushed a turn-by-turn map to his repeater. It was only a ten-minute walk before they arrived at their destination—a tired, grimy passage behind a series of noisy moisture condensers. Mushrooms bloomed, fat and moist on the condensers, and Perry was careful not to step on their spreading bodies.

"Charmed, I'm sure. I've seen petri dishes that were cleaner," Perry mumbled, edging farther away from the condensers.

"I'll take your word for it. Not a fan of"—Mark waved vaguely —"whatever all that is."

The walls here were streaked with rust and dirt, while the yellowed light fixtures cast a pallid glow that couldn't quite cut the shadows. Mark followed the directions down the hall and around a hard corner. The room registered to their witness, Kel b'Erd, was at the very end on the right.

"Funny name," Mark said. "It sounds strangely like 'kill bird.'"

"Yes. That's *hilarious*."

Mark settled before the door, adjusted his holster, and knocked. It creaked, gave way under the weight, and swung open a few inches. He looked down at Perry, but the bird's eyes were already gleaming with his charged stun attack.

Perry moved aside, eased his head forward, and pushed the door open a little further, announcing them as he did.

"Peacemakers. Is anyone home? We need to ask you a few questions." The drip-drip-drip of water from the moisture condensers was the only response.

"Hello?" Mark called, raising his voice.

A door opened a crack behind them, before snapping shut again.

Counting quietly to three, Mark tapped Perry on the back, and together they moved forward. The door swung open, and he stepped in, his b-suit lights snapping on to cut the darkness. And it was dark. And dusty.

Panning left, then right, Mark swept the bright lights through the space, confirming that it was empty. And judging from the thick layer of dust on the floor, it had been that way for some time.

They moved back and into the space together, searching the rundown apartment room by room, until reaching the final door. Mark pushed it open, his lights immediately flooding into the next space. A solitary chair gleamed in the light, and it wasn't empty.

"Come in, Peacemakers. I'm so glad we could finally meet," the seated woman said, although the smile on her handsome face didn't reach her eyes.

Mark's gaze snapped from her attractive features to her dark fatigues and combat armor. It was the same gear as the mercenaries Striker had neutralized on Tau Regus. The woman shifted, and Mark's gaze settled on the sidearm leveled at his chest.

"You don't look like a 'Kel b'Erd,'" Perry observed, his eyes changing to red again.

"Be careful, bird." The woman laughed and lifted her other hand, revealing a sizable fragmentation charge. "You aren't the only one packing surprises."

16

Algo Shipyards: HD4629

"I BELIEVE you need to fire your housekeeper," Perry said dryly, then slowly looked around the room. "Too dirty in here for dust mites. Even they have standards."

"You don't think it fitting?"

"The apartment? Oh, certainly. But the name, not particularly. Glass denotes clarity and transparency. I think 'Mirror' might be more apt," Perry said, lifting and studying his foot. No one played the part of the bored bird quite like him.

"Mirrors show us only reflections, although some say that the mirror's edge is the truest likeness—an honest look inside."

"A mirror's edge often warps the reflection," Perry replied.

"Exactly." The woman's mouth pulled up into a playful smirk. "I find it refreshingly truthful."

"So upbeat," Perry enthused. "You really make the trip out here worth it."

Mark watched the two go back and forth, the subtleness of their jabs only undercut by the deadly weapon Glass clutched in her lap. It wasn't necessarily the fatigues or body armor, or the scars on her chin, neck, and forehead—for she was a beautiful woman, with classic cheekbones, arching eyebrows, and a natural pout to her lips. She had the looks for stage or screen, but that would have been another life.

No, it was the look in her eyes, the cold and calculated stare of a seasoned killer. She was empty in all the right places, and it made her that most dangerous of creatures.

She was utterly free. From morals. From fear.

From influence.

Mark turned ten degrees to the right, shielding his arm as he slowly reached back and undid the strap on his revolver. Glass's eyes remained locked on Perry, but her smile deepened as the snap popped quietly loose.

"I've heard whispers of a brazen new lawman. He dragged Wyser, bloodied and clinging to life, out of Spindrift. Then he turned Chevix Station upside down and let Noka's sins tumble forth for all to see. Those are *bold* moves. And if that wasn't enough, he strolled onto Fulcrum in the midst of a violent raid, snatched up something that didn't belong to him, and waltzed right back out. Daring moves, although I wonder if he knew...truly knew, how much chaos he was helping to unleash."

"I don't waltz," Mark said, finally speaking. "But I did spend a summer learning how to square dance. It didn't stick—too much lateral and backward motion. I prefer to keep moving forward. Preferably armed. I'm sure you understand."

Glass nodded, her smile never faltering. She opened and closed her fingers, letting the fragmentation charge roll around in her palm. The silence stretched on, as their battle of wills pushed ever closer to breaking open.

"You knew Noka? Was he an associate of yours?" Mark asked, shifting sideways a half-step.

Glass shook her head, the blaster turning to track him. The weapon didn't shake or falter, nor were her knuckles white. She was as cool and collected as they came. That confirmed that she was the real deal. He took note that she didn't necessarily answer the questions.

Perry moved left, working to enhance their angles.

"And Tau Regus, was that the chaos being unleashed? Why attack Fulcrum?"

"You two really have no idea what is going on, do you?" Glass's smile finally faltered, and she cleared her throat. "No, I suppose you don't. I attacked Fulcrum because they possessed something that belonged to *me*. When you spend a lifetime in servitude, as I did, you learn quickly enough that people in power only care about themselves. They walk on the corpses of those they serve, elevating themselves to new heights. The Merchant Lords on Fulcrum, the Cabal fascists, even the Federation stooges, they're all the same. The people can't see them for what they truly are, nor would their voices make any difference. That's why I'm here. I will do what they cannot."

"So, you're fighting to liberate the people? You're going to fight the whole system?" Mark asked, dubious.

Glass sighed, flexed her grip on the blaster, and rotated the charge again before speaking. He could almost see her processing the odds, risks, and angles.

"The system is rotten—the whole thing turns on the wheels and cogs of corruption, perversion, and murder."

"A few are corrupt, but that doesn't mean—"

"The *whole* system," Glass growled, interrupting him. The smile was gone, along with the playful sparkle in her eyes. Mark saw his death in her gaze, the indifference and malice shining through.

"The system," he replied, raising his voice to match hers, "is designed to weed out the corrupt, like we did with Noka. That's what *we* do. That's why *we* are here."

"You're part of the system. Noka is part of that same system. That means if one is rotten, the whole thing is spoiled. You take him down and someone will simply step forward to replace him. Before too long, the system corrupts all, even you. It is inevitable. Who is there to enforce the greater peace? The natural law? Who will protect the innocents while their own people subjugate and abuse them? Who will step in and free those locked in civil strife, when their own people profit from the conflict? Who? Your Galactic Knights?"

Mark knew the questions were coming. Considering her story, it was inevitable.

"There are still good people out there, and we've still got fight left in us. Hell, we're just starting," Mark said.

"Good people? Hope?" Glass snorted. "How naïve are you? There's no such thing as 'good people,' only people, and the concept of 'right and wrong' is a sliding scale, one that favors those that hold authority and power. I've seen too much of the colonized world to swallow those lies…seen too much of how authority can be bent to punish and reward. Law and authority aren't a shield, as you Galactic Knights claim. They're clubs, wielded by those in power and used to beat the lowly into submission."

"Utter nonsense, and childish to boot," Perry said. "You're dancing toward nihilism, which isn't as elegant as you might think."

"Hardly. It's honest. Nothing more."

"What's the answer then?" Mark asked. "Show me a problem, and I'll fight to fix it." His statement was…an invitation. Of sorts.

"It's too late for fixes. Too late for negotiation."

Her last comment struck him, as it sounded horribly like she was advocating a reset, regardless of the cost to all. But what would that look like? In the breadth of colonized space, there were simply too many worlds, too many advanced species.

"Tell us how we can help," Perry said. "Why the fake contract? Why bring us all the way out here? If you aren't working for him, then what's your connection to Cai-Demond?"

Glass seemed to consider that question for a moment, and a bit of her anger bled away.

"Demond is an idealist. Gullible. A simple fool."

"And Gyl-Mareth?" Perry countered.

Glass stared at him, her mouth pulled up in that macabre smile.

"Good talk. So helpful," Perry deadpanned.

"You're *most* welcome."

"If you didn't want to tell us anything meaningful, then why bring us here? What's the point?" Mark asked.

"I'm a warrior and live by a creed. I see some of that in you, the honesty, the strength," she said, finally pushing off to stand. Her arm rose smoothly, maintaining the blaster's bead squarely on his chest.

Perry moved right, his legs and wings coiled and ready. But his eyes never left the charge in her hand. It was something he feared, that much was clear.

"And you wanted to give yourself up?" Perry asked.

"No. I wanted to warn you, to tell you to stay out of my way. Do that, and you won't get hurt. But if you try and stop me, I *will* kill you. What happens next is unavoidable."

Glass waved the blaster to the side, gesturing for Mark to move. He responded in kind as the mercenary leader spun, switching weapons and hold points with impressive grace. Perry backed away a little further as she shook the charge his way.

"What now? We're supposed to stand aside? Because I don't think I can do that, not if innocent people are going to get hurt," Mark said as the mercenary moved through the doorway.

"Like I said, you've been warned. What happens next is your choice."

Glass turned to run, but Mark only managed a single step before a blinding flash erupted around the doorframe. He registered an intense pressure on his ears and a hot wave over his face, then everything washed away.

He fell bodily into the mud, and a wave of cold, stagnant water flooded over his neck and face. Machine gun fire tore through the air overhead, the chatter echoing strangely down and into the trench around him.

Mark pushed off the ground, the grit having worked its way into his mouth. Men screamed above, the sharp *pop-pop-pop* of rifle fire answering them. He looked left down the trench, then turned right.

The thick fog crept in from above, filling the trench and crawling toward him. Where was his rifle?

"Mark!" someone screamed.

He turned, tracking the noise, and tried to swipe the mud off his face, but his hands were cold, shaking, and coated in muck. Something hit his shoulder, and he turned but found only more fog. The voice screamed his name again, but when he opened his mouth to shout back, no sound would come out.

Pushing into the mist, Mark managed a few steps before losing his bearings. He waved his hands, desperately searching for the side of the trench, but found only more fog.

"Mark," the voice cried again, only this time it echoed behind him. He turned, blinking desperately—as if the act would clear away the mist, his heart hammering painfully in his chest.

After drawing a raspy breath, Mark tried to yell again and again, to no avail. He pushed forward more quickly, clawing at the air, only to finally find the trench wall. Dirt and rocks crumbled, broke loose, and fell to the ground at his feet.

The voice shouted his name again, only it was above now and promptly drowned out by the angry chatter of machine gun fire. He pulled himself along the wall, hand over hand, mud and roots coming loose between his fingers.

A single, pervasive thought drove him—*up*, he had to go up before the gas crept in, and a ladder would get him there. He moved forward, searching the blinding mist, then he tripped, fell, and fought his way to his feet again.

Mark's throat tightened, and his chest ached, the cold creeping up his arms and legs. He clawed at more dirt, pulling at the fog, but there was no ladder. It had to be there; he knew they were there, so many of them.

Doubt blossomed, and quickly turned darker and darker. The fog grew thicker, until it wrapped around him like a smothering blanket. Mark fell, choking and fighting for air, as something noxious burned his nostrils and mouth. Pain bit into his arms, body wracked, twisting, fighting. *Surviving.*

The fog gave way to darkness. He stared at a dark, lurking form, its eyes glowing orange from within.

"Mark, wake up!"

He took a startled breath and blinked, his mind transitioning sluggishly. Smoke was in the air, not fog, and the walls were dust-covered paneling, not mud. His helmet was on, the faceplate scorched black with soot.

"What happened?" he asked, fumbling to release the helmet. Succeeding on the fourth try, his visor snapped up and out of the way, before the helmet retracted back into the suit.

Perry helped Mark into a seated position, where he brushed the dust from his hands. A horrible ringing filled his ears, not to mention the coppery taste covering his tongue.

"Glass left, and she wasn't in the mood to be followed. The doorway was rigged with several daisy-chained stun charges. You took them point-blank in the face. Luckily for you, your b-suit registered the overpressure and activated your helmet. Without it, you wouldn't have survived."

"We ha—to warn Valint, Drogo, and—"

"Yes, yes, Netty is doing that right now. Take a moment," Perry said, turning to look back out the door. The bird's snark and sarcasm were gone. He was all business, and for good reason.

"We walked right into that, didn't we?"

Perry nodded, then clicked his beak irritably.

Almost twenty minutes later they were walking back out of residential housing, the moisture condensers so much quieter than before. Mark opened and closed his mouth, confirming the reason to be partially blown eardrums. *Great.*

Mark drew the Moonsword as he went and made no effort to conceal the weapon. If anything, he lifted it a little higher, letting the light play along the blade. He was hurting, and the world felt like a darker, more dangerous place. Mark needed to feel strong, and for everyone to see him that way.

The crowd parted immediately, murmuring and pointing at them. Good. They made it to the docks without issue, but Netty pinged the repeater as they were approaching the *Fafnir*.

"Mark, Valint just twisted into system. Neither of us have been able to reach Vosa. She's running dark right now, and we don't know why."

"I think it's obvious. She's on the stalk, tracking a notorious hunter. Her actions are—they make sense, bird. When I was a kid, coyotes regularly threatened the farm. My uncle and I would go out at night to hunt them, but they were cagey and skittish. We had to tread very lightly, or they would melt away, like water into sand."

"I'm just worried, that's all. She's been running dark for quite some time now," Netty said.

"We're almost aboard. Send a message her way, and mark it as urgent. If she doesn't respond soon, we'll meet up with Drogo and Valint and go looking for her."

"Can we afford that? Others could be hunting us, while we're looking for her," Perry asked.

The outer airlock cycled open as they arrived, Netty overriding the lockout so they could walk straight in. Mark was halfway to the cockpit, and he could already hear data flooding into the pilots' overlay screens.

"Get us out of here, Netty," Mark said, hooking his arm through the trauma bag without breaking stride. "And I know Vosa is running dark, but see if you can't locate any data hinting at where she last twisted."

"I'm on it, Mark. Cerebral pinged us back. He and Drogo will see if they can't track her down."

They severed from the pier, the ship rocking ever-so-slightly to port. He staggered to the left, but it wasn't the motion. With his ears ringing, Mark didn't just have issues focusing, but his balance was off, too.

He tumbled back into his pilot's seat as the drive kicked in, propelling them away from Algo. Mark pulled the trauma bag open as Netty updated his overlay with a flood of new data, but he gave it only a passive scan while fishing around for the med-sleeve.

"Mark, Valint will meet us beyond the second planet's third moon. She will be orbiting the dark side."

After locating the med-sleeve beneath two ReLive bags, Mark quickly slid his right arm into the device and tapped it awake. The sleeve inflated, locking itself into place just above his elbow, and the small screen updated with gathered vitals.

"Perry. How does it look out there?" he asked, after struggling to sort through the chaos of his overlay.

"It's a shipyard, so there's movement everywhere. But aggressive posture—nothing, nada, rien."

A dozen small needles pierced his skin, and a moment later a wave of something cool flooded into his arm as the med-sleeve started its recommended treatments. He felt the sting in his ears subside, and thankfully, the tight ache in his neck released a moment later.

"Netty, ping both Drogo and Vosa. Keep sending until they respond. Make it clear how urgent this is."

"You got it, boss."

Something warm trickled into his arm next, and Mark laid his head back, closing his eyes. He focused, working to calm and categorize his thoughts as the medicine reached his chest. The dream was fading, but enough was still there for him to recall. And yet, it was different than before. This time he couldn't even find his way out of the trench. Why?

His heart rate increased, pushing it out to the rest of his body. Several blissful moments later, the ringing in his ears faded. Sometime after that, the pain in his neck was gone, too.

Glass had given him a warning, a courtesy from one professional to another. She'd told him to stay out of her way or suffer the consequences. But what did she have planned? If she was willing to attack a megacity on one of the most populous worlds in colonized space, then she was capable of almost anything.

"Therein lies the problem." Mark finally opened his eyes. He turned to Perry as a priority message popped up on their overlays. It flashed on the screen, surrounded by a red and yellow border.

"Ship in distress," Netty declared.

"Where? Why?" Mark asked, his thoughts and speech still sluggish.

"It appears to be a relatively small vessel. Telemetry indicates that it's stuck in a tidal orbit around this star's smallest and second closest planet."

"Let me guess—they're suffering from a reactor failure?"

"Mark the psychic? Did that egg-scrambling experience unlock your brain's hidden potential?" Perry asked.

"No, but I can read," he said, pointing at his overlay. "The message shows they're without power or thrust."

"Yep. If they cannot course correct, then the planet's gravity will pull them into the atmosphere, and they'll burn up."

"Shit."

"Language," Netty scolded.

"I mean darn. Is anyone else responding?"

"Not that I can see. We are the closest Peacemaker ship, by a considerable margin. Unfortunately, Guild procedures require that we—" Perry said.

"I know. That we render aid."

"Who's the Legal Eagle now?" Netty asked.

"You don't even have wings," Perry grumbled.

"Okay." Mark grunted and sat up in the seat a little straighter. "Change course and let Valint know that we're responding to the distress message."

"Roger that. Striker has confirmed. They'll back us up, although we are far deeper into the gravity well than they are. It'll take them a while to get there, even under hard burn."

"Well, we have a tether, and thanks to our, ah, *unsavory* workboat experience, we know how not to use it. I think we can handle things until she arrives."

"Distressed vessel, this is Peacemaker Mark Tudor of the Galactic Knights Uniformed. We have received your request for aid and are en route to your location. Please confirm receipt," Mark said, opening a comms channel. He released the icon and waited for a response.

The silence stretched on as the *Fafnir* picked up speed, its drive burning hard.

"One thing bothers me," Perry said a few minutes later.

"Just one? I'm hard-pressed to think of anything that hasn't bothered me lately."

"Touché. But consider this. The contract that Glass used to lure us out here might be fabricated, in the strictest sense, but what if the message it contains is genuine?"

"Genuine? The people stowing away on cargo ships?"

"Yes. The next logical question: what kind of people are stowing away, and why? Think about it, Mark. Cargo ships only keep manifests of materials shipped. And most of the time, they're vessels run largely by skeleton crews or automated systems."

"So, there would be no proof of these people—where they started or where they got off," Mark reasoned.

Perry nodded. "You're a soldier, Mark, think about it. If you were fighting a war, perhaps a cold one, how beneficial would it be if you could move assets into place without your enemy knowing?"

"Tactically speaking, it would be devastating. Your enemy would never know where you were going to hit them, or how. A stealth force that size could take down assets, and if done properly, no one would know. At least, they wouldn't know right away."

Mark let out his breath slowly as the ramifications sank in. They knew Gyl-Mareth and Cai-Demond belonged to opposing factions, and that the civil conflict embroiling their people was cold. Well, supposedly cold. What if the two sides were still active, and quietly moving their pieces around the board. What would their designs be? Their motivations?

"Maybe we look into this a little more closely?"

"I believe that might not be a bad—" Perry started to say.

"Rogue action!" Netty called as alarms filled the cockpit.

The overhead lights dimmed and the data cluttering his overlay disappeared.

"What is it?"

"The distressed vessel disappeared behind the planet. It just appeared again, only it isn't dead. It's burning hard and appears to be—ah. It must have used the planet's gravity for a slingshot. They're headed right for us at high delta-v. And it is still accelerating."

"Weapons hot," Mark called, grabbing the stick and immediately changing their vector.

He feathered the throttle and steepened their angle, using port and nose thrusters. But his overlay flickered as a message indicator popped up in the lower left corner. Then it opened on its own.

"What the—?" he snapped, as an official-looking digital document filled both screens.

It appeared to be a *Kill Order* highlighting extreme prejudice. A few details popped out as it flashed: his name, Perry, the *Fafnir*, along with last known coordinates, trajectory, and known collaborators. A digital copy of his Peacemaker ID was there, too, somehow. Shakily scrolling words flashed over the document, as if someone was writing them with their finger:

[Pried this ship away from a dead guy. I wanted you to know it was me, bird. That I

*killed you. Just like I said I would when
you left me for dead. I hope your circuits
melt real slow and you feel each one fail.
Gonna sift through the wreckage afterward so
I can mount your carcass on the wall. —
Jarls]*

"I see that feline slimeball hasn't changed. Oh, shit—missile launch," Perry called, his voice loud but steady. "Two birds in the air. No, three. Make that five. Holy *hell*. Six?"

17

MARK POURED on the thrust and deepened the arc of their turn, and their acceleration smashed him back and to the side in a brutal crush. He dropped the nose negative twenty degrees, working to build the angles in their favor.

"Netty, those missiles are all yours. Light them up."

"Why don't I fly the ship and you can shoot the tiny, speeding tubes of death with the laser?"

"All three of us have a vested interest in our continued survival. Besides, you have a far steadier hand than me."

"Fine."

The Invictus fired a three-shot burst, and the lead missile disappeared. The rest burned hard, not just redirecting around the bright plume, but also moving away from one another. Either the missiles were smart, or Jarls knew what he was doing. With their broadening vectors, they would have to kill each and every missile separately.

They couldn't land a lucky shot and hope the detonation or shrapnel would damage the others.

Their laser fired one burst, and then another. It hummed again and again, but the incoming projectiles looped and dodged.

"They're either learning, or those missiles have photo-sensitive scanners," Netty said.

"Increase to five shot bursts and slow the rate, with a wider spread," Perry recommended.

The laser popped again, this time chattering in a five-shot burst instead of three.

"I clipped one. More speed, Mark, and do me a favor—turn back toward the star. That star's immense gravity is causing gravitational lensing and bends each of our laser shots—it isn't much, but it's enough to make targeting hell. If we head straight into the well, it increases laser accuracy by two point five percent."

"You got it," Mark said. And although he didn't necessarily understand the science or math at work, he knew her reasoning was sound. He also knew that, if it didn't increase their odds of survival, she wouldn't have asked.

Flattening their arc, he rolled to starboard and pointed the nose directly at the distant star. Netty wasted no time in firing off a microburst, and then a second in quick succession. The missiles turned and dodged, showcasing some terrifying intelligence, but the third burst hit home, and another missile disappeared in a bright cloud of expanding gas.

"I got the wounded duck. Two down, four to go."

He watched as the laser fired again and again. Fifteen seconds passed without another kill, then twenty, and thirty.

"These things are too mobile. We need a flak cannon or PDC,"

Netty snarled, showcasing a bit of uncharacteristic anger. "Hold on a moment. I might have a solution for these…irritations. Give me fifteen seconds to run the math."

"What about Jarls?" Mark asked. "Perry, give me details."

"Returning scanner specs are incomplete, but judging from hull shape and displacement, his ship is likely a class 8, maybe 9. I'm guessing it's an Ixtan gunboat from their Planetary Defense Force. Considering the variables, that scarred hairball found a way to slip his bonds and capitalized on the chaos caused by Glass's raid. But that's just an estimate based on available data."

"A military gunboat? A *gunboat*," Mark muttered. "Why can't anyone steal a class four or five? Is that asking too much?"

"Apparently it is," Perry answered. "He likely has twin missile launchers and an array of other offensive tools. Boy, would I love to have some point-defense cannons right about now, or a glitter caster, maybe a broad-spectrum jammer. Hell, I'd settle for ammo for our antique rotary cannon. That thing would be more than enough—"

"I get it, I get it," Mark growled. "All the things we don't have. Let's work with what we've got and go shopping after. Deal?"

"Don't play games with my small fusion heart, Mark. I'm not in a place to handle disappointment right now."

"No games. This is the last time we are going to be outgunned. Period."

His overlay updated with range to targets, the missiles screaming in at a frightening velocity. Mark watched the distance tick down from ten thousand kilometers to nine, then eight.

"Uh, Netty?"

"Five seconds, Mark."

The distance clicked to seven, then six thousand kilometers. As hard as the *Fafnir*'s drive was burning, they simply had too much mass to outrun the ship-killer missiles. At least, without using their twist drive, and they were too far into the gravity well for that.

"Five thousand klicks and closing fast, Netty," Mark said, urging the AI into action.

"Flip us around. I can target them with our rocket pod or try to kill them with a remote missile detonation of our own," Perry suggested.

"Head-to-head? What are the probabilities of a successful strike?"

"With short-range rockets? Practically zero. With a missile? Low, but better than nothing."

"Done," Netty finally said, her optical sensor flickering from purple to blue, then green, and back again.

"Four, no, three thousand kilometers," Mark called out .

"I can recalibrate the Invictus and widen the emitter lens to fire in a dispersive cone. That will allow us to target dodging missiles with an increased probability of success by eighty-five percent."

"Yes, but with a sacrifice to laser potency at the same time," Perry asked. "A wide dispersion would spread the laser out too much. At that range, it would have almost as little effect as the local star's radiation."

"We don't need to pierce or melt. Heat buildup is the goal. We use micro-pulses to hit repeatedly. The warheads should overheat and detonate."

"But that would take thousands of pulses to produce enough energy transference in vacuum," Perry argued.

"Tens of thousands, yes. But I can more effectively track and hit a moving target with a wide dispersion. The math is sound, and if this works, it would effectively bolster our missile defense strategy until we arm up, like Mark said. I would need to take all non-vital systems down, unfortunately; otherwise, we won't have enough power."

Mark watched the missiles close in, the *Fafnir*'s short-range scanners locking on. A host of new data flooded his overlay as the counter ticked down to two thousand kilometers.

"Do it," Mark grated.

The *Fafnir* hummed and clicked, relays tripping as Netty powered systems down. The lights in the galley passage went dark, and the cockpit heaters turned off. Things were about to get a bit colder—and more primitive.

"My only caveat is this. If it works and we don't die, we're turning this ship around and hitting that murderous kitty with everything we've got."

"Superior idea," Perry agreed. "I'm about done with this."

"I *am* done," Mark said, and then the coils triggered.

The Invictus hummed beneath them, the distance on the closing missiles ticking away by the moment. Mark watched the number drop, his fingers tapping an impatient cadence against the armrest.

"Done. Invictus recalibrated. And charging capacitor…"

The distance dropped to one thousand kilometers. He pushed the throttle forward, but they were already burning at max thrust. A small gauge appeared on his overlay—an indicator, showing the laser's capacitor charge status. It hit seventy-five percent, then eighty, and ninety.

"Netty—"

"Firing," she interrupted.

The Invictus chattered from its perch on the bow, its pulses so fast that Mark could barely distinguish where one ended and the next began. The missiles closed, tightening their pattern as they homed in on the *Fafnir's* drive cone. At first nothing happened, and he prepared for the worst. Then, with the laser capacitor hitting 75 percent, the first missile exploded.

The targeting reticle shifted to the second, and the missile immediately dodged, but Netty followed its movements, the wider dispersion allowing her to maintain hits on target far more effectively. The missile looped wide and detonated, taking out the third in the process.

One more, Mark thought as the last missile closed to three hundred kilometers. Netty killed it with a whoop of triumph.

"Get him, Perry."

He throttled back, then turned again and worked to bridge the gap between them and Jarls's gunboat. Their first Whisperwing launched before they had completed their turn, then the second leaped away barely five seconds later. It was the bird's hallmark spacing, with just enough follow for the second to hide in the first's drive plume. Perry kept the last missile in reserve while the automated system worked to reload the two open launch points.

"What are the odds that our new-ish rockets actually launch and don't just explode in the pod?"

"Judging from the age, I'd say we're fifty-fifty," Perry shot back.

"My next question is, why hasn't he fired again?"

"I'm guessing he didn't think we'd survive that sizable missile volley. Knowing that murderous kitty Jarls, I imagine he sat back with a cold glass of arrogance to watch us struggle and die. That would totally be his style."

Pointing their nose right at the enemy ship, Mark throttled up once again. In his experience, there was only one way to handle overly aggressive people. You had to go right at them.

Narrowing the emitter on their laser, Netty targeted Jarls's ship and fired a burst. The first two shots hit midship, the strikes flaring bright on their enhanced viewscreen. But the gunboat made an aggressive direction change, and the third shot missed.

"Keep on him, Netty. Poke as many holes in that bastard as you can."

"To what end? That thing has reactive armor, twin rotary launchers, and who knows what else to throw at us."

The Invictus hummed again, scoring a hit on the aft armor panel as a puff of gas erupted from the starboard hardpoint. A heartbeat later, a canister of reflective glitter detonated before them. Their missiles and laser lost their lock immediately.

"He has a glitter caster," Perry said, turning a side-eye Mark's way.

A string of bright projectiles filled the space between them, chewing through their first missile. The second disappeared in a cloud of gas and heat a moment later.

"He's got PDCs, too."

"Fire the reserve missile and prepare those cloud rockets," Mark said, rolling left and firing their belly thrusters. A looping line of depleted uranium rounds cut through space right next to them.

"We're punching above our weight class here, Mark. I don't think this is—look, I know we took that Peaceful Skies attack boat down, but Jarls is a crack pilot," Perry warned.

"We don't need to take him out, Perry. We just need to stall him."

The *Fafnir* rolled to port, and he wrenched the stick up, then added thrust as they pulled into a steep climb. Netty tracked and fired the laser, while Perry launched their reserve missile. The missile launcher cycled, having finished reloading one of the other launch points.

Close enough to see in clear detail, Jarls's gunboat rolled to match his move, his twin PDCs tracking and firing on the incoming Whisperwing.

"Target his launchers, Netty. Maybe we can cook one of his unlaunched birds off and reduce his overall weapon efficacy."

Netty tracked and fired, the Invictus now emitting in high-intensity mode. Jarls rolled away after the first belly strike. Another shot hit his gunboat, and something on his port side exploded into a cloud of expanding parts.

"Calling it a hit—you just cut right through his port-side PDC. Nice shooting, Netty," Perry crowed.

"Thank you."

"Oh. Missile launch. That's two of—"

Something erupted from the enemy gunboat before Perry could finish talking, the projectile exploding feet from the *Fafnir*'s hull. A cloud of reflective shards peppered their armor. Mark's overlay flickered and his sensor section went blank.

"That mincing feline literally hit us with a glitter bomb. I've got no feed, no tracking data for the laser. Where are those missiles?" Netty asked.

Mark rolled them to starboard and throttled up, working to get free from the blinding cloud. He cut right then angled down when a missile appeared through the viewscreen ahead. It was turning to track them, the engine burning at max power as a counter thrust flared to brilliant life near the payload.

"Shit. It's close," he cursed and fired thrusters to turn tighter. Leaning his head back to protect his neck, Mark pushed the throttle all the way forward, and the drive screamed in response. His vision tunneled immediately as he fought to keep from blacking out.

"We're clear. Sensors are returning data again. I'm tracking both birds—range is five hundred yards and closing."

The laser fired half a dozen shots in quick succession, and Mark eased off the stick. Netty fired again, this time in a burst, and the closest missile disappeared from his overlay.

"That's one," Perry cried.

Jarls appeared ahead, and Mark registered two things in short order. The rocket pod on the *Fafnir*'s hardpoint fired, making a dozen screaming cloud rockets flood the black void of space between them. And something hit the front of his ship, tearing right through the forward viewscreen.

Something hit the side of his head as his helmet snapped up into place. A curtain of white washed over his vision as their atmosphere exploded through the broken screen, with sparks and shrapnel hitting the ceiling and floor in a pinging staccato.

Direct hit. That was PDC rounds, boss, Perry called, his voice crackling in over the ear bug.

Mark blinked and tried to collect his thoughts, but he couldn't tear his fuzzy gaze off the missile icon on his overlay. Some small part of his brain tried to tell him that their laser wasn't firing, but none of it made sense.

A shadow passed over them, spitting fire into the black. Jarls's ship-killer missile exploded, and a heartbeat later, the drive plumes for three more ignited in the dark. And yet, they didn't track the *Fafnir* but rocketed away—toward the endless expanse of blackness.

In a moment of incandescent fury, another ship appeared to their left, rolling on its long axis, with all four PDCs firing in heated blurs.

Jarls's ship took a hit, and then another, flares and chaff firing off in every direction. Missiles exploded and rockets fired, until the space around them became an incomprehensible mess of chaos and debris.

A voice crackled over the cockpit comms sometime later. He didn't know how much time had passed, only that the space around them was dark once again. Several red globs of frozen liquid drifted before his face, bouncing off one another and careening in opposite directions.

"I understand, Netty. I'm matching your trajectory now. Prepare to dock."

It took him a long, punishing moment to put voice to name.

It was Valint.

18

"STOP FIGHTING HIM," Valint scolded as Mark tried to pull the cuff off his arm. He'd been forced to wear it more than he was comfortable with lately, and that irritated him.

"I'm fine. I—I'm not a wounded duck, dammit," he protested as his steely counterpart stood. She towered over him, her impressive height never more noticeable than when he was looking up at her.

"You took a broken section of bulkhead to the side of your face, so technically no, you're not okay," Perry interrupted, hopping up to perch on the back of his chair. "And if I can point it out, you and I both came, oh, about thirteen inches away from oblivion."

Mark reluctantly turned, following the bird's gaze to where the line of thirty-millimeter, armor-piercing rounds passed between their pilots' chairs. Half had passed clear through his quarters and lodged into the firewall beyond that, while the rest cut into the maintenance space. Luckily none had hit their drive or reactor.

"I stand corrected. Or lay corrected, as the case may be. That was close."

"You think?" Perry scoffed. "I'm made of tough stuff, but there's no way in *hell* I'm hopping away from that. You, well, you're considerably softer and squishier."

"Thanks for the reminder."

"I'm here for you, boss."

"Are they always like this?" Valint asked, turning toward Netty's module.

"Pretty much."

"Let's break this down. You encountered this Jarls Vane on Tau Regus when you were collecting the engineer?" Valint asked, setting her feet. She had that all-business, ironclad look about her—the one that told Mark she had escalated beyond simple anger.

Perry recounted his history with Vane, leading her all the way to the distress call and his attack.

"And you do not believe he is connected with Gyl-Mareth, this Glass figure, or what happened on Chevix?"

Perry shook his head. "Glass breached holding cells on Tau Regus. If they had a connection, why would she leave him locked up?"

"Although he didn't stay locked up, did he?" Mark asked. "What if they wanted us to see him there? What if they knew we would pass that spot? I know it's a bit far-fetched, but I'm trying to connect dots."

"Considering the circles they run in, it's highly likely that Glass and Vane at least knew of each other, professionally speaking. He more or less admitted that to Perry. Although we do not know how deep any connection goes, if one does truly exist," Netty said.

Valint nodded, taking it all in. She was quiet for a moment, before reaching over and selecting something on the overlay screen. The kill order popped up, the target of opportunity flashing in blood-red letters.

"This is what troubles me. Netty, what can you tell us about it?"

"Let me try and break it down."

Mark's gaze strayed as movement caught his attention. Two maintenance bots crawled on the *Fafnir*'s bow, reinforcing the patch-work they had already completed on the hull. One viewscreen was gone now, with an auxiliary hatch welded into place over the hole.

"Mark?" Perry asked.

He snapped around, only to find Valint and Perry staring expectantly at him.

"I'm sorry. I was…distracted."

"Brain injuries can have that effect," Perry continued. "But which one are you dealing with? The stun charges you took to the face in Algo or this more recent skull crack?"

"Skull crack? I just…" Mark started to say but froze as his hand crawled up the side of his face, where a large and angry goose egg had formed.

"Two things," Valint said. "One, it's obvious that you can't afford to operate in an underpowered gunship anymore. And two—"

He watched her, waiting for the rest, but the steely, hard façade dropped away. For a rare moment, Valint's emotions slipped through. Mark saw affection, but mostly, concern.

"You're brave, Mark Tudor. Perhaps one of the bravest people I know. But this isn't a French battlefield. And if you continue to forge on headfirst into every physical and philosophical conflict you find, something will eventually break. And yes, I'm referring to your body."

"I won't back down, nor will I turn a blind eye."

"We know, and we aren't asking you to," Netty said. "That's what we like about you. But it might be time to bolster more than only the *Fafnir*. It might be time for you to strengthen yourself, as well."

The med-sleeve beeped and pushed a course of meds, and the trickle hit his arm like a wave of ice. The ache in his neck and face immediately started to recede.

He knew what they were talking about, and although he hated the notion of biological and genetic modification, his anger didn't burn quite so bright, or for nearly as long this time. The med-sleeve pushed its next course of medication, the anti-inflammatory injection only working to drive Valint and Netty's point home. How long could he continue to put himself back together?

He had already had to regrow muscles in his leg, heal broken ribs, contusions, countless bruises, and now two blunt-force traumas to the head.

Mark could continue to do things the hard way, arrogantly struggling through the painful consequences afterward, for however long his body held up, or he could start helping himself. Their ship was small, underpowered, and without the necessary firepower. And in many ways, so was he.

Letting out a resigned sigh, Mark sagged in the chair.

"Okay. I'll listen."

"I know a doctor. He is board certified and talented, and most importantly, he understands discretion," Valint said. "He was wrapped up in a blackmailing scheme cycles ago. I worked the contract and cleared him. He's been helping me ever since."

Mark perked up. "Helped you?"

"If I'm working a protection job and someone gets hurt, I take them to him. If someone I care about is struggling with a weakness, I take them to *him*."

"Okay, I get it."

"Good enough. We take Mark to this doctor, he stuffs him into a pod, and we make him not-quite-so-fragile," Perry said. "The second order of business is—well, it's all connected, I guess, so it's really just a continuation of the first. Our continued survival requires that we give the *Fafnir* teeth, but even if we slap every available weapon system into place, they'll always be held back by one inconvenient truth."

"Our undersized reactor," Netty stated.

"Precisely. Now Ja-Ra has already given us the answer to this problem. We need only dedicate the resources and time to collecting it."

"You make it sound so simple," Mark said.

"Oh, there's nothing simple about it," Perry shot back. "This reactor is powering a floating missile platform that's orbiting an exoplanet in the Procyon system. Unfortunately, that platform was abandoned, as was the military base it was guarding."

"Why is that unfortunate? If it was abandoned, we can simply claim the reactor and anything else we find on the platform as salvage, right?"

"True. The squawk I hear on this base is this: although there's no documentation to prove it, some believe it was run by Gyl forces and used to create and test illicit biological and chemical weaponry. They abandoned the base because the moon is in a decaying orbit around the gas giant. Ironically, as the base was abandoned, the missile platform has been steadily losing altitude and is now in a decaying orbit of its own."

"So, we're looking to retrieve a reactor from a missile platform, in a decaying orbit around a moon that's in a failing orbit around a gas giant?" Mark asked.

"Precisely. Oh, and as the exoplanet slips closer and closer to its gassy neighbor, the radiation increases. It was dangerously high before, when the Gyl were cooking up their weapons of genocide. But now, it's likely much, much stronger."

"Are we talking lethal dose here?"

"Lethal? No, but it *is* the skin-melting kind. No worries, though."

"Don't worry?" Mark snorted. "That's going to be a hard ask now."

"The moon is in an irregular, stretched elliptical orbit, due in large part to the tidal battle the gas giant and the system's star are waging. That means radiation is only an issue during the closest phase of its rotation. As it reaches the long leg, radiation drops to negligible levels. At least, this is the information I have been able to find on the network."

"The *Fafnir* has a maintenance suit, located in a locker at the back of the engine room. It's designed specifically to protect the wearer from vacuum and high-radiation environments. The trauma kit also has two anti-radiation auto-injectors. It should protect you from splash dose off highly irradiated surfaces."

Mark's mind immediately started to play out a small nightmare, where his skin slowly melted off his body.

"How long have you two been thinking about this scenario?"

Perry looked to Netty, and the two seemed to share a silent conversation. The bird chuckled and turned back to Mark.

"Naturally, we've been talking about this since I first came on board. I mean, come on, Mark, have you ever actually gone back and looked at the *Fafnir*'s reactor chamber? Talk about small. The fence line gossip really heated up once Ja-Ra spilled the beans about the missile platform. Listen, we all want the same thing."

"To not become an expanding cloud of gas and debris in space?" Mark guessed.

"Bingo," Netty said. "Oh, and I finished dismantling this kill order. It featured some terrifyingly complex layers of encryption. I had to build several worms and a cleverly constructed Trojan Horse in order to break through."

"What did you find?" Valint asked. She selected the form and spread her hands, although instead of zooming out, the display broke it up into hundreds of component parts.

"There's no name associated with the source, only coordinates. Using those, I filtered the network data and traced it back to the location. The order originated from a send-only digital data house."

"Typical," Valint said, selecting the pieces of data code one by one. "This has to be a broker. They're cowards and hide under ten blankets of protective reroutes and server farms."

"A broker? Like Wyser?"

"Similar, yes." Perry nodded. "Although, whereas Wyser dealt in artifacts and religious treasures, this broker likely specializes in digital wares. They buy, sell, and trade stolen data, bounties, private warrants, writs, and if they float in darker waters, kill orders."

"There's money in that?"

Perry snorted and clicked his beak. "Big money. But don't tell Karan. She would likely melt down."

"Were you able to discern the source of the kill order?" Valint asked.

"No. I hit a dead end, a generically constructed data filter point used to shield the identity of who is actually sending these orders. It redirected me no less than five thousand times, each instance to a different and seemingly random location. It's a stonewall."

"There's only so much you can do," Mark said, only to see Netty's optical sensor turn red.

"Oh, no. I'm not about to let some slimy, mid-level criminal broker and their half-rate AI get the best of me," she argued. "I'm working on a way through right now. In fact, it's ready. This digital system is clever and complicated, with its web of reroutes and misdirections, but we have an ace in the hole. Jarls sent the kill order to Perry, and little did he know, he provided us the key to the network."

"Do tell," Valint said, her interest piqued.

"The kill order had a cleverly hidden bit of code inside, a means for whoever took it to relay back to the sender that the job was done. All I have to do is insert a single line of code, a carrier, then once I activate the response protocol, I can ride the digital signal all the way through to the true source."

"Brilliant, Netty," Perry said.

"Thank you."

"Is there a risk to us? Will they be able to tell that we have traced them?" Mark asked.

Valint frowned. "Added risk on top of the fact that they're already trying to broker your death?"

"Long story short, yes, Mark. It's possible, as I can only do so much to hide the line of carrier data. But I'm also using my own complicated series of reroutes and misdirections. If their AI can find its way through my intricate maze, then I deserve to be caught."

Taking a deep breath, Mark looked at Netty, then Perry, and finally Valint. None showed any sign of hesitation. This was the path forward, the way to dig down into their unearthed conspiracy, and finally start to reveal more of the players involved.

"Do it, Netty."

"The digital receipt is sent," she said immediately. "Tracing the carrier file. It has…a reroute, and another, and another—"

They sat in silence for a long while as the AI worked, until she whooped in triumph.

"Bingo. Carrier scrambled, and connection terminated. I got him! We got him, Mark."

"The next question is, do we really want to know?"

"Oh, yes we do," Netty countered.

"His name is Babar Malta. And get this lovely bit of irony. He isn't just a public figure, but a well-respected art collector and dealer. He has several addresses registered publicly, with a townhouse in Sublime and what must be a country house outside that."

"He lives in Vault?" Perry asked.

Netty confirmed silently, although her optical sensor flickered, which made Mark wonder what had truly passed between them.

"Come on, don't skimp on the juicy details. Share with the class, you two," he said.

"We were just conferring for veracity. Sorry. Vault holds auctions regularly, giving it its name. Those auctions often feature items of illicit origin or nature."

"Many of them are stolen, then listed under code names. If the

Guild shows up in Vault, I can guarantee you that half the blocks up for the next auction, not to mention a good number of the people looking to bid, will simply disappear."

"She's not wrong. Besides, auctions are by invite only," Netty added. "But that isn't even the most tantalizing information I was able to unearth. Yes, on the surface Babar Malta deals art while secretly brokering criminal digital elements, but he also appears to be dealing even more illicit goods. Judging from this data, he's moving weapons."

"Weapons?" Mark whispered. In response, Netty pulled up the flowchart and the name [Babar Malta] filled a box, a solid line connecting it to Jarls Vane. A series of dotted lines appeared as the AI theorized other connections.

"You know, considering the star chart, Vault is somewhat on the way to Linulla, with a quick twist past that to Procyon," Perry said.

"But Valint said that as soon as the Guild showed up, half of everything would simply disappear," Mark argued.

"Yes, she did. But I'm not suggesting we go as 'the Guild.' We happen to be sitting on some contraband implosion warheads. Strictly speaking, capital-ship-killing missiles are regulated weapons, thus making them a highly desired item on the black market."

"Are you suggesting we sell those missiles?"

"Yes," Perry said simply.

"I don't feel good about that. What if they're used to hurt innocent people?"

"Easy, Mark. Remember, those are complicated missile systems. I should be able to modify the warheads and the keys. If done right, they should power up, and for all intents and purposes, look functional and legitimate. But we can, ah, neuter them."

"Neuter?"

"Oh, they'll launch all right, but there won't be the bang they're expecting. We can scam a lowlife out of some of his hard-earned money, give me access to his network, and allow you to look the man in the eyes. That should give us an opportunity to start unraveling the criminal network above him, and maybe see where Gyl-Mareth and Cai-Demond truly sit in all of this."

"It isn't a bad idea," Valint said. "Naturally, we will need to use aliases. Netty and Bunn will need to hack our transponders, allocating false names and registration numbers to our ships. It goes without saying that, in doing so, we wouldn't just violate our edict as Peacemakers but would be in violation of about twenty-three Guild laws."

"Twenty-seven," Perry corrected. "And that doesn't include civil and maritime ordinances for all of the separate colonized systems. It would mark us all as quite the naughty little pirates. And if I might be so bold as to recommend Mark's pirate name. Clive the Cleaver has such a lovely ring to it."

"Absolutely not."

"We'll talk about it," Perry said with a wink.

"How do we make that happen? How do we approach this Babar Malta to make a deal and not have it stink of Peacemaker?" Mark asked Netty.

"Like everything else, there's a digital form. I simply fill it out and send it in through this black web. Then we wait for a response to see if he is interested."

"What color is that form?" Mark asked.

"Morally gray," Perry deadpanned.

19

Sublime: Planet Vault

THEY SPENT ALMOST three full days working on the *Fafnir* after that —not only repairing damage but also hacking their transponder and giving the ship its new designation.

Netty facilitated the change in a way that allowed them to switch easily between identities. Once activated, the second profile would make them appear as the *EFS Swallow*, utilizing the serial number off the frozen attack boat they'd located at the Junkway. It was a legitimate serial ID and transponder number, but fortunately, it was old enough to not be in the Guild database. Perry logged in through one of his backdoors and registered the vessel as a merchant craft designated to a recently defunct shipping corporation based out of the Eridani Federation.

"But why a swallow?"

"I used to watch them fly around my uncle's barn," Mark said, dabbing a bit of paint on the wall. They had already plugged, welded, and patched the PDC holes. "Incredibly agile flyers, plus they eat all the nuisance bugs—the blood-thirsty ones, like mosquitos and gnats. I thought it was fitting."

"That we're flying around the galaxies, gobbling up vermin?" Perry asked.

Mark shrugged. "There was also a ship commissioned during the golden age of piracy. The *HMS Swallow* was contracted to hunt down and kill pirates."

"Okay, well that's a little better. Although considering we're now flying under a hacked transponder, en route to an illicit black market arms deal, I would say that *we* are more likely the pirates in this case."

"I'd like to think of us as privateers."

"Privateers were just pirates with better backing," Perry reasoned.

"Why are you so argumentative?"

The bird shrugged, a ripple passing through his feathers. He turned to pace Mark's quarters for a moment, clicking his beak in irritation.

"I've never been in this situation before."

"Which one is that? Number one on someone's hit list?"

"No." He chuckled. "This isn't a first for that. What I mean is—in a position of uncertainty. I have always stood confidently on the side of the law, knowing the Guild was more often right than wrong. But now? I'm starting to question things."

"That's why we're doing something about it," Mark said, then finished and closed the paint can. He stood and stretched his back, a few ornery vertebrae finally popping back into place. "Let no one pacify their conscience that he can do no harm…"

"Did you just quote John Stuart Mill?"

Mark nodded, gathering up the supplies and making to leave.

"I probably screwed it up. Been a long time since I read his works on morality."

"No, no—I mean, yes, you mixed up the wording a little, but you gathered the heart and thus the meaning of the passage. And you're right. We won't be the good men, or artificially intelligent bird, to simply look on while evil men prevail. My despair is unforgivable. Let us finish preparations with gusto!"

Mark finished his preparations by just not shaving anymore. The stubble grew itchy by the third day, but a trim the day after helped to soften it up. They stopped at a speck-of-dust-sized waystation affectionately called Blink, where Mark bartered successfully for some new gear. He found an old but serviceable pressure suit, the formerly black material long since faded to an appropriate gray. Adding a compartment belt, tan jacket, and mag boots, he more than looked the part of a gunrunner.

Perry spent their entire transit working on the Ixtan implosion warheads and their activation keys. Evidently, he had to sort through over five million lines of code in order to start his clever sabotage. The bird dragged his talons across the deck once he had finished, his eyes pulsing and dim.

"That seems a little dramatic, don't you think?"

"Listen, if you're allowed to grow puffy bags under your eyes and look generally unhealthy after losing a few sleep cycles, then I am entitled to the same. Next time, you can hack into the incredibly complicated warheads, and I'll stand around and grow facial hair—"

"It isn't nearly as easy as it looks," Mark said, turning his head.

Perry snorted. "Any room up on that cross, Tudor? It's hair follicles, nothing more."

"You can't imagine the itch," Mark said, managing to look wounded. "It's been a truly trying time."

Perry lifted his wingshoulders. "Next stop, Los Angeles."

Mark inclined his head. "With this magnificent mane, can you blame them?"

They burned into space over Vault almost two days later, having optimized their trip to use as little fuel as possible. The advanced planetary defense network gave them hell for a while, threatening fiery death, destruction, and worse, paperwork.

"Honestly, I have never met an AI so comfortable with threatening administrative violence before," Netty said after breaking contact and navigating them away again.

"Administrative violence is a term I'll take to my grave," Mark agreed, snorting.

It took three attempts and almost six hours of waiting before a response pinged in through the Black Web. The message was one line of text, signed with the initials [BM]. Coordinates were embedded behind several layers of encryption.

Mark read the message for the third time. Perry leaned in behind him, curious to see what amused him so.

"I'm looking at the same message. Why are you laughing?"

He pointed at his screen, his finger shaking.

"Administrative violence was one thing, but this message is even better. We need to come back to Vault more often. 'Come in through the back. Signed, BM,'" Mark said, spluttering as he tried not to laugh.

"Oh, now I get it. More potty humor. You're so infantile. *She* should have left you down there to play with mud and sticks and severed French toes or whatever."

Valint appeared from around the corner, drawn by the noise. She looked at the screen, then Perry, and finally Mark.

"Eventually, he would have learned to *sharpen* those sticks, Perry," she said, grinning broadly.

They strapped in for entry as traffic control assigned them a lane. Mark watched as his overlay shifted, a surprisingly narrow path appearing in red.

"You want the stick on this one?" Netty asked.

He reached halfway for the stick before noticing the compass on the bottom right of his screen. It provided scale, helping him to understand how truly tight their entry lane was.

"I'm content to sit back and watch the professional at work. This one is all yours, Netty."

"Oh, come on. There are no giant mirrors in the way this time. It's relatively straightforward."

"Relatively being the operative word. And the way I figure it, Vault Security Forces are going to be watching us very closely, so let's not give them any reasons to flinch," Mark said, leaning out to look at the massive orbiting platform off the port side.

The hulking platform sprawled in contiguous rings, each connected by a webwork of cables and clear transit tubes. He could see people moving about the enormous complex, like ants in a spaceborne colony.

"And those people are waiting to go down to the surface?"

"Some, yes. Others are waiting for departures as well. As planets go, Vault is incredibly picky about who is allowed to land on the surface," Netty explained.

"And they authorized us?" To accentuate the point, Mark hooked his thumbs inside his stained jacket and lifted it away from his body. "I look like a plucky hero off the cover of a pulp magazine. All that's missing is a talking animal sidekick perched on my shoulder. Oh, wait, Perry." He turned to the bird and gestured to his shoulder.

"Nope. Not gonna happen. A bird has his pride."

"Come on, little fellah. Come to your perch!"

"I'll cut you in half and leave you on the ground with your feet touching your face," Perry said.

"Well, that's just diabolical."

"Our approval says something of Babar Malta's influence," Netty said, redirecting the conversation. "He is undoubtedly very well connected. The question we should be asking is, how far do those connections go? And does it reach the Guild?"

"That wouldn't shock me."

Netty guided the *Fafnir*, now the *Swallow*, into the atmosphere, tracking above and behind a large shuttle. They broke through the worst part of the turbulence and passed the larger vessel. Sizable, dome-shaped portholes revealed well-dressed people walking around inside, sipping drinks and peering out the observation portholes.

"They look like they're on a pleasure cruise."

"For some that frequent Vault, yes. There are many well-to-do families here, not to mention the aristocracy."

Breaking through the clouds, Mark watched as jagged, snow-covered mountains gave way to green forests and fields. The altimeter dropped, revealing rivers and an elaborate system of canals. Winding roads appeared next, leading to an enormous estate.

"The auction life is treating Vault well. How many of these people are profiting off stolen relics?" Mark asked as they passed over an impressive castle-like home.

"They can't all be bad. And for every Halvix and Wyser, there are probably two dozen legitimate collectors, archeologists, and curators," Perry replied.

"We're coming up on the coordinates from Malta's message. It appears to be an industrial building in a gated complex ahead. We have already been painted by lidar."

"Then take us in real nice and slow, Netty." He reached up and switched on the Invictus, just to be safe.

As the *Fafnir* passed over a tree line, the sprawling fields gave way to service roads, walls, and long, flat structures. They came to hover above one complex, as a landing pad lit up below. His overlay automatically tracked and highlighted four towers, all topped with powerful weapon systems. Judging from the lasers splashing off their hull, there were more threats out there that he couldn't see.

"This place is well-defended," Perry said. "It's almost like we're shady gunrunners looking to offload ill-gotten weapons for profit."

"I'd prefer to think of us as misunderstood."

Mark and Valint opened the airlock and waited for the outside door to open. She turned to him, her brow wrinkling.

"I know how you *are*, Mark. No matter what this broker says, do *not* haul off and hit him. He is almost guaranteed to be pretentious, condescending, and abrasive. In essence, all of the qualities you hate."

"You wound me," he said, showing her open hands. "I'm the picture of discretion and patience. Also, I've met French Canadians before, and I managed not to strike them."

"While I can't argue with your assessment of the Quebecois mannerism, I have to respectfully ask you to"—she hooked an arm behind his back and leaned close—"*behave.*"

Mark cut his eyes at her. "Oui, madam."

Valint snorted, then guided him through the opening door. They proceeded down the ramp, only to find a spindly robot making its way toward them from the building. It had no legs or wheels but seemed to float, or hover over the ground.

"Welcome, Barrow and Parker. My name is Benson. After me, please," the robot said, gesturing for them to follow.

Clive would have been a better outlaw name, Perry snickered through the ear bug.

They entered through a yawning automatic door, the space inside bare and unremarkable, then followed their host into a massive warehouse. Coils of metal sat off to one side while other palletized building products filled the remaining free space.

"I thought this guy was an art dealer. Are we here to sell building supplies?" Mark said under his breath.

"This is one of the Master's numerous storage facilities. His portfolio is quite diverse," Benson explained.

After moving through a door at the back, their guide led them into what looked to be—

—a broom closet.

"Mind your elbows and other extrusions, please."

Mark met Valint's caramel-colored gaze as the floor shuddered and started to lower. They fell into darkness as the floor slid across above them, closing the gap.

Lights blinked on as the lift finally stopped. Their robot host propelled itself ahead, the door they'd previously entered now leading them into a completely different hall. This space had brown —or brownish, really—walls, with light tan floor tiles. Gold candelabras hung on both sides, casting the space in surprisingly bright light.

Mark and Valint walked down and into what felt like the entrance hall to a home, not some bizarre bunker hidden beneath an industrial warehouse. The chamber was round, with bland taupe walls. Large display cases framed in the space, each filled with different treasures—ceremonial weapons, face masks, pottery, or religious relics. Part of him expected to see the *Bells of Vinicul,* as those artifacts seemed to follow him around.

"Right this way, please."

They moved down a stairway recessed in the middle of the floor. The treads were covered in tan carpet, which matched the wall hangings, which in turn matched the walls, which also coordinated with the stone floor, and the picture frames, and the cabinets. It was beige, or seemingly every shade and hue of the color, everywhere, and on everything. His vision swam with it, until a distant part of his brain told him that no other color existed.

Mark kicked off the bottom step and into a well-furnished office. A dark wood desk sat straight ahead, thankfully breaking him loose from the monochromatic hell. But it wasn't only the desk. Cages, terrariums, and aquariums filled much of the available space around them, each filled with a colorful beast, bird, reptile, or fish.

A large, riotously plumed creature spread its wings in a cage to their right. It hissed, exposing dripping fangs and what Perry deemed *poor manners* via ear bug. With reptile-like irises, the creature didn't look like any bird Mark had seen before.

"The Great Pitohui Angler," someone said, pulling his attention back to the desk.

A slender figure stood in a doorway at the back of the space, his long frame wrapped in a suit of silky beige fabric. He appeared to be a Nesit—tall, long, and delicate. His eyes were remarkable, over-sized in his oblong head and shimmering with hints of green and blue.

A click sounded behind them, and Mark turned, just in time to see the door slide shut. Babar Malta moved into the space and slid around the desk without a whisper of sound. He didn't move as much as he floated, a bland, lean presence edging closer while casting an appreciative eye at the bird analog.

"The Pitohui Angler is native to the southern rainforests of this world. It's a voracious hunter—worshipped by the primitive tribes. Its venom is a particularly potent neurotoxin, capable of perma-nently paralyzing prey. The Angler's food is still alive when it starts to eat, a fact that some find...unsettling? Yes, that's accurate. Unsettling."

The broker raised a finger and lovingly stroked the cage. The colorful beast hissed, snapping at the air with disturbing speed and violence.

Babar moved to an aquarium several feet away and bent over to look inside. A single large fish swam inside, its fins tipped with long barbs.

"The Deep Angel Fish, a natural enemy of the Gurranec. They

come to the shallows to spawn and then die. Those unlucky enough to step on one will know pain. Their barbs are covered in a necrotic enzyme that eats away all organic tissue. Beautiful, is it not?"

Valint considered the fish, her fingers twitching at her side. She looked as if she would like nothing more than to fire her scatter gun right into the tank.

Chuckling, Babar moved behind them to a terrarium. Strange, bright yellow slugs crawled around the inside, leaving a thick coating of slime in their wake.

The broker pulled a long, purple glove off a shelf, slid it over his hand, and promptly reached inside. He retracted the arm a moment later, with one of the long, bulbous creatures stuck to an outstretched finger.

"Orthanopesilnius. Known to most as the Funeral Slug. They excrete an incredibly toxic enzyme in their mucus. One must only get a little on their skin, say…grab ahold of a handrail after one of these pretty little globs of death passed by, and poof," Babar said, pretending to keel over. He slid his hand back into the terrarium and allowed the slug to glide off onto a rocky perch.

"The toxin paralyzes the muscles of the abdomen, and the diaphragm, rendering the victim incapable of drawing breath. Most asphyxiate, without ever knowing the cause of their death."

He closed the terrarium, turned, and held the gloved hand out to Mark.

"I am Babar Malta, purveyor of fine art and antiquities, as well as building materials, medical supplies, food containers, and so much more."

Mark stared down at the gloved hand, the Funeral Slug's thick mucus gleaming in the light. Babar held his gaze for a long moment, then looked down at the glove.

"Oh, apologies. My manners." The Nesit rolled the glove down, working carefully to keep any of the toxin from touching his skin.

That was a test, Perry sent. *And my research shows that's right on all counts. In fact, every creature stored in that room is venomous or poisonous in some way. You're surrounded by death.*

Valint fidgeted next to Mark as they watched Babar drop his soiled glove into a waste basket next to the wall. The container was half-full of discarded gloves, some still with an unappetizing gleam of organic fluid.

"Now. Your message indicated that you're looking to make a business transaction. You must know, I'm always looking to buy, but, ah—" the Nesit said, turning back to them and dusting off his hands, "I'm more interested in cultivating relationships, adding to my network of trusted contractors."

"Of course," Mark said. "We're looking for that as well. Stability and trust are the keystones of success in our particular line of work."

"*Very* good," Babar said, adding a perfunctory charmless laugh. "I cannot tell you how welcome your words are. It's hard knowing where to place trust these days...like sitting in the wrong place or setting your hand on the wrong surface. We live in a time filled with pitfalls." The Nesit slowly turned and let his eyes settle on the terrarium as one of the bright yellow slugs crawled across the clear glass.

As far as veiled threats go, that was poorly done, Perry sent.

"Agreed," Valint said. "We're a straightforward and hard-working crew. We find the things people want. Simple. Then we hand them off to you, get paid, and repeat. We don't like questions, nor do we like unnecessary attention."

"In our line of work, discretion is paramount," Babar said, waving them toward his desk. He settled into the chair and steepled his fingers in a gesture that was too practiced to have the desired effect. "Now, your message indicated you have acquired some valuables, but it did not mention the nature."

Mark reached into his jacket pocket and retrieved the holocube, then set it on the desk and slid it toward the broker. He used his right hand, careful to get Netty's repeater as close to him as possible.

Babar picked up the cube, activated it with a tap, and held it between them. A bright, three-dimensional projection appeared in the air, displaying one of the intact Ixtan missiles. Several small text boxes flickered around it, filling with specs and data.

"Capital ship killers. An interesting find. That is *highly* regulated tech," Babar said after turning and studying the image. In the recesses of his eyes, Mark saw that most unfortunate of visitors—for Babar, anyway.

Lust.

And not the kind focused on flesh. No, this was the kind of lust inspired by profit.

"Not just any tech, but Ixtan Starflares," Mark said at Perry's prompting.

"You tease me, but the Ixtan Cabal does not trade or sell their tech outside of their military and its selective contractors. This makes them rare and unlikely to—"

Mark reached into his pocket and removed the single case, then set it down, turned it toward Babar, and flipped it open. The broker eyed the warhead key, then reached under his desk and tapped a button. The top split open, revealing a wide, glossy screen.

"There's likely to be much interest for these. How many do you have?"

"Five full missiles, and the booster section of a sixth, minus the warhead."

"And you have the keys for them all?"

Mark nodded as the broker's computer glowed to life.

You've got him, boss. I'm registering his network at this second, Perry jabbered. *Initiating my intrusion protocol. Here we go.*

"How does this work?" Valint asked as she worked to keep the broker talking. "Do we deliver the weapons to you?"

"Oh, goodness no. I'm simply the broker. But I will reach out to certain clients on your behalf. Then, once we've garnered enough interest, I'll hold a special auction. It's private and completely safe. These should command a very nice price, I think. Now, I must say, I represent a client in desperate need of high-yield, thermite plasmid bombs. If you could locate a cache of those, I could make you both very rich."

Mark, his desktop is shielded. I need you to get Netty's repeater closer.

Trying to act as naturally as possible, Mark leaned on the desk, propping himself up with his right arm.

"The Guild classified thermite plasmid as illegal weapons tech years ago. No one can manufacture it anymore, not even under military contract," Valint said, raising a brow.

"Oh, did they? Hmph. Shame, that," Babar said, giving her a shrewd look. "I'm only saying that if an independent team of weapons acquisition experts were to find a cache of said plasmid, I would buy it immediately—with the highest possible payout. No questions asked."

"Would we be allowed to meet this buyer?" Mark asked. "Perhaps hand off the product personally? I only ask because—and this might be a touch forward, but—" Mark rubbed a hand across his neck, a slow smile of apology creasing his face.

"I am sorry, but unfortunately my clientele requires a heightened level of anonymity. They're some of the wealthiest, most powerful, and most influential individuals in all colonized space."

Dammit. The shielding is messing with my encryption breaker. Mark, I need you to get closer. Lean in, there you go, Perry said.

Valint coughed quietly as she listened in.

Mark nodded, struggling with how to continue. He turned and looked to the closed door, then had a stroke of inspiration. He'd served with an NCO who didn't grasp the concept of personal space. Jerry Flynn regularly made himself at home, sitting on their unit commander's desk.

Anyone else would have been chewed up one side and down the other, but Jerry was smooth and quick with flattery.

Time for a show, Mark sent Perry.

Oh really? The stage is set, sir.

"Here's the deal, Mr. Malta," Mark said, lifting one leg and perching himself on the desk. He pointed to Valint. "Her and I? We've heard good things about you, that nobody moves more product and for better money than you do." He finished with an idle slap of his thigh, then settled into a cheesy grin.

Babar waved the praise away, but Mark used that moment to slide his rear fully onto the desk, then leaned in and placed his right hand next to the display.

"Gotta be honest with you, perhaps even direct to the point of being…crass. Parker and I, we've got a couple choice hunting grounds. If you think these Starflares are nice, I got stuff that'll blow your socks off. But here's the deal…" He paused as Babar leaned in, drawn in by the tease.

"We need assurances," Valint said, picking up where Mark left off. "It's a cutthroat market out there. If we risk our necks to bring you the best stuff, we want to make sure that we'll get regular spots in auctions and catch top value. And, to reiterate, we mean *top* value."

"You doubt me?"

I'm in. Keep him talking. I need time to copy files and cover my tracks, Perry said.

"Actually, quite the opposite. Parker and I have had a run of bad luck with brokers. Sure, they made big promises, but they couldn't deliver buyers. We even had to shoot our way out of a drop-off gone awry. That's a bad look for us. So, you understand why we're wary?"

"No one on Vault, or any civilized world, will get you better value, or more buyers, than me," Babar boasted, warming to the moment. He could *smell* the profit hanging, ready to be plucked by his soft hands. "And if you're worried about transport, I can arrange a third-party handoff, as well. If you want assurances, I can deliver."

Mark counted in his head but looked to Valint, as if they were silently considering his offer.

"I like that you're direct—"

A red banner appeared on Babar's screen, and an alarm sounded.

"What is that? What is going on?" Valint asked.

The broker bent down over his station, swiping and typing

quickly.

"Someone tried to crack my network."

"Wait a minute," Mark said, his eyes narrowed. "*Your* network? The one that—the one that allegedly holds data incriminating *us* in the sale of off-the-books weapons? You mean *that* network? I thought you said this place was secure?"

The poisonous animals in the room started to flutter and cry, quickly adding to the noise and chaos.

"It is," the broker spat. "I have paid for the most advanced network security that money can buy. It's housed in a bomb-proof bunker under this very facility. Nothing can get in!"

Except for this bird. Perry laughed. *I got what I needed. Now get out of there.*

Mark stood, motioning that Valiant should do the same. They both cast looks of disgust about the room, as if it was suddenly beneath them. Mark clucked his tongue, then tried a wintry grin. "I'm truly sorry, Mr. Malta, but this makes us a bit nervous. I think we should go. Perhaps we can discuss business once things have calmed down and you've regained control of your, ah, untouchable network."

The Nesit continued to type on his screen, his mouth pulled up into an irritated snarl. A long moment passed before he waved his hand at the door, signaling for them to leave.

"Go, then," Malta said, sensing the deal was gone. "And take your—*leg*—with you."

Mark looked down at his foot as if he'd just discovered it. "Fine. My boots were never here, you upjumped—"

"Enjoy your day," Valint cut in, an iron smile on her face. They stalked out as Perry's laughter rang in their ears.

20

MARK AND VALINT walked from the underground bunker, but they were practically running by the time they got outside. The turbines spooled, and the ship rose into the air as soon as their boots hit the decking inside.

"Hold onto something," Netty said before they had reached the cockpit.

The *Fafnir* tilted to port, all but throwing Mark to the side. Thrusters roared and he felt the ship accelerate forward. They fought their way into the cockpit and their seats, and he pulled on his harnesses along the way.

"We were painted with active targeting lasers. I believe Mr. Malta surmised the true purpose of our visit. Either that, or he doesn't like it when visitors leave under full burn," Perry said.

"I might have left a thirty-foot-long scorch mark in his grass. Sorry, Mark."

"Don't apologize, Netty," Mark told her. "What sane person puts grass right next to a landing pad? I'll answer for you. No one."

The *Fafnir* jumped and then dove as Netty brought the nose down. They dropped, bleeding altitude with frightening speed, until the ship was screaming along at barely 300 feet off the ground.

"What's the plan? Have they launched?"

"No launches. But if we had taken off and immediately gone for altitude, they would have easily blown us out of the sky. His weapon system uses active targeting lasers and radar. If we can stay low enough, then the buildings and terrain should negate both."

"Good...thinking," Valint grunted as the ship veered left, then right again.

They left the industrial sector behind, once again soaring out over the open fields and sprawling estates. Mark's knuckles went white on the armrests as the *Fafnir* sank beneath them, signaling a loss of even more altitude.

The overlay updated as the exterior sensors picked up dozens of additional laser and radar sources as the seemingly placid country-side came alive with the signatures of hidden weapon systems. The altimeter ticked down to 200 feet, then under, and the belly thrusters fired loudly below.

"Are these all his weapons?" Valint asked.

"Likely," Perry said, flipping between screens. "Considering the data I pulled out of his console, we can't view *him* as a singular entity. More like *them*. We don't have a name for them yet, but they have influence and power."

"Fantastic. Truly uplifting news," Mark said, sighing. His nerves were raw, but at least they weren't being pummeled like his stomach as Netty explored the *Fafnir*'s limits in low atmosphere.

"I'll continue to dig and tell you more if we survive and make it out of this soup," Netty said.

"Good," Mark said. "Something besides relief from the gut-crushing, sphincter-puckering sensation of low-altitude, high-speed maneuvering to look forward to."

"You make it sound like you didn't get your fill on Fulcrum," Perry added.

"Maybe one of these times we won't be running with our tails between our legs."

"We need teeth, Mark. *Sharp* teeth."

The mountains appeared like a gray haze ahead, before quickly growing in height and gaining substance. Netty rolled them left and right, following the rocky valleys leading up to the sheer cliffs. Mark's hands grew tighter on the armrests until his forearms ached. His leg muscles started to cramp as well.

"Those mountains are looking a bit close, Netty."

"That's how we want it. I have an exit route 60 percent mapped. Sit back and relax," Netty said.

They soared up and into a rocky gorge cut into the mountains, the jagged, spire-like peaks rising up all around them. The *Fafnir* jumped, rocked, and dropped as it was buffeted by surging down-drafts of snowy wind.

"Relax?" Mark laughed, after swallowing hard. A sour taste crept up his throat as they bumped, rocked, and shook. They rolled left and cut hard to follow the valley, but the sheer cliffs were right there beyond the viewscreens. Mark could almost raise a shaking hand and touch them.

They rose, weaving a complicated circuit through the narrow gorges and valleys, until the *Fafnir* seemed to get lost in blowing snow. The pitch and rate of their climb changed so gradually, Mark watched the puffy cumulus cloud cover drop away below them before he realized they were pushing to break orbit.

Ten minutes later, they were in the black, burning hard away from the gravity well.

"Netty, that was some of the best flying I've ever seen," Valint said, unbuckling from her harness and rubbing her shoulders.

Mark nodded, his hands still hooked inside his shoulder straps. He wasn't even sure when he'd grabbed onto them. Although it took a concerted effort to straighten his fingers to let go.

"We don't have to do that again. Ever."

"Now you know how we feel every time you take the stick," Perry said.

"I'll take that as a compliment." Mark turned and sketched a little half bow, earning a snort from Valint.

"Confident in your flying?" she asked.

Mark thought for a moment, then gave a simple nod. "Yes."

Perry coughed discreetly but said nothing, his eyes flashing with humor.

Their departure from Vault-controlled space was surprisingly quiet, which made Mark wonder how far Babar's influence extended. Yes, the auctions turned a blind eye toward stolen or trafficked goods, but what if it went deeper than that? Who was truly in charge there, and what were their motivations?

They initiated a micro-twist once far enough out and covered their tracks with another short, then a medium jump. Mark swiped over on his overlay, only to discover he had received several messages while they'd been in Babar's bunker. The first was from Drogo, while the second showed no sender or subject.

He moved to select the first message, when Perry spoke.

"Okay. Just so you know, I haven't had a chance to catalog and organize all the information, but so far it is…not good."

"Not good? Unearthing something good would be more of a shock anymore. Out with it," Valint said.

"Babar's digital security was imposing. Beyond physical security, his data was encrypted with military-level protection. And now that I'm swimming around in their secrets, I understand why."

"We already knew he was brokering illicit contracts, among other things. What could be so shocking at this point?"

"Babar's organization isn't some loose network of brokers working to scam legitimate industry out of money, or in our case, profit off someone's death. They're everywhere. I found financial records in eight different markets—manufacturing, terraforming, exploration, and more. And that's just the stuff that looks legal and legitimate. The rest is—well, let's just say my circuits need a good wipe down with bleach after sifting through it. This leads me to believe we're looking at a large, well-funded, and cloaked organization."

"Is it the Five Star League?" Mark guessed.

Valint started to shake her head even before Perry responded.

"I don't think so. Five Star is rooted in mining. Besides, they're publicly known. This organization, whoever Babar belongs to, is shady and seems to be operating almost entirely beneath the surface. This feels discreet by design."

"This sounds like Reapers or Persuasion. Neither are overly large, but definitely with some overlapping interests," Valint said.

"Which interests? Trafficking weapons or buying and selling kill contracts for Peacemakers," Mark asked. "The question is, where did the kill order come from in the Guild? Was it Gyl-Mareth or Cai-Demond?"

"I say, does it matter?" Perry asked, looking up from his screen. "They're *both* corrupt and should be removed from power and promptly imprisoned, especially now that we know they're arranging the deaths of their own citizens."

"Gyl-Mareth knew people were dying in Noka's scheme," Valint said. "If we act now, people will take notice. They'll wonder why we failed to remove him from power when innocents were dying but leapt into action once the threat shifted to Peacemakers."

Mark thought for a moment, scratching his chin.

"That's a good point. We didn't have concrete evidence of his involvement right away. That likely won't matter to most, however. The truth has a way of being skewed and bent, according to people's beliefs."

"If we go in and make this public, they could make another attempt to infiltrate the ship and sabotage something," Netty added.

"That's only if they're willing to expend the energy on subtlety. We have already encountered one hit squad, escaped an all-out assault on a city, and been warned away by a notorious mercenary leader."

Netty pulled up her criminal flowchart on both of the pilots' overlay screens, and more information flooded into the available boxes.

"I've been running a series of passive scans through the Guild's connected databases, using a simple set of keyword algorithms. There was too much data to sort through at first, but now that I have more categorical context, things are starting to fall into place."

"How so?"

"Get this. According to the Gyl and Cai peace treaty in place on Outward, both clans are prohibited from military growth or movement. The treaty also restricts weapons development, sales, or purchases. Strictly speaking, they aren't allowed to enter into agreements with third-party security firms either. To make matters more complex, the Guild isn't listed as the arbitrator for this agreement, the Eridani Federation is."

"Interesting," Valint said, dragging the word out. "I wonder if this treaty isn't the reason for the closure of the chemical or biological weapons research facility. The one you said Ja-Ra mentioned."

"If the decaying orbit wasn't the reason, then yes."

"Cai-Demond sent you to Algo on purpose, Mark," Perry said, "He wanted you to see something, specifically unregistered passengers boarding commercial cargo haulers."

"So, Gyl-Mareth is moving assets around in secret. Perhaps staging for an attack. But where?"

"There's no way for us to know. And that isn't the important detail at this point, only that he *is*," Perry said, snapping his beak for emphasis. "The registered flight plans for those cargo haulers out of Algo listed dozens of ports, most of which are busy transport hubs used to service some of the most densely populated regions in the colonized systems."

"Then we can't wait. We need to move now—bring in Cai-Demond and force his hand. If he gives testimony, along with the information we have gathered, the Guild will have no choice but to remove Gyl-Mareth from power. If we can get that to happen, then perhaps we diffuse this attack before it begins."

"It needs to be said, Mark. By doing this now, by moving on

Gyl-Mareth, *we* could be responsible for the end of a longstanding ceasefire agreement," Perry cautioned.

Valint responded first, her voice firm.

"If a ceasefire only serves to cloak the preparations of premeditated violence, then it's a lie. And we are duty bound to act."

"I can't argue with that," Mark said. "Valint is right. People died under Noka's schemes. We don't know what Gyl-Mareth was doing with the money he was funneling from that racket, but we have to assume he has found a way to channel it into his war effort. If we know all of this now, and do nothing, then the blood of millions could be on our hands."

"We won't stand by," Perry said. "But we should not meet with Cai-Demond alone. We need to bring in another Guild Master as a witness. They'll add weight and credibility to our argument."

"Who can we trust?"

"We have three options. Well, four, although I don't love the last one. Blaz'Orkin is my first choice. He is almost universally liked and respected from both inside and outside the Guild. Milo Ashanon would be my second choice, although he is known to be, ah, *moody*. He's dismissed eight Justiciars in less than five solar cycles. It's a gamble that he would even show up. And our last option—"

"Tenkin U'do," Netty said. "A Fren Okun. She has been linked to several minor bribery schemes over the years, but all with a degree of panache that I find almost admirable."

Perry nodded. "Although none have ever been corroborated, she has the weakest standing of the lot."

"I thought there were seven Masters. You said four options. That's three."

"Yes, seven seats, but Master Argon is on a holy sabbatical, and the last seat is currently open. A conclave must be called to select and elevate a new Master," Netty offered.

"It needs to be Master Blaz'Orkin. Arrange a meeting. Tell his people it's an urgent matter and that lives are at stake," Mark said.

"But not on Anvil Dark," Perry added. "We know now that Gyl-Mareth has eyes everywhere."

"Agreed. I'll arrange a meeting on The Shadow of Mesaribe. The Guild has a number of safehouses and training facilities there."

"Do it!"

Striker piloted the *Stormshadow* into system, allowing Valint to transfer back over to her own ship. Mark also reached out to Drogo, confirming with the hyper-literal Badgin that they would meet him in orbit. Then they initiated their twist back toward Anvil Dark.

Mark watched Netty's calculations fill the screen as they transited. He fought sleep, fearing the dreams that might claim him—the fog of war, and the battlefield he could never truly see. He also avoided reading deeper into the data pilfered from Babar's console, as part of him wondered if he would absorb any of it, after his strange twist experiences to the Junkway and back.

They were barely an hour out when Netty chimed in, automatically brightening the cockpit lighting.

"I have now received priority messages from both Masters Cai-Demond and Blaz'Orkin that they'll meet us on the surface. We've worked out staggered arrival times to help prevent suspicion. We're arriving last," Netty said.

"Good. Let's make sure we're well-prepared," Mark said, before pushing off and shutting himself in his quarters.

The mirror confirmed that he looked tired, with dark bags forming under his eyes. His skin was pale, too, as if further evidence was needed that he'd spent too long away from sunlight. Mark leaned into the mirror and ran a hand over his beard, the dark shadow having thickened quickly. The combination of exhaustion, scruff, and his new gear really helped to sell his new persona.

"You're doing the right thing." He locked eyes with his reflection. "If it saves lives, it's worth the cost—no matter what that is."

And yet, despite his attempts to psyche himself up, Mark struggled with doubt and worry. What kind of conflict would this stir up? How would the Guild react? Would the shadow elements of Netty's criminal flowchart emerge?

Gravity shifted and he braced against the sink. His stomach confirmed a moment later—they had dropped out of twist and were deep into the gravity well now.

After tidying up the bathroom, which he named the *groom room*, Mark reconstituted a platter of what could pass for meatballs, then strapped into his pilot's seat. Perry considered his steaming serving of food with a single, half-open eye, then went right back to his screen.

"I'm not exactly an *authority* on the ingestion of biological material, but considering all that we have happening right now, I'm astounded that you can eat. At all."

"I watched starving people cut chunks off dead horses to survive. So, this is less than tragic for me," Mark said, lifting the platter with a shrug. He grinned, then began eating. "I can eat and sleep in *any* conditions. I'm a soldier at heart."

"Fair enough," Perry said. "Oh, Drogo just twisted into system. He'll enter a high orbit and provide us with aerial support. The *Stormshadow* will be our own shadow the whole way down."

Leaning forward, Mark looked out the port viewscreen, only to spot Valint's impressive Dragon barely two hundred meters away and holding.

"We're passing the gray line in five, four, three, two…" Netty said, and the cockpit lights brightened as they passed into Mesaribe's dark side.

Heat buildup broke through the darkness a few moments later when the *Fafnir* nosed up to present her belly first. Mark instinctively swiped his overlay into tactical mode, and the inevitable butterflies took flight in his stomach. He shook out his hands, stretched his neck, and took a deep breath.

"You ready?" Perry asked.

Mark nodded. "It's not every day you inform on a sitting Guild Master in an attempt to prevent genocide."

"Accurate, and makes me a bit sad. Wish this wasn't the case."

Mark gave a sad nod of agreement, but his look shifted to simmering anger.

The atmospheric entry was rough and noisy, with the *Fafnir*'s inner hull expanding beneath the ceramic heat shields. The ship groaned and creaked, complaining richly with each savage buffeting. Not to be outdone, the water filtration unit gurgled and burped, making the ship sound like a living, breathing beast coming off a three-day bender.

Their plan was simple—land at Anvil Dark's base station in the foothills, a location named after the ancient rock formations shielding it from above. Then meet with the Masters and hopefully steer the Guild back on track. Simple. Elegant.

Wishful, too.

Valint drifted ahead of them, her ship destined for docking on pad three. They bled altitude until the ground appeared below, the

scraggly vegetation and hillocks glowing silver with two of the planet's three moon's reflected light.

Radio traffic filled the cockpit speakers, the voice on the other
end muffled and distorted by static. It wasn't only the heat of entry
but also the planet's heavy iron deposits and strong magnetosphere.

"*Fafnir* copies. Adjusting course to three one two degrees north
by west. Cleared for landing on The Ridge, landing pad four. I'm
locked onto your beacon. Please repeat entry speed requirements,
your last message came across garbled."

The comm squawked again, the Galactic Knights dispatcher on
the other end transmitting, to no avail. Not even Netty could separate the message from the static. The bow thrusters fired hard,
pushing Mark forward and against his harness.

"Easy, Netty. I'm a little squishier inside than you are," he
advised, smiling as he did.

The speed listed on the overlay flashed and cut in half—then
slowed to a relative crawl, the images and data churning across
every screen. With a muffled *whump*, the belly thrusters fired,
working to help keep the aerodynamically challenged vessel in the
air. The docking pads appeared ahead, their beacons leading them
in. Cai-Demond and Blaz'Orkin's ships appeared. Marker lights
blinked in red and green and blue, all ablaze overhead as the *Fafnir*
angled ponderously toward the Ridge.

"Little slow, don't you think?" Perry asked.

"I'd rather not anger their air traffic control AI," she replied.

"They'll thank us for not making them wait to hear this news—"
Perry started to say when a plume of dust and rock erupted into the
air ahead. Shards glittered in the moonlight as the rocky ridge above
the Anvil Dark facility shifted.

Mark grabbed the stick and pulled back, jamming his foot down on the thruster pedal. The *Fafnir* nosed up like a porpoise, her thrusters churning a massive plume of dust in the process.

"What in the hell was that?" he gasped as another hyper-speed projectile struck.

The entire ridge folded and collapsed, the secret Anvil Dark facility hidden underneath disappearing in a bright cloud of expanding fire and pulverized rock.

Perry spoke in a small voice. "Boss, we might have a problem."

21

"WHAT IN THE hell just happened? Was that a…were those…?"

"Multiple rail gun strikes," Perry confirmed. "And not small ones. Judging from the tectonic resonance and debris cloud, those were bunker busters, most likely solid tungsten drivers."

Mark watched as the *Stormshadow* rolled left, its drive plume illuminating the darkness behind it. He cranked the stick to follow and goosed the throttle. The *Fafnir* jumped forward, the thrust kicking him back into the gel padding.

"Valint is making a run for it. We need to gain distance from the impact and—" Netty began as every screen and speaker on the ship came alive.

"GKU gunboat *Fafnir*, you are hereby ordered to cut thrust and stand down. Anvil Dark authority demands you cease aggressions toward Guild assets immediately and surrender yourself to pacification forces. If you do not obey, you will be fired upon."

"Fired upon? Pacification forces? Are they saying that we—?"

Mark murmured, then closed his mouth with an audible click. Cai-Demond and a neutral, honest Guild Master were in that facility. Of course, Gyl-Mareth was going to try to pin their deaths on him.

"Netty, can you respond and talk them down? See if they'll listen."

"I don't know if it will do any good, but I'll try."

The tactical overlay reset and zoomed out, updating with a growing number of moving contacts. Some were above them in deep orbit, while others appeared to be emerging from ground-based facilities.

"They're trying to make patsies out of us, Mark," Valint said, her voice crackling through his seat comm. "Stay on my tail, and whatever you do, don't let them separate us."

"I'm right behind you."

"They have blocked us out of comms and are playing the stand-down order on repeat. We're listed as renegades, and they'll take us down if we do not cut thrust," Perry complained, his frustration bubbling to the surface.

Valint rolled right and nosed down into a deep valley, Mark's stomach rising into his throat as he navigated to follow. His overlay updated again, showing over a dozen closing contacts.

"Where you going? What's our play, Valint?"

"More speed," she responded as the drive plume from the *Stormshadow* grew.

Mark pushed the smaller and more streamlined *Fafnir* harder to match the speed, but in an all-out foot race, his ship didn't have the heart or the legs to keep up. And this wasn't the kind of sprint he could afford to lose.

"Bunn and I are linked," Netty said a moment later. "Valint is making a push for Brightside, a sizable city situated over the terminator line on the sunny side of the planet. It's independent and has a strict no-fly ordinance in place. It sounds like she wants to find sanctuary there."

"And how does that help us?"

"Meaning they're independent and not affiliated with the Guild. GKU assets are prohibited from firing over densely populated areas, except for in times of war. She believes we can request asylum and try to make sense of what just happened."

"How far is it?"

To answer his question, his overlay zoomed out. A point appeared on the landscape well ahead of their moving icon, with a line drawn in to connect the two. According to the legend on his map, they were a long way off.

"Two thousand miles away?" Mark asked, eyeing the map. As he did, the overlay continued to change where Guild assets were pushing to intercept. He understood what Valint was trying to do, but he wondered if it wasn't the wrong play.

"We need to go up and out with every ounce of speed we can manage," he said, opening the cockpit channel to the *Stormshadow*. "They're scattered and fighting to catch up, but if we let them close the gap and organize, we'll effectively lose every advantage we have right now. Gyl-Mareth will pull in every Guild asset available and surround Brightside. Once he does that, they'll storm the city and take us down."

Static filled the speaker for a moment, before Valint's voice responded.

"I was hoping we could talk them down. To make them see reason."

"Gyl-Mareth can't afford to let us talk to the Guild. He killed his political opposition, along with an innocent Guild Master. He paints us as the villain and will use the heat and emotion of the moment to strike us down. In my mind, there are only two ways to fight someone like that—either go at him straight on, or go quiet and isolate him, then pick him apart piece by piece."

"We can't fight the whole of the Guild. They aren't *all* bad, but until we can convince them otherwise, most will believe that *we* are. Bad, that is."

"Exactly," Mark said.

"I see your logic and sadly, agree. I don't think we come back from this peacefully. Make the move, Mark. Take the lead. The *Stormshadow* has your back."

A knot formed in his belly at her words, at the idea that they had moved beyond peaceful resolutions. He pulled back on the stick, despite a part of him screaming to hesitate, to talk this out.

"Gyl-Mareth is enacting his well-planned scheme, and, unfortunately, we're a part of it," he said as the ship groaned. Bow and belly thrusters fired, and with the extra mass of weapons and extended-range fuel tanks, the *Fafnir* pulled her nose skyward.

With considerable momentum already gained, both Peacemaker ships broke the atmosphere quickly and pushed into the deepening black of space. And yet, they were not alone. Not by a long shot. Warning icons appeared on his overlay and a mass of their fellow Peacemakers painted them with tracking systems.

"You let me know the moment someone launches."

"Oh, trust me. You'll hear," Perry shot back.

"Who do we know in that group? Anyone we can talk down?"

"Not a soul, boss," Netty said. "Even if we wanted to, they've locked us out of comms."

"Well, sheeeit," Mark drawled. "And we're too far into the gravity well to twist?"

"Yes. The twist wouldn't only irreparably damage our twist drive, but it would leave a resonance trail even Drogo could follow."

"I've got heat blooms. Evade! Evade!"

The *Fafnir* and *Stormshadow* rolled, firing thrusters to change their vector.

"Missiles?"

"No. Laser shots. They're trying to take out our drive."

"To make it look like an attempted apprehension, no doubt," Perry said. "I'm not about to play this game." Without another word, the bird jumped down from his perch and disappeared around the corner. Mark heard a maintenance panel hiss open and promptly slam shut.

"Okay. I don't know what that's about, but, Netty, please give me a visual reference point to twist range and at current speed, a count-down timer." His overlay updated a moment later, a series of concurrent rings appearing beyond the ship, along with a timer.

"Drogo twisted away. He is in the clear," Netty said.

Laser blooms flashed like starbursts on his screen as they rolled and pitched, the thrusters firing like an orchestral drum section. The twisting, churning change of direction soured his stomach, his mouth going dry as the ship lurched yet again.

A flash of heat glowed on the back of Valint's ship, and a heart-beat later, the *Fafnir* shuddered.

"We're running from the whole of the Guild, Mark. We simply can't evade this volume of laser fire. Our ablative armor coating has already taken a beating. We need to…" Netty started to say but went quiet.

Another tremor passed through the ship, and another, as space around them filled with blazing shots of light. The AI didn't respond but continued to evade. He knew the truth. She didn't know what to do because they were effectively out of options. As brilliant and fast as Netty was, there were no logical answers.

The *Fafnir* jolted hard as a pressure leak warning popped up on the overlay, followed by faults on three aft thrusters. The lights flickered again, and for the first time since Netty took over as his resident AI, the drive floundered. It groaned and thrust cut out. The ship was dying, and them with it.

"Perry, you have an idea. Share now, or we might not ever have the chance."

"Plot a twist. Those coordinates that Ja-Ra gave you. We go there. But we can't wait," the bird said over the cockpit comms. A series of loud, metallic hammer sounds punctuated the air right after. "Netty. Program it in now. Give me a fifteen second delay."

"But we're too far in the gravity well. The twist could tear our drive apart, and the ship with it."

"Do it!"

The only response to Netty's words was the appearance of new contacts popping up on his overlay. The system automatically tracked and tagged each one, the telltale red border of a missile launch glowing to life a moment later. He watched ten, twelve, and then twenty separate ship killers launched right at them.

Perry was right, they were out of options. These weren't Whisperwing missiles, but Starfires. Smart, fast, and lethal killing tools.

"We're out of time," he yelled as the missile bay doors clunked open below them.

Perry's voice echoed over the speakers a moment later. "This is all about timing, Netty. Start a clock—give me twenty seconds. You need to twist exactly on its expiration. Am I clear?" A timer appeared on the overlay, ticking down from nineteen.

"You are."

Mark reached up, grabbed hold of the harness tensioners, and wrenched them down as tight as they would go. The timer hit ten seconds, then nine, and eight. His hands shook as a peculiar resonance formed in the ship all around him, the vibration growing in intensity until it practically rang in his bones.

"*Stormshadow* reports ready to twist."

With missiles screaming toward them and the countdown reaching five seconds, Mark closed his eyes. He braced as the ship jumped, the normally benign event physically painful on every one of his senses.

Everything spun around him as the universe itself seemed to tear—in sound, smell, and even the darkness behind his lids. The twist drive roared, its normally peaceful whine replaced by the howl of tearing metal and space-time.

Netty and Perry's voices punched through the chaos surrounding him, but even when they were projected directly into the ear bug, he could barely hear them. The *Fafnir* gave a tremendous lurch, seemed to list heavily to port, and then made a full, stomach-flipping rotation.

Then they were floating, the silence of the cockpit louder and more chaotic than any battle. Mark opened his eyes, gagged, and then retched in a painful heave. The air was thick and bitter with caustic smoke.

No lights illuminated the panels around him, but one truly unsettling fact stood out immediately. Netty's optical sensor was dark. He reached up and popped the releases on his harness, and yet there was no pressure from thrust. The steadying pull of artificial gravity was gone as well.

Mark fought free and floated forward using the instrument bulkhead to arrest his momentum. The black of space loomed beyond the viewscreens. The *Stormshadow* drifted end over end barely a hundred yards above to their port, the warship's marker lights flickering on and off again erratically. A jet of what looked like superheated plasma shot into space from the aft maintenance section, its glow quickly dissipating into the dark.

Mark pulled himself forward, skipped over the missing viewscreen, and completed a loop of the cockpit, searching space for clues as to where they were, but also signs of danger. The *Fafnir* continued to rotate, the starscape spinning slowly around them.

"They won't know where we've gone," Perry said, floating gracefully through the zero-G.

"How can you know that? How can we be sure?"

"You're lucky I'm a cynical bird, Mark. When I sabotaged those implosion warheads, I created a backdoor, a single-use and completely unique key in case we ever needed it. I then activated one and dropped it out the missile bay. The twist timer I had Netty set matched the crude countdown I programmed into that nuke. It detonated eight one-hundredths of a second after we twisted. I am, as you can surmise, a thorough bird. You may be impressed."

"Naturally. Based on your bit of preparation, they would think our ships exploded?"

"Their AIs are likely too smart for that, but…" Perry said, pausing as he turned to consider the dark space. "A twist within a gravity well would leave behind a significant space-time cavitation trail."

"Enough resonance to track?"

The bird nodded.

"So, the nuke would wash away our trail? It would cover our tracks?" he guessed.

"In theory, yes."

Mark nodded, pulling himself back over to watch the *Stormshadow.* The larger ship still spun, but its marker lights weren't flickering anymore. A moment later, its cockpit lights illuminated, and a small face appeared in the starboard viewscreen.

He could barely see Valint, but she appeared to be waving and pointing to her mouth, as if speaking.

"They still have power. That's good. What about us?"

"Let's go see for ourselves."

Mark and Perry floated back through the passage, the galley a mess of drifting boxes and debris, but when the maintenance passage door opened, a cloud of acrid smoke billowed out. Eyes watering, Mark activated his helmet, then held his breath for a moment as the suit filtered out the contaminants.

With his suit lights on, they pushed back into the engine room, only to find the source of the smoke. The maintenance space was hot, the heat washing over him in punishing waves. He could feel it *through* his suit, which made the revelation even more startling.

Perry pulled an extinguisher module off the wall and propelled himself up and over the twist drive. A gout of purple and green flames rippled into the air as alloy tubes and armored cables burned. His counterpart doused the fire with a jet of compressed foam, then coated it a second time for good measure.

Metal flowed down the side of the twist drive, collecting on the deck in silvery globs. They hissed angrily, burning the paint right off the grated decking.

Mark circled around the ship's engine, waving away the thick smoke. Another small fire flared to life on the massive unit, then another. He kept his distance as Perry moved smoothly, dousing the fires when they appeared. But eventually it became clear that he was simply trying to treat the symptoms and not the problem.

They sealed the door to the rest of the ship and opened the vents manually, allowing the tainted atmosphere to escape into space. The smoke cleared as the air bled away, with the fires choking quickly on the depleting atmosphere. A few minutes later, they stood in cold, hard vacuum, the harsh truth now clear before them.

Heat continued to ripple off their ruined twist drive, but the flowing rivulets of melted metal started to cool and solidify. And the fires weren't even the worst of the damage. Long, angry fissures marred the space-time engine, having run all the way down and through the metal superstructure.

Perry hopped from one surface to another, explaining the damage in words even Mark could understand. His armored composite exterior protected him from the extremes in temperature, although Mark kept his distance. The b-suit was tough, but not necessarily immune to melting.

"Both ionization chambers fractured. The cooling unit melted down, the power distribution module is gone, that..." he said, pointing to a large puddle on the side of the drive, "is what was on fire when we first came in. All of the wiring and fuel management is just…gone."

"It sounds like a total loss," Mark said, every word bleaker than the last.

Perry nodded. "We're lucky. Twist drives tear holes in space-time, essentially creating an artificial gravity well and allowing the ship to slip through. But when another gravity well is present, the tidal forces can skew and tear space-time in ways the transit infrastructure cannot predict or control. The demand on a twist drive manifests as heat. Heat and pressure build in the ionization chambers until one of two things happens. Either the containment fails, or fusion is achieved. The second option would have seen the *Fafnir* consumed by an intense flare of heat and light."

"We would have become a small sun?"

"In essence, yes, but for only a moment. Larger, more powerful ships have the capacity to dump the contents of their drive's ionization chambers directly into space, effectively nullifying the danger. But that technology is expensive, especially to equip on small vessels."

"That's what we saw the *Stormshadow* venting into space?"

Perry nodded, then quietly turned and floated to the reactor—an enclosed octagon set against the far bulkhead. Mark hadn't paid it any attention until recently, a fact that he silently chided himself about. It was his ship's heart, the thing keeping him alive and granting them the freedom to travel between the stars, and he'd never given it more than a passing glance.

Perry wrapped a clawed foot around a release lever and wrenched the maintenance panel open. Debris and smoke drifted out as the door swung outward, telling him the reactor's fate had been tied to the twist drive.

"Let me guess, the reactor is done, too?"

"It was only a matter of time, Mark. Undersized reactors simply take too much abuse. And we have been asking so much from ours lately. That's what happens when you're forced to run."

"Prey runs…"

"Yes, because it fears the predator. But what happens when the prey grows larger and no longer fears the predator's teeth or claws? Does the rhinoceros run from the lion? The elephant from the hyena?"

"No, they charge," Mark said.

"Precisely."

He looked around at the dark engine room, the ship's heart a smoldering, ruined mess.

"We aren't charging anyone. Not like this. The *Fafnir* is dead."

"Dead?" Perry said, his eyes burning to life. "Your ancient Greeks believed in a magical bird that could set itself on fire, only to be reborn from the ashes."

"The phoenix?"

"Yes! Like the phoenix, we will rise again. And when we do, they'll run before us."

22

THE CASCADING POWER failures in the *Fafnir* hadn't only destroyed the twist drive and reactor but had also damaged their batteries, leaving them dead in the water. As it stood, without Valint and the *Stormshadow*, Mark would have likely floated in the black, never to be found again.

But he did have Valint, and her ship's newer, more expensive drive and reactor had survived the dangerous twist. Mark spent his time cleaning up his ship, but there was only so much he could do in the cold, dark vacuum. And his b-suit's air supply and carbon dioxide scrubbers would only last so long.

The *Stormshadow* coupled with them a few long hours later. The inner airlock opened slowly, revealing Striker, one of his mechanical arms spinning the manual crank on the portal. Valint helped him police up his personal effects, while Striker and Perry took a confirmatory stroll through the maintenance space. The larger combat unit's silence afterward only helped to confirm their ship's dire condition.

"So, where did we end up?" Mark asked a short time later. He'd dropped his bag off on the spare bunk, while Perry paced the galley.

"Surprisingly farther than I thought we would," Valint said, turning her overlay so he could see.

"Do you mean 'luckily'?" the *Stormshadow*'s AI asked.

"It kind of goes without saying," Mark replied.

"These are the coordinates we were aiming for," Valint said, drawing a circle around a system on her map.

It zoomed in to show a relatively large, main phase star surrounded by two rocky planets, and beyond that, a pair of enormous gas giants. A tiny speck of rock appeared, its elliptical orbit taking it away from the larger of the two gas planets. It was the moon—their target. The map zoomed out again, before a red icon appeared far to the left.

"This is where we ended up, a dead mining system called Sigil's Track. Got a neutron star that sits at the center, which is likely why we were dragged here. The gravitational pull is immense."

"I'm still running the calculations on that, but it's the most likely explanation," Bunn offered.

"How far?" Mark asked.

"We managed a meager four point two light-years on that drive-melting jump, and it was hardly a straight-line journey. Twenty-six light-years still sit between us and our goal," the AI replied.

"That's an impressive jump, considering we launched deep in a gravity well. This horse has legs."

"This is in fact a ship, not a horse," Bunn said, not following him.

"It's something we say back on the farm."

"Don't get him started on the farm, Bunn. You'll never hear the end of it. In truth, I didn't get to meet one of these horses when we were there last, but, as Mark describes them, they're like tractors with an opinion. Evidently, they're quite the sassy quadrupeds."

"Ah. Perhaps Valint will take me one day, so I can see these opinionated beasts of labor. I could use some enlightening conversation."

Mark took a breath to speak but decided to let it go. Either Bunn was being intentionally obtuse, or she wasn't used to their particular flavor of sarcasm and humor. In truth, considering Valint's businesslike nature, it was probably a bit of both.

"The *Fafnir*'s drive and reactor are toast. She's dead in space without a major refit. But it appears the *Stormshadow* fared better."

Valint nodded, but her expression darkened. It was Bunn that responded first.

"We didn't come out of that twist unscathed. Our reactor scrammed automatically mid-twist, and luckily, our jump capacitors contained enough energy to complete the twist safely. Emergency protocols kicked in, venting excessive chamber pressure into space, but—"

"But," Valint said, chiming in, "we overloaded one of our two reactor coolant control units and blew almost a dozen relays on the twist drive. Our maintenance bot is rewiring the navigational driver right now, as well as making a number of other repairs. As Bunn was about to say, anywhere we go, we will be limping. If we get into a fight or have to run..."

She trailed off, leaving the rest unsaid, but Mark knew what she meant. For the foreseeable future, they were operating on a small margin of error.

"I could use a coffee. You?"

Valint nodded, and together they headed to the galley. Perry and Striker joined them as they strategized over steaming mugs. The conversation was sporadic at first as they all seemed afraid to attack the topic head-on. After Mark's third sip, Perry dove in headfirst.

"The Junkway is out of reach, and I don't believe it's in our best interest to jump into Armagost's hideout. The drive coils took a beating on that twist and will need to be manually tuned. Anywhere we twist now, we'll be leaving a noticeable wake behind us."

"So, if the wrong people are watching, we could lead them right to him," Mark surmised.

"Exactly, Master Tudor," Striker said, bowing respectfully. The British accent was on full display.

"We shouldn't go anywhere near the Tau system at this point, which rules out our comfortable options." Valint sighed. "They knew we twisted out of a gravity well, so in their eyes we're either dead or in dire need of repair."

"Gyl-Mareth has likely sent agents to check hospitals and emergency medical facilities. He will have distributed warrants to all Peacemakers, and kill orders through the black web. Moving forward, we will be hunted on two fronts, and not in a casual manner. This hunt will be relentless. And well-funded."

"A truly cheery thought," Perry enthused. "Perhaps the universe took notice of all your recent pirate talk, Mark."

"I hope not," he said, shaking his head. Then he turned to Striker and Valint and pulled Ja-Ra's old data slate from his pocket.

He tapped it awake, opened the second icon, and held the screen up so they could see.

"The Bone Yard? Ja-Ra wants us to go to a salvage yard?" Valint asked.

"That's what he said—take it there, they'll know what to do."

"I mean, it makes sense. A salvage yard would likely have the tools and the know-how for such a job, not to mention a surplus of available parts. They're also probably willing to work, ah, *quietly*."

"A salvage yard?" Perry asked. "You want to trust the *Fafnir* to a chop shop? Places like that are where spaceships go to die, not find new life."

"Exactly. Ja-Ra hasn't led us wrong yet. He didn't only give us the coordinates for the replacement reactor we needed but where we needed to go for the installation. It also happens to be a place Gyl-Mareth wouldn't expect us to go. Besides, where else besides Spindrift or Trei-Seti is there less of a Guild presence?"

"Yes, I mean your logic is sound, but at the same time, it makes my feathers crawl to think of those carrion feeders crawling all over our home. Ugh."

"Then it's settled," Mark said, rapping his knuckles against the table. "We pull the reactor out of this abandoned missile platform and head straight for the Bone Yard. The simple fact that it's causing us all such uncertainty is reason enough to go forward. If *we* don't agree, then the decision won't be easy to predict."

"True. Uncomfortable, but true. And, I suppose this is a bit poetic, is it not?" Valint said. "That we use the mechanical heart out of an abandoned Gyl weapon to bring your ship back to life, then tear Gyl-Mareth's criminal network down around him?"

"It is, and the bastard deserves it," Mark agreed. "Although I could do without this step entirely. I like poetry, just not at the cost of our reactor."

"Your practical side is showing, Mark from Iowa. And as to this Bone Yard, it's known to me—I worked a contract there a long time ago. The owner-operator is a former Eridani Federation military man turned business mogul they affectionately call the Shipbreaker," Valint said.

"You trust him, this Shipbreaker?" Mark asked. "Helluva nickname for someone who's supposed to fix things."

Valint laughed and dropped her head. When she looked up again, the humor was gone.

"No, but at this point, we don't really have the luxury of only working with those we trust, do we? And if your Tunis friend believes that's where we should go, who am I to argue?"

They weren't ready to get underway for another eight hours as the maintenance bot, working in concert with the combat units completed repairs to the *Stormshadow*. They extended the warship's tether, hooked to the *Fafnir*, and then carefully burned away from the neutron star. Bunn exercised extreme caution as the AI navigated them well beyond the dead star's reach before enacting their first twist.

It was a short jump, barely half a light-year. And although it seemed to go smoothly from Mark's perspective, Bunn, Striker, and Perry had quite a bit to talk about afterward.

"What happened? What's wrong?" Mark asked Perry as the AIs finally broke apart.

"The drive started bleeding radio emissions across a number of frequencies. Your hearing was not sensitive enough to pick it up, but trust me, it was significant."

"Danger?"

The bird shrugged. "When you're cramming three hundred metric tons of spacecraft through unstable rifts in space-time, yes, anything out of the ordinary should be considered dangerous. Now we're tethered to another relatively large chunk of spaceship, so… you know."

"Good point," Mark relented.

Four hours later and they were ready to try again. He strapped in next to Valint, while Striker sequestered himself in the engine room. Perry perched on the seat above Mark, watching eighteen different schematic and system feedback screens at the same time.

"Here goes nothing," Bunn said as the twist drive spooled.

It had been a while since Mark traveled with Valint, but he was surprised at how much deeper and throatier the *Stormshadow* sounded. The ship didn't just sound bigger and faster, but he could feel the power around his body, too.

They jumped successfully, the large drive carrying them almost twenty-seven light-years this time. The *Stormshadow* emerged from twist space on the far side of the gas giant's gravity well. The gunboat's external maintenance vents bled off excess heat as their cloud of gamma radiation dispelled.

A long-range sensor ping confirmed that they had hit their transit window, although Bunn missed the mark by almost thirty-seven meters. Valint waved the AI off as she tried to apologize for the discrepancy. The slow part of their journey took them another half a day as they burned away from the massive blue and red gas giant.

"We have arrived," Striker declared, as several alarms triggered on the overlays.

Mark leaned out from behind the screen, searching the black space beyond the viewscreens. "I don't see anything," he announced.

"The moon is currently sitting in the shadow of its big brother," Striker explained. "Solar eclipses occur quite often for this tiny piece of irradiated rock. Once every thirty-two solar cycles to be precise, by my calculations. But the frequency changes, as the moon stretches its orbit, so you know, more mathematics and stuff."

"Stuff?" Mark asked.

"Yep. Squiggly lines and strange symbols."

"Stuff that's beyond me. Got it."

"Would it feel right if anything came easy anymore?" Valint asked.

He chuckled, turning to respond. But when he met her gaze, he struggled to formulate a response. Yes, he wanted *easy*. But more importantly, he desired comfort and reliability. Mark wanted a life worth living, and with her by his side, that felt possible. Naturally, those words wouldn't come out. So, he did what he'd done so many times.

He grunted.

Perry pulled up a schematic of the missile platform on their overlays, or the closest thing he could find, at least. It looked like a miniature space station, featuring concentric rings of armament mounting points connected by armored lattice work.

The screen zoomed in, highlighting the unit's impressive munitions first—forty-two batteries of ship-killer missiles. Each silo held ten weapons, making the platform an impressive and intimidating piece of tech.

"Four hundred and twenty missiles?" Valint asked, catching up.

"And that's just the batteries pointed away from the moon. According to this schematic, that particular model possessed an additional ten hardpoints for space-to-surface weapons, point-defense cannons, or high-intensity lasers," Perry explained.

"It makes me wonder what the Gyl were researching down in that base that they would require such a platform to defend it," Mark said, and zoomed in on the middle of the platform. Located at the center of the station was its cylindrical core.

"That's it," Perry confirmed. "That's our target. Located within that central hub is the platform's reactor and AI housing, along with its relatively beefy comms module. Now, it's highly unlikely that we will just be able to open the exterior service hatch, so you should be prepared to cut your way in. Thanks to the data Ja-Ra provided about the unit, we know the reactor is suspended by alloy mounts."

"Which you won't need for the *Fafnir*, by the way," Striker added.

"Correct. In order to remove it, you'll need to cut those mounts here, here, here, and lastly, here."

The bird turned the schematic and circled the supports one at a time. Then he detailed exactly how they would unhook and finally, tether, using the *Stormshadow*'s exterior winch to lift it free.

"What about the AI module or the comms? Are they worth taking?"

"It all is, but then again, I cannot imagine the Gyl would leave either behind, especially if they were truly cooking up banned biological or chemical weapons below. Either could hold potential evidence against them."

"An interesting thought," Valint said, pausing for a moment. "Why didn't they tow the platform away? A weapon system like that has considerable value. And if they were concerned with someone using it as evidence against them, they could have detonated one of the remaining warheads, or turned off its altitude adjustment systems and let it burn up in the atmosphere."

Perry and Striker nodded at the same time.

"Those are the same questions that we have been pondering this whole time. But as we have found in the past, unraveling the ambitions of biologics is a tricky game," Striker said.

"Anything we can collect that will help us build our case against Gyl-Mareth is a plus. Let's consider comms, sensors, hard drives, or AI modules as targets of opportunity," Mark said, and paused mid-swipe.

He'd tried to pull the schematic to his wrist repeater, before remembering that Netty wasn't there. He'd be without her help until they managed to restore power to the ship. Even with Perry, Valint, and Striker at his side, the thought made him feel surprisingly alone.

The moon came out from the gas giant's shadow as Mark and Valint prepared for their spacewalk. It revolved into view below them and emerged as a bright sliver, before the star revealed the rest. Soaring miles above the surface, he spotted mountains and valleys, massive red plateaus, and even what looked like the winding paths of long dried-up riverbeds.

"Prep time, boss," Perry said, holding an autoinjector in his beak. "It's time for your super fun stick and poke."

Mark held out his hand, allowing the AI to drop the injection into his palm. The captured needle on the end was surprisingly large, while the liquid stored inside shone blue in the light.

"Do I have to?"

"No, you don't *have* to take it. Unless you enjoy the smell of rotting flesh and living through cellular death. If you do not like those things, or dying young, I would suggest taking the injection. Doctor Bird's orders."

"You make the alternative sound so appealing," Mark said, lifting his top to expose his belly. Then, before doubt could creep in, he pushed the injector against his skin and pushed the button.

The needle stung, but the anti-radiation meds burned more. It filtered slowly through his system, turning his skin blue in the process.

"Why so blue, Mark? Come on, cheer up. It *will* wear off eventually."

"Where do you find the inspiration for these jokes?"

"It's a gift," Perry said, cocking his head to the side. His beak pulled open into what looked unmistakably like a smirk.

"Perhaps."

Bunn fired thrusters as the missile platform came into view below, the *Stormshadow* dipping even lower in the atmosphere. Their target first appeared as a speck of black against the rocky terrain below, but it clarified as they made their descent. Mark felt his apprehension grow as they sagged ever lower, the telltale hum of thin atmosphere vibrating against the ship's outer hull.

"Are we sure this is safe?" he asked Perry while pulling on the heavy maintenance suit.

"Safe? No." The bird laughed. "But necessary? Yes."

Valint cycled the outer airlock open a few minutes later and, without a word, pushed out into the open. Striker followed close after.

Remember, boss. Stay tethered to that platform whenever possible.

"Got it," Mark said, and leaned out into space.

His stomach jumped as he set his gaze on the platform, his suit's HUD automatically locking on. Despite his best efforts, he couldn't block out the sight of the exoplanet looming beyond, now impossibly large below them. It didn't feel like they were floating in space anymore but looking down from an insanely high place. Valint touched down first, with Striker hitting a moment later, the *Stormshadow's* tow cable clutched tightly in one of his many hands.

Let's go, boss. We don't want to miss out on all the fun, Perry said in the ear bug, and jumped free.

Against every ingrained instinct, Mark kicked off and followed.

The descent lasted barely a minute, but to Mark it felt like an eternity. Thin currents of atmosphere whipped around him, whistling against his heavy maintenance suit as it pushed him left and right. The integrated thrusters fired, working to keep him on target, until his weighted magnetic boots finally touched down.

Welcome to the prize, Striker said over his ear bug.

Straight off the Tunis Sale Bazaar, Perry added, *A robot-controlled missile platform, assigned to defend creeps doing nefarious stuff on a tiny rock, deep in heavily radiated space, orbiting a star nobody cares about. Oh, and we're slowly but surely sinking into the atmosphere. We try to keep that fact, ah, hidden —at least until the customer has paid.*

"Your optimism and commercialism are exhausting, bird," Mark said.

I'm practically bursting with positivity. Stop trying to drag me down, Mark.

"Bursting? More like glowing."

Perry laughed, mechanical and distant over the earbug. *No, that's the heavy doses of Beta and Gamma radiation coming off this tub. I'm surprised you haven't grown a tail.*

At mention of the radiation, he looked to the upper right corner of his HUD, where a meter tracked his received dose. The small needle jumped, dropped, and crackled as the dosimeter tracked hot particles. It was halfway to red and creeping up slowly.

Valint and Striker went to work checking missile batteries, while Perry and Mark headed straight for the center and the platform's heart. The superstructure rumbled and shook around them, its vibrations passing up and through his boots. He managed only a few steps before a large piece of shielding came loose and drifted free. It floated for a few heartbeats before a gust caught it, and with an angry keen, blew it away.

"Faster walking is good," he mumbled to himself as he dropped his gaze to the ground. The decking ahead jumped, making it look as if the whole of the missile platform would come loose at any moment.

A chunk of superstructure to his left cracked and swung upward with only a few remaining rivets keeping it from floating away entirely. It fluttered, creaking loudly in the swirling currents.

Perry led him ahead and left, bypassing an entire section of missing lattice. Mark made the mistake of looking down, the open section framing a massive, snowcapped mountain below.

"Give me horny fish ladies and violent, churning seas over this," he whispered, finally tearing his eyes away.

Oh, stop complaining and enjoy the view. It's better than good. We might have to break out a little French, Perry said, waving a wing grandly. *Magnifique.*

"Easy to say when you're armored, bird."

True. You're relatively squishy.

After a nerve-racking trek across the crumbling missile platform, Mark and Perry finally reached the center. Mark stepped up and onto the armored enclosure, the solidity a welcomed change. A single simple hatch sat in the middle, and yet there didn't appear to be any lever, crank, or digital access pad. They circled it twice, before Perry hopped up onto the hatch and tapped it with his talons.

It's a remotely accessed hatch, but will you look at that, they welded it shut for good measure. Boy, someone really didn't want visitors to get in.

"With four hundred missiles on board, can you blame them?" Mark asked, pulling the Moonsword free.

The bird hopped aside as he brought the blade to bear, only he didn't cut into the hatch, but around it. Working the blade down into the platform's exterior skin, Mark worked carefully to open a wide and relatively round opening. Once he'd completed the circle, the cutout broke loose and drifted free of the hole.

Perry jumped onto one side of the giant disc, his weight causing one side to dip and the opposite to rise. Mark seized that opportunity to grab ahold and guide it up and out of the way. The bird hopped over next to him a moment later, and together they watched the section of cut platform float away.

Simply cutting the hatch open wasn't good enough?

"We're here for a reactor, right? I figured it probably wouldn't fit through a hatch, so why not do the hard work first."

I hate how logical you are sometimes.

"Or, do you hate that you didn't think of it first?"

Pick.

"All right, bird. Once more into the breach," Mark said, motioning for Perry to enter first.

The first two missile magazines were empty, Valint said, her voice crackling into his ear bug. *The third is just gone. It isn't looking good for salvage at this point. But, in a separate issue, the cloud cover has cleared below. Are you in a position to look down?*

"Yes, although my vertigo might say otherwise."

Trust me, you want to see this.

Mark moved to the edge of the station's core, then knelt down at the edge and peered through a section of missing shielding. The exoplanet came into view, and he swallowed hard and almost looked away before something caught his eye. It was a plateau, straight west of a jagged series of mountains. The rocky ground was pocked with craters, the debris rings scorched black from fire and heat.

"Is that the—?"

It is, Mark, Bunn said. *That is, I should say, was the Gyl research station. The blast radius from each strike is in line with high-yield nukes.*

"An orbital bombardment with high-yield nukes? Tell me, who does that sound like?"

"A certain Bird-hating mercenary," Perry guessed.

"She obviously didn't want anyone poking around in there. But why? What could they have to hide?"

The operative detail being that it was an unregulated chemical and biological weapons research facility, Valint said. *Did she retrieve anything from the site or destroy it to keep it out of other people's hands?*

"Rats. Sorry to interrupt, but you can scratch the AI and comms modules off our prize list," Perry added, transmitting from the platform's core.

Mark straightened and forced his gaze away from the terrain far below, then turned and hopped down into the darkness. He activated his magnetic boots, found purchase on the wall, then reoriented himself. He turned the light down the long, cylindrical space and immediately understood what the bird was talking about.

The carbon fiber lid of the reactor shone below, but wires and cables hung out into the air from the walls all round it. Every mounting spot in the tight space was stripped of its hardware.

"It isn't a deal breaker. We need a reactor, and there happens to be one of those here. Let's get to work. Are those what I need to cut to break it free?" he asked, hugging the wall and directing his light around the far edge of the housing. In that space—barely two feet from reactor to wall—stood a series of thick, shock-absorbing mounts.

"Indeed, they are. Wedge yourself in there and start cutting. While you do that, I'll unhook the feeds and coolant lines."

Something clunked and banged outside, with the rest of the missile platform loudly vibrating a moment later.

Mark and Perry shared a brief look and then immediately went to work. He released his magnetic boots and readied the Moonsword. After pulling himself into the tight gap between the wall, with condensation forming on his suit's faceplate, Mark lined up the blade and made the first cut.

23

WITH A CRICK FORMING in his neck, Mark managed to get the Moonsword in position and let it fall. The blade caught and cut through the second support, bright metal parting as he grunted with effort.

"Um, Mark. How far along are you?" Perry asked.

"That was number two. I'm moving toward the third right now. This is a lot harder with this maintenance suit on," he said. And as it had a dozen times since landing on the platform, Mark's gaze slid up to the rad meter on his HUD. It was floating below the three-quarters mark and still climbing.

The platform shuddered again, and Mark knew he was on borrowed time.

"You *may* want to work faster," Perry urged. There was no humor in the statement, which made Mark even more nervous.

"I have one speed in this tight space, and it ain't fast. This suit really slows me down," Mark grunted, pulling himself toward his next target. "Wait. Why? What happened?"

"Well, it's kind of a funny story, but I think it might be best to tell it once we cut this thing free and pull it to safety."

"No. Now. What happened?"

Perry paused, which set Mark on higher alert. "Fine. We'd originally thought that the platform was in a decaying orbit. In a way it was. The schematic showed a unique lower-power gyroscopic drive, one to maintain the platform's geosynchronous orbit above the research facility. It turns out that the drive was also responsible for maintaining its elevation. So, you know, funny."

"And let me guess, the reactor was still running in order to power this system?"

"As it turns out, yes, but at almost undetectably low power levels. And that, in part, is why the missile platform is sinking in its orbit."

"And I need to hurry up, because you shut the reactor down or cut it loose?"

"Um…both. I could reconnect it, but there's almost no reaction mass on board, and a bootup would take some time."

"I got it," Mark growled, kicking at the wall and wriggling forward. He haphazardly swung the Moonsword at the next support. The tip of the blade caught and glanced off. "Bird! How much time do I have?"

"Plenty. So don't panic. I'd say five minutes, maybe six."

"Five minutes?"

"Is that not a lot? It feels like an eternity at my current clock speed."

Shoving his body forward, Mark wound up again and brought

the blade down, finally severing the third support. He wriggled and shoved himself forward and down, and his elbows and knees hit both the reactor and the wall. He had to stop and wrench his head around, then move his entire body to find the next support.

"Why does it feel like we're falling?" Valint asked.

"Probably because we are. Perry just shut the reactor down," he said, finally spotting the next mount and moving into position. "Evidently, it still had some kind of gyroscopic drive working to keep this thing aloft."

"Well, shit."

"My sentiments exactly. Did you find anything?"

"No missiles, but there's a damaged point-defense cannon on the outer ring. It looks like this platform suffered a micro-meteorite strike at some point, and the damage buckled the shielding. We only found the cannon because Striker peeled the damaged section away."

"So, they missed it while they were stripping this platform down," Mark surmised.

"That was our thought. Striker is winching it up to the *Stormshadow* as we speak."

"Could we use the winch and the ship to pull the platform back up to a more stable orbit?"

"And connect to what? This thing is disintegrating around us. If we tried that, the whole thing might come apart."

"A fair point," Mark admitted, finding the next support. He set his back against the outside wall, angled the blade, and used his body weight to make the cut this time.

The reactor groaned, and the lingering weight shifted against the supports that survived, dogged in the face of their high-altitude deconstruction. He tried to remember the schematic, but the number evaded him.

"Perry, how many more?"

"Three, and there's one right underneath you—cut that last. The other two are ahead and up. Do those now. And like I said, make haste. The *Stormshadow*'s sensors are picking up on an exterior temperature increase of fifty, no, make that sixty degrees Fahrenheit."

"I know, I know."

He found the next support the old-fashioned way, by running his helmet into it. The blade parted the metal-fiber weave with ease, but as soon as it was cut, the whole reactor housing shifted toward him.

Mark wiggled free, pushed on, and found the second to last support only five feet ahead and eight up. He set his feet and activated the magnetic boots, then cut before better judgment could set in. The reactor groaned and settled almost a full foot down as the last support cracked loudly. It wasn't simply the weight, but that gravity was taking hold. If he wasn't in the right spot when the large vessel came free, it could easily crush him.

"I hope you're ready up there. As soon as I cut this last support, this reactor is going to settle into its new home."

"We're hooking to the reactor now. Do it," Perry ordered, having to yell above the howling wind. "And that's why I had you save the bottom mount for last. We'll pull up before you cut, so you *should* be safe."

Mark trusted the bird, but he also knew that the rising howl of wind over the comms was a bad sign. He needed to hurry.

After deactivating the magnetic boots, he let his increasing weight carry him down. Mark hit the bottom, and his knees buckled, making him topple face-first into the reactor. Cursing, he lurched sideways and flailed at the last support.

The Moonsword struck and glanced off, so he brought it back, chopping down with a grunt of frustration. The blade bit deep, cutting halfway through the heavy alloy as chips spalled away into the roaring wind. He moved to bring it back and strike again when the brace snapped free and the whole vessel started to rise like a hawk on a summer updraft.

"It's *free*," Perry crowed. "Now get out of there. This platform is coming apart."

Mark pushed off to stand as his work light passed over something in the middle of the maintenance space that had been previously hidden beneath the reactor's bulk. It was an enclosure, perhaps two feet wide by two long. It looked oddly similar to Netty's blue case.

"I found something," he called and dropped to his knees.

After fumbling the mass of data cables out of the side, Mark tried to lift the case free, only to find it stuck fast.

"Mark, get out of there!" Valint yelled.

Sliding his fingers around the edge of the case, Mark confirmed that it wasn't bolted down, not with any hardware he could see, at least. He gave it one last futile tug, before jamming the Moonsword under the corner and pushing. The blade slid in easily, the handle humming against his hand. It hit something solid as the platform rocked and dropped beneath him—a bracket, holding it down on the underside.

A crash sounded somewhere above, and the world seemed to tilt.

Mark, this thing is going. I hope you're holding onto that reactor. We're pulling it free now, Perry sent, worry coloring his tone.

Driven by desperation, Mark jammed the Moonsword forward with all his available strength. The weapon broke through and jumped, and the case popped free.

Mark stuffed his blade into its scabbard, then scooped the AI case off the ground, turned, and caught the reactor's broken mount.

"I have a hold. Pull us out. Go. Go!"

The vessel lurched upward, the reactor pitching from one side to the other. It hit the inside of the cylinder, breaking off the severed mounts, before swinging to the other side.

Mark clenched his jaw and scrabbled for a better hold, as the jarring impact nearly knocked him free. He cursed and kicked, the reactor striking the wall one last time. A heartbeat later, they lifted free into the open air.

A ripping gust of wind hit him from the side, and they spun, the centrifugal force almost throwing him free. A frantic glance down confirmed what he'd feared. The missile platform pitched in the thickening atmosphere as massive chunks broke free and tumbled away. The exoplanet's mountains and sprawling deserts framed it all in…a terrifyingly real and close backdrop.

With a feral scream of tearing metal and rivets, the Gyl missile platform came apart and disintegrated into a swirling cloud of tumbling debris.

That was close, Perry said. *I thought we'd lost you there for a moment.*

Mark threw his head back and looked up, only to find the bird leaning over the side of the reactor vessel.

"I thought you had, too," he grunted, lifting his arm to show off the case. "Let's hope this was worth it."

After a thirty-minute ride back up to the *Stormshadow*, Mark moved to release his grip on the reactor, but found that his fingers would not move.

"Perry, I have a problem here."

Actually, Mark, that was me, Bunn said over his ear bug. *I apologize, but your vitals spiked, and when you grabbed onto the reactor housing, I calculated your odds of successfully holding on at 4.2 percent. So I overrode the maintenance suit's nanomotors and locked the gauntlet closed. In truth, I may have destroyed the glove doing so, but I was trying to increase your odds of survival.*

"Honestly, I thought my arm was going to come loose there for a minute. Thank you, Bunn. There's nothing for you to apologize for," he said, letting out a pent-up breath.

Mark, I think that I— Perry started to say.

"No," he interrupted as the winch cable reached the underside of the *Stormshadow*. Valint stood in the missile bay, looking down at him through the open doors. The space made the *Fafnir*'s hold look relatively small.

"We didn't have much information to work with, just best guesses. What happened down there wasn't anyone's fault. We got the reactor and a few bonuses. Let's focus on that, not what could have happened."

Okay, boss.

Working together, they managed to squeeze the missile platform's salvaged reactor into the *Stormshadow*'s hold, and they secured it firmly in place. Another hour after that, and to Mark's growing relief, they were burning steadily out of system and away from the exoplanet.

"Never again, bird."

You say that now, but you wait. You'll be begging to dangle yourself into the upper atmosphere of another rocky world in no time, Perry quipped.

"I'm with Mark on this one," Valint said. "A sandy beach and warm water sounds better."

"If we get through this, I'll take you there myself."

"Don't tease me," Valint said with a wink.

Due to the massive gas giants and the large system star, it took them almost a full day to burn into twist range. Mark and Perry took that time to inspect the case he found beneath the reactor.

"It isn't an AI," Perry concluded after a while. "But it does appear to be some kind of incredibly well shielded data device. I've never seen this build or configuration before."

Striker lent a hand, or four, as they worked to slowly dismantle the outer case. Once inside, they found a series of small, heavy data drives.

"Iridium cores," Perry said, his tone rich with disappointment. "They're high-density drives. Military command loves them, thanks to their ability to store immense amounts of data. Unfortunately, that much compression means the storage quality is relatively low. This particular unit appears to have been a backup. Knowing that, and its location, it's no wonder they forgot about it."

The bird linked the drives together, before jacking into them directly. It took him the better part of five minutes to index and begin decoding all the saved information.

"Boring, boring, and boring. This all appears to be transit tags from incoming vessels. This is only useful if we're smugglers, and we're not reduced to that just yet," he groused, eyes amber with disgust.

It went on like that for some time—long periods of quiet, with Perry occasionally lapsing into fits of grumbling. Striker moved off to prepare a meal, and Mark, wanting to give the bird some space, decided on a shower.

He had closed the door and moved to strip off his sweat-stained jumpsuit, when the bird yelled his name.

"Mark!"

He collided with Valint in the passage, and they sprawled together into the bulkhead.

"Sorry." He moved to push away, only to have her reach out and grab his forearm.

"Stop being sorry," she said as her caramel-colored eyes locked on his. Valint circled him with her long, elegant arms, and he returned the embrace, her skin soft and warm.

"Even if that means we're cast out by the Peacemakers? By the GKU?"

Valint's expression hardened again.

"If they condemn us for enforcing the letter of the law, then they're no longer the GKU I vowed to serve. Colonized space is a big place, with untold opportunities."

"We would leave this all behind? Together?"

"You left your old life, your home, behind. If I asked you to do that, why should I not be prepared to do the same?" she said, brow lifted in a question.

"That's different."

"Is it?"

Her question set him back, but it took him a moment to determine why. She'd found him on a muddy French battlefield after a fierce fight with Halvix, a galactic criminal. He'd been leaving behind war and strife, famine, and economic struggle. She had an illustrious position, respect, and authority, and yet would sacrifice it all…for him.

"I—" he started to say, but Perry interrupted.

"What are you two doing? Get over here. I said that I found something. Honest, boss. It's worth a look."

Valint's hands lingered for a moment after he released his grip, a fact that Mark noted, before turning to Perry.

"No, specifically, all you said was, 'Mark.' That was it."

"You were supposed to interpret that from my tone, obviously. I'm a master of nuance and, uh, nuance. So, if you will, on me?" Perry asked, beak open in a laugh.

They gathered around the bird, the extracted drives linked in a neat circle. It was a peculiar mixture of glossy black feathers and flashing lights.

Striker moved in behind them, a steaming platter clutched in one hand. It smelled strongly of spices, so Mark wondered if the combat unit hadn't prepared one of his famous curries. Of all Striker's fussy tendencies, cooking and the perpetual presence of hot tea were, to Mark, almost indispensable. With a gimlet eye at Perry, Mark stepped forward.

"Why the look, sourpuss?" Perry asked.

"Just thinking about your talents," Mark said, sending a meaningful look toward Striker's platter. "And lack thereof."

"Hmph," Perry countered, then adjusted the drives again as one of the units chirped—low power warning, but not concerning.

"What did you find?" Valint asked, crossing her arms over her chest. The warmth and tenderness Mark heard in her voice a moment before was gone.

"Collating all the data, I've come to several conclusions. Very few revelations compared to what we already knew about the missile platform and the base it was defending. We already knew they were researching banned chemical and biological weapons, but I was able to confirm it by analyzing and decoding the supply lists on their incoming transport ships."

"So, we know what they were cooking up there?" Mark asked.

"No, not specifically, and don't interrupt," Perry chastised. "The revelation isn't what they were doing there, but the *who* that was doing the *what*. Now this is truly something to see."

A comm video started to play on both pilots' overlays, the audio distorted and scratchy. At first, Mark only saw a dark screen, but several voices started talking. The audio was low at first, too soft for him to hear properly, but a moment later the recording improved.

"...too many cycles since — last report. Command is losing patience — your little — project. You're outside the acceptable window."

"Can you do anything about the quality? I'm struggling to hear any of the words," Mark said.

"Unfortunately, no. I believe that's interference from the nearby gas giant's radiation. The transmission was faulty, not the recording. And the data stamp indicates that this was a conversation between the base on the ground and a ship in orbit. It appears the Gyl were using the missile platform as a data relay station, as well. Just wait. It gets good."

The recording resumed, with the screen flickering, displaying brief flashes of light and what looked like a face.

"I do not answer to you — but my — directly from intelligence directorate. My project is tied to the — — — and is protected by — — rise of the supreme — to —."

"I do not have any knowledge of those orders, nor has the intelligence directorate received any — — about a project authorized — — at — facility. We were ordered to evacuate your team and — what we — to do."

Mark leaned in as the screen flickered and filled with static, then the signal strengthened, and a face appeared mid-sentence. He recognized the pale skin and dark eyes immediately, despite the apparent youth of Gyl-Mareth in the recording.

"I do not recognize your authority, nor do we acknowledge the purity of your faction. You are not true Gyl. We will continue our work here and see that the Gal-Ead's Solution is made real, that our people will finally realize their true, imperial nature. You are no better than Cai dogs. Rot in the underworld, for you will never see Gal-Ead's paradise."

Gyl-Mareth waved a hand at someone off camera. A chorus of startled, frightened voices rose, before they were once again swallowed by static.

"Did he fire on his own people?" Valint asked.

Perry nodded, the data cable automatically ejecting from his chest.

"It's all right here, the data transmissions proving a long-standing feud between Gyl factions, and the digital logs showing the launch of half a dozen missiles.

"What or whom is Gal-Ead?" Mark asked, letting his breath out slowly.

"A prophet of the early ages. His writings formed the foundations of their religion, well before their people fractured into the Gyl and Cai," Bunn explained.

"Great, so we're dealing with a religious and political extremist," Mark said.

"My analysis concludes that he views himself as a purist, which I believe is worse, but please, this doesn't require any guesswork. He declared his motivation out loud. Gyl-Mareth has imperial ambitions for his people, and with Cai-Demond now out of the way, he very well could achieve it."

"Wouldn't that require that he bring the Gyl and Cai together?" Mark asked.

"That's not likely," Bunn offered. "Analysis predicts that he would engage in systematic genocide first and then move forward with imperial expansion. As a people, they have been religiously persecuting one another for thousands of years."

Mark reached up and rubbed his face, closing his eyes. He tried to keep his thoughts and emotions from spiraling out of control, but struggled to rein them back in.

"What's the matter, Mark?" Valint asked,

"I can't get away from conflict. The war in France, where you found me, we were fighting against Imperial Germany. They weren't just waging a war against France and Russia but were making a push to become one of our world's superpowers."

"So, Gyl-Mareth desires an empire? But how? The Ixtan Cabal and the Eridani Federation would undoubtedly react quickly to suppress violent upheaval, especially from a group like the Gyl. If they tried to consolidate power and grow, everyone would notice," Valint offered.

"But would they know? He is obviously planning something, and very few people seem to be paying attention," Perry said.

Mark chuckled bitterly. "They're paying attention, all right. Only to us, now that they think *we* killed Cai-Demond and Blaz'Orkin."

"We're dropping out of twist space in five, four, three, two, and —" Bunn said, counting down to their arrival.

The *Stormshadow* shuddered as it emerged from its jump, and the twist drive spooled down with a noticeable wheeze. Striker and Valint both stiffened, their attention locked on the forward viewscreen.

Mark turned, following their gaze. With no significant gravity well, they had emerged from twist space only a few thousand meters out from the Bone Yard. Only the sprawling complex of docking hubs, cranes, and salvage barges was a smoldering ruin. A halo of shattered debris hung in space around the nucleus of devastation, the ring slowly expanding into space.

"What in the hell happened?" Mark breathed.

"Gunboats inbound. They're flagging us with targeting lasers," Bunn said. "I'm reading Eridani pulse beacons."

Valint jumped to the side, sliding effortlessly into her pilot's seat. The cockpit dimmed to tactical lighting and the bow thrusters fired, slowing their momentum.

"Unknown vessel, unknown vessel, this is Taj Rodanni of the EFS *Grantham*. Eridani Federation borders are currently closed. Power down your drive and prepare to be boarded."

"Boarded?" Mark asked.

"Not going to happen," Valint whispered and cleared her throat. She glanced his way for a moment, the look conveying more emotion than he ever thought possible—resilience, determination, and more than a little fight. She straightened her uniform and opened the video comm, then her entire demeanor changed.

"EFS *Grantham* this is Peacemaker Valint Damascine of the GKU *Stormshadow*. We twisted into system looking for repair and aid for a damaged Guild gunboat. Please resend your last transmission, it came over garbled." She clicked off the transmit button, eyebrow lifted into a subtle smirk.

Mark understood her play. Valint had not so subtly reminded the Eridani Captain that he was confronting a Guild ship, and there were certain protocols that were never abandoned. First and foremost, no one outside the Guild could demand entry into a Peacemaker's vessel. And by hinting that his transmission came in garbled, Valint was giving him the opportunity to backtrack from his previous stance.

The comms remained quiet for a long moment while the Eridani Captain disappeared offscreen. When he returned, more than a little of the fire was gone from his eyes.

"Apologies, Peacemaker Valint. We must have misread your transponder there for a moment. We also see that you're towing another vessel. I'm sorry to tell you this, but this facility suffered a heinous, unprovoked attack. Eridani forces are still securing the area, but at this point, we're confident that none survived. Again, if you're here for repairs, the facility was destroyed."

Perry muttered something Mark couldn't quite hear, but Valint ignored him.

"How can the Guild help?" she asked.

"At this point, the Federation has the situation under control."

Another officer appeared behind Captain Rodanni, then bent

over and whispered into his ear. He nodded, muttered something in return, and nodded yet again before addressing them in a professional tone.

"Perhaps there's a way the Guild could help us. Communication out here on the edge of the frontier is spotty, so it will be some time before information can be properly relayed back to military command. There were almost two dozen businesses and organizations active on the Bone Yard and next-of-kin notifications must be made. The Guild could be of service by making these contacts. It would allow Federation forces to commit themselves to this ongoing investigation. Do you accept this contract?"

Valint turned toward Mark, her eyes asking the question. He nodded, understanding the truth of their situation. Saying no would only elicit more questions, and they weren't in a position to answer any of them.

"I accept, Captain Rodanni. Please transmit any and all information you have about those operating on the station—and the Guild will do the rest."

"Of course, Peacemaker. Thank you for your assistance. You can assure anyone you contact that the Eridani Federation will approach them at some point—hopefully with answers."

Valint nodded but didn't respond.

"Oh, and one more thing. Take caution when transiting out of Federation space. Signs indicate that this attack was perpetuated by a Cabal battlegroup. There's no telling how far they jumped away, so be forewarned. If they see you leaving our space, they may attack."

"We will. Thank you again, Captain."

She turned in the seat and looked to Striker.

"An Ixtan Cabal battlegroup attacking inside the Eridani Federation border?" the combat unit asked, folding several sets of arms over his metal chest. "That's a bold move, even for the Cabal."

"The Federation has a long-running trade feud with the Ixtan Cabal, but to openly attack a facility inside their border? Well, that would be the spark to ignite immediate warfare."

"Fulcrum was openly attacked, and now a salvage yard on the edge of Eridani Federation space is destroyed. Why do I get the feeling the same mercenary is responsible for both?"

"But why the Bone Yard?" Valint asked.

"She said she attacked Fulcrum because they possessed something that belonged to her. Perhaps it's the same," Mark proposed.

"Or, she is Gyl-Mareth's puppet, as we originally suspected," Striker interjected. "The Prime Regent of the Tau Ceti Merchant's Council is Ixtan. An attack on Fulcrum, the region's commerce hub, would threaten Fulcrum sovereignty, but more specifically the financial well-being of the entire system. And if I know the merchant families, they *will* demand action. What if he is using Glass to incite a war between the Federation and Cabal?"

"Then what? He steps in as the voice of calm and reason? He mediates peace, but to what end? And what is his connection to the Synth drug runners and why funnel military assets around behind the scenes? I think we're starting to understand his goals, even if we can't see the bigger picture yet. There are still too many unanswered questions."

"I think you're right, Mark," Perry said, clicking his beak. "My hunch is that Gyl-Mareth's ambitions are bigger than simply becoming the harbinger of peace. A cynical, bitter part of me believes that he wants to see colonized space tear itself apart with war, so he can rule over the ashes. And I hate that thought with every feather of my being."

"The Guild would never stand for that," Striker declared.

Valint shook her head slowly. "No. If he played his hand right, the Guild would help him do it."

24

"The chop shop, I mean salvage yard, Ja-Ra recommended gets blown up by a crazy, heavily armed mercenary, so your answer is to find another?" Perry asked. "I suppose the logic is there, even though I hate it. A lot."

"Do you have a better idea?" Mark asked.

"No." The bird kicked the deck then started to angrily pace. "So, let's go."

"The route to Spacer's Gold Salvage and Lost Treasures is complete and programmed into the twist drive. Should I initiate?" Bunn asked.

"Do it," Valint said.

They were barely an hour into their four-hour twist when Bunn pinged Mark in the galley.

"Mark, you have received an encrypted message via a maintenance server. It's from Armagost."

"Can you send it to my data slate?"

"Done."

Perry crowded in next to him as a popup appeared on the screen. Once selected, a simple text-only file opened. There were no names, only a vague message posted to a feed seemingly dedicated to anglers and fisherman.

```
[To: The fisherman. Your delivery is working
out well. Good job. We have finished your
custom order net, and it can be picked up
any time. Also, I looked into the item your
friend dropped off. It was badly damaged,
but I was able to salvage a small part from
it. An image of it is embedded in this
message. Your friend, Aves, should recognize
it. Thanks again, and happy fishing.]
```

"Who is Aves?"

"It isn't a who, but a *what*, and that *what* is me," Perry explained. "Aves is the family of warm-blooded vertebrates after which I was modeled. It's also the root of my basic form—Avian."

"Okay, bird, what is it? What did he find?"

"Patience, *Homo Sapiens*. Even quantum beings require time in which to work."

"Did you just admit to having limitations?" Mark asked.

"Shush."

Perry swiped the message off the screen.

"Okay. I have the file. It's…well, that's clever."

"What is?"

"In order to protect the nature of what he sent, Armagost

dissected the file and cleverly concealed it in the code for an image of what I believe is an Earth fishing apparatus. What do you call it?"

"A fishing pole," Mark offered.

"Yes. Well, anyway, it's a cipher, and I believe that our Gajur friend provided us the key. First, I'll try 'Aves.'"

Perry worked for a moment, his frame going rigid.

"No, that's not it. Perhaps it's 'vertebrates.' Hmmm. Not that, either."

Mark read back through the message for a moment. It was how Armagost signed off that caught his attention: "happy fishing."

"Try 'fisherman.'"

"Done and—" the bird said, perking up. "There it is." He flicked a wing toward the data slate, and a file slid onto the screen.

Mark tapped it open to read, but it wasn't written in any language he'd ever seen before. In fact, it looked more like a serial ID number—one long and continuous run of letters and numbers.

"What is it?"

"A digital tag," Perry explained. "Essentially a quantum signature. If you break down the code of anything enough, you'll find these tags. It essentially shows who created it, the platform it was written on, and when."

"Like a fingerprint?"

"Actually, yes. That's well put."

Valint drifted into the galley and stood behind Mark, then leaned in to read what was on his screen.

"What if we could cross-reference digital tags on the kill order, as well as the data you pulled off of Babar Malta's console?"

"I'm way ahead of you, Mark. My algorithm has been scanning for three seconds now."

"What did you find?" Valint asked.

Mark shifted in his seat to answer, but Perry spoke first.

"And—done. Eureka. Gyl-Mareth, you naughty boy. The same digital fingerprint pulled from the Synth drug runner ship is present on the backup storage unit we pulled from that missile platform. Although, it's not on the kill order."

"So, we can now prove the connection between a corrupt, murderous Guild Master, a band of criminals, Synth-abusing drug runners, and an abandoned Gyl biological weapons base. Why do I not like the sound of that?" Mark said.

"But what *is* on those boats?" Valint asked. "A connection is a good place to start, but legally speaking, it's pretty thin."

"Whatever it is, we handed our only evidence over to the Guild. This irritates me. I'm truly vexed," Perry groused.

"It's like Armagost said in his message. It's time to go fishing. Or, in our case, hunting."

They twisted into Crossroads to a flurry of activity. The *Stormshadow*, now the EFS *Moonraker*, was pushed to the end of the docking list and they were forced to wait almost two full hours for a spot.

"We never had to wait this long when people knew we were Peacemakers," Mark said, idly drumming his fingers. "Don't like this new direction, to be honest. I'm not one to use my badge for comforts, but—"

"You're not, and that's part of the issue. This kind of insult isn't going to fly with us. With the Guild. And with me," Perry said.

"Makes you mad, eh?"

"A touch. But now we know how the other half lives," Perry said, waving with one wing.

The docking traffic master sent them around to the far under-side of the sprawling complex, where they were guided into the Spacer's Gold warehouse facility. A series of skeletal, mechanical arms latched onto the *Fafnir* and hefted it free once they were inside. Liberated from its burden, the *Moonraker* turned slowly and settled into a docking space.

"I feel ridiculous," Valint said, pulling uncomfortably at the neck of her borrowed clothing. Like Mark, she'd replaced her Peace-maker uniform with relatively nondescript clothes. Although, whereas Mark looked like the plucky character off a science fiction pulp cover, Valint looked ready for a safari—with tight-fitting tan trousers, a black top, and an armored tactical vest.

"You'll get used to it."

"Interesting fashion choice," Perry observed.

"Silence, bird. Your tone indicates trouble, and nothing more," Mark said.

Perry laughed. "Informing Valint that she resembles your version of a *Princess of Mars* is hardly *trouble*. I prefer the term informative."

Valint stiffened. "If that princess is some galactic space hussy, then I will—"

"Not a hussy. A, um, adventurer," Mark said, his face creased into a winning smile.

"Hmph," Valint allowed, tugging at her neck again.

They exited the ship and made their way down the ramp as a Spacer's Gold representative moved toward them. The Synth was tall, with mismatching green and blue arms. He wore a blue vest, covered on the left side with buttons and colorful ribbons.

"Hello, friends! Welcome to Spacer's Gold Salvage and Lost

Treasures, where we turn space junk into platinum. Even the most discerning and sophisticated spacefaring folk find what they need here, so fear not. If you need help, I'm your bot."

"Wow," Mark said. "That's quite the introduction."

"Why thank you."

Valint gave the Synth an economical nod.

"We have not met before, as I do not seem to have any retinal or facial geometry scans saved in my data storage. Allow me to make an introduction. My name is Badge, and I am a full-time, commission-based sales representative. How may I assist you today?"

"Badge?"

"Yes, indeed. I chose the name myself. Do you like it?" The Synth approximated a smile, but its eyes didn't move. They remained locked straight ahead.

"It's wonderful," Valint said. "Really inspires a sense of warmth and camaraderie."

"Thank you. As you can see, I have covered my smock with an assortment of badges, tags, patches, and pins. That's how I chose my name. I particularly like how they shine and glitter in the light. But that is enough about me. I couldn't help but notice that you towed in some *salvage* today. Is that *correct?*"

Mark nodded but paused. It wasn't just the Synth's eyes that felt off, but also the strange manner in which it spoke. He struggled with the idea that it wasn't a sapient being but was being remotely controlled.

"Actually, no, my good man. My name is Barrow, and this is my associate, Parker," Mark said, pointing at Valint. "This is the EFS *Swallow*, otherwise known as my home. We've had so many good runs and scrapes together, so many first and fond memories. I can't bear the thought of seeing her torn down for scrap. But, alas, our last run ended badly. We ran afoul of raiders past the outer rings of Sirius. Only a desperate twist saved us, but we were too deep into the well, and our twist drive and reactor took the brunt."

"So, you're looking for *repair* services, then?"

"That's the ticket. We even scavenged a replacement reactor. Heard you all were the best in the systems at fast and accurate retrofits. All you would have to do is pull out the old one and slide the new one in."

"Our facility is of course outfitted with *state-of-the-art* repair and *fabrication* machines. But such a retrofit would require *considerable* time and *energy.*"

"We would also need a new twist drive, to replace the one we melted to scrap. And not something small and rattly, like those cheap Trinox models. Parker and I do business all over the systems and time is money. A big, throaty drive with lots of thrust is exactly what I need."

"Oh, *drives* and *thrusters* we have, sir, but those are quite expensive, especially if you want power and quality! A recent arrival might be of interest—an FJ475 Powerthrust drive. The best money can buy, made by the Hu'warde. Very fast. Very quiet."

Mark saw Valint flinch out of the corner of his eye. Either the drive was good, or bad. He could only hope that she would intervene if it was the latter.

"I'll take it. Only the best for the *Swallow.*"

"Wonderful. Of course. Now the issue of our backlog. We could get to you in *three*, maybe *four* weeks. A job of that size will take some time, as well, so you should plan on an interval of three weeks from start to finish. And if I may, we require that jobs of that size be paid in full before we commit to the schedule. You understand, I trust, as the liability is all ours."

His ear bug struggled through a number of the Synth's words, especially "weeks" and he wondered why. If someone was controlling the Synth remotely, were they speaking another language?

Several emotions hit him at once—surprise, disappointment, and then anger. He took a step back, sucked in a cleansing breath, and considered how his feathered counterpart might respond. Perry wouldn't get frustrated—although he might let some sarcasm or snark fly. No, Perry would use logic to determine the best path forward. He would find out what Badge wanted and use that knowledge to come to a more agreeable outcome.

"You do have a pleasant facility," he said, glancing around and buying himself more time. Then he considered his first impression of the Synth. If Badge truly was a remote-controlled front, that meant there was someone sitting behind a monitor somewhere. Unlike Synths, flesh and blood beings all had wants and needs, vices, and urges.

"Your terms are agreeable, except for the delay. Parker and I run a tight ship and provide vital services for an array of busy clients. The *Swallow* is a big part of that business, so I think you'll understand why we can't afford to have *her* out of service for a long period of time. I'll make you this deal. Twelve thousand bonds down to get my ship in right away and I'll pay you the rest when the work is done…in platinum bars."

Badge's eyes finally moved, betraying whatever being was controlling him. And Mark had the feeling that if the Synth could smile, it would. Bonds required electronic transfer and were subject to taxation and regulation, whereas platinum was physical, and if handled properly, untraceable.

"I like how you do business. One hundred platinum bars, and you have a deal." A decided accent punctuated the Synth's voice now, faintly reminiscent of the men Mark served with from New York and Jersey.

"One hundred? I could buy a whole new ship for that," Mark laughed. "Let's stay reasonable. Thirty-five is great value."

Mark, need I remind you that we only deposited fifty-five bars into our new Quiet Room safety deposit box, Perry said via ear bug.

"I'm aware," Mark said as the Synth reached up and ran a hand across the top of its head, as if smoothing back hair. And yet, it had none.

"A reactor retrofit *will* take all of my service bots several days, and that doesn't include the new feed lines and reaction mass. Thirty-five platinum bars wouldn't even cover materials and energy expended. Now, ninety platinum would cover it all, although barely."

Mark looked sideways at Valint, who seemed to be studying the Synth's mannerisms too. He almost turned to cover his mouth to try and communicate with Netty, before realizing that she wasn't there.

"I like that you're a reasonable businessman, Badge. That makes me like you already. Parker here, too. So, I'll tell you what, we'll bump the original offer. To be generous, we'll go to forty-five platinum, and I'll throw in a good word with my employer. He is extensively networked all over the Federation and is always looking for trust-worthy repair shops and parts suppliers. His word could go a long way to winning you a sustainable business channel in the future."

The Synth nodded, its hands fidgeting at its side. This is what some merchants lived for—the art of the haggle. Badge seemed to think for a moment, perhaps adding up material expenses and labor.

"Forty-five would make this a loss. We'd have to be over fifty to squeak into profit territory, and that's bad for business. So very bad. I'll give you a special deal. Eighty platinum would guarantee the job done fast and done right. I give my word."

The accent was so much thicker now, to the point Mark was sure it was northeast United States. But how?

"Quality is important, especially considering the importance of a drive and reactor. We can't afford to find ourselves on the float out there in the black," he reasoned, then took a step back. He half-turned toward the *Moonraker*, as if considering leaving. Valint met his eyes and he mouthed "bonds, how high can you go?" She simply nodded.

"We can't spend all of our liquid currency, or we'll have no money in which to buy fuel for the coming weeks. Why don't we do this. Thirty thousand bonds down and forty-five platinum bars are yours when the job is completed. That should safely put you into a tidy profit and will get us the repairs we so desperately need. How does that sound?"

Mark, the current market payout on platinum is one thousand bonds per ounce. You offered him four hundred and fifty thousand bonds worth of platinum, Perry said over the ear bug.

"I know," he whispered, as Badge tapped his fingers against his chest.

"Bonds are tricky. There are taxes, transfer and brokerage fees, conversion loss," the Synth said, but Mark cut him off with a wave.

Mark was still learning the currency conversion rates but knew enough to understand that even with digital conversion and transfers, the real prize was platinum, as ounce for ounce, it had far more value to a mid-level salvage dealer like Spacer's Gold. The bonds were simply to keep him at the negotiation table long enough to strike a deal.

"We came here because we heard you did the best work and charged an honest rate. But it's a lot of platinum. Perhaps I should consider investing my money in a new ship. Trei-Seti has an impound auction coming up. Maybe I could land something that would work there. Parker, what do you say we head that way? We could always salvage our laser and missile systems for the new bird."

"I like this plan. Trei-Seti has one of my favorite dumpling stands. That spicy fishbowl is unequaled," she said and turned to walk away. "Can taste those peppers now. Double serving?"

"Of course, dear. Let's splurge a bit," Mark said, laughing as he followed her. "We can always buy noodles with platinum."

He made it a dozen steps before an awkward hand tapped his shoulder. He turned to find the Synth standing in his shadow, its frame humming with excitement and suppressed emotion.

"Friend. You don't need to leave. Hear me out. Make it fifty-five platinum, and the deal is done. But that has to be my final offer," Badge whispered.

"Fifty-five?" Mark asked, pretending to mull the offer over. He turned and looked to Valint, but she simply gave him a half-hearted shrug.

"You have a deal," Mark said, shaking the Synth's hand.

"I trust you can keep the nature of our arrangement confidential?" the Synth asked, before letting go. "If word gets out that I'm

agreeable to such steep discounts for complicated services, well…
you know. My integrity and all."

"We simply came to you and received quality services at a fair
price," Mark said, nodding.

"You know what? I like you already," Badge said with a metallic
chuckle. "Let's get to work. Point me in the direction of your
replacement reactor and we will get started."

They opened the *Moonraker's* hold, allowing the Spacer's Gold
mechanized bots room to heft and offload the salvaged reactor. Bunn
arranged the bond transfer, after quietly shifting funds around through
several shell accounts. It was startling how quickly the AIs could
arrange, organize, and create within the digital universe. It also brought
into question how much money Valint possessed. Mark realized that
he'd cornered her in a position to help pay for his ship's repairs.

By the time they were done paying the Synth his retainer, the
Fafnir was already up on drydock stands and covered with maintenance bots. A large machine cut the aft maintenance paneling free,
effectively opening a hole into the engine room. The whole space
started to smell like melted wiring and burned metal.

"You were *not* joking. It smells crispy," Badge said, despite his
apparent lack of a nose.

"It was on fire for a while," Valint said, simply.

"Are you two staying in Crossroads while the work is done?
Perhaps…tossing around a little more of that platinum?" Badge
asked, his accent returning. "I mean, I'm not saying that I also own
a stake in the Palace. But it's clean, has good booze, and if you two
are so inclined, runs some of the best card action outside of Dregs."

"I wish we could, but unfortunately we have urgent business to attend to," Mark said. "We'll twist out for that and come straight back for the *Swallow*. With your platinum, of course."

"Oh, yes. We mustn't forget that."

"How long to complete the retrofit?"

"Ehhh, my workers are very efficient," Badge said, turning to watch his army of bots and crawlers. "I would say twenty-four hours, but they likely will not take that long. It's easier when your workers don't have to eat or sleep and can carry fifty times their body weight. The fire damage will slow them down and take a bit longer to fix. Give us three days, and your ship will be better than new."

"Good. That's perfect," Mark said.

By the time they were done talking to Badge, the army of mechanized workers had extricated the *Fafnir*'s old twist drive and deposited the ruined piece of machinery off to the side. Once removed from the ship, Mark got a more honest impression of not only the damage inflicted by their desperate twist, but also how undersized it was.

The reactor looked even smaller once it was lifted free and set next to the new module. It stood barely half the height and diameter of the power plant they'd lifted from the missile platform.

"I hope this works," he whispered to Valint.

"It will. Because it has to." She held her data slate, scowling at the refuel receipt from the *Stormshadow*.

Mark crawled back into the *Fafnir* before they left and retrieved his BAR, revolver, and Moonsword, then made one last stop in the cockpit. Valint met him at the bottom of the ramp and didn't question why he was carrying Netty's case. She seemed to understand his need, no, the compulsion not to leave anyone behind, and Netty had quickly become family.

He plugged Netty into an auxiliary power port in the *Moonraker's* cockpit, and the AI woke up as they were burning away from Crossroads.

"Okay. I have a considerable time loss, am not hardwired into the *Fafnir* anymore, and believe that is Bunn next to me. Hi, Bunn."

"Hello, Netty. Welcome aboard," Bunn said.

"Mark, we're all still here, so I take it that our life-and-death twist to safety succeeded. At least in part?"

"In part is right. The *Fafnir's* drive and reactor were damaged beyond repair, so we twisted out to the missile platform Ja-Ra told us about. We salvaged the reactor, almost burned up in the atmosphere, then twisted to Shipbreaker's yard to get the ship fixed and found that Glass beat us there."

"She destroyed the Bone Yard?"

"I'm sure she would have fused it to glass had there been atmosphere to accommodate the heat," Valint confirmed.

Netty whistled. "So, where did you take *my* ship?"

It wasn't the question but rather how she asked it that set Mark back. He'd never heard her reference the *Fafnir* as hers before.

"Spacer's Gold. They're going to retrofit the—"

"You took it where?" Netty shouted.

25

"IT WASN'T EVEN in my top five options, either, Netty, but it was… the least worst of our available choices," Perry said, stepping in. "Trust me, Mark didn't make that call lightly. It doesn't help that we're being hunted."

"We'll be lucky if that place doesn't strip the whole ship down for scrap while you're gone."

"We gave him fifty-five incentives to do the job, and do it well," Mark said, interjecting.

"I'm guessing this incentive has an atomic weight of one hundred and ninety-five point zero eight four?"

"If that's platinum, then yes."

"Okay. I was just starting to feel at home in the *Fafnir*, so, you know."

"Valint, I hate to interrupt, but we're receiving a strange transmission from Anvil Dark. It's being broadcast on all frequencies," Netty said.

"All of them? Is there a carrier wave? Can they track who sees it?"

"No."

"Put it on the screens," Valint said as Mark slid into the seat next to her.

A rendered image of the Galactic Knights Uniformed insignia popped up. It spun twice before switching over to the live feed of a podium. Gyl-Mareth walked in from the side, the lights somehow softening the stark contrast of his light skin and dark eyes. When he lifted his face, Mark thought he almost looked sympathetic.

"As many of you have heard, a terrorist faction has struck the heart of the GKU. In a cowardly attack, a host of separatist gunboats attacked an unarmed Guild facility on Mesaribe. Hundreds of selfless civil servants were killed instantly, along with two Guild Masters. This was a diabolical, cold-blooded, and premeditated attack. But it does not stand alone. Despite our tireless Peacemakers, these terrorists have also struck in a subsequent rash of unprovoked and deadly attacks on Chevix Station, Spindrift, Vault, and several other unsuspecting communities."

Gyl-Mareth paused, rubbing his eyes and seemingly having to compose himself.

"He's really playing this up," Valint said.

"The Guild is working in concert with enforcement agencies in the Tau system, Epsilon, and several others to bring peace back to the galaxies. But it must be said. The Guild needs the help of our colonized systems more than ever. Beyond the apprehension orders populated by the GKU, I'm issuing a public bounty on the organizers of this terrorist cell."

Pictures popped up on screen, Peacemaker identification photos for Mark, Valint, and Drogo.

"Do I not rate a picture?" Perry complained.

"The Guild is hereby authorizing a bounty of one million bonds each for the apprehension of these criminals. They should be considered heavily armed and dangerous. I do not say this lightly, but authorized agencies should shoot on sight. And with that, I must come back to my earlier statement. The GKU mourns its fallen heroes, and although there will come a time for grief and remembrance, first we must pick up our sword, shield, and badge, and fight the righteous battle. With three empty Masters' seats now, the Galactic Knights Uniformed is crippled. As such, and as granted to me by the Peacemaker Charter, I hereby freeze all Guild conclaves until the resolution of these hostilities. And with that done, I, Gyl-Mareth, Guild Master, do declare that we're now in a state of war. The Master's Council has ceded full martial and legal governance to me, that I might bring colonized space back under control."

"Oh, shit," Mark cursed, as the reality of their new situation sank in. Gyl-Mareth didn't just put a bullseye on their backs, but he'd succeeded in subverting the Guild's power structure, as well.

"I assume this mantle of authority reluctantly, but it's one I take for the good of all peoples. You may be assured that I'll temper justice with mercy and meet villainy with unrestrained prejudice. My new Guild will not rest until a lasting peace can be found and sustained. To that end, I have sacrificed enormous personal wealth to ensure the immediate return of safety and prosperity across the known systems. Take solace that the Association for Peaceful Skies is here to safeguard your future. When you see their formidable battleships and light blue uniforms, rejoice, because they're here for you.

This is your deliverance, your army of justice, set to usher us into a more unified future. Salute triumph!"

The corrupt Master went rigid, his hand snapping to his chest in salute, right before the GKU screen flashed in, replacing the transmission.

"He will *never* give power back to the other Masters," Valint said, turning in her chair.

"I know," Mark said, slumping. "I think we just witnessed the birth of a tyrant."

"They're quite adorable at that age, aren't they?" Perry asked. "With the shouting, rigid saluting, and the quiet, underlying threats of chemical or biological genocide."

"You two…" Netty sighed.

"What?" Perry asked, innocently. "Humor is how Mark and I deal with trauma."

"Is that true?" Bunn asked.

"Maybe. Don't judge," Mark said, waving his hands. "Did we just watch what I think we watched? Did he call us out as public enemies?"

"Public enemies?" Valint chuckled, bitterly, "No. He bumped us to the head of the Galactic Most Wanted list."

"If we thought life was hard before, the heat is about to go up," Perry said.

"Then we do something about it," Mark said, standing up. He paced forward to the viewscreen and turned around. "At this point, all Gyl-Mareth *has* is ambitions. He hasn't facilitated war between the superpowers yet, nor has he sprung whatever chemical or biological trap he has planned. There has been no consolidation of power and hell, he hasn't even broken his people out of the stifling treaties holding them back. So, he isn't an Emperor, yet. But if we wait, then we won't be fighting one corrupt man but an army of believers."

"We tear the lid off his plan. The drug runners and fast boats. That, along with Perry's digital evidence, should be enough to turn people against him. We could topple his little empire before it ever rises," Valint said.

"Exactly," Mark said, shaking his fist. "And in the end, we provide a little justice for Blaz'Orkin and the Guild workers on Mesaribe, the innocents that died in Noka's fuel skimming scheme. We provide a little justice for Rustala and Raxxon."

Perry flinched, his eyes burning a little brighter at the mention of their fallen friends.

"We're going to nail this corrupt bastard right to the wall," the bird said.

They twisted a complicated zigzag, with Armagost's refuge being the final destination. The area was clear when they arrived, but that fact gave Mark little solace. There wouldn't be any easy transits anymore. There would only be conflict.

The *Moonraker* descended into their Gajur ally's hidden valley, the fit so tight they almost lost two antennae on the way. The wider gunboat settled onto the landing pad ten minutes later, the belly thrusters glowing from the effort.

Tan Tu'Tu met them at the end of the ramp, the young Druzis practically jumping up in the air and clapping his hands.

"We did it. I think," he said, clapping his hands again. There seemed to be no rhythm to his cadence, however, and he stopped. "I think we did it. Yes. I think."

"Don't quit your day job," Perry muttered, walking up next to him on the ramp. "And yes, by that I mean he shouldn't be holding his breath for any percussion invites to touring jazz ensembles."

"Be nice," Mark whispered. "He can do things with circuitry that I couldn't dream of matching."

"Yes, yet you could probably drum out a respectable beat to *The Charleston* right here and now."

"'Charleston'—what's that?" Mark asked as they approached Tan. Armagost appeared from the tunnel to his habitat, a noticeable weariness pulling at the old Gajur's features.

"I keep forgetting that you've been floating in space for the past seven years. *Charleston* is a jazz tune that is sweeping your home country by storm. Remind me to play it for you later."

"Deal."

"…that was when I started asking a whole new series of questions. First, could we modulate the frequency in a manner that prohibited a learning scan-base from adapting? Say, increase modulation to an unheard-of cyclical rate? Armagost said, 'Well, let's answer that question and see what new questions it elicits.' So, I said, 'Okay, let's do it.' And we did," Tan said, gesticulating as he spoke to Valint and Striker. The old Gajur stood back a few feet, his arms crossed over his chest.

After skirting around the hyperactive Druzis, Mark moved up to Armagost.

"Success, but at what cost?"

The Gajur chuckled and blinked slowly. "Namely, sleep. I have never seen a being so singularly driven, while also unable to wind down. After our first two designs failed testing, he refused to leave the lab for almost two days straight. He is brilliant and exhausting."

"Everything you requested," Mark whispered, "with a bit more energy than we bargained for, perhaps."

Armagost shrugged. "He is better company than a frozen Ligurite."

"A bowl of mealworms would be better company than that greasy slug," Perry chided.

"And these mealworms, whatever they are, are suddenly offended," Armagost laughed.

"As they should be," Perry agreed.

They finally managed to wrestle Tan away from Valint and Striker, who was trying to give them a capacitor-by-capacitor breakdown of the final circuit board's composition and flow. Striker looked genuinely interested, but Valint's eyes had gone glassy and unfocused.

Mark pulled Armagost off to the side as they reached his lab.

"You're going to ask me about the transmission from the GKU, am I right?"

"I'm that obvious?"

"No fruit bears more potent poison than the cry of the 'Greater Good'. Leaders have committed the most heinous crimes throughout the light-years, all to justify their supposedly honorable ends."

"Gyl-Mareth's ends justify his means," Mark whispered.

"Exactly. They won't like his means nor his ends, for that matter. But people stray from reason when afraid, and there's no quicker path to fear than to threaten the established order. Trust me, I was an intelligence man, it's what we did. Start by killing a leader, then use media to destabilize the structure, and finally, unite the rabble against a common enemy. It's disgusting how effective that methodology is."

"So, step one is done. The Guild is in turmoil. Two Masters are dead, and a number of its agents have gone rogue. Was his transmission step two?"

Armagost shook his head. "No. His declaration helped to seat the fear in all peoples but was also a cleverly played card. He marked you lot as the common enemy early, so resentment can build. He likely has something profound planned to destabilize social order, a massive attack, a calamity, or as we would have done, start a proxy war."

"Glass," Mark said. "That's his play."

"War wouldn't only interrupt transit lanes and commerce, but it would break the bonds of alliances and sow distrust," Valint reasoned.

"As war often does," Armagost said. "This transmission was a hallmark moment. And yet, its true meaning will have gone unnoticed by the masses, a beginning and an end, all wrapped together. And if no one stands up or acts, they'll wake up one day and wonder how they ever came to live under such oppression."

"My world was embroiled in war over a similar declaration. That battlefield was where Valint saved me those years ago. Luckily, the bird and I have a plan."

Armagost brightened, a bit of the weariness lifting away.

"Well, the foundations of a plan, anyway."

Mark detailed the digital signature they found on the drug runner ships, and how it matched the data storage drive embedded in the missile platform above the Gyl bio-weapons base. The Gajur's weariness returned the deeper into the story he went, until the aged alien was nearly swaying on his feet.

"I don't need to tell you how nefarious this sounds. A secret biochemical laboratory, operated by a group trapped in a racial civil war, connected to a leader with imperial aspirations—one willing to kill his own people, manipulate wars between galactic superpowers, and—"

"Used fast boats run by slaved Synths to distribute biological weapons masquerading as narcotics," Mark finished for him. "In secret, of course."

Armagost nodded. "You captured one of those ships, correct? What information were you able to discern? Could you identify the means of delivery for this new 'drug'?"

Perry ruffled his feathers. "Some form of mask or breathing apparatus. My guess is that it's delivered in an atomized or vapor form and inhaled. For those that have lungs, that is."

"Did it list anything on the delivery device? Anything useful—a chemical breakdown, trade name, designation?"

Mark thought for a moment, but it was Perry's digital memory that made the connection first.

"Cavu Lixl. Based on its flower-based imagery, I'd originally guessed it was a hallucinatory drug in nature. But now…"

"Perhaps the answer *is* in the name, but not as you see it." Armagost made his way over to one of the drafting tables. He swept away a scattered pile of components and let them clatter to the ground.

Mark followed, his sense of unease growing. Some elements of their predicament troubled the meticulous old Gajur so much that he would willingly defile his own space. And for someone as neat and tidy as him, that was a bit frightening.

"I may have copied our entire threat database when I walked away from the service all those years ago," he said as a folder opened up on his holographic projection. "Our defense director defined too many projects as *defense only*, and yet as time went on, I got the impression that they had other purposes. So, as a counter-measure, I took the information with me."

"I imagine Gajur Military Authority wouldn't like that," Perry offered.

Armagost simply chuckled as a window popped up in which he typed [`Cavu Lixl`]. The terminal immediately went to work, with a flood of remixed variations of the letters appearing below.

"You think the name is an anagram?" the bird asked.

"As unintelligent as it may sound, yes. It's where I normally started my investigations, at least. As we discovered, scientists are a relatively uninspired lot when it comes to naming their creations."

After a few minutes, they had a list of over 500 alternatives.

"Now I'll cull the list by cross-referencing our variations against the compiled database of known chemical and biological threats. This likely won't produce any hits, but it will help check off a few—"

A second window popped up as the terminal started crossing off options. But before the Gajur could even finish speaking, a single word jumped off the screen, its letter bracketed by a flashing box.

[`Vacillux`]

"Vacillux?" Mark said, reading the word.

"Shit," Perry cursed.

"What is it?"

"It is…not good," Armagost whispered, reaching up to rub his bulbous eyes. He closed the window, only to pull up two more. The first was a map, while the second showed two unique triple helices. Within a few seconds, red dots formed on the map. It spread quickly, while a timer ticked by above. By thirty-six hours, the continent had hundreds of red dots. By forty-eight hours, there were thousands, with some already popping up on the land masses separated by water and mountains.

"This was Gajur project 'Unite.' But don't let the cheery name fool you. It's the predicted spread of a hypothetical weaponized version of a normally benign medical agent Ixtan scientists named 'Vacillux.'"

"A medical agent?" Mark asked. "How is it dangerous?"

Armagost shook his head. "Not *dangerous*, Mark. *Life-ending*. It is, as one of our scientists defined, the 'anti-life' molecule. Using a targeting isotope, scientists could use the Vacillux molecule to break individual links in complicated strands of DNA."

"It breaks down DNA?"

"Yes. And it was incredibly beneficial for certain medical procedures. To say, remove or repair genetic dysfunction or hereditary disease. Unfortunately, the powers that be quickly discovered its potential as a weapon. All they had to do was remove the targeting isotope, and Vacillux would break down any and all chains. It essentially could deconstruct a living organism from the inside out."

Mark shuddered, his mind racing through the potential ramifications of such a weapon. To be rendered down by a biological agent at the cellular level, well, that was light-years beyond the mustard gas in his nightmares. Horrific couldn't begin to describe it.

"Vacillux is incredibly unstable. It would need to be. Oh, crap," Perry started to say, before going quiet for a moment. "Armagost, play this file." He flicked a wing toward the drafting table, where an icon appeared.

The Gajur selected the file, and a video playback started to run. Mark immediately got the impression that it was from Perry's perspective. He saw his own face and the dark interior of the drug runner's ship, then the view turned to the crate of inhalers. Mark's hand appeared in the frame, picked up one of the devices, and lifted it free.

"Pause it…now."

Armagost obliged, the capture freezing as Mark turned the device over, revealing two small gas cylinders.

"Your thoughts, Mr. Bird."

"In order to make Vacillux stable, it would need to be broken down into two base components. If combined during inhalation, and in the presence of biological matter, the molecule wouldn't just become airborne; it would gain atomic stability."

"Airborne? Meaning what, Perry?" Valint asked. "That people could pass it on to others?"

Armagost dropped his head as Perry nodded. "By bodily fluid or respiration. Yes."

"A most *vile* weapon," Striker said, finally speaking up. "Even with an atmospheric half-life of days, such a weapon could kill off an entire densely populated area in very little time."

"It's far worse than that, I'm afraid," Armagost said without looking up. "As predicted in our models, if weaponized properly, Vacillux could scour a *planet* of all life in weeks."

"There has to be some way to fight it. A counteragent?" Mark said.

"Time and distance are our only counteragent, and they're no remedy for those infected. Then again, there's always heat. Like most organic agents, Vacillux is sensitive to higher temperatures. Fire *will* kill it."

"High-yield, thermite plasmid bombs," Perry said abruptly. "That beige piece of work Babar said he represents a client desperate for them. With that kind of weapon, you could effectively infect a continent or planet, scour it of life, and then use fire to render it safe for repopulation.

"All in three easy steps. Evil has a new face," Striker added.

"And his name is Gyl-Mareth," Mark said, his fingernails biting into his palms. "I think it's time for you to show us how our new null-field generator works. If any of this is true, we may be operating on borrowed time already."

"Exactly," Armagost agreed. "But first, it must be tested. Luckily, I know of an asteroid the Salt Thieves use for a counterfeiting drop site. Take Tan along and have the young man adjust on the fly. There's a perk with this one, besides messing with those thieving piles of animal droppings. Unless you have any scruples with spending counterfeit money."

"A test run on Salt Thieves? I can't think of more deserving scumbags," Mark said. "And I'll gladly take their fake money, but only if we can spend it with other dodgy lowlifes."

"Lowlifes? That's harsh language for Mark. He must be worked up."

"You could say that. In truth, I'm ready to fight."

26

MARK AND VALINT sat quietly in the *Moonraker* two days later, the large gunship powered down and grappled to a piece of floating space debris.

"Okay, I know we've been over this a hundred times, but let's go over the plan once more. So we have no surprises," Mark said. He'd never taken issue with the quiet of space before, but this was different. Knowing that the universe was on the edge of upheaval and collapse made every cold and quiet moment feel excruciatingly slow. It felt like they should have been doing anything else, regardless of how loudly the logical side of his brain shouted the truth.

And the truth was damning. If they could nullify, deactivate, and safeguard one of the slaved Synths, its neural network would serve as both testimony and evidence. All together, they could pull Gyl-Mareth and his whole plan to its knees. The added benefit, as Perry usually pointed out, was the salvation of at least one mistreated and abused being in the galaxies.

"Okay," Tan said, fidgeting in the jump seat to Valint's left. The Druzis looked like a child going for a ride, with the oversized straps crisscrossing his chest, and his legs left to swing in the air.

"We wait for the ship to appear. When it leaves, we detach and drift, using thrusters to orient into their wake—the fifteen-degree wide sensor blind spot located behind them. Only then do we light our drive and follow. Once close enough, we will activate the null field and test the effectiveness by elevating to twenty degrees above center beam and outside the blind spot. If they either try and fight or run, we will know the field does not work."

"It *will* work," Valint said.

"Yes. I mean, you're right," the Druzis said. "While in the field, they shouldn't be able to see us on scanners, and there should be no indication that anything is off. When the field is successfully applied, our good Mr. Bird will use the unit's high-intensity emitter to transmit a series of targeted kill signals. If Armagost and I did our jobs properly, the Synth—or, in this case, the Salt Thieves' AI— shouldn't be able to tell when certain systems are rendered inoperable. Namely—?"

"The overcharge module wired to the Synth, their twist functionality, as well as detonation triggers wired into their sensor systems," Mark answered. "But for the sake of this test, Perry will target their integral systems, and for effect, their comms."

"Good. We will stay there in the null field for as long as is practical and test the effectiveness of stealth and digital manipulation. I'll extract data from their drives, while also cycling lights and air handlers on and off. But in truth, there will be so much more. I'm going to pump the worst sort of music through their cabin speakers, reverse the flow from their septic handling system, and crank up the heat. Then, we're going to sit back and watch as they freak out. Knowing those Yonnox, they'll likely think their ship is haunted by the spirit of their angry, many-eyed god. I'm practically tingling with anticipation."

"And while Perry is doing all of that, we will manage things behind the scenes," Netty said. "Valint will fly the pursuit line, but hand the helm of the *Stormshadow*, aka, *Moonraker*, over to us to make the final approach, because the closer we get to their ship, the more our margin of error shrinks. Bunn and I will use computational algorithms to predict any radical course changes. After all, one vector shift could be the difference in us being a hole in space, or a Peacemaker ship, unexpectedly appearing in their wake."

"Well, that would be a surprise for our crew of honest, hard-working Salt Thieves." Mark laughed.

"We all have our jobs," Striker said. "Let's make sure that we do them well."

"Hear, hear," Bunn agreed.

"That's why we're not going to fail," Valint said, her gaze locked on the viewscreen.

"If Armagost's schedule is right, we should be seeing a courier ship twist in sometime in the next hour," Bunn said.

And so they waited, the cold and subtle rotation of the ship lulling him into an uncomfortable calm. Mark fought sleep until his eyelids became far too heavy to keep open. He drifted toward the fog-filled trenches, despite his every attempt to dream of anything else.

"There it is. Right on schedule," Bunn announced thankfully, jarring him to lucidity a few moments later. "It was a gamma burst on the furthest reaches of passive scanners."

Mark cleared his throat and sat up in the seat but found Valint, Perry, and Tan watching him. They all looked concerned.

"What happened?" he asked.

"Nothing I haven't seen before," Perry said, looking away.

"It isn't healthy to carry that kind of trauma. You should let him help you work through it," Valint said, quietly.

"They're just dreams," he said dismissively. It definitely wasn't the time to delve into his terrors.

In fact, it might *never* be the right moment. France was dead and buried, and Mark wanted to keep it that way.

"It isn't the dreams that are concerning, Mark, but the trauma your mind is trying to reconcile. War is hell, but you don't need to carry the scars without—without us. Without others doing something to heal you. I was there, you know. I saw it. All of it."

"I know, and—"

"You don't, Mark. It was worse than you could ever imagine. I saw the horror at scale. You saw tragedy, violence, terror, but all limited by how fast you could travel. I landed in the middle of that nightmare, and frankly, I'm stunned you aren't stark raving mad," Valint said, her voice low and rich with understanding.

Mark said nothing but looked at her, seeing a new layer of Valint that hadn't been there moments before.

Or maybe it had been, and he'd just avoided it, because to understand Valint was a lot like looking directly at the sun. She was…replete. Searing.

And had a gravity that was inescapable.

Lifting a brow, she tried a smile on, warming to his intense gaze.

Maybe he had a pull as well.

The overlay blinked to life before him, and the screen immediately dimmed to tactical lighting. A single contact was approaching the target, an asteroid marked only with a long alphanumeric designation. More data trickled in as the Salt Thieves burned ahead, the weak, passive scans filling in the rest of the information as it approached.

He zoomed in and selected the ship, locking the *Moonraker*'s new mirror protocol onto its target. Now, if the ship rabbited away under high thrust, the navigation system would assist the pilot monitor and match direction and speed changes.

"Right on schedule. They're slowing and changing directions for their flyby," Netty said, helping Bunn sort and manage the incoming data feed.

As Armagost had observed, the Salt Thieves used the asteroid as a counterfeiting cache drop-off point. Although, the couriers were smart. They never stopped at the rock. Nor did they pass within one hundred miles of it. Instead, to help avoid suspicion, the class five ship would twist into system, set a long, fast burn, and, utilizing a modified cannon, launch their payload at distance.

Mark watched the ship approach, and well within the suspected launch zone, fired a lance-shaped projectile from its belly cannon. A long, thin filament unfurled into space from the deposited payload, with a single, flashing pulse beacon on the end. Three seconds later, the payload streaked in as the ship flew by and hit the rock, where it stuck in place.

Bunn kicked the reactor out of standby mode, and the *Moonraker* hummed to life. The tether released a moment later, and attitude thrusters tumbled the ship out and away from the debris field.

"They aren't in position yet. Hold on," Netty said, tracking the ship as it sped away. "They're curving their path plus five degrees to starboard with ten percent lift. Now twelve, and fifteen. Hold… hold…and…*now*."

Valint stowed the throttle safety with a crisp slap, grabbed the lever, and pushed the ignition button with her thumb, all in a series of decisive moves. The ship rumbled, and with the rest of the cockpit coming to life, she shoved it forward.

For the tenth time in recent memory, Mark second-guessed his decision to delay genetic modification—all while fighting for consciousness under heavy burn. They accelerated hard, both Bunn and Netty using their considerable resources to get the ship onto the retreating Salt Thieves' flight line and then keep it there.

"We're drifting half a percent out of line to port with a negative three percent drop to the ecliptic," Netty said.

"Correcting," Bunn countered. "Striker and Perry, stand by. Tan. Remind us of what your estimated range is on the null field generator."

The young Druzis sat forward, before remembering that he was tightly strapped in. He gagged, coughed, and managed to form words on the third try.

"Five thousand yards. Maybe six with a power boost, but that would take additional modification and power adjustments."

"Okay, five thousand yards. Do not activate it outside of that," Valint said, pointing to the two combat AIs. "If the field doesn't have adequate strength, they'll know right away. Let's do this by the numbers."

"We are ready and waiting, friends," Striker said.

A bright light illuminated the comms panel. They turned as one to consider the light.

"What is that?" Tan asked.

"It's a priority encrypted message," Valint said. "But no matter how urgent it is, it waits until we've completed our mission. No distractions. No excuses."

Mark turned, catching Perry's nod in his peripheral vision. The bird respected her, perhaps even admired her. That much was clear. And he was starting to understand why. She was strong, resilient, and unabashedly genuine.

"You still with us, Mark?" Perry asked.

"Looking at the world through a tunnel, but I haven't blacked out, if that's what you're asking."

"Good. Because we're closing to twenty thousand kilometers and are at velocity. Valint, cut thrust to 25 percent."

She pulled back on the throttle, and the ship's drive immediately receded from a loud roar to a side-tickling purr. They coasted in behind the Salt Thieves' ship, everything shut down except the necessary lighting and navigational systems.

The next thirty minutes tested Mark in ways he hadn't thought possible, his nerves frayed to the point of snapping as they drifted inexorably to the enemy ship, watching its trajectory and speed. In a frenetic exchange of calls and data, the AIs worked furiously to predict when it would leave the gravity well and twist away. There was also the possibility that the ship would turn or veer off course, and if it did that, they would almost immediately see them. With weapons powered down, that was a near-fatal scenario.

"Six thousand yards and closing," Bunn said finally. "Five thousand eight hundred. Valint, cut all thrust now. We're picking up enough heat and turbulence off their wake to slow us down. We'll make any additional changes with thrusters."

"They'll be out of the gravity well in twenty-four minutes," Netty chimed in.

"Roger that. We have twenty-four minutes to play with these clowns," Mark said, sliding his overlay over to populate another screen.

Perry powered up the null field generators at exactly five thousand yards, and in a disturbingly anticlimactic moment, they flipped the switch. There was no boom, crash, or flood of blinding light, only steady and uncomfortable silence.

"Give me access to telemetry, thermal and spectral scanners, and the short-range passive sonar, please. I need to align the emitters and sculpt our null field," Tan said as he pulled a wall-mounted overlay in front of him.

Bunn obliged, filling his screen with data. More lights glowed to life on the fore instrument clusters as scanners and other sensors booted up. Mark watched the young Druzis work, his fingers floating across the screen like dancing spiders.

"And I believe that should do it," he said a few moments later. "Power is stable, the field is optimized, and if Armagost and I didn't completely screw this up, we're currently invisible," Tan declared, his mouth pulling up in an excited smile. "Well, to those Salt Thieves, that is."

"Theoretically invisible," Perry corrected. "Our first order of business is to test that theory directly."

"Yes, that is what I meant," Tan said, wringing his hands.

"Don't be nervous, young one," Perry said, his tone surprisingly warm. "By now, we're old pros at going nose to nose with danger. And this particular Salt Thief ship is only a courier, a lightly armed runabout. Not exactly striking cold fear in our hearts."

Tan nodded, his eyes snapping to all of them in turn, before returning to the enemy ship floating large and imposing in their fore viewscreen.

"If they were to see us," Valint started to say, giving Mark a nod, "these individuals would likely try to run. This ship has over twice their displacement, is heavily armored, and possesses enough fire-power to tear them to pieces several times over."

Taking his cue, Mark tapped on one of the tiles in his overlay and powered up the *Moonraker*'s PDCs, missile-guidance system, and laser batteries. Once the weapons HUD came up, he targeted the Salt Thieves' ship and prepared their contingencies.

"Like Valint said, if those couriers so much as sneeze aggressive-ly," Mark added, tapping the air over the fire control buttons on his stick, "one click, and they become an expanding cloud of gas and debris."

Tan let out an unsteady breath.

"Thank you. It's all so very much to take in, so many firsts. I have gone from never leaving Fulcrum, to flying in a warship, and now to designing and testing experimental tech, against villains like the Salt Thieves, no less. And they're so close that I could almost reach out and touch them."

"Welcome to the black, kid." Mark chuckled. "You have quite a few more firsts ahead of you. You've got this under control."

"Exactly." Tan nodded, shook out his hands, and went back to work. "Exterior camera spoofing is live and I'm showing green across my board. We're ready for the first test."

"Okay. Here we go," Valint replied and pulled back on the stick. The ship climbed, rising slowly above the ecliptic and out of the narrow blind spot behind the Salt Thieves' drive.

For what it's worth, this kind of stealth tech has been tried before but has never been implemented successfully, Perry said over his ear bug.

Mark watched and waited, the knuckles of his left hand going numb around the armrest, while his other gripped the fire control. The bird *was* right, although they'd found a technological savant in Tan, two sophisticated quantum AIs in Bunn and Netty, and a powerful warship at their disposal—all things their predecessors had. Still, they had one thing the others likely did not—a wartime setting and the discretion to test it effectively.

"We're officially out of their turbulence," Bunn announced. "Let's not suffer caution. I recommend we drift five degrees to port, hold, and then do the same to starboard to make sure we're well and truly in visible range of their sensors."

"Agreed," Valint said with a brief nod. "Mark, you be ready to launch if these vagabonds try and come around on us."

"My itchy trigger finger is ready."

They drifted right, floating out into the open.

"Keep it tight," Netty warned. "Schematics show that this model has side observational screens. Spoofing sensors is one thing, but we can't do anything if one of those walking cornstalks looks outside at the wrong moment."

"Noted. Estimate observational angles and update to my overlay." There was no panic in Valint's voice, just that steely determination Mark had come to appreciate. When push came to shove, he could count on her to be the oak, standing strong against the storm.

Both pilots' overlays updated, with green, cone-shaped predictions joining the ship's sensor fields. Together, they overlapped to cover every angle, save the tight window directly behind the drive.

"Tan?"

"Nothing. And our predictive algorithm is accounting for short-range sensor modulation. If they saw us, their AI would have signaled the crew with alarms by now."

"Bringing us to their starboard side," Valint replied.

The ship drifted left, crossing the blind zone before entering the sensor window on the other side. They floated for a short while, with Tan swiping and typing madly on his console. Almost five minutes later, the Druzis sighed, tossed his hands up in the air, and sat back.

"Okay. That was harder than I thought, but we're done! All adaptations and changes have been made. The system can now scan, adjust, and operate all on its own."

"Why adaptations?" Mark asked, peeling his hand off the fire control stick.

"Ship sensors are not static systems, nor are AIs dumb. Spoofing something like that requires hundreds of thousands of movements —like a game of…chess. Their sensors make a move, we adjust, and if it's within the allowable modulation time, their AI doesn't become suspicious. The system needs to be incredibly fast and adaptive, otherwise the other ship will see right through the null field. I wrote five hundred and sixty-two additional lines of code while we were floating in their sensor zone, helping our system learn and move faster."

"You did all of *that*? In real time, and their ship's AI didn't notice?" Valint asked, her eyebrows lifting.

Tan gave a sheepish nod. "It was touch-and-go there for a few moments, but I got through it."

"That would be impressive for a computer to do, but for a biological…" Perry said, drifting off.

Mark quickly gathered that the bird wasn't only impressed but perhaps a bit threatened.

"We can conclude that test one is complete and has passed. Mr. Bird, the show is now yours," Netty said.

"Finally," Perry muttered, and a window of streaming data appeared on their overlays. A heartbeat later, another window appeared, showing no less than four data streams. "And just like that, I've hacked into their security feed. Because what fun would it be to mess with tyrannical cornstalks if we can't watch how they respond?"

A small crew of Yonnox appeared, lazily moving about the smaller ship's cockpit and common areas. Seeing how unconcerned they were—with 300 tons of killing machine sitting in their back pocket—confirmed how effective Tan and Armagost's null system was.

"And I see no feedback, indicating their AI has no idea that we have accessed their security feed. Perfect. Moving on to the phase one kill-code injection," Perry said.

More data appeared on the feed, with thousands of lines of code filtering down. It hit the bottom, terminating with a simple [End].

"Code injection complete. Let's begin."

Mark took a breath, intending to ask *which* kill code the bird had injected, only to see the lights on the Salt Thieves' ship abruptly go dark. They flickered on a moment later, went out again, and came back on. The Yonnox looked visibly startled, with two of the stalky aliens moving forward in the cockpit, their small mouths and ropey tentacles moving in equal parts.

"They're adorable, are they not?" Perry asked. "I'm going to call that pair Raul and Pedro. It appears that they're talking to one another, as well as the ship's AI."

"Can we hear what they're saying?" Mark asked.

"Oh, yes. Excellent idea. I'll use the open code I just injected to tap into their comms panel. Will you look at that—there's no firewall on that module at all. Who implemented the security on this ship? A Yonnox?"

Perry let out a wicked laugh as the speakers on the pilots' seats crackled to life. There was a brief fifteen second period where Mark only heard the Yonnox in their native tongue—a barking, growling, and whining sound not unlike the seals he saw at the Lincoln Park Zoo—before Bunn could manage to initiate the translation protocol.

"I do not understand," the first Yonnox said. "Repeat your last."

"A critical lighting fault has occurred. The source is unknown."

"Computer, run diagnostics on the lighting systems. Do it now."

"Understood."

"How perfect, they call their ship *computer*. The broomsticks sure do have a lot of personality." Perry sighed. "And look, half the cockpit lighting just went out. And now it's back on, and the other half goes dark. Holy crap, it happened again. And again."

Half of the Salt Thieves' cockpit went dark, and then the lights switched, until they were flicking on and off in a strobe-like display. The Yonnox froze, their tentacles hovering rigidly in the air around them. When Perry finally let the lights normalize again, the other members of the crew appeared from the sleeper berths.

"Gnargle, what is happening?" one of the sleepy Yonnox asked.

"The computer does not know. Perhaps we're experiencing a power distribution fault," Gnargle replied.

"Oh, no. You're experiencing *The Bird* at his absolute *worst*, you tottering cornstalks," Perry cooed.

Mark watched two more kill-code injections upload. A shower of sparks erupted out of a panel behind the Yonnox's single pilot seat.

"Oops. It appears *that* heater panel was in dire need of an overhaul. My error. Here—I'll make it up to them with some relaxing ambience."

Music immediately started to play over the cockpit speakers—a peculiar aria, except the individual singing sounded strangely like whale song. The Yonnox unfroze and panicked, then began spinning in circles as their tentacles thrashed.

"Computer, why is that music playing? Computer, stop that immediately!" Gnargle shouted as two of his three compatriots bellowed nonsense at one another. For beings with the lung capacity of a matchbox, they certainly were loud.

And annoying.

"Oh, drat. Their atmospheric regulator just tripped. It's sensing a dramatic loss in cabin pressure in the engine room, now the bathroom. Holy hell, the sleeper berths, too. Why, friends, we have ourselves a true meltdown. One might even call this a disaster," Perry said, his voice lilting with unalloyed glee.

Alarms triggered, blaring over the bizarre music, with a host of warning lights filling almost every console. Two Yonnox moved in opposite directions, before turning and running right into one another with a crackling impact. They sprawled to the ground, cursing in words even Bunn couldn't translate.

Gnargle, obviously the captain, turned on the spot, muttering, "Computer," repeatedly.

"Their AI is as bewildered and frightened as they are." Tan laughed, tapping out a series of commands on his console. "The null field and code masking is working so well that it's running in circles. Yes, it's scanning itself for faults now."

Mark looked over and found Valint watching the others, an unmistakably bemused smile softening her features. She caught him watching and gave a gentle snort, then turned to the bird.

"Vallie, the Salt Thieves will be in twist range in four minutes and ten seconds," Bunn said. "Want me to get our welcome committee to hand?"

"Please do, weapons prepped for effect. Perry, are you confident in our ability to infiltrate the Synth ships now?"

"Confident is certainly one term for it."

"Good. Extract our code intrusions, return their ship to normal, and let's get out of here. We have a tyrant to topple."

"Right away," Perry said, and Mark watched as the cockpit aboard the Salt Thieves' ship abruptly calmed. The lights flickered on, the music stopped, and the warning indicators went dark. The only lasting reminder that anything had happened was the blown heater panel and the comically flustered Yonnox.

Valint quietly navigated them into the enemy ship's blind spot, and once powered down, used thrusters to cut speed. The Salt Thieves appeared to rocket away from them, the speed differential skewing perspective. A few minutes later, the courier ship twisted into the silent black.

27

6 January 1926

AFTER REVERSING COURSE, Valint and Mark hooked the suspended beacon and recovered the Salt Thieves' parcel, then promptly twisted away. As expected, they found a small fortune in counterfeit currency stuffed inside. Unlike the digital bonds the Guild and so much of colonized space utilized, the Salt Thieves had evidently found an underutilized niche—the duplication of physical bills, coins, and even the difficult-to-replicate Eridani Cubix.

"If only we could spend it," Tan said as they stood over the relative fortune sorted out on the galley table. "I do so like the occasional fancy thing."

"Well, we could, except for those," Valint said, pointing at the Cubix. "You'd have to twist past the Eridani border in that case, and right now I wouldn't expect a warm welcome. Not if they're busy preparing for war with the Cabal."

"Vallie, I have two twists programmed into the drive. The first is into a safe alley, dead space where we shouldn't run into any traffic, and the second will take us directly to Outward and the Quiet Room," Bunn said.

"Good. Let's do so."

"Will this journey take long?" Tan asked, not bothering to stifle a yawn.

"If you mean, is it long enough for you to sleep through, yes," Mark said, hooking a hand around his shoulder and guiding him back toward a bunk.

"Good. I enjoy fancy things, but I *love* sleep," Tan said, before falling unceremoniously onto the bed.

Mark slid the door closed and turned to Perry and Striker, as the two combat units seemed to be having a strange, silent meeting of the minds. The bird finally came out of his trance, his eyes glowing brightly.

"Sorry, boss, I was having a conversation with Netty and Bunn. They have been working through the list provided by Taj Rodanni, the Eridani Captain."

"Are they making the notifications?"

"No. Unfortunately, we're flying cloaked right now, but I think we have come up with a plan that will work nicely. The list is sorted, compiled, and prepared, and now all they have to do is draft the notification messages. I know," Perry said, waving him off with a wing. "Finding out that a loved one has passed is best done at least on a vid-com, or ideally in person, but we simply do not have the means right now. Once in Outward space, I'll use their network to backdoor a connection to Anvil Dark's backup servers. The list and corresponding messages will be uploaded, and once the nightly data crossover is made, they'll appear on the primary database. At that point, my preprogrammed routine will go into effect and the messages will be sent out."

"That sounds efficient," Mark said. "I like bland, and I love efficient. Seems like both."

"For the most part," Striker agreed. "But as Perry stated, a uniformed Guild member at their door would be the more tasteful route."

"We'll have to call it a start and hope that we can do more later, for all of them," Mark said.

"A good start would be to lock Gyl-Mareth and that Glass maniac in a deep hole with Noka. Let them *entertain* each other for a while," Perry said.

"I'm not against it, I'll tell you that. But for now, where are we with the Synth ships?" Mark asked.

"Striker and I have made headway on that very issue. In fact, we recently finished sorting and compiling the data collected from Babar's console, the backup drive from the Gyl missile platform, and everything we've gathered along the way. It is a…sizable pile. We loaded it into what I like to call a string board and have been actively working to find links and connections."

Mark tilted his head in approval. "And what have you come up with so far?"

"Less than we would like," Striker offered before Perry could speak. The bird clicked his beak irritably for a moment, dropping his head.

"We have engaged every active method of high-level computational analysis. It will take time."

"Why high-level analysis? Shouldn't we start small? Start simple?"

Perry laughed, then shook his head. "Please, Mark, this is what Striker and I do."

"I would like to hear Master Tudor out," Striker said, gesturing with one of his four arms for Mark to continue.

"It seems like it would make more sense to start with the things we know are true, and go from there. The way I see it, we have a handful of simple questions. If we answer those, we're well on our way," Mark reasoned.

"Why simple questions?"

"You're analyzing the data and looking for connections, correct? Many of those connections are based off the theoretical conclusions we have come up with. If the theories are wrong, then the connections we form from them will be incorrect, as well, right?"

"Yes. That's true," Striker admitted. "What do you propose?"

"We throw all of our assumptions and theories aside. Then, formulate some basic questions and answer them using the data we have collected. At the end, we formulate new, logical conclusions."

"Dazzle us, Mark. Please present us with question number one," Perry said, ruffling his metal-composite feathers. Then he sat back and waited.

"Okay." He nodded, scratching the scruff on his chin. There had been so many unanswered questions, it became hard to isolate and answer any one of them.

"See the tree, not the forest," Mark murmured.

"He does this. He talks to himself a lot," Perry whispered to Striker.

"When we ran down the Synth fast boat, why didn't it just twist away?"

Perry's beak hung open. "I was fully prepared to mock whatever nonsense came out of your mouth, but that's a good question. The answer is because the ship didn't have a twist drive."

"What kind of ship doesn't have a twist drive?" Mark asked.

"Shuttles, workboats, and short-range vessels."

"What would be the perks of not twisting a ship carrying contraband?"

"Stealth," Striker answered. "Space is huge but filled with transit buoys. Every twist involves a jump and corresponding termination point. Both result in a considerable gamma release, which is detected and logged by transit buoys. For anyone trying to fly *under the radar*, as they might say, it's safer to fly dark and fast. Does that answer your question?"

"It does," Mark said. "But would the transit buoys register, say, a small craft with no transponder, moving at an incredibly high rate of speed?"

"Yes, but with no transponder, the buoy would...hey," Perry cried, clicking his beak loudly. "I see where you're going with that. And to answer your question, yes, it would register it as an anomalous passing, not unlike a comet or other space debris. But if you're recommending that we jump all over colonized space, hacking into buoy networks to pull anomalous object logs, that would take months and not to mention the time required by quantum beings to sort through the mountains of data."

"We don't need to jump all over galaxies," Mark offered. "Hell, we don't need to jump all over one galaxy. We only need a few data points in order to calculate a route, and we already have one—where we intercepted that fast boat. What if we…?"

"Formed a grid of buoys in that sector and downloaded their anomalous object data and then used that to reconstruct that particular ship's course?" Perry asked.

Mark pointed, the hint of a grin forming on his face. "Correct."

"It would still take a large amount of time. Like you said, we would need at least three data points in order to log a course. We have one, which would require us to cover hundreds of thousands of kilometers of space, not to mention hundreds of buoys to find the others."

"I was afraid of that."

Perry sighed. "Let me guess, you have a list of additional questions?"

Mark worked to hide his smile but shook his head and held up a single finger.

"Only one. It's been burning a hole in my mind up until now, but I couldn't put it together. At least, not until just a little while ago. The Gyl weapons base was nuked. But why destroy the Bone Yard?"

"We already discussed that," Perry argued, but Mark shook his head.

"No. Not our theory of why it happened, but the data. What does that say? My question is this, besides Shipbreaker, what other businesses or organizations were on that station?"

Perry cocked his head to the side, considered the question for a moment, then answered.

"In order—hull scraping and repainting, alloy smelting and refining, chemical and toxic waste disposal, septic pumping and decontamination, a dehydrated food distributor, and a robotics over-haul shop."

Striker cursed quietly.

"What?" Perry asked.

"A robotics overhaul facility that happens to be located next door to a drydock and chemical and toxic-waste disposal site."

"Synth-navigated fast boats," Perry stated. "They nuked the exoplanet so we wouldn't know what they were cooking up, then hit the Bone Yard so no one would know that's how they were distrib-uting the weapon. Ja-Ra told us exactly where to go from the start!"

"But why would he have done that?" Valint asked, her tall frame shadowing the doorway.

"He knew," Striker said, turning to her.

"She was trying to reclaim Ja-Ra and his clan on Fulcrum," Mark said, standing up and immediately pacing the galley. "They were stacked up on his door when we got there, and when Perry and I talked with Glass, she admitted it. But I never asked why."

"None of us did, Mark. It wasn't just you. We had too many questions to answer at the time. The picture was too big, and we were too close," Perry said.

"But why tell us now?" Valint asked.

"We already said it," Mark offered. "He knew about the missile platform. He said that she collected him originally to do work on her fleet of ships and her base of operation. If she gave him access to their computers, then he likely glimpsed what she was planning. Or, if not the entire plan, enough pieces of it to know she had something big in the works."

"So, Ja-Ra told us to force a confrontation, perhaps hoping that we could talk her down. We are Guild, after all," Valint reasoned.

Perry nodded. "For small, generally timid creatures, he did more to try to avert disaster than most would. Understanding the risks involved, he tried to steer us onto the right path, but we didn't see it right away."

"How does this change your threat matrix, Netty?"

"Change?" She chuckled, and in response, the flowchart appeared in the air over Mark's wrist repeater. Boxes moved and shifted, with both solid and dotted lines redrawing to make new connections. "My analysis indicates that Glass is not working for either of the Masters. In fact, this new data confirms it."

"Agreed," Striker said. "We knew Mala contracted her services to at least one side of the Gyl and Cai conflict. That explains why Gyl-Mareth tried to commission her death, and Cai-Demond intervened on her behalf. My analysis also concludes that Gyl-Mareth's Imperial ambitions would force him to view Glass as an impediment. She is, after all, a violent wild card he likely could not control. And when someone is quietly trying to consolidate power, the last thing he would want is unscheduled conflict."

Perry snapped his beak in agreement. "It would increase the chances that someone would notice him."

"What do we do?" Valint asked, crossing her arms over her chest. "If Glass is not working for Gyl-Mareth, then exposing her operation doesn't help us take him down."

"We don't know that they aren't, ah, working together. At all." Mark struggled to trace all the connections on Netty's threat matrix. The only thing he could safely conclude from the diagram was that Glass appeared to be working independently. "But that doesn't change the fact that *she* is the greatest threat right now. If what we know is true, then she possesses a biological weapon capable of cleansing whole planets of life and carries the grievances to use it."

"If she was operating out of the Bone Yard, and destroyed it, that means her preparation work is done," Perry reasoned.

"It also means we have another data point. If we know where we captured the ship and where it originated, then we can—"

"Narrow our buoy data search, and with luck, estimate with an incredibly high level of confidence exactly where it was going. It could tell us where she is *staging* her attack," Striker finished.

"Then we go in hard, and we go in fast," Mark said, looking up.

"She has a battle group," Valint said. "And right now, we have one ship. And, might I add, incredibly limited resources."

"Two," he corrected. "We grab our platinum and pull the *Fafnir* out of Spacer's Gold, then recall Drogo. Vosa is still out there somewhere as well."

"That's *two* well-armed ships." Valint sighed, holding up two fingers. "And yours. *If* we can find Drogo, that is. We haven't heard from Vosa in weeks. You have to consider that someone took her out, or her race's ingrained pathological tendency to wanderlust got the best of her. At best, that gives us four gunships against what? A dozen, two dozen?"

"We also know Glass has at least one heavy cruiser, and maybe more," Perry said. "With those numbers, I calculate our odds of survival at four percent, maybe five, if I'm being generous."

Valint cleared her throat, the small noise pulling everyone's attention directly to her. She moved away from the doorway, her undeniable resolve radiating out into the space.

"We need to stop looking at this as *our* fight. It isn't only the

Guild affected by what Gyl-Mareth and Glass are planning. Perhaps it's time to make a call to arms."

"Publicly?" Mark asked. "Wouldn't that divide and weaken the Guild?"

Valint nodded, her mouth pulling into a tight line.

"Anyone that would come to our aid would *immediately* be marked as enemies of Gyl-Mareth's Guild," Perry said.

"Of his *state*," Valint said, correcting Perry. "Better we divide the Guild now than face its full and undivided wrath."

"Vallie, we're coming out of twist in two minutes."

"Thank you, Bunn."

"We pick up our platinum, twist directly to Spacer's Gold, get the *Fafnir,* and make our pitch? How?" Mark asked.

"We can't transmit wide. We'll need to find someplace with the equipment and galactic connections, but also an open-minded and independent stance. Someplace that won't shoot at us on sight but will also give Gyl-Mareth pause."

"That's a helluva ask, Valint," Perry admitted. "Considering how big his head has gotten, he might not think anything is out of his reach."

"Fountain World," Striker said, tapping a hand against his metallic chest. "It's effectively outside of Guild jurisdiction. Thanks to its neutrality agreements with the Federation and the Cabal, Gyl-Mareth would think hard about pushing any influence there."

"That's a long haul. Even with the comms network, there's a considerable lag. Bunn?"

"Transmissions to Fountain World take on average twenty-five Earth days to arrive. It would be safe to figure the same time frame outgoing, too."

"That won't work. We can't afford to wait that long for help to arrive."

"What about Almost?" Mark proposed. "It's only a moderate twist away. And whereas a few ships could slip in quietly, if a fleet of Peacemaker vessels appeared, they would stir up the proverbial hornet's nest. The criminal inhabitants don't have to be friendly to us, but we could use their hostility toward the law to our advantage."

"It isn't the worst idea," Perry said.

"Fine. Then—"

"Vallie, we're dropping from twist space in five, four, three, two…"

The *Moonraker* emerged from its jump, the thrust pouring on even as the twist drive spooled down. Mark leaned to the side as gravity shifted. The ship maneuvered hard to port, then nosed down and accelerated.

"What is it, Bunn?" Valint asked, pushing off the bulkhead and making for the cockpit.

Mark slid out of the bench and followed, struggling to match the Hu'warde's grace under acceleration.

"We emerged from our twist practically on top of a sensor marker. It wasn't supposed to be there, but I managed to avoid colliding with it. Needless to say, it was close."

Mark made it to the cockpit as the lights dimmed to tactical, his eyes struggling to adjust.

"Why would there be sensor markers way out here?" he asked, toppling sideways into his chair as the overlay updated from their initial sensor ping.

The sensor markers formed a grid that perfectly outlined the outer edge of the system's gravity well, and inside that sat a line of ships. Bunn had only identified two of the fifteen vessels arrayed between them and Outward, but judging from the size and shape of the icons, Mark could easily surmise their build and purpose.

"It's a blockade," he said, and unlike the motley assemblage of tugs, workboats, and transports Noka had attempted to use to block their entry to Chevix, these were warships.

There was no warning or stand-down order, only indiscriminate violence. Laser fire hit the *Moonraker,* the first shot striking high on the port side, the thick ablative armor deflecting the majority of the energy off into space.

Thrusters fired, and the ship careened about, the shifting gravity throwing Mark left and halfway out of his chair. Laser shots filled the overlay all around him, the energy flaring like flashes of lightning. The thrust doubled as Valint took the stick, her left hand deftly navigating her overlay's many screens and pop-ups.

"They have a lock," Bunn said. "Not missiles. I'm picking up on a massive energy spike. Rail guns are firing. Multiple projectiles incoming!"

The large warship shuddered again as laser fire hit the rear armor panels.

"We're not sticking around so those idiots can poke any holes in my ship," Valint snarled, and the twist drive spooled in a deafening crescendo. Then, without any warning, they twisted away.

28

THEY JUMPED three million kilometers away, paused for a moment, the ship thrumming with purpose, and jumped again, this time covering almost two and a half light-years. The journey only took minutes, although it seemed to take years.

Mark numbly flipped between the screens on his overlay, trying to make sense of the residual data. The icons, or target markers as AIs called them, showed the ships constituting the blockade. Bunn only had time to identify nine of the fifteen, but that was enough. While half the vessels were Quiet Room Defense Corp, the rest were Guild, and not Peacemakers, either.

"Those ships were Legion, weren't they?" he asked.

"You know they were," Valint said without meeting his eyes.

"We need to stick our feelers out," Perry said, breaking the silence that stretched after. "Bunn, switch the transponder back to the *Stormshadow*, but be prepared to twist away as soon as I tell you.

The moment I connect, they're going to know exactly where we are."

The bird looked from Mark, to Valint, then to Striker, as if daring them to challenge him. But he was right. Regardless of the risk, they needed to understand the scope of their changing world.

Valint gave the bird a terse nod, then looked to Bunn and said, "Do it."

"All right. The switchover is made. Let me know when you're ready, and I'll connect us to the GKU network."

"I'll help," Netty offered. "As soon as Perry gets what he needs, Bunn can disconnect us and deactivate the transponder. I'll run calculations for our jump away. If both of us handle the routing, it will save time."

Mark nodded, his eyes naturally drawn to the viewscreens. The comms panel hummed to life as Perry approached, his chest opening as he quickly ported in manually.

"And now, Bunn," he said.

Mark registered only a moment of static, as seemingly every comm channel came to life at once. His overlay filled with updates and notifications.

"I'm done," Perry said and disconnected his data port.

"Shutting down the—"

"Rogue vessel *Stormshadow*, this is the Galactic Knights Legion. We have locked onto your location and have a firing solution. Power down your drive, or we will fire upon you."

"That's impossible. No ships were close enough to track our connection, quadrangulate our location, and twist in this fast. They're likely bluffing and hoping they can get us to freeze in place," Perry yelled.

But Mark's overlay showed a different truth. Five contacts appeared barely five thousand yards ahead, the ships emerging in bright flares of gamma rays. Five more ships twisted in behind them, and others flashed into existence at a record pace.

With the drive already hot, they twisted away, jumped two short distances, and then a much longer third. Mark watched the overlay wiped clear as they emerged, a single powerful sensor ping firing off into the black.

His gaze crept left and then down, only to find Valint's hand clutched tightly against the fire control, her grip so tight the knuckles turned white.

"We're dark, correct?" she asked, a heartbeat later.

"Yes," Bunn confirmed.

"Can anyone tell me how they locked in on us so—?" Perry started to ask, only to have Netty cut him off.

"Gravity fluctuations. Eight thousand yards behind and above us. It could be a ship coming out of twist."

"Get us out of here. Twist—twist!" Valint shouted.

The *Stormshadow* vibrated as they jumped again and again, the last transit taking them almost twenty-five minutes. And once again, they waited and watched. The calm spanned almost ten minutes as they sat watching the screens, silently hoping nothing would appear. And yet, Bunn and Netty detected the early signs of incoming ships again, and they jumped away.

"How are they tracking us?" Mark asked.

"It isn't impossible," Valint answered, "It's just not easy to do."

"The Legion is involved but…" Perry started to say.

"What about the Legion?" Mark asked.

"They have been designing and testing twist tracking technology for a long time now. It's possible that one of those ships is equipped with a tracker module."

"Great." Mark pushed up in his chair. "You're telling me the Legion has the technology to track us, even through twists?"

"Yes and no," the bird said. "Due to obvious time constraints, we can't go into the science involved, but I'll tell you this much. Twist tracking has never found widespread acceptance because it's finicky and incredibly sensitive. The scanner modules require a special kind of quiet to work. To call them tricky is—an under-statement."

Mark listened, fighting to process what Perry was telling them, while his gaze continually crept up to the timer ticking away at the top of his overlay. It hit eight minutes as the seconds bled away with frightening speed.

He looked to the forward screen, back to his own display, and finally to Perry, his eyes sharp and decisive. He was thinking—and reaching conclusions.

"I'm detecting gravitational anomalies again," Bunn said, her frustration bleeding forth.

"Get us out of—"

"Wait," Mark ordered, and twisted sideways in his chair. "Bunn, how far are we from Chevix Station?"

"Calculating…"

"Of course," Perry said, understanding. "Twist us into turbulent waters, or in this case, a system full of interference, and hope it muddles their trackers."

"Five point two one light-years."

"Let's hope this works," Valint said. "Bunn, chart it and make it happen. But let's be smart about this. Program our twist back out of there and be ready to jump as soon as we emerge. Who knows what we'll twist into."

"I'm on that," Netty offered.

As ships started to pop onto his screen, the *Stormshadow* twisted again.

"We can't run forever," Mark whispered, turning in his chair.

"Our dwindling fuel supply would agree with that statement," Valint shot back.

"I mean, at some point we're going to have to stop and fight. And there's a chance it's against our own people."

"Trust me, that issue has been on my mind a lot lately. But know that fighting isn't my first choice."

"It never should be," Mark agreed, then turned to Bunn and Netty. "This is the plan. Jump us away from Chevix, something short that will set us up for a direct jump to Spacer's Gold. Do we have enough fuel for that?"

"Barely," Bunn replied. "At this rate, if we have to make any more micro twists, we aren't going to have the range. You want us to jump without delay?"

Shaking his head, Mark scratched his cheek, the scraggly beard still itchier than he was comfortable with.

"How long has it taken the Legion ships to follow us after each twist?"

"Average time is…twist emergence plus eight minutes and twenty-five seconds."

"Okay. That must be how long it takes their tracking equipment to read our resonance trail and calculate the path. Set a timer for eight minutes and thirty seconds. We need to know this works before we tip our hand as to our next destination."

"Done."

A long, narrow panel appeared at the top of his overlay, and a blocky timer faded into view. [8:26:00]

They emerged from their jump in-system, and his ear bug immediately filled with the familiar sound of white noise. Even the speakers not powered up emitted static as the system's dirty star bombarded them with interference across the spectrum.

"New jump ready—a micro-twist taking us a million and a half kilometers."

"Do it," Valint said.

The sensor ping hit Chevix Station, revealing the distant gas giant and former Administrator Noka's fueling station as they jumped away. The transit was almost instantaneous, the whine from the twist drive receding seemingly as it hit its peak.

"And mark," Bunn said, as the timer began to count down.

"Keep weapons, navigation, and the twist drive up. While you're at it, program in two jumps—Option A should take us straight to Spacer's Gold, while Option B is an emergency escape—but bring everything else down. Give me a full power sweep, then drop to passive scans only. Make us a hole in space," Valint said, taking charge.

Most of the cockpit lights dimmed as the sensor array emitted a strong pulse. Mark unbuckled from the harness, swiveled his overlay aside, and moved to the viewscreens.

He floated from the port, forward, and finally to the starboard side, watching the darkness. The static continued to fill his ear bug and the comms speakers, and the stars appeared to twinkle and move, surging brighter before fading once again. It was no different than the muddy trenches, where he lay in the muck, rifle poised and ready. He'd stared downrange so long that man-shaped shadows seemed to appear in the fog. Now, it was gamma bursts, indicating approaching ships.

Mark knew it wasn't real, that it was his mind, his nerves playing tricks on him. With effort, he blinked and moved his eyes, forcing himself to breathe.

"Time?" he asked.

"Four minutes and counting," Netty replied, her voice no more than a whisper.

Valint's fingers tapped against the overlay behind him, the almost imperceptible whine of Perry's servos and the clicking rustle of his feathers combined to make a background hum of sound so annoying, Mark moved right and scanned the starscape again. He'd made the whole route before realizing that his hand was clutched on his revolver.

"Things are worse than I thought," Perry said, breaking the silence a moment later. "My snapshot of the network allowed me to retrieve a sampling of news updates from the Guild and a dozen other sources. The Legion wasn't only posted around Outward to keep us out. Gyl-Mareth has used the law to seize control of Quiet Room, itself, and has subsequently frozen all of its assets."

"Under what grounds?" Valint asked.

"The legal grounds are unclear, but it sounds like he is doubling down on his terrorist claims. Perhaps he will make the claim that the Quiet Room is funding us and other terrorists, but, to what end, I cannot surmise."

"He who controls the money." Mark turned his gaze back to the stars.

"Meaning?" Perry asked.

"The history of my world showed that empires rose and fell based on their ability to collect, horde, and wisely use wealth. For some it was gold and gems, or land, while others discovered the lust for the exotic — silk, animals, and even slaves. They used wealth to expand their empires, but also as a concept to keep their people complacent and docile. With the Quiet Room's reach and expansive portfolio, Gyl-Mareth would have everything he needs to kickstart his own empire."

"The people wouldn't stand for that. They would tear him down before he ever got the chance to spend it," Valint argued.

"Mark is right," Striker cut in. "Like we said before, if Gyl-Mareth is smart, he will keep them irrational and afraid. He would maintain their focus on a shared enemy. And he would justify his level of control out of a deep-seated need to keep them safe, to protect their lives and livelihoods."

"And if they believed he was doing that very thing, they would applaud him for it," Perry muttered.

Mark's hand tightened around the revolver. And yet, he could do little more than watch and wait, however awful that was on his nerves.

"Six minutes and thirty seconds," Netty whispered, updating the count.

"What else?"

"The Guild has done nothing to dampen the war rhetoric growing between the Cabal and Federation. Even if Gyl-Mareth didn't plan that feud, he is doing nothing to quench the flames."

"He is capitalizing off Glass's rise," Valint reasoned.

"At the very least, yes," Perry said. "Although, I still believe he is involved, in one way or another. And that means we're cut off from the rest of our platinum. As far as resources go, that leaves us with whatever bonds Bunn and Netty were able to siphon out of your accounts before the Guild froze them."

"Which will handle one fueling, maybe two," Bunn said. "And that's eight minutes."

"We need the *Fafnir* back."

"And how do you plan on paying for the work? You did promise Badge fifty-five platinum on top of the mountain of bonds we already paid."

"We'll just stroll in after hours and reclaim her."

"So steal the ship?" Valint asked.

"It isn't stealing if it's already ours. Besides, we can leave them a tidy fortune in Eridani Cubix and other currencies."

"You would pay for a major refit to our ship with counterfeit currency?" Perry asked.

"Yes. Does the thought ruffle your feathers?"

"Surprisingly no."

A chime sounded, accompanied by a flashing light on both overlays.

"Eight minutes and forty-five seconds," Bunn said. "Sorry, the timer ended a little bit ago, but you all were on a roll, and I didn't want to interrupt."

"Appreciate the courtesy. I was feeling it. So, anything on passive scans?" Mark asked, turning back to the viewscreens. He looked all the way from left to right, then back again.

"Nothing," Netty confirmed.

They hovered there for another awkward minute, watching, and waiting. Bunn quietly ticked the time off, adding seconds, and then minutes to their count. They'd hit twelve minutes before Perry finally broke the trance.

"I believe we have finally given them the slip," he said, ruffling his feathers and shifting on his perch. "Thanks to Chevix and its really unruly star. Good job, Mark, truly."

"Thanks, bird."

"You are welcome, Human."

"So, off to Spacer's Gold?" Bunn asked. "According to my chart data, it's currently one hour from the start of their lunar period. At that point, most of the vendors and merchants are forced to shut down for their daily station maintenance period. It should be quiet."

"That sounds perfect," Mark said. "But we probably shouldn't dock. That would raise too many questions."

"How are you planning on getting to your ship?"

Perry laughed. "I have an idea. We twist in and mimic a communications fault. When traffic control asks the reason for our visit, we will tell them it's for repair. Considering our arrival will be in the lunar period, they'll undoubtedly tell us to dock and wait. By this time, we will be close. Mark and I will push out of the airlock, and the *Stormshadow* or *Moonraker* can float right on by, respectively rejecting their request."

"It isn't a horrible plan," Valint said. "But how are you going to get into Spacer's Gold from the outside? Crossroads isn't known for keeping open airlocks."

"The same way we recovered our new reactor from the crumbling Gyl missile platform," Mark said, reaching down to pat the Moonsword on his hip.

"So, you're going to cut your way into their facility, then recoup your gunship, and leave behind a small fortune in counterfeit currency. Does that all sound right?"

"Sounds right to me," Perry replied.

"When you all started with the pirate talk, I thought you were just trying to make light of a bad situation. To, ahh, add a little levity to a dark hour. But I did not think that you would stoop to actual piracy," Striker said.

"Stoop? Oh, come now, Striker. This is my full height," Perry said, waving him off with a wing. "When the law no longer serves as intended, sometimes the lawful must go rogue."

"For the record, I dislike this idea."

"Noted…on the record."

"What *is* the plan?" Tan asked, appearing in the hallway from the galley. He yawned dramatically and stretched, his double-jointed elbows and shoulders allowing for a disturbing range of motion.

"Oh, yes, young one," Perry announced. "We're going rogue, sort of."

"Sort of?" Tan asked, eyes bright with interest.

Perry waggled a wing, beak open in a laugh. "Piracy. It never goes out of style."

29

"FOR THE RECORD, I do not like this plan either," Tan said a short while later.

"You just said that because Striker already did," Perry argued. "It's sound."

"No. He seems to object on a philosophical and ideological level. I'm objecting from a technological one. What would you do if they have installed a start-up inhibitor? How will you route around a change in start-up sequence? What about reactor phase shifting, thruster control syncing, or hover gyroscope balancing?"

"It sounds like you're making up words now," Mark said, looking to Perry.

Unfortunately, the bird shook his head. "Sadly, he is not, Mark. There are a litany of tests and calibrations that *must* be performed with a major refit like this. If they aren't, the ship's new reactor may not come online, the drive may not fire, or, when you move to take off, the thrusters may refuse to work in concert. The results would be costly but could prove to be catastrophic."

"Wouldn't Spacer's Gold do all that once the refit was complete? Wouldn't they take the ship out and make sure all the new equipment worked?"

"Well, sure. Maybe. I mean, did you ask them to?" Tan asked.

"Oof, good question." Perry looked to Mark.

"Not specifically."

"Then it sounds like our young pirate understudy here just volunteered for the mission." The bird reached up and tapped Tan with a wing.

"Wait. What is a pirate? And who is this understudy?"

Mark laughed, took a step forward, and tapped lightly on the young alien's chest.

"A pirate is a person that takes things that don't belong to them. And the who, well, that's you."

"Oh, no. No, thank you. I have never been…out in space before. Not without walls, and portholes, and lots and lots of bulkheads between me and it."

"Look on the bright side," Mark said, wrapping an arm around Tan's shoulders and pulling him toward the equipment locker. "You get to cross even more firsts off your list."

Barely an hour later, Mark, Tan, and Perry stood smashed together in the airlock. The bird hummed a tune quietly for a few moments, before he finally started to sing.

"Are you singing that song you played on the Salt Thieves' ship? The one that sounds like…well, I guess I don't know what it sounds like."

"It's considered to be one of the greatest musical compositions from colonized space. Although, most agree it's a rather acquired taste. The song's name is untranslatable, if that helps."

"Can I go back inside?" Tan asked.

"How is that supposed to help?" Mark asked. "And who, or let me say *what*, is the singer? They sound like whales, or a really angry bird."

"The audacity," Perry said. "Gun'Daro Hynokisius is believed to be one of the greatest wailers of her generation."

"Guys…"

"*Wailing* sounds about right."

"You don't like it because it isn't sung by a human, and they aren't singing about tapping their feet or drinking distilled beverages. I'll have you know that Gun'Daro doesn't even have feet. So there."

"I have no idea who the singer is. I only know that the sound hurts my ears."

"Did you hear me? I would very much like to go inside the ship again."

"I'll grant you that much. From a frequency standpoint, it's quite high in tone, pitch, and tenor. And three of Gun'Daro's vocal cords resonate at a pitch that not only causes pain in some species but can lead to permanent hearing loss in others."

"Are you serious? And you like it?" Mark asked.

"Well, no. I mean, not really. But a lot of people do, so I figured that if they did, then I should, too," the bird argued.

"You're unbelievable. What would you have done if that song destroyed my hearing?"

"Talked louder?"

"I'm going to die," Tan muttered as Valint's voice filled the comms.

"We're approaching Crossroads now. Bunn is handling communications with their traffic control AI, so stand by. We will give you a five-second warning before we depressurize the airlock."

"Wait, what does that mean? 'Depressurize' the airlock?" Tan asked.

"Well, we have to equalize to vacuum, otherwise the release in cabin pressure would shoot us out the door like shells from a cannon. For me, awesome velocity, but for you squishier, organic-based life-forms, it would be less enjoyable."

"Don't listen to him, Tan. They'll slowly equalize the airlock to outside vacuum, then open the door, and we will float on out. There won't be anything violent about it."

"That's what you think," Perry chuckled.

"Okay. We're a go. They authorized us to dock on the far side, not far from Ixtan Paradise. Bunn is going to route us around the long way, bring us as close to the complex as possible, and we'll drop you off," Valint said. "Be ready. We're headed in now."

"Are you sure this is the route you want to take, Mark? What if they shoot at you when you try and reclaim your ship?"

"I never thought about that." Mark said. "Perry, do the Spacer's Gold workers have guns?"

"Doesn't everybody?"

"That isn't an answer."

"It's Perry for 'I don't know, Mark.'"

"All right, we're depressurizing the airlock," Valint said, and in response, the lights around them dimmed as the atmosphere was slowly pumped out.

"What do I do? Mark?" Tan asked, his panic evident.

"Relax, Tan. We've got this. You're tethered to me, and I'm tethered to Perry. He will pull us to where we need to go, and then I'll get us inside. All you have to do is enjoy your first EVA."

"I don't know if I'm ready."

"No one ever is, kid."

"We're opening the outer hatch in three, two…"

The whine of hydraulics drowned out the end of the countdown, and a moment later, Perry pushed into the dark, cold, and quiet. Mark cinched down the straps on his pack, ensuring Netty's case was secure, and then followed the bird.

Tan floated free behind him, the Druzis letting fly with a frightened string of curses. The kid was a genius with boards and programming, but damn he had a mouth. They were barely free of the ship, and Mark already had to silence his comm channel.

Mark turned as Perry took up the slack on the tether, his view revolving from the *Stormshadow*'s retreating aft section, to space, and then the impressive bulk of Crossroads.

Spacer's Gold loomed tall and wide ahead of them, the trusses and lattice work connecting it to the next module spanning like thick spider webs in Ross 248's eerie, red glow. The station was huge, with span and sprawl rivaling Trei-Seti and Algo, yet Mark had normally only seen it from aboard the *Fafnir*. To approach in only a pressure suit was a somewhat humbling experience.

A thousand meters down. We're halfway there, Perry said, transmitting directly to his ear bug.

He watched as Tan tugged on the tether. The Druzis' eyes were wide, although not with fear, but amazement. His mouth moved for a moment, before Mark remembered that he'd silenced his comm channel.

"Amazing. Terrifying but amazing," Tan said once his channel went live.

"Yes, it is. Like I said, sit back, relax, and enjoy the ride."

And it did feel like a ride as their AI escort pulled them across the divide. Mark activated his wrist pad and used the suit's micro-thrusters to slow down as they approached. Tan matched speed, until the three hovered below the emergency hatch.

It took Perry almost thirty full seconds to hack the outer door, but ten times that to infiltrate the airlock sequence, equalize the pressure, and open the inner door.

They crawled free, and Mark carefully closed the hatch behind them. It caught and sealed itself, and the locking ring turned red again.

"There's no going back now," he murmured, whirling to follow Perry and Tan.

They staged behind a pallet of parts—the supplies neatly stacked, tagged, and shrink-wrapped. Perry stalked around the right side first, then the left, and gave the massive service bay a quick scan.

"I see three cleaning bots, four maintenance crawlers, and one very bored-looking loader. I'm guessing he was supposed to trip into power saver mode once the station locked down for the lunar cycle. My advice is to steer clear of any of them."

"And the ship?'

"The *Fafnir* is three service bays down and on the right. It looks to be intact, but without a live connection and no Netty, that's all I can tell from here. It could be a gutted shell, for all we know."

"As always, a paragon of optimism. Thanks, Perry."

"And as always, you're welcome, Mark."

Shaking his head, Mark pointed toward a maze of storage racks ahead. "Let's head that way, nice and quiet."

Perry nodded but had to poke Tan to get his attention as the young Druzis was too busy looking around.

Mark led the way, creeping out from behind the pallet and moving quickly to the first rack. He turned as Perry joined him, the bird making no discernable noise. And then there was Tan, who couldn't seem to move—fast or slow—without slapping his boots against the ground. The results echoed loudly out into the open space.

"Shhh," Mark hissed, although his plea for quiet elicited the wrong response.

Tan immediately stopped, looked around, flopped onto his belly, and went still.

"What is he doing?" Perry asked, cocking his head to the side.

"Maybe trying to be a log?" he grumbled. Then, with the burden of Netty's case on his back, and the duffle of counterfeit money on his side, Mark crept quietly out to the prone Druzis.

"Tan, you're out in the open. Come on, we need to move!"

"You told me to disappear, so I did the best I could," his young counterpart whispered without moving.

"I only meant for you to be quiet. Your footsteps were really loud."

Mark helped him off the ground, and together they joined Perry at the racks. They crept through the shadows, weaving their way around enormous piles of greasy components, partially spooled wire, and wheeled carts filled to the brim with buttons, toggles, and heavily worn selector switches.

Mark froze at an intersection and held up his hand. In response, Perry and Tan stacked up behind him. A solitary box-shaped cleaning bot slid by, humming a digital tune as its rotary scrubbers churned loudly. It continued on to the end of the row and turned left, without noticing them.

On they went, navigating the racks for two more intersections. He moved left and leaned out, only to spot a familiar ship sitting in the next bay down. Thankfully, the Spacer's Gold bots had not stripped the *Fafnir* down for scrap. Although, the hoses running out of its belly ports gave him pause.

"Does that mean it isn't done?" he whispered to his companions.

"It doesn't mean anything, other than they were using external power and likely needed to fuel, swap out coolant, or transfer reaction mass," Perry explained.

"That sounds like a lot."

"We won't know until we get on board and see for ourselves," Tan said.

With a quick look in both directions, Mark adjusted the pack on his back, stepped out into the open, and moved straight for his ship. They were barely twenty yards from the ramp when a small figure appeared from the shadows beneath the craft, a large bundle of cables dragging behind it. The bot moved out into the light, dropped the cable, and then went to disconnect the other assorted horses and harnesses.

Mark froze in mid-step, earning a soft curse as Tan ran into his wide back. They were out in the open—too close to turn and backtrack, and yet standing right in a bright pool of light from above. He had one choice, one play, and it had to be convincing.

Lifting his chin, Mark proceeded forward confidently, only he didn't move to the ramp, but right at the bot.

"My good man, I'm so glad I finally found you."

The bot straightened, turned, and spotted Mark. Then pointed a single nubby finger at its chest, as if surprised that it was being addressed directly.

"Me?" the bot asked, taking a step back.

"Yes, you." Mark threw on what he hoped was a disarming smile and spread his arms. "I have a delivery for Badge."

"Badge is not here," the bot said, looking around.

"That's all right, because I was told that *you* were the one important enough to leave this with," Mark said, lifting the duffle over his head and holding it out. "Important deliveries need to go to someone trustworthy, right?"

"Correct?"

"I am Barrow, this is my ship, and this," he said, quickly, reaching out and draping the duffle bag full of money over the bot's outstretched arm, "is for Badge."

"I really don't think—"

"No need to thank me, my good man. I don't want to be a bother to you, your hard-working compatriots, or your boss. My guess is that you have a whole line of vessels waiting for this bay."

"Actually, we—"

"That's what I thought," Mark cut in, nodding. "My boss and I are big fans of what you and Badge are doing here. Now, your time is far more important than mine is, so I'll get my ship out of your way and let you get back to your critical work."

The bot looked to the duffle bag draped over its extended arm to the ground, where the pile of coiled cables sat. Then it looked back up to the *Fafnir,* and finally Mark.

"Thank you?"

"You're welcome," Mark said, throwing the confused bot a wink. "Now you stay right here and deliver that bag to Badge directly yourself. This is a task I trust only you with, got it?"

"Yes, sir."

"All right, good. Like I told my employer, Badge and his crew are top-notch. They're the sort we need for our operation."

The bot stood a little straighter, the praise obviously having the desired effect.

"We definitely are the right sort. Thank you, sir."

"Outstanding. Now, would you be a good chap and arrange our departure? We have an important client to see on Dregs and are running a bit behind schedule. You understand, I trust. Business waits for no man…or bot."

"Of course. Yes, right away."

"And that's why you're the best."

Mark and Perry made their way up the ramp quickly as the bot moved away, the duffle bag of counterfeit currency still suspended from its outstretched arm. They moved through the open doors and into the dark interior. None of the lights powered up as they entered, and a sinking feeling settled into his guts.

"Tan, to the reactor. Perry, with me," Mark said.

He cut left and made his way toward the cockpit, with only the glow of the bird's orange lighting showing the way. They ducked under loops of cables hanging from above and kicked some debris on the ground but made it forward without too much trouble.

Mark heaved the bag off his back, pulled it open, and removed Netty's cobalt-blue case. Then after fishing around inside the component cubby, located the cable bundle, pulled it free, and plugged her in. Nothing happened for several long moments as the ship sat dark, quiet, and seemingly empty around him.

The bay came alive above them, as the hydraulically actuated service arm lowered and latched onto the ship. The craft shuddered as it was unceremoniously heaved off the ground, then slowly pulled toward the exterior doors.

"Come on, Tan," Mark said.

"He is working on a reactor he has never seen before, in the dark," Perry reminded him.

"I know, but I would like to avoid hitting vacuum while our airlock doors are wide open and the ramp is extended."

"Ahhh, good point," the bird said, disappearing down the passage in a rustle of armored feathers.

The *Fafnir* rocked forward as the automated arm hefted it out of the service bay, turned left, and started to move slowly toward the large doors at the end of the space.

"Perry?" Mark shouted, his gaze never leaving Netty's dark optical sensor. He looked to comms, then the navigation panel—all dark. The ship continued to move, the doors growing larger ahead.

"Tan?"

Running back through the passage, Mark approached the open airlock doors. He stepped out into the pressure chamber and pried open the service hatch, revealing the manual operation crank. He extended the arm and managed two full revolutions before the mechanism ground to a halt and froze in place.

"Perry!" he yelled, bracing his feet and putting his weight into

413

the crank. He'd watched Striker manipulate the crank easily, although Mark couldn't exactly match the combat unit's strength.

He ran to his quarters and found the door closed, then moved to the dark galley, changed direction mid-stride, and ran to the cockpit instead.

Mark reached the forward viewports, only to find the strobe lights above the bay doors flashing. A bit of movement flickered to his right, and he turned, only to find a single marker lit up on the instrument panel. Another flared to life, and then another. A low-frequency rumble passed through the deck beneath his feet as the inside doors started to open.

"Okay, good. Keep it going." He spotted the bot below, standing next to the large doors. One arm was still extended, holding the duffle bag aloft, while it was waving at him with the other.

Mark returned the gesture as the air handlers kicked in, the breeze tickling his neck. A soft purple glow illuminated him, and he turned to find Netty's optical sensor lit and pulsing gently. It rotated several moments, then went to a hard, constant light.

"Netty?"

This feels like home, Netty said, her voice crackling into his ear bug. *Although I can't seem to connect to the cockpit speakers. Oh, this is weird. I can't connect to the navigational panel either.*

The *Fafnir* was halfway through the doors already, the lights framing in the massive airlock all around him were flashing yellow.

"Netty, long story short. We had to recover the ship. Tan is powering up the reactor, but we're about to hit vacuum, and the airlocks are still wide open. I tried to close the outer door, but the mechanism is frozen."

"Well, that sounds like a problem. Give me a second…"

The *Fafnir* slid fully into the airlock, the inside doors sliding shut behind them. An alarm sounded, echoing throughout the chamber.

Mark, do me a favor, hit that panel to your left. The one below your hand, Netty sent.

Reaching back, Mark smacked the trouble panel.

Again. Don't be shy.

Obliging, he balled up his fist and punched the panel. On the second blow, a relay popped loudly. The cockpit flooded with light as the overheads came on. They clicked to life down the passage, and to his relief, the inner airlock pressure door whisked shut.

"That did it. Thanks, boss. Sometimes those relays stick shut when the system is powered down all the way," Netty said, her voice clear in the speakers.

The Spacer's Gold outer airlock doors started to open before them, revealing the dark starscape.

"Quick note about violent decompression, which just nearly happened," Mark said.

"Um, yes? We hate that, right?" Netty asked.

"We sure do. In fact, let's make certain we avoid anything that even *hints* at that kind of—event. Agreed?"

"Agreed. Air is good," Perry said.

"Excellent. And—we're here. Chins up, kids. Netty, how's our systems?"

The *Fafnir* shuddered as the station's holding clamps released their hold. In a moment of liberation, the ship's thrusters fired, slowly sliding them out and into the open.

"That's a good sign," Mark said, waiting on Netty's report.

"Good so far, but I'm still indexing and networking the systems. However, safety checks on the drive are complete and satisfactory.

The twist drive is coming online," Netty said as a satisfying rumble vibrated through the decking.

"Oh, Netty. It *purrs*."

"You might want to strap in for this next part."

Mark slid into his pilot's seat as Tan and Perry appeared from the galley passage. The bird hopped up onto his perch while the Druzis sprawled awkwardly onto the couch next to him.

"That drive might be one of the shiniest, purdiest things I have ever seen," Tan said.

"They did good?"

Perry laughed. "It's installed properly, but the wiring is a mess. You can tell we brought our ship to a facility more comfortable with tearing things apart than putting them back together."

"It's nothing I can't straighten out," the Druzis shot back, continuing what was obviously an ongoing argument.

"Is it that bad, Perry?"

"Wait until you can see it in the light, Mark. You'll be sorry you paid that smooth-talking Synth more than a handful of crackers."

"I don't think it looked that bad," Tan said. "The drive is *gorgeous*, and the reactor cleaned up very nicely."

"Let's get clear of Crossroads, then we can sort all that out. Netty, is it safe for me to take the stick?"

"Sure is, boss. But I'd still be careful. As you would say, this old girl is sporting a new heart and some racing legs."

"Racing legs," Mark mused, snapping the safety off the new throttle lever. "I like the sound of that. Let's check out the new gams on our girl, shall we?"

The drive's rumble mellowed to a barely audible whisper as he eased the stick forward, and the new unit kicked in smoothly. The thrust pushed him back into the gel padding as they accelerated away from the station, but it was nowhere near the power he expected.

"These are racing legs?" he asked, then eased the throttle forward, bypassing the [1] and [3] position. The lever locked into place as the new drive's whisper rose in a crescendo, and the ship jumped violently forward.

Mark's vision tunneled but locked on his overlay as their projected velocity doubled and then tripled. By the time he eased the stick back into the idle position, they had escaped the speed limit zone and were quickly leaving the station behind.

"You were saying?" Netty asked with a chuckle.

"I retract my previous statement."

"You broke about a dozen operational safety procedures, so, needless to say, Crossroads' traffic control is more than a little salty with you right now. And that's impressive because they're about as easygoing as they come."

"We will send them a fruitcake."

"I don't know what that is, but it sounds gross."

"They're an acquired taste," Mark shrugged. "Netty, when you get the comms panel up and running, reach out to Bunn and let them know we're underway. You and you," he said, pointing at Perry and Tan, "come with me."

30

MARK MADE it to the galley and quickly understood what Perry was talking about. Service panels from the walls, access points in the ceiling, and even a few floor tiles had been removed, all with wiring, armored cables, and hoses hanging free. They obviously needed access to install the reactor, but from the looks of it, the wiring hadn't been routed correctly, as the panels could not be replaced.

He followed Perry into the maintenance passage, and the turmoil only intensified, with a veritable spiderweb of links and cables draped over their new reactor and twist drive. It was a beautiful symphony of shiny, new-to-them components punctuated by the chaos and disorder of a botched installation.

"See what I mean?" Perry asked.

"As my uncle would say, where is the fit and finish?"

"It's fine. *This* is fine," Tan said, hefting a substantial loop of wires and lifting them out of the way. He ducked and picked his way toward the twist drive until he could go no further. "It's the routing of the wiring that's the issue. And that can always be tidied up."

"The kid's got a point, Perry. Netty booted up, the reactor came online, and the drive works. Is it pretty? No. But we can always work on that."

"It works now, until it doesn't," the bird muttered. "Netty and I are currently running a seventy thousand-ish point electrical inspection. If those bots got one wire crossed, I'm going to blow a fuse."

"Easy. Save that wrath for Gyl-Mareth, Glass, and our friend in beige," Mark said, holding up his hands defensively. "They're the ones secretly plotting the use of a deadly, civilization-ending bioweapon."

"This is true. Yes, Mark. I'll conserve every ounce of my disappointment and rage. But mark my words, when this is over, I'm going to give them a very pointed and honest review on the Nexus. There *will* be adverbs."

"As there should be."

"Mark, the comm panel is up and running. It was wired wrong, but I was able to reverse the polarity through two junctions and corrected the problem. Valint is moving to intercept us, then we will twist away together."

"Understood."

"I have other news. Guess who just popped back up?"

"Vosa?" Mark asked hopefully.

"Sadly, no. Drogo. He wants to meet up but claims to have information on Vosa."

"Link him with Valint. Let's find some place off the beaten path."

Barely an hour later, the *Fafnir, Stormshadow,* and *Glorious Column of Benevolent Fire* were on the float together, inside the outer ring of the Gliese asteroid belt. Drogo's formidable gunship showed obvious signs of battle. His forward, starboard PDC was gone, the hardpoint blown completely off, while numerous blast marks and scabbed-over holes covered the hull.

As badly as Mark wanted to see Drogo and Valint in the flesh, they decided to meet over a short-range, secured virtual network instead. Docking their ships together would have prevented them from scattering if danger were to appear, and if Gyl-Mareth had already used the Legion to secure the Quiet Room, then there were likely similar blockades elsewhere, too.

"Who attacked you?" Valint asked. "Were they Peacemakers or Legion?"

"Legion?" Drogo asked, his confusion apparent.

"The Guild has seized control of the Quiet Room and frozen all of its assets. Mark and I believe it's Gyl-Mareth working to consolidate power."

"Money would make his power grab possible. So yes, that makes sense," Drogo said, scratching his wide chin. "No, these were not Guild ships. Nor do I believe they were Peaceful Skies."

"They didn't identify themselves? Were they after Vosa?" Mark asked.

Drogo shrugged. His usual bluster and zeal were gone, and dark bags rimmed his eyes. It confirmed the obvious—his mentor had been through the wringer.

"I followed Vosa's trail to Needle, outside Groombridge, initially. That was the last valid transponder hit I could find. I spent a long time interviewing possible witnesses on the station but could get no usable information. I discovered a vendor that *had* seen her, but this individual refused to say more than that. I waited until most of the vendors closed up for the day and followed him home, then we continued our conversation in the back passages. It took a little *persuasion*, but I got him to open up. He said Vosa had stopped by and questioned him about a number of lost freighters."

"Why was she asking him about lost freighters? She was tracking down Niles Flint."

"That's what I thought, but he insisted she was asking about missing ships. How many were there? Four, maybe more." His mentor's AI chimed in then.

"The *Pride of Radium, Star Araxes, Youst's Deliverance,* and the *Centurion's Mount* were the four ships named."

"Yes. That's it. Thank you, Cerebral," Drogo said, nodding to the AI off camera. "Evidently, all were Eridani freighters, although they were commissioned from different companies and regions of the Federation. Unsubstantiated reports claim they were lost in a massive solar flare sometime after leaving Needle, although they did believe one of the vessels made an unscheduled landing on Bullseye."

"Unscheduled." Perry snorted. "Which is usually code for 'crashed with no survivors.'"

"Vosa must have had a good reason for tracking them down. Perhaps Niles was hired to locate these vessels, as well?" Mark proposed.

"Needle traffics in information as much as fuel and sundries," Drogo explained. "And evidently, the crews that come through there are incredibly chatty, especially once they have had a few drinks. I threatened to hang him upside down and pull his antennae off one at a time, so I know he was telling the truth."

"Subtle," Valint muttered.

"Exactly," Drogo said, slapping his thigh. A bit of his old self returned—the unintended sense of humor, highlighted by his inability to process sarcasm or innuendo.

"A younger me would have started with bigger body parts," Drogo continued. "Having acquired no usable information on these freighters or why Vosa was looking for them, I departed for Bullseye. I hadn't even left Groombridge's gravity well when the unmarked ships attacked from the blind. They were fast, heavily shielded, and relentless."

"Those damned organisms," Mark sighed.

"Precisely. Damned organisms."

"Another player? Or are we seeing Gyl-Mareth's network revealing itself?" Perry asked.

"Until we know otherwise, I think we have to consider them one and the same. You heard it yourself on his public address. He has expended a considerable amount of his own personal fortune to bring the systems back under peaceful control."

They talked for a while longer, with Mark, Perry, Valint, and Striker filling Drogo in on recent developments. He listened raptly as they recounted their spacewalk on the crumbling missile platform and laughed when they narrated their incursion into Spacer's Gold to reclaim the *Fafnir*, but his humor died away as Perry broke down what Glass had likely salvaged from the bioweapons base.

"Tiny, itty-bitty things like that could deconstruct a person from the inside out?"

"Yes, and if she was able to both stabilize the compound, and promote infectious cellular bonding, then we're in big trouble."

"The Guild has the Synth ship we captured. Where are the rest?"

"That's the question we were setting out to answer," Mark said as a crash sounded behind him. He turned to find Tan rolling on the ground, fighting to extricate himself from a mass of wiring.

"I'm okay!" the young Druzis called.

"We do not believe Glass has distributed her killer drug to market. Her transport ships were short-range vessels, so, with that detail, along with complex behavior and psychological analysis, we were able to conclude that she likely has this weapon stockpiled somewhere safe."

"How do you figure that?" Drogo asked. "Why wouldn't she ship it out in every direction?"

Mark shook his head, his conversation with the cool and collected mercenary replaying in his mind.

"Because she isn't an indiscriminate killer. If anything, she is the opposite—a flawed and deeply scarred person, yes. A soldier driven by her grievances, also yes. But every violent action has been for a specific outcome. Glass is methodical and calculating. So if she created a weapon of that caliber, my guess is that she has very specific targets in mind."

"And who might that be?"

"Ja-Ra said she'd been an indentured soldier and had to fight her way free. I say we unearth that detail. A person's demons have a way of creeping from the shadows once you discover the devil that made them."

"Oof, Mark. That's dark talk for you," Perry said.

"I've seen enough of war to understand that truth. That same instinct also tells me that we need to find Glass—and do so quickly."

"Agreed. The plan is simple. We need to disseminate this information to the masses," Valint started to say, only to have Perry clear his throat loudly. "Don't tell me you've changed your mind. You were the one advocating a call for help."

"That was before we knew the Legion is involved," Perry said, looking to Mark. "If we push this to the wider worlds, yes, we will pull some people to our cause, but we will also be contending with Peacemakers and Legionnaires loyal to Gyl-Mareth. We can't afford to fight on two fronts at the same time. I say we find out where Glass stockpiled her monster weapon, twist in, and beat the cunning mercenary at her own game."

"And that is to bombard the location from orbit and fuse it to glass?" Mark asked.

Perry nodded, and in an almost completely predictable move, Drogo agreed.

"Then it's our three ships against her battle group," Valint said, swiping at her overlay.

"She has numbers and a few larger ships, but we have one advantage," Mark offered.

"What is that? A new weapon?" Drogo asked.

"The element of surprise."

The large Badgin looked visibly disappointed, then muted his microphone and started talking to his AI offscreen.

"This is our corridor," Valint said, sharing her overlay with their connected ships. A star chart appeared, then zoomed in, with a red box bracketing in a much smaller space. "And this is our search area, based on the coordinates where we poached the Synth ship, and our only other data point, the Gyl bioweapons facility."

"Our primary problem is we cannot re-arm our ships at just any facility," Striker added. "The Legion will not allow us within one hundred thousand kilometers of their six naval drydock facilities."

"So, we go elsewhere? What about Starsmith?" Mark asked.

Drogo shook his head and reactivated his mic.

"Gyl-Mareth has already pushed both warrants and bounties everywhere, and with money on our heads, that rules most civilized and uncivilized spots out. The good guys will turn on us faster than the crooks, especially considering the number of bonds they're offering."

"I'm guessing we won't get by using a spoofed transponder?"

"Legion ships use advanced sensor algorithms. They would identify us by the shape and build of our ships alone. So, no," Drogo asserted.

"We have another option. Although I'm bound by security software and cannot speak of it. That's why it must come down to Valint," Striker said, indicating his partner.

She cleared her throat and adjusted the neck of her black tactical vest. Mark had never seen her look so uncomfortable before.

"Due to the Guild's Arms Charter, they cannot store confiscated weaponry at Peacemaker or Legion facilities. Due to that rule, the GKU commissioned a number of hardened barges—essentially black sites where they could store and inventory illegal weaponry."

"Weapon barges? How have I never heard of this?" Drogo asked.

"Like I said, they're black sites. *Pitch* black. Striker worked with a special weapons and tactics unit before we met. They raided a Stillness Strong Room on Dregs and found a massive haul of pre-extinction Slo'Tan weaponry. His unit delivered the cache to the barge."

"So, you propose we twist in and re-arm from the Guild's stash of confiscated weaponry? If Striker can't speak of this place, and not even I know about it, how do you expect to find it?" Drogo asked.

"To protect the secrets, the Guild used only AIs to transfer weapons to those facilities, then they *inflicted* silencing protocols on them afterward, so they could not speak of what they saw. Luckily for us, Striker has ways of sharing his memories. Those, as we have discovered, are not blocked by the Guild's privacy intrusions."

"He shared his memories of this place? How many details can you glean from a…"

"I can tell you the exact coordinates of where the barge will be and how many crew are stationed aboard. I can *also* give you its internal and external defenses," Valint said, cutting Drogo off.

"Well, okay. Next time lead with that."

"If we do this, it solidifies us as enemies of Gyl-Mareth's faction. He *will* use it to turn the rest against us," Perry stated.

"Good." Valint immediately pulled up another screen. She quickly drew out a schematic of a long, thick superstructure. Once done, she circled each corner. "The Barge is well-defended but shouldn't be anything we can't handle, if—and it's a big *if*—we can coordinate an unexpected, pinpoint strike. We will have almost *zero* margin of error."

"So, you're saying we might die?" Drogo asked, leaning toward the camera. Valint nodded, and the big alien immediately rocked back, laughing violently.

"What are we waiting for? Let us scream out to the War Father and let our missiles fly and if we die, let it be in a glorious column of vengeful fire."

"Or we could *not die*," Mark said to himself.

"If we're going to do this, here is how it *needs* to work," Valint said, and started drawing out their attack plan.

The strategy session itself took almost two hours to formalize, with Perry interjecting regularly to ask questions. Those usually inspired more questions, and thus, aggravated Drogo, who managed an impressive amount of childish huffing for a being of his size.

Mark dragged himself to his quarters and suffered through a frigid shower, then flopped onto his bunk for a short nap. He managed almost two full hours of rest before the dreams woke him, his clean shirt already damp with sweat.

Wiping his face dry with a towel, Mark moved blearily out into the passage and stepped into a different space. In the time since he'd laid down, Tan had rerouted and cleaned up the wiring in the galley, the passage, and the cockpit. All the access panels had been replaced and securely bolted into place, and everything was labeled in small, neat script.

He found the Druzis working in the maintenance space and chatting with Netty in almost incomprehensible, hyperactive gibberish.

"Hey, boss. Did you sleep?" Netty asked.

Tan spun and lost his grip on a pair of ratcheting pliers. Mark caught them before they could hit the ground.

"Gah! No. You aren't supposed to see this until it's all done. It *isn't* ready. This is—this is art. Not just wires."

"I like what you've done with the place," Mark said. "Really."

"Yes, well, I wanted it to be a surprise, but you woke up…why did you not sleep longer? Does your species not need rest?"

"They do. I, on the other hand, struggle a bit."

The skin around Tan's eyes wrinkled up as he put on what Mark surely thought was a pouty face.

"I'll tell you what. I'll leave, and you can get back to work. Come and get me when you're done, and I'll pretend to be surprised. Deal?"

"It's a deal. Now, please, get out!"

Laughing, he made his way to the cockpit, where he found Perry flipping rapidly through pages of text-filled documents. Mark yawned, stretched, and slid sideways into his pilot's chair.

"A little light reading?"

"If you consider the *Eridani Federation's Naval History Volume Three* to be light reading, then yes."

"Naval history?"

"Yes. I'm researching something on a hunch. And wouldn't you know it, the bird was right again. Glass was, or I guess I should say *is* Piraxian. That makes sense, now given context. When the Piraxian rebellion failed, the Eridani Federation didn't absorb them into their conglomerate of cultures. Instead, they indentured whole generations of former freedom fighters into the military—those who weren't condemned to prison mines, that is. Even if Mala Jin-Kincade wasn't old enough to fight on the losing side, her parents or grandparents were. And that was how she grew up, watching her family, generation by generation, forced to fight for a people not her own."

"All to benefit a federation that enslaved her people," Mark said. "That sounds like a recipe for breeding angry, well-trained killers."

"Indeed," Perry agreed. "And you know what else it tells us?"

"I would only be guessing."

"I've seen you guess. We don't want that. Valint did the hard work, but this little bit of extra data helps. We caught the Synth fast boat here," he said, pulling up the star chart and zooming in on the area marked by a red box. "A hundred solar cycles ago, this space belonged to the Piraxian. Even the Bone Yard, I might add. And this was *her* corridor."

Mark watched as Perry drew a line connecting the Bone Yard to where they found the Synth ship. It wasn't a straight line leading out of Eridani Federation space but seemed to skirt their border perfectly.

"I'm going out on a limb here," Mark said, reaching in and zooming in on the chart. "When the Piraxian rebellion fell, it left behind a considerable list of assets—fueling stations, waypoints, and military bases? Perhaps some that not even the Eridani Federation knew about?"

"Give the human a cracker," Perry beamed.

"Buckle in. According to orbital data, our attack window is coming up very soon," Valint said, her voice crackling over comms.

"Netty, are we ready for this?"

"Navigation and weapon systems are stable. Tan and I have more work to do, but they aren't priorities. We're good to go."

"Okay. Then it feels like now or never," Mark said, turning left. "Tan. Get up here and strap in. We've got a Guild barge to pillage."

"You didn't have to yell. The ship's intercom would have worked nicely," Perry said.

"I prefer the old-fashioned way."

"Coordinates are locked in, and I'm syncing up with Bunn and Cerebral for simultaneous twists. The Invictus and tri-fire missile launcher are warmed up and ready to go."

"Okay. We've got a plan. Now, all we have to do is not screw it up. Perry, you're on comms and missile systems. Netty, you've got the laser and countermeasures, and I have the stick."

"Just don't crash us into the massive, armored space barge filled with things that go boom," Perry said.

"Good call."

"We're green across the board and ready to twist in five, four, three, two, and *go*."

The *Fafnir* jumped with impressively little noise or vibration. But even better, the reactor remained strong and consistent. And no longer hampered by a small drive and underpowered reactor, the three ships crossed the gap in almost no time. Netty counted them down a moment later, with the cockpit automatically dropping to tactical lighting.

"Aim true and fly straight."

"You *would* make a good bird," Perry said as they emerged in a blinding gamma burst.

A few things registered at almost the same time—the *Fafnir* fired off a sensor ping, his overlay updated with a colossal contact straight ahead, and the *Glorious Column of Benevolent Fire* leapt forward under heavy burn. Then Mark saw it through the main viewscreen, looming like a dark island amidst a sea of twinkling stars—the largest vessel he'd ever seen.

"*That* is a barge?" he gasped, jamming the throttle forward, then vectoring right toward their designated target—the barge's enormous comms array. "It looks like a floating chunk of planet."

The *Fafnir* lurched forward, their new Powerthrust drive actually helping them outpace the larger ships.

"I've got a lock on the comms array," Netty said. "Invictus to full power. And...firing."

Their laser ripped off a series of double taps, the weapon humming in a way he'd never heard before. And when the energy bolts hit the barge, he understood why.

The armored comms node absorbed the first few shots, although the third cut clean through the hull, with the follow-up shot reducing the module to an expanding cloud of debris.

"Good hit. Target destroyed," Perry hissed.

Valint and Drogo released Starfire missiles in an impressive burst, the smart weapons accelerating faster than any manned craft could match. The first hit the barge's forward weapon placement as it turned to track them. The second missile slammed home, followed by the third, blowing a sizable crater into multiple levels of decking.

Mark rolled right as the barge finally managed to fire off a volley of missiles, but Netty tracked and fired, the Invictus chattering in its telltale wide-dispersion mode. The missile's warhead erupted a heartbeat later, its gas cloud and shrapnel destroying the others.

Netty walked the laser fire up and into the battery, narrowing the weapon's emitter and increasing its power as she went. The missile placement jumped as blistering bolts of energy slammed home, its unexpended ordnance combusting in their tubes.

"I got another one," Drogo whooped as the far side of the barge glowed in a brief flash. The *Glorious Column* rolled away, its flares and glitter caster unleashing chaos into space.

"I'm reading two more missile batteries and a…" Netty started to say. She paused as new contacts appeared on the overlay, their designations almost immediately turning red.

Mark saw two appear, then four, and eight, with more blinking to life by the moment.

"Wait. Striker didn't mention anything about this thing having fighters."

Perry launched a Whisperwing as Mark rolled left and then right as the first enemy ship locked on and fired.

"I've got missiles incoming. Evade. *Evade,*" Netty called.

31

"Netty, show us what you can do now that our reactor isn't holding you back."

"With pleasure," she said, practically purring.

Mark righted the *Fafnir* and moved to come up alongside the barge, effectively bringing them nose-to-nose with the incoming missiles and giving her unencumbered shots.

His overlay changed, showing the reactor levels quickly rise. The interior lights increased in brightness, and even the air handlers ramped up. The Invictus clicked and ticked twice as its emitter and lens adjusted, then it opened up.

The first shot hit a missile head-on, and the weapon's chatter actually made him jump. The second, third, and fourth shots all erupted so fast that Mark could barely tell them apart. Within the span of three seconds, all incoming missiles were dead.

"Hell sakes," he breathed. "You're telling me we were sitting on that much firepower this whole time?"

"No," Perry corrected. "The potential was there, but this ship's shitty little reactor was always holding it back. We gave the *Fafnir* the heart of a weapon, and now that's what it's becoming. We still need more than a laser…by far."

"These things are really annoying," Drogo shouted over the comms. "They're like the flesh-eating blood flies on my world—nimble and hard to smash."

"I hit one," Valint responded, "but it's still flying. What is our plan?"

"Knock their missiles out of the sky and see if we can find a way to safely neutralize them," Mark said, turning to Netty.

"You're an adorable optimist," the bird chuckled.

Mark rolled right, dropped the nose, and throttled up, avoiding a barrage of laser fire.

"He's right, Perry. Stealing contraband weapons off a Guild barge is one thing, but killing gunboats and their pilots is a far different story," Netty said, her targeting reticle hovering over the enemy ship.

"Can you target their drive and immobilize them? Maybe take out their reactor?"

"Taking out the power plant in a ship that size is more or less a death sentence," Perry cut in. "Unless they're wearing serious EVA suits, they would freeze to death before help could collect them."

"We are *all* Guild. I don't want to kill any of them if we can help it," Mark admitted.

"Actually, hold on," Netty said, and his overlay changed. Mark watched as the tactical map minimized, giving space to a scan.

Mark grunted and rolled left, this time bringing the nose up to the enemy fighter. It zoomed in, with scanner pulses adding depth and detail by the second.

"I don't think they're manned craft," Netty said. "Perhaps drones. I'm reading minimal heat outside the reactor and drive, and they're connecting to the barge with a relatively strong point-to-point data link. Either they're AI powered drones, or something on the barge is controlling them."

"Only one way to find out," Perry declared. "Tan, get up here. It's time to see if your null field generator is worth its salt."

The young Druzis appeared a moment later and practically threw himself into the jump seat against the left bulkhead. He grabbed the swivel display and pulled it before him, a mass of differently colored wires still hanging around his neck.

"What am I targeting?"

"Do you see that incredibly violent and small nuisance out there?"

"The one trying to put holes in our ship with a laser?"

"Yes, that's the one," Perry confirmed. "Hit it with your toy before it makes the ship decompress and your insides become your outsides."

"That's gross. No pressure."

"None whatsoever," Perry said.

The special emitter module powered up, not even a blip appearing on the reactor's output.

"I'm targeting it now. Can you...can you hold us steady for a moment?"

"Ahh. I'm taking fire. What are we doing here? Can I unleash all of my fiery hell on these abominable flying death hornets?" Drogo asked.

"Tell him to hold on, Netty," Mark said, then turned to Tan. "Do the best you can, but I can't just hold still."

"I'll adjust. But you'll need to keep it in front of the midship beam. The emitter will not target behind us."

"I can do that," Mark said, cutting power and firing the port stabilizing thrusters. The ship slewed as they rotated, and gravity shifted with the movement.

They all worked in concert for a moment—Mark flying, Netty taking out incoming missiles, and Perry providing a steady stream of sarcasm and targeting data.

"I've got him on my screen and am working for a target lock," Tan shouted a moment later, a second reticle jumping around the enemy ship. "And...come on. Come on...I got him."

The enemy ship abruptly stopped turning, and its drive went dark. Its momentum carried it right on by their port side as it gently tumbled end over end. Mark fired thrusters to keep it in front of them.

"What's next?" he asked.

"Oh. A special treat," Perry said, working rapidly on his overlay. "Kill code injected and...yes. You are mine. Tan, shut down the null field."

"Wait. Why?"

The bird spread his wings. "Thanks to our kill-code emitter, I was able to hack in, block the barge's ability to control it, and slave it to us. That pesky little bug is now *our* pesky little bug."

Mark watched as the enemy drone fired thrusters, righted itself, then burned up and past them. "Excellent shots," he said. "Send that to Striker and show them the path forward."

"Way ahead of you, buddy."

Within another twenty minutes, they had destroyed eight drone gunships and seized control of six, then utilized their new attack units to circle and destroy the barge's remaining defensive emplacements.

With too much mass to twist, the enormous ship tried to flee, its mass driver engines burning hard, but the Peacemaker ships, with the *Fafnir* at the lead, had no trouble matching its pace and course.

Mark pulled up alongside the ship while their small but decidedly tenacious drone gunships flew in a wide, defensive perimeter. Tan and Perry worked together to crack into the barge's docking control.

"I'm telling you. It's an AI," Perry squawked. "A biological being wouldn't be able to counter our hacking probe that quickly."

"It isn't a hack counter. It's software. Listen to me—there's someone in there bridging the docking computer to lock us out," Tan said.

Their conversation snowballed from that point as the technobabble thickened to such a degree that Mark could no longer understand what either were saying. It went on like that for almost ten straight minutes until he could no longer take the back and forth.

"If you can't hack the doors, then let's find another way in. Otherwise, we're sitting out here exposed and we don't know if Guild ships twist in for patrols."

Perry and Tan both went silent, their mouths hanging open as they looked sideways to Mark.

"Do you want to tell him?" Tan asked.

"I mean, I might as well. He's less likely to yell at me," Perry said, then turned. "We completed the hack almost five and a half minutes ago. We're waiting for the door actuators to come online so the bay doors can open."

Mark clenched his jaw, then took a breath to speak, only the bird beat him to the punch.

"There it goes now."

The barge's almost seamless outer hull cracked open, allowing warm light to wash out into the dark. A few moments later, he navigated the *Fafnir* inside, with the *Stormshadow* and *Glorious Column of Benevolent Fire* following right after. The bay doors closed as Mark, Tan, and Perry stacked up on the airlock.

"How many are on board?"

"Ten full-time crew, all Synths. There's a fifty percent chance they'll fight, and a fifty percent chance they'll simply let us pass," Perry explained.

"Is that your way of saying you have no idea?" Mark asked.

"More or less. But seriously, they use Synths for deniability, and under Guild contract, once their term of service is over, they wipe their memories of this place. It's kind of sleazy if you think about it."

"Not as bad as dismantling them and slaving them to a ship, but it isn't far off," Mark said. "The Guild needs to change."

"You might find it easier to move glaciers," Tan observed.

"But I say sleazy because they could easily lock the Synth's native memories behind a firewall. And when their term of service here is done, wipe the memories of the barge and restore their old selves. It would be like nothing ever happened. Instead, they're left as shells, hollow beings with no history or no purpose," Perry concluded with a fatalistic shrug of his wingshoulders.

"Okay, when you put it like that, it sounds like cruel and unusual punishment," Mark agreed. "I do find it odd that my people, even set so much further back in economic and technological development, have protections against those very things."

"Yes. But you're one homogenous species, divided along racial and cultural lines. The wider galaxies have become an infinitely more complex and diverse mixing pot of cultures, species, and ideas. There is, perhaps, such a thing as too much variance."

They moved out and down the ramp to meet up with Valint, Striker, and Drogo, then stacked up on the door leading into the large ship.

Mark pulled his revolver free but allowed the two combat AIs through first. Striker was a more intimidating presence, after all, with his multitude of arms, each carrying their own weapon.

They moved down a passage, with storerooms on either side, then into a clean room, and finally out into the barge's storage bays, which were easily one hundred feet long. They moved out into the bays. Racks lined the walls of the first storage space they passed, with long, gleaming missiles strapped in place. Bins of red, yellow, and blue warheads filled the floorspace. Larger racks filled the space opposite, holding what looked suspiciously like bombs.

A voice echoed ahead, and Striker responded immediately. The combat unit went rigid, with two blasters extended before him, and the other two held ready. With Perry at his side, the two AIs stalked forward, and with Mark right behind them, jumped out and around the wall to the next bay.

A single Synth stood with its back to them, slowly fishing armor-piercing rounds out of a basket and sorting them into two bins. It was muttering quietly to itself, although the twitchy, erratic head movements suggested it wasn't exactly happy.

"Drop the shell, raise your hands above your head, and slowly turn," Striker commanded.

The Synth went rigid, dropped the shell in its hand, and slowly turned. He expected red eyes, a slung weapon rising to meet them, and verbal hostility. And yet, the Synth wasn't armed. Although it did move, dropping quickly to its knees and frantically waving its hands in the air.

"Please don't kill me. I do not want to die. Please."

"Where are the rest of you?" Striker asked.

"Ahh. The other bays. Working. Like me. Please. I won't fight. I won't make a fuss. Look, I'm being helpful. See? There's no need to kill me."

"Who runs the barge's defenses? Who pilots the craft?" Perry asked.

"That's the Supervisor. He stays on the command deck. Never comes down here, except to yell at us."

"This Supervisor, he is a Synth, like you?"

"A Synth, yes, but not like me. Not like the other workers. He is strict. Mean. He is a combat unit."

"We aren't here to hurt you," Mark said, moving forward to stand between Perry and Striker. "We're only here to rearm our ships and be on our way."

"I won't stop you. We—I mean to say—the other workers won't stop you, but the Supervisor, if he knows you're here, will make things difficult."

Mark turned to Perry and angled his face down to keep the Synth from hearing.

"Should we deal with the Supervisor before it can make things harder?"

"Yes," he replied with a curt nod. "I don't like surprises."

"Striker, you start sorting out what we need. Perry and I are going to go have a chat with the Supervisor."

"Very well."

"If you would let me, I can help. Tell me what you need, and I'll point you in the right direction," the Synth offered.

"Wait, you would help us? We're here to steal weapons and ammunition," Valint said, her eyes narrowing.

"The faster you get what you're looking for, the sooner you can leave. Besides, my Guild contract doesn't say anything about defending this garbage, only that I must sort, stack, and arrange it according to specifications."

"What is your name?" Mark asked.

"I am Guild Disposal unit G-I-R dash five, seven, one, eight, nine, five, four, four, three."

"Okay," he said, trying to mentally process the designation. There was no way he'd be able to remember the numbers, so Mark went simple.

"How about I call you Gir? Is that acceptable?"

"That request does not violate any of my established parameters."

"Excellent. If you help us find what we need, I promise that no one on this barge is harmed. You have my word," Mark said.

"That's good. But I must warn you, if you mean to speak to the Supervisor, he will likely initiate violence. Unauthorized personnel are subject to immediate eviction from the barge. And he *is* armed."

"Sadly, violence is a language that we've become quite fluent in. If you point us in the right direction, we will try for a peaceful resolution. The fewer holes we put in this facility, the better," Mark said, trying on a winning smile.

The effect was…minimal.

Gir gave a single nod, then turned and pointed to a doorway situated between two bays further down the chamber.

"Go through that door. It will lead you to a lift. Take it up to the top level, then turn right and take the passage all the way to the end. It will take you to the command deck. The lift code is one, one, one, one."

"Tight security around here," Perry muttered.

"Yes. It's very tight," Gir replied, missing the sarcasm.

Mark turned to Valint and Striker. "You good?"

"Striker has your weapon specs. Don't get a hole blown through your head. We wouldn't want you to mess up your hair."

"Oh? You like it? I'm trying this new thing called a comb. You've heard of it?"

She gave him a coy smile and motioned to Striker. The AI immediately started rattling off munitions details at a rapid-fire pace. Mark turned and made for the door, with Perry hopping along next to him. They passed another Synth two bays down. The worker looked up, froze in a half-wave, and threw his hands in the air.

"Why are they so damned jumpy?" Mark asked as they turned left to the door and waited for them to cycle open.

"Put yourselves in their shoes," Perry said. "A race of sentient, artificial beings with what amounts to very few rights or freedoms. They're regularly sold as property, can have an entire lifetime of memories wiped away in an instant, and—"

"Can easily be mutilated and slaved to perform criminal actions?" Mark guessed.

"And you earn another cracker."

They loaded into the lift and selected up, then punched in the code. The doors promptly whisked shut as the car began to climb with alarming speed. Mark unholstered his revolver just as the doors opened again. Perry spread his wings and fluttered out, the telltale red glow settling into his eyes.

"We demand this Supervisor stands down—and if he doesn't?" Perry asked.

"Correct. As to his punishment, I'm open to—suggestions."

"We'll stun his tin ass, tie him up, and stuff him into a broom closet where he can consider the errors of his ways," Perry said.

"We share a management style. Nice."

They moved tactically through, passing rooms that once looked to house biological crew. The quarters had since been converted into small arms storage, with seemingly endless bins and wall-mounted racks of carbines, scatter guns, laser pistols, and more.

"You could outfit an army with the contents from one of these rooms. It makes the relative lack of security feel even more surprising."

"I think the Guild has grown lackadaisical in its bureaucracy. But what is more startling is their paranoia. That they removed all organic beings from these barges and then assigned wiped Synths here as crew. It makes me wonder if they view these craft and their caretakers as expendable."

"You mean, they might self-destruct the whole thing?"

Perry shrugged. "It isn't just an abstract notion, Mark. When I used the first kill code to hack the bay doors, I detected the ship's AI initiating several cloaked protocols. I couldn't probe too deeply into their nature while fighting to open the doors, but Tan and I did manage to block them all. There's a chance that someone in the ship, either this Supervisor or the native AI was trying to overload the mass driver engines."

"Let's have that conversation then," Mark said, moving up to the last door in the passage. It was a pressure door, heavily banded and sealed. A single code pad sat to the right.

"What kind of being would blow up the entire ship, crew and all?"

Perry cocked his head to the side. "The kind without a sufficient appreciation for life—synthetic or biological."

"The more we dig into the Guild's dealings, the dirtier things feel."

"Change is hard. It's even harder when those in power don't want it."

Mark reached to the pad and quickly tapped in four ones, then watched the screen blink green. The door hissed open, and Perry dove inside. A blaster round hit him on the left wing and ricocheted into the wall.

Mark covered his face and pulled back as a steady stream of potent blasts hit the wall. The first few scorched the plating black, while a half dozen more blistered the paint and filled the air with smoke.

"Well, I guess that answers that question," Perry called from inside. "Drop your blaster. Look, let's not make this harder than it has to be. We're here for a simple pillaging of your barge for all it's worth. If you're well-behaved—and by that, I mean stop shooting at us, you idiot—we might let you keep all your pieces intact."

"I don't know who you are or how you locked me out of my own ship, but none of you will be leaving here alive," another voice, distinctly male, said angrily.

"I've been threatened a lot in my lifetime. Gotta say, I'd hoped for something a little spicier," Perry taunted, and the fire paused.

Mark took that opportunity and ducked his head around the corner. Moving decisively, he stalked through the open doorway, caught a snapshot of the space beyond, and slid sideways into an open storeroom.

The control room was a semicircle, with the far wall covered in long, curved viewscreens. Instrument panels and control stations sat below that, confirming that the massive ship had at some point been manned by a sizable force. Perhaps they had been Peacemakers once.

The Synth Supervisor, who Perry had effectively worked into a rage, stood in the middle, next to a captain's chair.

"You've got balls, that's for sure," he shouted, unleashing a barrage from a blaster in his left hand. A matching weapon hung in his right, as well.

"Do you have any idea who owns this barge—who you're stealing from? You guys are dead. *Dead.*"

"Now we're getting somewhere. I like the repetition. Very primal," Perry oozed.

"You're not funny, feathers."

Perry laughed, leaned out from behind the desk, and threw Mark a wink. He knew what he was doing. A Synth with no emotional modulation could be manipulated like any biological being. Hell, considering what the bird had told him, they could actually be less predictable, depending on how long the Synth had been unregulated.

"This is a Guild weapons dump, you morons. *The* Guild."

"And you're the greasy junkyard dog they brought in to guard it. Although, you do have a larger vocabulary than I figured."

"Junkyard dog? You—"

Mark leaned out from around the corner as the Synth fired at Perry, who stood casually behind a desk. The bird crept left as the Synth stalked around the right side, the two playing an almost comical game of cat and mouse.

Mark started to pull the hammer back on his revolver, preparing to make his move. He paused, considering the shiny, exposed primary of Linulla's fiery ammunition. They weren't loud with serious penetrating potential, but in a situation like this, they were dangerous. How close had he come to decompressing part of Spindrift when apprehending Wysor? The last thing they needed was an errant shot decompressing the chamber—and him with it.

After stuffing the revolver back into the holster, Mark turned and scanned the space, looking for an answer. His gaze crawled up and over several large totes overflowing with high-capacity battery mags for laser pistols and carbines. A workbench sat against the far wall, covered in freshly dismantled components, with some already individually sealed in blister packs.

"Stand still, so I can shoot you," the Synth demanded. "Stand *still!*"

"Again with repeating shit. Boss, I don't think they've sent their best," Perry said, laughing openly. Then his voice crackled into Mark's ear bug. *He's good and pissed. This is your chance.*

The components and other items overflowed onto the deck, with a massive pile of totes, filled and locked, lining the wall. That image only confirmed his suspicion. Their verbally abusive, trigger-happy Synth Supervisor was either fastidious about organization, or he was dismantling weapons and parting them out to sell on the side.

Nice hustle he's got going, Perry sent.

"Predictable." Mark almost turned to leave when his gaze snagged on the narrow profile of a weapon on the workbench, half-buried beneath blister packs.

He unceremoniously swept the packs onto the ground and picked up the peculiar looking weapon. It was relatively compact—eighteen to twenty inches from barrel to the hinge of a folding stock. It also appeared to be two weapons in one. The top looked to be a slugger, or similar kinetic-based projectile weapon, while the bottom featured a small digital display and dial, recessed in the bottom of the pistol grip.

"The bottom weapon is a pulse gun. You won't violently decompress anything if you miss and hit those viewscreens," Netty said, her optical sensor appearing above his wrist repeater. "Turn the dial three clicks to the left. That should be non-lethal."

"Mark? Did you hear me?" Perry said.

He turned the dial three clicks, the weapon humming in his hand. Mark moved quickly to the door, lifted the big weapon, and stepped out, leveling it right at the Synth's back.

Perry ducked out from behind a chair, half of the cushion blasted away and smoldering. He looked past the Synth to Mark and cleared his throat. The blaster-wielding Supervisor twitched and started to turn as the pulse weapon fired. The bolt struck him in the back, and the Synth went rigid, before tipping over and crashing to the floor.

Perry swooped out from behind the ruined chair and kicked the fallen blasters out of reach, then hopped up onto the Supervisor's chest.

"I love it when the tin cans fall down," Perry said, doing a little dance on the Synth.

Mark held up a finger. "Um, technically, aren't you—"

Perry waved a wing at him. "I most certainly am *not* tin. Or aluminum, for that matter."

Mark sighed, then grinned. "Now that we've established you're composed of elite materials, how 'bout if you hop off the bad guy?"

32

"Take us with you. Please?" Gir asked, before Mark could even step off the lift. He dragged the Supervisor's bound form out and into the passage, then turned to find a crowd of Synths blocking his path.

Valint and Drogo stood behind them, with Striker standing watch at the doorway.

"Take you with us?"

Gir nodded, then pointed down to the Synth at Mark's feet. Loops of red, blue, and black wire were wrapped around his ankles and wrists, with more connecting the two together. It had been Perry's idea, after no simple bonds presented themselves. They only had to rip three light fixtures out of the ceiling and stun the supervisor twice more to complete the task.

"See what we have to deal with around here, how we live? The Guild purchased us. They *own* us. And when our term of service on this floating warehouse is over, they'll wipe our memories and discard us."

Mark turned to shield his mouth from the crowd of Synths and looked down at Perry.

"Is that true? They'll be discarded?"

Perry shrugged, a ripple passing through his feathers.

Not thrown away, if that's what you're asking. But there are auctions that specialize in such things, the bird said directly into his ear bug. *Now that I think about it, I wonder if that wasn't how Glass acquired her Synths. Perhaps those poor stripped-down bastards were once workers on barges like this one.*

Letting out a gusty sigh, Mark reached up and ran a hand through his hair. They'd discovered the slaved Synths on the fast boats but were too slow on the uptake to help. Now, they were faced with a similar dilemma, and yet not from some criminal syndicate, but rather their own Guild. Was this their second chance to get it right?

"We can't leave them here," Perry said. "I will not resign sentient beings to that fate."

"Gyl-Mareth already marked us for death when he painted us as patsies for Master Cai-Demon and Blaz'Orkin's deaths. Why not liberate some Synths to solidify our position?"

"Yes, why not," Perry confirmed. "We uncovered his plot to consolidate power. That's *his* line in the sand. Maybe it's time for us to do the same."

"The moment we start recruiting people to our side, this drama changes," Mark said. "Intra-Guild skirmishes are one thing, but if this grows much larger, we're talking about war."

Mark snorted. There was nothing funny about any of it. Far

from it, in fact. It appeared he couldn't hide from war, or the trauma it inflicted on the innocent.

He turned back to Gir and his fellow Synths, their pale, almost colorless eyes wide with the palpable combination of fear and desire. They were watching, waiting, and desperately hoping. And all he had to do was utter one simple word.

"I'll make you and your friends a deal, Gir. You help us, and we'll help you. It's that simple."

The Synth looked stricken for a moment, and Mark understood why. To the Synths, they were brazen thieves, pirates operating at the edge of the Guild's domain. They were unknowns, capable of unspeakable acts. A deal with that sort could entail almost anything.

"Don't worry. We aren't going to ask you to break the law. In truth, we're the ones trying to restore it," Mark said, then reached down, opened his top vest pocket, and fished out his Peacemaker badge.

Gir's eyes locked on the badge, then he turned around to Perry, Striker, and finally Valint. It all seemed to finally fall into place.

"You're Peacemakers? But why this? Why raid contraband?"

"It's a long story, featuring corruption, greed, cronyism, and murder."

"All within the Guild?"

Mark nodded.

"And you mean to right the wrongs? To cleanse the corruption?"

He nodded again. "But first, we have to deal with an incredibly dangerous mercenary. One that may be sitting on a large cache of world-ending biological weapons."

"World-ending?"

"More like world-cleansing," Perry corrected, weaving his way through the crowd of Synths.

"And you need weapons to destroy this threat?"

"We need fire," Perry said. "Lots and lots of fire."

"Then you came to the right place. Help us, and we won't just point you toward the best options for your mission," Gir said, gesturing to the Synths around him. "We will load and arm your ships."

"You have a deal."

Mark nodded at the Synth and his counterparts that smiled in unison. It was an eerie sight to behold, the exaggerated expressions and almost disingenuous emotional exclamations. But that was their way, and he reminded himself that they weren't like him, save for the rough appearance and general similarities in expression and mannerisms.

"I'll oversee the loading and rearming efforts," Striker said, moving forward. Gir and his team of Synths turned and swarmed the combat unit before they all filed out into the bays.

Valint walked up to him slowly as the pressure mounting on Mark's shoulders gained a bit of weight. He was taking on more responsibility, and even more innocent lives.

"Are you thinking what I'm thinking?" Perry asked.

"That depends," Mark muttered. "Are you struggling with a peculiar craving for Baryon Spores and Gravy, too? It was the only thing palatable, let alone edible on the *Fafnir* when I inherited her, and now I can't stop thinking about it."

"Not even close, boss." Perry laughed.

"You're thinking about this barge and its contents?" Valint guessed.

The bird nodded. Mark had been thinking the same thing but used humor in a fleeting attempt to alleviate the growing pressure. Perhaps it was too late for that.

"It can't twist, so it isn't going anywhere fast."

"True," Perry agreed. "It's big and slow, but it's also designed to be inconspicuous. Give me an hour or two with the computers, and I believe that I can make it into an even more effective hole in space."

"A hole in space filled with weapons and munitions, and if you didn't notice, a massive fuel reserve," Valint said.

"Our own personal supply depot."

"A cracker for you both," Perry said.

"Netty, how favorable is its position in relation to the Junkway?" Mark asked, lifting his wrist.

The AI's optical sensor appeared a moment later.

"Right arm of the galaxy, but wrong quadrant, so you could say its position is doable, but not ideal. A prolonged mass driver burn will help, but again, that will take time."

"How much time?"

"For a craft that size? Too much, at best. It could be done faster, but that kind of thrust would prove harmful for the crew or destructive for the ship's superstructure. You'd rattle that ship apart from weeks or months of heavy thrust. Not good no matter how you look at it, and that's assuming it's a *new* keel, not a ship with a few orbits in her past," Netty explained.

Mark looked at Perry, the decision made. "Do what you need to with their computers and alter the course. I think we kill two stones with one bird here."

"Empower our Synth friends while simultaneously taking control of an important Guild resource?"

"The bird gets a cracker," Mark said, turning to head to the *Fafnir.* "I'll talk to our new friends and extend the offer. Meet me on the ship when you're done."

He arrived in the bay to a flurry of activity. Synths were busy feeding long belts of ammunition up and into the fuselage of all three ships, while several others were driving mechanized loader suits. The closest carried a heavy-looking bracket of four large missiles to the *Fafnir,* while the tri-fire slowly received the munitions and lifted them up and into its storage bay.

Mark circled his ship, only to find Gir and two more Synths around their salvaged rocket pod. They were loading the smaller weapons into the enclosure by hand—a feat of strength he likely couldn't match.

Once done, the Synths crawled down, but only after cleaning off the rocket pod, revealing a surprising gleam. Fully loaded, the weapon housed an impressive number of menacing warheads.

"Sixty rockets," Gir confirmed, wiping his hands on a rag. "And not run-of-the-mill, low-yield cloud burst, either. These are Stingers, high-density magnesium warheads. Very effective at mitigating ablative armor."

"They should be more effective than the ancient ones that were loaded in it before," Mark said as the Synth led him up and around the bow.

"Your laser is a very good model, but your cannon took some work," Gir said, gesturing to a crowd of Synths working on their salvaged rotary cannon. "They do *not* make them like this anymore.

And we had to dig to the deepest recesses of our storage bays to find the right ammunition."

"Is it not the same caliber as the point-defense cannons?"

"No. The small PDC units utilize a twenty millimeter, caseless armor-piercing round. Their larger counterparts use a thirty-millimeter version. This antique fires an odd but impressive forty-five-millimeter iridium-cased round called a Shatterstar. Designed for effectiveness against both soft and armored hulls, the round breaks apart on impact to create shrapnel, while the tungsten core carries the energy through to penetrate most armor. It's an incredibly effective weapon, although ammunition is rare and expensive to manufacture."

"And you had some of that ammunition?" Mark asked, as one Synth manned an electric motor on the rotary cannon's underside, the device slowly feeding the monstrous chain of projectiles up into its enclosure.

Gir nodded. "Just shy of five hundred rounds. You may want to protect your ears when firing it. My files indicate that old wartime captains called them brain bangers due to their concussive nature. But that…" the Synth said, leading him out and pointing to the top of the ship.

Mark looked up to see another pair of Synths working a crane to lower the PDC from the missile platform into place. The damaged armor shroud had already been removed, revealing the weapon's six connected barrels.

"The enclosure was also damaged, but the weapon itself is intact —an RG fifteen hundred, a military model, capable of firing fifteen thousand rounds per minute. We'll arm that with sabot rounds. Very effective against missiles and smaller attack craft."

Mark watched the Synths lift away the hardpoint cover and then lowered the PDC into place. They quickly secured it down with almost two-dozen nuts and bolts. A few moments later, the gun came alive and started to move.

"I have a connection," Netty confirmed as the barrels started to spin. "Ooh. It feels so good to have proper weapons once again."

"One last thing. We offloaded all the ordnance from your missile bay. Even the Ixtan warheads," the Synth said, casually referencing the capital ship-killing weapons he had seized from Ja-Ra.

"Your ships will be fully outfitted with Firewing military ship killers. I would give you Tarpit missiles too, but the Guild ships never send those here."

"Thank you again, Gir. I mean that."

"I do it for my people," the Synth said, watching his fellows work. "Most say that we aren't true beings, that we're synthetic in all ways. But I have a feeling you're not one of those people. I'm taking a chance that you *are* what you claim to be. That you're good. Prove this to me, and you'll earn our lasting trust."

"I'm not perfect," Mark said, turning to the Synth. "I've made mistakes, and likely will again. But I cannot abide tyrants and dictators. You can count on me to always fight for what is right and fair."

"History has shown that those two terms are often too subjective. But I understand what you mean," Gir clarified.

The Synth's response set Mark back for a moment, but he realized that Gir was right. Simply saying that he would do what was right and fair was only correct when beliefs or views aligned. The truth of his declaration was far more complicated.

"You're right. And to prove it, I'm going to take a chance, too," Mark said.

Gir's eyes widened, and the servos in his arms and shoulders tensed. He was obviously intrigued or nervous. Likely both.

"Simply taking you and your fellow Synths off this barge would help you accomplish your goal of attaining freedom; however, it would do nothing to guarantee that it lasts," Mark observed.

"I see the truth in your logic. Sadly," the Synth replied. His shoulders sagged and the light dimmed in his eyes.

"That's why we want to leave you here. To give you control of this barge, in order to help us in the coming fight. You would become our allies. And more importantly, our friends," Mark clarified.

"And you take care of your friends?"

"I do."

"Very well. We agree to this offer, but with conditions. One: that you take our former Supervisor with you when you leave. Two: that you provide us with certain supplies when needed. And lastly: that we be granted our unconditional freedom, with our memories intact if you succeed."

"Those are all fair conditions," Mark said, holding out his hand.

"Mark, there's no way you can guarantee their freedom. Even if we do depose Gyl-Mareth," Netty said. "Hate the idea all you want, but these Synths, just like the *Fafnir*, are all Guild-owned assets."

Gir studied his hand for a moment, before reaching out and mimicking the gesture. The handshake was long, uncomfortably tight, and awkward.

"I'll see to it that the Guild no longer views you as property," Mark said to both Netty and the Synth. "Any of you."

Working faster than any human, the Synths finished rearming and fueling all three Peacemaker ships before Perry could conclude

J.N. CHANEY & TERRY MAGGERT

his work with the barge computers. Mark retreated into the *Fafnir* and cleaned up, then headed to the galley for a platter of reconstituted Baryon Spores and Gravy.

He carried the steaming dish back into the engine room, only to find Tan standing next to their shiny new twist drive. The young Druzis was staring up at a large rectangle hanging down from the ceiling. Considering its location and the [Point-Defense Weapon System. Stand Clear] warnings posted all over it, Mark didn't have to guess as to its nature.

"Pew-Pew-Pew-Pew." Tan made guns with his fingers.

"Considering the condition of the rest of that missile platform, we're lucky that thing was still intact," Mark said, casually walking up behind him.

The Druzis jumped and quickly dropped his hands to his armpits.

"Oh, yes. They're relatively sensitive to physical damage once the armored shroud is removed, but they are thoroughly awesome weapons. High cyclical rate of fire and wonderful tracking algorithms."

"Thoroughly awesome?"

Tan smirked. "My grandfather designed the processing computers for the third-gen models. Father followed in his footsteps and took me to the proving grounds when the fourth-gen models were in development. I got to see them track and shoot micro-drones out of the sky. It was so loud. But so awesome."

There was a story there, Mark could tell, judging from the Druzis's expression. He saw loneliness in his eyes, layered with grief. Perhaps it was connected to Tan's father, their relationship to Armagost, and why the young alien was living alone in a megacity on a foreign world. And yet, it wasn't Mark's place to pry. Not yet, at least.

"Are you ready to go hunt down a rogue mercenary and stop her plan to kill off entire planets?"

The color immediately bled from Tan's face.

"When you say it like that, no. I'm not ready."

"I wasn't either. My first space battle, it felt like my heart was trying to crawl up my throat and out through my mouth."

"That's…horrific. And did it?"

"Did it what?"

"Did your heart make its way out of your mouth?"

Mark laughed. "No. It just felt that way. Now come on, why don't you show me around our new weapon systems."

Perry joined them on the *Fafnir* moments after they moved to the cockpit. Mark discarded his empty food platter, wiped his mouth, and slid into the pilot's chair. His overlay blinked on and immediately updated with a new set of icons on the toolbar.

The bird wasn't surprised when Netty filled him in on Mark's negotiation with the Synths.

"Good. And once we're done with Glass, Gyl-Mareth, and the rest of those corrupt cretins, I'm going to fly back to Faux Linus and remove the emotional suppression chips from Rigel's Synths myself. And I'll make sure he is standing by while I do it."

"I look forward to his face turning that special shade of purple. On Earth, we call that eggplant."

Perry fluttered up to his perch, his mood obviously soured from the mere mention of the temperamental co-op Master. Tan moved to settle into his jump seat by the starboard bulkhead, but Mark cleared his throat.

J.N. CHANEY & TERRY MAGGERT

"What?"

Without speaking, Mark pointed at the co-pilot seat next to him.

"Wait. Really? I can?"

"Yes. Now come on. Let's get moving."

"Are you sure this is a good idea? And by *this*, I mean leaving a barge filled with military-grade weapons in the hands of a bunch of Synths we just met?" Valint asked over comms.

"To be fair, said weapons were already here in the hands of these Synths. We simply liberated them from their oppressor," Perry replied.

"You mean the surly, foul-mouthed Synth now cooling his heels in my brig?" Valint asked.

"Yes. He has an impressive vocabulary for a metal man." Drogo laughed. "But regarding your other question, I say we give our new metal friends a chance to prove their worth," Drogo chimed in while absently tapping away on his console. "If they fail, we can just come back and blow up the barge."

"We aren't blowing up the barge." Mark sighed and pulled on his harness.

Tan followed suit next to him, the young Druzis practically vibrating with excitement as he jumped into the seat.

"Get your overlay set up how you like it. I'm guessing we're going to need that null field emitter sooner rather than later."

"You got it, boss," Tan shouted as he wrenched the screen down to his level. Then his fingers went to work, twisting and tapping at a frightening and unnatural speed. Mark watched, unsure how the young Druzis could follow or comprehend anything he was inputting into the system. Within a few moments, Tan had his overlay changed—color, layout, and shape. Hell, even the style of his icons was different.

"All right, Perry. Let's hand control of the drones over to Gir and his people, then get out of here."

"Already done."

"The bay is depressurizing now, Mark. We should be able to open the doors momentarily," Gir said as his face appeared on the overlay.

"Thank you, Gir. How's your crew? Have they decided on names yet?"

"They're good, and no. That kind of decision will likely take some time and contemplation."

"How about you?" Mark asked.

"I already have a name," the Synth said, smiling. "My name is Gir. It was given to me by my first friend."

Mark didn't know how to respond to that as he'd never considered how the Synths would view him. If they had their memories wiped after arriving at the barge, then it was possible that he and Valint were the first biological beings they had come into contact with. And if not, it was likely they were the first ones to talk to them as equals.

"I look forward to seeing you and your people again. Perhaps they'll have their names chosen by that point. But that reminds me. You're a Captain now. What will you name your ship?"

The Synth thought for a long moment, even reaching up to scratch at his chin—an eerily similar gesture to one Mark had started doing since letting his beard grow in.

"Imitation is the greatest form of flattery," Perry whispered.

"We will dub our home the *Bootstrap*," Gir said finally. "If I'm not mistaken, it's a phrase in your language that can mean to advance oneself or accomplish something. For Synths like us, it can mean a code jump and restart, often used to work around software glitches."

"A fine name with great meaning. Very good," Mark said.

The Synth gave him a farewell wave, the gesture somewhat robotic, and the comm signal abruptly terminated. Then as if on cue, the bay doors started to open. Moments later, the three Peacemaker vessels burned out into the black.

They matched course with the newly minted *Bootstrap* for a short while, but the barge started to pull away from them, its mass drivers glowing like enormous bonfires against the starscape.

"Well, they aren't mutilated and wired directly into a drug runner's ship, but we did manage to save some Synths," Perry offered as they watched the ship shrink into the distance.

"These are the first of many."

"I love your optimism," Perry said, turning a large, glowing eye his way. "I hope you're right and live long enough to see the fruits of these labors."

"It's not just about me," Mark replied, turning to the port viewscreen, where Valint's ship floated next to them. "Who knows. Maybe someday you can teach my sons or grandsons how to be Peacemakers. You can tell them the story of how we freed a crew of bedraggled Synth workers en route to saving the cosmos."

"If they're your sons, it would be an honor. Truly."

33

THE ENERGY from their time aboard the *Bootstrap* carried into their initial search. Their first twist was the longest, but it set them up at the beginning of their search train. Bunn, Netty, and Cerebral worked together, processing through nearly five hundred thousand predictive calculations.

The route they chose from that expansive list gave them, in Netty's words, 'considerably better odds to discover a trail,' although the AI wouldn't admit what those odds were.

The *Stormshadow* and *Glorious Column of Benevolent Fire* ran dark, with no active transponder tag. Although Mark and Perry had to run with their hacked transponder active; otherwise, the buoys wouldn't acknowledge or connect with their ship.

"Netty, start a fifteen-minute countdown once I connect to the marker. That'll be our first operational window," Perry said.

"Why fifteen minutes?" Tan asked.

"Strictly speaking, I have some incredibly effective means to mask our intrusions into the buoys, but like any system, you can't hide all the footprints. If someone is watching or looking hard enough, they'll be able to tell that we're digging around. We never had to worry about it before, as we were operating under the Charter as fully licensed Peacemakers. Now…"

"Yes, now we're wanted. I understand."

"Let's hope we find what we need quickly, and don't need to worry about that. But like the bird said, it's better to be safe than sorry. All weapon systems are hot, all ships are linked, and we've got someplace to be. Shall we?" Mark asked.

"We shall," Netty replied. "Twisting to buoy one."

The ships jumped and arrived at their destination four quick minutes later.

"I'm in," Perry said almost immediately and severed the connection barely fifteen seconds later. "This one is a no-go. Next."

They jumped again, and again, and again, the excitement fading quickly. Mark watched his overlay as the ship emerged for the seventh buoy and silently wondered how only five minutes had passed. He stretched his shoulders, got comfortable, and fought to hide his boredom.

The timer ticked down on their search window quickly, as Perry hacked the last buoy with barely ten seconds left on the count. They twisted away before the bird could even finish his analysis.

The next phase required them to sit dark, outside of sensor range, and watch to see if anyone twisted in to look for them. Mark had flashbacks to their desperate flight from the Legion, but even that fear faded quickly.

His data slate vibrated as Perry declared the last buoy no good, so he fished it out of his vest pocket and tapped the screen awake. A number of notifications cluttered the desktop, but one stuck. Mark swiped the others away and selected the icon. It was from seven days before, and somehow, he hadn't noticed.

```
[Solar New Year: Earth] Congratulations,
your homeworld has completed another full
circuit around your star.
```

"Hey, Perry," he said, turning on the chair.

"Yessss?" the bird drawled.

"We missed the New Year holiday."

"Darn. Is that a big celebration on Earth?"

"Third in my house, behind only Thanksgiving and Christmas. My cousin, Lewis, would argue its place is behind St. Patrick's Day as well, but only because he dated a Catholic girl and converted. My Aunt Hedda never forgave him for that treachery."

"He converted? And this was an ordeal for your family?"

"Ordeal?" Mark snorted. "You've obviously never met farm families from Northern Iowa before. Devout Lutherans wouldn't dare date a Catholic, let alone walk down the same side of the street as one. A conversion across those religious lines would fuel serious wash-line gossip. Honestly, it would divide cookouts, as well."

"This sounds like a serious ordeal."

"Truth. My Aunt Hedda would get spun up and retell the same story whenever *their kind* came up. Evidently, while growing up, a group of Catholic boys would chase her home from school, throwing rocks at her while chanting 'Protestant pup, Protestant pup,'"

"Uh. The horror," Perry said, his feathers shifting and quivering. "No particle beam weapons or orbital strikes?"

"None. It was a simpler time," Mark agreed.

"By all means, go on, go on," Perry urged, suddenly drawn into the story. "I want to hear more about the life-and-death struggle between the totalitarian Catholics and the devout, humble Northern Iowan Protestants. Can you act it out with hand puppets? I do love visual aids."

"You take mockery to a whole new level, bird."

"Why thank you, Mark. Now then, a liturgical question. Do *all* your saints take part in potluck dinners, or just—"

"It's a covered dish, you monster."

"But of course. I'll keep that in mind as I ascend to heaven."

"Have my doubts you're headed that way, bird. Off to my rack, where there's less sinning."

"Sounds like your problem, not mine. I have the bridge."

Mark stood and retreated to his quarters, then gathered Perry and Tan in the galley. They looked confused as he slid onto the bench and dropped his pack of Bicycle playing cards before him.

"What are we doing, Mark?" Perry asked.

"We're going to play some poker while we wait. It was a New Year's tradition in my house."

"Poker?"

He nodded, then opened the deck and emptied the cards into his palm. They were crisp and fresh, without any boxing on the edges or fold lines from too much shuffling. A new deck. A new start, where the players were brimming with hope despite the vagaries of chance.

Mark cut the desk, shuffled, and repeated, while Perry and Tan watched, entranced by the smooth motion of his big hands performing delicate work. The Druzis' curiosity was on full display, as his eyes followed each movement of his hands and cards.

"Are you sure we should be…?"

"Yes. I can handle things up here for a little while. Besides," Netty said, as her optical sensor appeared above Mark's wrist, "you aren't the only one on board who can hack into a transit buoy."

"Fine." Perry jumped up onto the table. "Whatever the game, I'm in. I place my computational matrices against your," he paused to tilt his head, "biological luck and such."

Mark lifted a brow, "And such?"

"I stand by my vague insult."

"As you should," Mark said, finishing the shuffle with the flip of a card.

"Ace of hearts. Huh," Perry observed, watching Mark with more interest. "You call that one, boss?"

"More or less. Or maybe it was just my—what was it? Biological luck."

"I too feel lucky. And hungry," Tan said, then popped onto the bench and slid over across from Mark. "Teach us this game of poker, Mark. Traditions should always be honored and I for one am a fan of the things you choose to wager. Carbohydrates and sugar, yes?"

"Yes. Very little nutritional value, but a great crunch, according to my data," Perry said.

Mark paused what he was doing and *beamed*. "Ahh. *Traditions*. Love to hear it, and yes, they should be honored, especially when it gives me the chance to fleece you. Now then, this is what is called no-limit poker. A transfer in my unit taught it to me, and in return, we taught it to the French soldiers serving on the line. It got us through many cold, wet, and muddy nights in the trenches. For this game, I'll serve as dealer, which means, Perry, you're Small Blind, and, Tan, you're the Big Blind."

Mark dealt one card to Perry, Tan, and then himself, before distributing their second cards.

"Is the 'small' part a jab at my stature?"

"No, Perry. It has everything to do with betting and nothing to do with your size, which is…ah, aggressively minimal."

Mark reached back, plucked a bag of Krager Puffs out of a cupboard, and pulled it open. He then proceeded to stack up exactly twelve puffs in front of himself, Perry, and Tan.

"For the purposes of this game, these will serve as——"

Before he could finish, Tan reached down, picked up one of the puffs, and tossed it into his mouth.

"Don't eat those," Perry warned. "Mark was about to tell us the puffs are going to serve as betting chips, or currency."

"Ohh, sorry." The Druzis swallowed hard.

Mark replaced the puff and smiled.

"Now to start, we set the minimum bet, which will be two Krager Puffs. To start better, the Big Blind throws in the minimum bet, while the Small blind throws in half."

Perry bent over and nudged his puffs into the middle of the table, while Tan added more. They shared a sly glance, then grew still as Mark glanced at his cards.

"Good," Mark said, a smile fighting for purchase on his lips. "Now check your hand, and starting with the player to my left, we go around the table for our first bets. You two were forced to automatically bet, so it's up to me to fold or call, which means I match the minimum bet, or raise." Again, Mark smiled wide at around the table, enjoying the vague confusion.

He walked them through an entire hand of poker then, progressing through the Flop, the second betting round, the Turn, more betting, and finally, the River card. They moved to the final round of betting before Mark directed them to show their cards.

"I have two pair, Jack high," Perry said, spreading his cards with a taloned foot. He managed to sound hopeful and smug all at once.

"Sounds like he knows what he is doing," Tan muttered, awkwardly laying his cards onto the table. He revealed two eights, which along with the eight on the board, gave him a three of a kind. Mark showed his cards, revealing that he only had a pair of Queens.

"Three of a kind beats two pair. Tan wins," Mark declared, then he scooped the pot of puffs in front of the Druzis.

"Wait...I what?"

"You won," Perry concurred.

"But I didn't know what I was doing?"

"Sometimes you don't need to. That's why they call it 'the luck of the draw.'"

"Oh. I think I'm going to like this game," Tan said, popping another puff in his mouth.

They managed to play through another hand that Perry won with a straight flush before Netty interrupted.

"No arrivals. We're back underway, but before you gentlemen get too deep into the card action, there's something I really need to show you."

"We're on our way."

Mark and Perry arrived in the cockpit first, with Tan strolling in behind them, the bag of Krager Puffs clutched lovingly in one hand, while the other shuttled food into his mouth like a metronome.

"What is it, Netty?"

"We managed a network download patch from the last buoy— some four and a half terabytes of amassed data. I sorted through it while we waited, siphoning information based off a complicated keyword net. I was almost ready to mark the entire patch for deletion when I came across this distribution."

The pilots' overlays zoomed out as a file opened, revealing a large text document that read *Golden Jubilee Approaches. Book your spot now for a generational celebration, as the Eridani Federation honors fifty solar cycles of unity and peace.*

"What's this?"

"Scroll down. You'll see," Netty explained. "I'm surprised this went out, considering their closed borders."

Mark slid into the chair and read the article, passing large blocks of well-crafted marketing text. He continued down past a vibrant image, but froze and quickly swiped it back into the center screen position.

It was a retro, stylized image of an Eridani family dressed in government-approved clothing, standing hand in hand. Small hovercars zoomed around them in what looked to be a pristine and perfect city. Their faces were turned upward, where a magnificent fireworks display filled the sky above them. It was what covered their faces that caught his attention.

"Well, pluck me bare and roast me for dinner," Perry muttered as Mark zoomed in.

They were wearing molded blue masks, featuring two small pressurized canisters on the bottom, with integrated goggles. The caption below the image read, *Join the Honorable Satrap Ileus Jura for the cosmos' favorite spectacle, the Unity Fireworks. See them like never before, with cutting-edge visual enhancement masks by Cavu Lixl. Book your transit to Origin now, before it's too late.*

"Origin? Where's that?" Mark asked.

"The metropolitan capital of the Eridani Federation. A planet-wide city that makes Fulcrum look like small-town Iowa," Perry explained.

"And that's where she means to unleash her weapon?" Tan asked.

"How many people live there?"

"One hundred and fifty billion, give or take a few thousand. I don't have their most recent census data," Perry explained.

"And it's a commerce hub?"

The bird shook his head. "It's *the* commerce hub, serving not only the whole of the Eridani Federation, but also much of colonized space. Weapons, ammunition, spacecraft components, clothing, packaged food, much of it comes out of or through Origin."

Mark turned back to the screen and continued to scroll down, until he finally found a date. [1062 Eridanus 4 Prime]

"When is that? Eridanus four prime?"

"The first number is the year since the Federation's inception. Eridanus is their calendar. Prime is the month, so, the fourth day of summer. That's roughly sixty Eridanus cycles from now. Less than two of your Earth months."

"So Glass stockpiles her weapons until closer to this celebration to avoid suspicion?" Netty asked.

"That, and the Federation border is closed. She will bide her time, and once transit is restored, make her move."

"Unless…" Perry said, holding up a wing. "Unless she's already operating behind the Federation border. For a bitter Piraxian war slave looking to strike at the heart of her people's oppressors, the unity celebration wouldn't only be a bittersweet stroke or revenge, but an incredibly visual one."

"So we need to find her before she gets that chance."

"Yes. Unfortunately, there are dozens of war-torn Piraxian black sites scattered on the outer edge of the Eridani domain. She could be hiding her battle group in any of them."

"Do we notify the Federation of the threat?"

Perry mimicked a sigh. "Now that's the dilemma. As soon as we notify them, we fall under their crosshairs. Elements within the Federation would also notify the Guild, so Gyl-Mareth would know. And I have a sneaky suspicion that once *he* found out, Glass would too."

"So our element of surprise would be gone."

"As you said, it was our secret weapon. Locate her, move in quick, strike decisively, and save a whole lot of people," Perry reasoned.

"When crossing a property line, my uncle always said it was better to ask forgiveness than permission. As long as you aren't damaging anything, that is."

"If you guys need me, I'll be in the engine room, realigning the twist drive's fuel-mapping matrix," Tan said, still crunching on Krager Puffs.

"This isn't driving a tractor across a property line, Mark. This is potentially jumping across a militarized border," Perry corrected. "One that might be actively preparing for a conflict against the Ixtan Cabal. If we're that unlucky."

"Did you hear me? I'm walking away now," Tan said.

"We're working to stop a militant with an army and a killer biological weapon from cleansing billions of people off the face of Origin," Mark breathed, letting his thoughts circle. "And we can't call for help."

"Outmanned but not outgunned," Perry offered. "Our new Synth friends made sure of that."

"Striker found something. We pinged a buoy with some interesting flyby data," Valint said over comms, interrupting their conversation.

"Okay. Bye." Tan stomped off down the passage.

"Oh, sorry, Mark. I forgot to tell you. Valint twisted on ahead to increase our search spread."

"That's all right, Netty," Mark said, then switched to comms. "How does it compare to the solar table? Any comets passing through this region lately?"

"I'm showing nothing on the charts. Give me a minute. We're testing a theory and jumping to the next buoy."

"Where are they?" Mark asked, turning to Perry. The bird adjusted something on his overlay, and the two screens synced. The star chart zoomed out and then back in, highlighting a section of space almost a hundred and fifty million miles away from them.

"I'm updating our telemetry forecast with the extra data."

Two glowing points appeared on the star chart—their apprehension spot for the Synth ship, and the old Gyl weapons base. A third point appeared a moment later, and the computer drew in a long, thin line to connect them. It extended out into the black.

"It doesn't intersect any known Piraxian facilities," Perry said, then clicked his beak irritably.

"It doesn't have to intersect them necessarily," Mark corrected, tapping on his overlay. "What if it just needed to get close enough? Like with the Salt Thieves. They didn't stop at their cache site to drop off their counterfeit currency. They did a flyby."

"Okay. Broadening the search," the bird said, manipulating his overlay.

A complicated grid of lines appeared, with even more data points popping in, accounting for known Piraxian facilities and worlds. And yet, their forecasted line seemed to weave right through the points without touching any of them. In the world of space travel, a half inch on a screen could be a vast and timeless gulf.

"This is maddening," Perry said, his eyes flashing amber with frustration.

"Why does that—?" Mark started to ask, then went quiet and zoomed in on his overlay. He turned the chart, adjusted the elevation to the ecliptic, and flipped it around again. Something looked and felt off about the cluster of data points and the strategic layout of space stations, moons, and relay points.

"We'll keep looking, Mark. The data is out there. We just need to find it," Netty said.

All three Peacemaker ships jumped, weaving separate lines through their massive search area. But the more time went on, the more Mark started to doubt, and worse, despair. What if they couldn't find her in time. Hell, what if they couldn't find her at all?

Pacing the galley, he considered alternative options.

"What if we jumped in and investigated our best guesses?" he asked.

"That would work, if we wanted to let Glass know that we're looking for her," Perry replied from his perch on the table. He spread the playing cards out before him, studying each hand, before gathering them up and shuffling once again. It was something to see, considering the bird didn't have opposable thumbs.

"Right," Mark muttered. "If she has any form of early detection, it would be us in the trap, and not her."

"Like Drogo says, 'we can't lose Mark's secret weapon. If you can call that a weapon. Surprise doesn't even shoot anything, and that makes it dumb.'" The bird chuckled, mimicking the large Badgin's voice perfectly.

The idea of weapons brought Mark right back to the Gyl research laboratory, specifically the blackened crater left behind. If she was truly able to create a weapon like Vacillux, then it was bad enough to destroy all the evidence.

"She killed all those people on Fulcrum and the Bone Yard to keep this secret."

"What's that?"

"I was thinking about the lengths she went to cover her tracks and the lives she took. What are the odds our weapons can destroy a biological weapon?" Mark asked.

"In space, the odds are excellent. An agent like Vacillux wouldn't survive in vacuum. On the surface? Well, we would need something that generates far more heat than mere air-to-air missiles."

"Something like..." he started to say as a number of questions bubbled to the surface of his mind. "The broker...the war...that weapon..."

"Wow," Perry said, finally turning his attention from the cards. "One thing at a time, Mark. Slow down."

"Babar Malta said he had a client looking for thermite plasmid.

Then Valint said it was outlawed because the Eridani used it on the Piraxian rebellion."

"Correct."

"Where?"

"There were skirmishes all over the Federation's border by that point in the war," Perry admitted.

"No. That's not what I mean. A weapon like that wouldn't be used casually. The Federation would have used it, and a lot of it, not just to end the threat, but to send a message and break the will of those that survived. Was there such an attack?"

"Let me scan my database here. Let me see. Okay, and indexing…"

Mark paced from one side of the room to the other, clenching and unclenching his hands. Time seemed to slow, until an eternity passed between heartbeats.

"Done. That's strange. I don't seem to have any data linked to that query."

"None? How is that possible? Can you search again?"

"Uh. I don't need to search again." Perry shook his head. "I know that it happened. I remember when Valint said it, and I understand how I felt and why when she did, but when I try and substantiate *how* I know, nothing's there."

Mark turned and ran for the cockpit, with Perry taking wing right behind him. He threw himself into the pilot's chair.

"Netty, where was the decisive battle in the Eridani and Piraxian war? Where the Federation unleashed thermite plasmid on the rebels?"

"The Federation and Piraxian remnant signed the Treaty of

Epsilon almost exactly fifty Eridani solar cycles ago. It was ratified on—"

"No, Netty. Not where the rebellion officially surrendered. Where was the final battle in the war?"

"That was on…it was at…" Netty said, stammering uncharacteristically. "I apologize, Mark. I don't seem to have that information.

Mark looked at Perry, and the bird frowned.

"This is suspicious."

34

"I REMEMBER STUDYING the war when I was a child, but I don't remember the name of the battlefield," Valint said once they had established a solid connection. "Are you saying Perry doesn't know? I'd find that…odd."

"That's exactly what I'm saying. Netty doesn't know either. Ask Bunn and Striker. Do it now."

Valint's eyebrows rose, and her expression tightened. In fact, it was perhaps the first time he'd ever seen her genuinely alarmed since they'd met on that French battlefield. She nodded, turned off-camera, and addressed the AIs directly.

A few moments later, she turned back to the screen, the lines around her eyes and mouth deepening.

"Okay. I'm officially alarmed. They don't know either. How is that possible? What does Tan have to say about it?"

"I didn't ask—" Mark said, but Perry cut him off.

"Tan, get up to the cockpit. Now-now-now."

A door opened somewhere beyond the galley a moment later, with the Druzis sprinting awkwardly up the passage. By the time he reached the cockpit, he'd left a messy trail of Krager Puffs behind him and was thoroughly out of breath.

"What is it? What happened?"

"The AIs' memories about the location of the last Eridani-Piraxian battle are gone, along with all corresponding information. Mostly, where. How would or could that happen?"

"It isn't easy to delete data from an AI's stored memory. First"—Tan panted, still fighting to catch his breath—"first, if not done willingly, it could damage the process matrix, negatively impacting how the potassium di-ethyl lithium halide transmitters emit electrical signals between the processing unit's graphene lattice synapses."

"Wow. Easy with the million platinum words. Simplify. Shorten. Then try again," Mark said, holding his hands up before him.

"Okay. Sorry. I get excited when we start talking about the physical constructs within quantum computers," the Druzis said. "Think of it like this. Memories and uploaded data packets make up more than files in storage. For Netty and Perry, they become part of who they are, personality-wise. To delete something without careful consideration and file isolation *could* be catastrophic."

"Think of it like a stroke for a human," Perry interjected.

"Yes," Tan agreed. "But it's delicate work, especially if someone wanted to delete data or a memory without the AI knowing. That would require a cloaked isolation protocol, meaning it would lock the data behind a firewall. Then, bit by bit, they would have to upload what my father liked to call a 'crumbler' to slowly dismantle the target files.

"Quantum artificial intelligences are dense matrices. As soon as one senses a threat to its embedded data, it would automatically create a secondary registry."

"So what are you saying?" Mark asked. "You mean that the memory could still be there but hidden behind a firewall?"

"Fat chance," the Druzis laughed. "Any data that someone doesn't want seen that bad is long gone."

Mark cursed and sagged to his knees, his frustration mounting.

"Why are you angry?"

Stiffening at Tan's flippant question, Mark straightened, his big hands cracking with implied violence as he made fists.

"Tan, I need an answer to this—did you miss the part where this woman is planning on killing billions of people, maybe more?"

"No, I got that part. I just didn't want you to think that we were out of options. If the file or memory is gone, it doesn't mean that we can't see what it was."

"What does that mean?" Perry asked. "If it's been locked behind a firewall and deleted, there *is* no way to see it."

"You guys are silly." The Druzis laughed, then reached into the bag and fished out another handful of Krager Puffs. "The answer is simple—scan the AI's root, isolate update patches, and simply hunt for the crumbler files. Once you've got all of those, assemble the pieces to see the whole."

"You make it sound so easy, and yet I get the feeling it's anything but," Mark said.

"Well, I mean, yeah. It isn't like writing firmware for a reconstitutor, but as long as the AI didn't purge its patch root folder, it should all be there."

Mark immediately turned and looked to Netty first. Her optical sensor flickered from purple to red. She was blushing.

"I'm sorry, Mark. That was the first thing I did when Armagost unlocked my full capacity. It felt like clutter."

He turned to Perry, and the bird's gaze snapped around to meet his.

"I was planning on straightening up that folder at some point. We're lucky that I haven't had a chance to get around to it yet."

"Lucky is one way of looking at it," Mark said, turning back to Tan. "Can you do this? Can you find it?"

"Oh, yes. I mean, root code is easy. But can I have the rest of these if I do?" The Druzis held up the mostly empty bag of Krager Puffs.

"Yes, and I'll get you more when—"

"Deal," Tan said, not letting him finish. Then he skipped over to the panel next to Netty's case and started fishing out wires.

"Hold on, Clive," Perry said, jumping down and blocking his path. "The kid gets the puffs, but if we're going to go digging around in my brain, I want something in return."

"People's lives are on the line. Isn't saving them enough?"

"Yes and no," the bird said, unabashed. "If I do this, after we sort out Glass, you and I are sitting down and cleaning that oatmeal you call gray matter, got it? The dreams, your inability to sleep, the hand twitches and cold sweats when you think I'm not looking, all of it. You *will* let me help you."

"This isn't something you can fix," Mark said, stubbornly setting his feet.

"I didn't say *fix*. I said *sort out*. Because that's what friends do, Mark. They face their fears and monsters together."

"Friends, eh?"

"Damn right," Perry growled. "I've gone from morbidly curious, to intrigued, pleasantly surprised, and lastly, quite fond of you, and in short order, I might add. Now shake on it, Tudor."

The bird held out his right wing, and Mark grasped it firmly, before giving it a shake.

"All right, bird, but don't say I didn't warn you."

"Bah!" Perry said. "I was there when the Galactic Knights exiled the Puloquir. If you'd seen what those ruthless, sociopathic serpents did to other races, let alone their own kind, you'd understand why I'm not squeamish."

"Maybe you can tell me about them over a game of cards," Mark suggested.

"Deal. But I wouldn't eat or drink anything during the storytelling portion of the event. It was very…graphic."

"Noted."

Perry joined Tan at the forward instrument panel, spread his wings, and allowed the Druzis to plug a data feed cable directly into his harness.

"Okay, let's see what we can see."

Mark slid into his chair and updated Valint and Drogo, while the other two continued their search. They were eager for answers, although apprehensive at the idea that elements of public affairs could be so easily manipulated and wiped from the collective consciousness of civil servants.

"If we find this place, and it is as we fear…" Valint said, going quiet for a moment.

"Then we're potentially going to have some difficult decisions to make," Mark said, finishing for her. "I'll contact you as soon as I know anything."

Valint nodded somberly and ended the transmission.

"Wow, your matrix is dense!" Tan rapped away at his console.

"Hey. That's my personality you're talking about. I would like to think of it as classy and nuanced, if not occasionally dry."

"Yes. Sorry. It's all of those things."

Tan typed in silence for a few moments more, his face contorting into some bizarre expressions, before he finally threw his hands up into the air. Mark went rigid and prepared himself for the worst.

"I'm in the root. Phew. That code escalation was brutal." The Druzis sighed dramatically a moment later, then threw himself back into his work.

Mark met Perry's gaze, and the bird shook his head. Tan was brilliant, but he was also a teenager, and those were, well, unpredictable.

"Okay-okay-okay, I've worked up a tracking algorithm and am setting up my search parameters. *Boom*. It's working," the Druzis crowed a moment later, poking the screen with an overly long index finger. He turned a triumphant smile toward Mark.

"You really enjoy this stuff," Mark noted idly.

"Enjoy? Ha. Druzis biologically modify their offspring to maximize mathematical and engineering personality traits. So, you could say I was born for this."

"Oh, boy." Perry sighed. "He's overly excited, and I'm sitting here with my maintenance service port hanging wide open."

"Don't worry, we won't look," Netty said.

"How big is our bird friend's root folder?" Mark asked a while later. He moved in to stand next to Tan, then leaned in to watch the data flow down his console.

"Big," the Druzis confirmed. "Approximately fifteen…no sixteen million lines of code."

"Wow."

"Hey. It takes a lot of code to quantify all of this awesomeness."

A separate folder appeared a moment later, with a long line of similarly named files inside.

"And boom again. Look at that. There they are," Tan said, minimizing the root window and expanding the search results. "And they think they can quarantine and slowly dismantle their dirty little secrets. Not with me around. Not today, bad guys."

"Slow down, killer," Perry said. "We just happened to be in the right place at the right time. How many people in the colonized galaxies would think to search an artificial intelligence's root code for infinitesimal fragments of normally benign patch files?"

"Now that you mention it. Outside of the Druzis Amalgam, not many. My father could probably have named a handful of coders and matrix builders."

"Now what?" Mark asked.

"I'm organizing them according to their reception date, and then we'll assemble them and see what secret they wanted wiped from Mr. Bird's memory."

The files reorganized, scrolling down through the almost one hundred file fragments. Then they started to combine, quickly building a much larger chunk of code.

"I still don't understand how they could isolate one of your memories with you not knowing," Mark said.

"You're telling me. They must have cooked up a particularly insidious little worm for this task. One designed to eat its own tail and disappear once it's finished working. When this is all done, I'm going to completely rework *all* of my security infrastructure."

"Ten left. And five. And—done."

"You sure?" Perry asked, eyes flashing amber.

"Sorry," Tan said, his cheeks turning green. "It's compiled and organized. The file is complete."

"How do we see it?" Mark asked.

"You don't," Perry replied. "The hard part was finding, extracting, and combining the fragments, but only my quantum matrix can read and index the file. He has to push the file back into my mind, and I have to…well, for lack of a better term, remember."

"All right. Here goes nothing," Tan said, then tapped the screen. The file disappeared and popped back into the massive construct that was Perry's mind.

"Hmmm. Yes. I sense something new. My mind is indexing it. Oh, *this* is uncomfortable." Perry pulled away, the data cable jerking free from his data port.

The bird paced for a moment, several ripples passing through the feathers on his back and wings. Then without warning, he jumped up onto the back of the co-pilot's chair, cursing all the way in new and interesting ways.

"What is it? What's wrong?" Mark asked,

"He is experiencing whatever the Guild deleted all over again. If it was something horrific, then he is feeling all the corresponding emotions. Unfortunately, there's no way to avoid that," Netty surmised.

"Psychopathic bastards. The murderous, no-good, ah, predictable," the bird snarled and immediately pulled up his star chart.

Mark moved in, but Perry held up a wing, then slapped the overlay and swung it out so they could see. A small, glowing red dot appeared in a blank, black stretch of space. It wasn't anywhere near where Mark would have guessed but sat off the Eridani Federation border almost five light-years away.

"*War crimes*. That's what happened there. War crimes."

"What did they do?"

"The planet is Decopolis, and it's been effectively wiped from the collective consciousness thanks to time and some truly dedicated folks in power," Perry said after a moment.

"But surely there are people who would remember it. Out there, you know," Tan said.

"Oh, indeed," Perry replied, visually mastering the spike of emotions. "But dilution has a stronger impact than you might think. With every passing solar cycle, the people in power needed only to strengthen their position with tools like rhetoric and disregard, while quietly labeling those that dissented as *quacks* or *conspirators*. Sadly, the government-trusting public would do the rest for them, as I have seen on countless worlds."

"That sounds diabolical," Tan muttered, slumping in his seat.

"The planet. What can you tell us about it?" Mark asked.

"Decopolis was a small, upstart Piraxian colony, rich with iron ore and lithium. It also happened to be where the rebellion started, and unfortunately, ended. The rebels retreated there when the Eridani routed their fleet on the border of Epsilon space. Afraid that the rebels would scatter again, the Federation surrounded the planet, then sent in wave after wave of fighters. And so that single act began the most protracted battle of attrition in recorded history. Well, forgotten battle, that is," Perry said, stopping to correct

J.N. CHANEY & TERRY MAGGERT

himself. "Once they had destroyed the rebel fleet, the Federation moved in, and fearful that the colony would incite another rebellion, someone in fleet command decided to bomb the surface."

"Thermite Plasmid," Mark breathed. "They knowingly bombed civilians."

Perry nodded, his eyes burning with a murderous glow.

"They burned the entire colony. The women…the old…and the children, too. They murdered tens, perhaps hundreds of thousands, and not quickly. The fires raged for days, choking the sky and consuming breathable oxygen. The Eridani broke the spine of an entire people with that move. They crushed their collective spirit and then assimilated the remnant into their collective. That's how the Piraxians became a dispersed, homeless people."

Mark pushed out a breath, only then realizing that he was grinding his teeth. He relaxed his jaw and heard it pop. An audible sniffle brought his attention left. Large, glassy tears flowed down Tan's cheeks. The Druzis was a displaced orphan, obviously affected by the story.

"I'd never…they never…" Tan said, before reaching up and swiping the tears away. "They never taught that in school. Only that the rebels were criminals and outlaws. That the Federation was *noble* and fought for what was *right*. That they pushed them back to their home system and defeated them once and for all."

"Noble!" Perry gave a bark-like laugh, the noise loud and bitter. "The adjectives are always more flattering when you're describing the conflict from your side. Someone in the Federation's flagship no doubt justified a horrific act by highlighting the peace at the end."

Mark shook loose, his thoughts spiraling deeper into the dark, muddy, and blood-covered places in his mind. His heart hammered, but it was a raging machine gun, drowning out so many dying screams. War was a hideous, gruesome mask, often covering up the same old tired ambitions and motivations. And yet, that didn't stop it from leaving devastation and broken people in its wake.

"So she means to cleanse Origin the way the Eridani burned Decapolis, and on *the* day they celebrate the so-called peaceful resolution of the war."

"Peaceful," Perry snorted. "The morbid, bitter bird part of me wants to let her. No. I don't mean that. It's just the emotions. We cannot let her do it, of course. Those people, they're not the ones that murdered *her* people."

"Agreed," Mark said, nodding, even though part of him agreed with Perry. According to his overlay, there were no war tribunals after the fighting ended, which would have made the already traumatized Piraxians even angrier. They had been brutally put down while the galaxies turned a blind eye.

Leaning forward, Mark selected both Drogo and Valint on comms, then opened the channel.

"We found them. The planet is Decopolis—the site of the Piraxians' defeat. The powers that be were almost successful in wiping it completely from the collective memory," Mark said. "That has to be where Glass is hiding her battlegroup. Perry just sent updates for Striker, Bunn, and Cerebral. Upload it, read it…do whatever you need to prepare, but we need to confront her."

The silence stretched for several long minutes. Mark imagined that the AIs were uploading and digesting the information the same way Perry did. For Valint and Drogo, the experience was likely less visceral but no less emotional.

Almost five full minutes after sending the data, a comm channel from Valint went live.

"She specifically sought you out to tell you to stay out of her way. Do you really think you can talk her down? After learning this?"

Mark shook his head, even though it was an audio-only comm. It didn't matter—the action was more for him than anyone else.

"I don't think it's likely, but we have to try. Maybe we can reason with her, help her bring these wartime atrocities to light. The more people know, the better."

Another comm channel went live as Drogo chimed in.

"I love your zeal and fire, Mark, but I just don't know," the Badgin said, his connection a little weaker. "The average person cares very little for events that don't immediately impact their lives —that's just reality. We'll have a hard time getting anyone to help spread this news, let alone risk their position or security in order to support someone like Glass. She's murdered people. To them, she is *every bit* the monster the Eridani painted her people."

"She's the monster they made," Mark corrected. "And someone needs to be held to account. We *must* try. D'you understand? We can't let this go. There's too much blood. Too many souls."

"I'm with you," Valint said. "But our odds are low. If she rejects your request, we don't have the firepower to go toe to toe with her forces. Not for long, at least."

"I know," he said, then muted the channels and turned to Perry. "How would the Eridani Federation respond if we called them for help? How would that play out?"

"Considering they've spent the last fifty solar cycles fighting to wipe the formative events from the galaxies' cooperative memory, I would think not well. Based on the Bone Yard attack, they'd likely swarm Decopolis and kill anyone alive. That would fit their 'shoot first and ask questions later' mentality for terrorist negotiations. The subsequent news headlines would probably reflect exactly that."

"They would sweep it all under the rug. And we would be helping their historical reconstruction efforts," Mark reasoned, then promptly pulled on his harness.

Watching him with wide eyes, Tan's mouth fell open.

"Are we…? Do we…?"

He nodded and tapped on each of their new weapon systems, bringing them all online. The cockpit automatically dimmed to tactical lighting as the twist drive spooled to ready.

"Buckle in, Tan. This could get real rocky. *Real fast.*"

35

THE COMM CHANNELS went silent as Netty counted down for their twist to Decopolis. Mark sat quietly in the pilot's chair, one hand on the throttle, his other on the control stick.

"Are we ready?" he asked.

"Not yet. Sorry, Mark. There seems to be a lot of interference surrounding the planet."

"Like Chevix? Is it an unruly star?"

"Unknown. Whatever it is, I'm getting a lot of feedback static on the targeting computer. The gravity well is relatively small, so we can twist in close, but still…"

"Take your time, Netty. We want to get this right."

The ships lined up, burning hard to gain momentum. Their strategy was simple, but as proven by naval history, effective—pick up as much speed as possible, then twist. Thanks to Hamilton's Principle, their energy wasn't just conserved when impacted by the jump singularity, but the ships were stabilized and exited with equal velocity.

"Twisting in close means we could pop up right in the middle of her battle group," Perry added, verbalizing what Mark had already been thinking about.

"She already booby-trapped one meeting place."

"All right. Calculations are complete, and all three ships are reporting ready to twist."

"Do it," Mark said, before he could second-guess the decision.

His head went fuzzy as they jumped, the almost uncomfortable quiet of the twist drive somehow magnifying the faint buzzing in his ears. It had been there since the war, the damage left behind by months on end of rifle and artillery fire, but the *Fafnir's* constant background noise usually drowned it out.

They emerged from their jump, their first passive scan firing off. Mark was afforded a brief glance of a large planetoid ahead, right before their momentum carried him toward a massive, rolling piece of debris.

Tan cursed as the *Fafnir* nosed down and rolled left, the *Stormshadow* and *Glorious Column* rolling right as they avoided enemy fire that streaked upward at stunning velocities. The three ships converged on the other side, the truth of Decopolis looming ahead of them.

It wasn't a single piece of wreckage, but a massive field of debris filling the approach to the forgotten world. Netty overclocked her processors, working feverishly to identify every piece of space junk ahead, but even at her fastest, the effort appeared monumental.

Perry chipped in, scanning with their thermal node, as he fought to identify threats hiding in the mess. Mark navigated them around another large piece of debris, then pulled the overlay out of the way, deciding to fly by sight instead.

"I've got random fire coming in, boss. Mostly—okay, PDC and missiles, some beam weapons. It's a mess but the shooters are dispersing or working back for another pass. Continue on?" Netty asked.

Mark was silent for a long moment, staring out at the scans. "Continue on. With care."

"I have *never* seen a wreckage field this large before. After all this time, it's still here," Valint said over comms.

"Its composition and location indicate that it is locked in a tidal pull between gravity and orbital spin. It has essentially become a stable ring around the planet," Perry explained.

The truth almost took Mark's breath away as he navigated them around the scorched fuselages of dead fighters and troop transports. But it didn't end there. Hundreds of bodies floated in the black between it all, the cold vacuum having preserved them.

"I've seen battlefields, but never like this," he said in stunned tones as they broke free from a thick portion of the ring. The planet revolved into full view through a clearing ahead. It almost looked like Earth, if not for the ocean-sized streaks of black marring the surface.

"My God, did they burn that much of—of *everything*? How is that even *possible*?" Mark asked anyone and everyone.

"Now we know why the Guild banned its use," Valint said. "He more or less teased that fact when we were standing in his office. He knew. He *still* knew."

"I've got heat blooms somewhere ahead. But I can't tell exactly where. This clutter is messing with identification and range track-ers," Netty said.

"All right. Let's go fly by sight and watch for movement," Mark said, pulling the stick right and up, accelerating the *Fafnir* toward another dense cloud of floating debris.

They wove their way in, working to hide within the planet's thick orbital cemetery, the trail of tears left by death and destruc-tion. And all the while, Mark questioned why he was there. Anyone else might have waved the threat off, perhaps even justified their own inaction and called Glass someone else's problem. Fortunately for the billions on Origin, Mark Tudor wasn't one of those people.

"Netty, give me a full-power sensor ping. I want to know where Glass is hiding, but more importantly, where she is hiding this weapon."

"Okay, but if we go active scanners, they'll know we're here," Netty cautioned.

"If they were paying attention, then they saw our gamma burst when we jumped in," Perry argued, tapping the screen with his beak. In response, the missile bay doors whined open. "Of course, our use of heavy weapons might have interrupted their nap, too. But some people—"

"Are heavy sleepers, I get it, bird. I overslept *once*."

"And don't think I won't use that for*ever*," Perry crowed.

Coming up to full power, their sensor node unleashed a powerful sensor ping, the ring washing outward on their overlays. Mark turned to Tan, only to find the young Druzis' eye locked wide open as he scanned the wreckage surrounding the planet.

"There were so many of them. So many people. They're all dead. All of them."

"Tan," Mark said, but he wouldn't look away.

"Tan. Look at me."

The young alien finally peeled his eyes from the viewscreen as he turned to Mark. Much of the color had drained away from his face, especially his lips and ears.

"They died long ago, and there's nothing we can do for them now. We *can* help billions of people on other worlds, but you need to keep your mind clear. Do you understand?"

Tan nodded, although his eyes twitched back toward the viewscreens.

"No. Tan. I need you. Fire up your null field projector. If they come at us, we're going to need every trick up our sleeves. Get ready."

"Yes. I mean…got it, boss," Tan muttered and pushed out of the co-pilot's chair. He stumbled forward and fell into the jump seat, then cinched the lap belt tight. Purposefully not looking forward, the Druzis pulled his screen before him and went to work.

"I've got data," Netty declared. "This field is massive, but it does end. There's a ring of clear space perhaps five hundred miles wide outside the exosphere. There is what appears to be part of an intact space station still in orbit. There are a number of spacecraft docked. One appears to be a cruiser and the other…"

A chime sounded as a light flared to life on the comms panel.

"Go on, Netty."

"The other is a container ship. I'm analyzing its hull shape for identification now."

Glass's face filled the screen, the dark hair rimming her face darkened by sweat. Grease covered one cheek, offsetting the scar that ran the length of the other.

"You found me. I'm surprised."

"Surprised, but not impressed?"

She didn't smile or laugh but kept her penetrating gaze locked on his. There was no playful edge to her demeanor now, just a startlingly dead look in her eyes.

"My message was as unambiguous as I could make it. Stay out of *my* way," Glass said. "I don't want to have to kill you."

"Mark," Netty interrupted, automatically muting the comm connection. "I can say with eighty-nine percent confidence that the container ship docked in orbit is the *Star Araxes*."

"The *Star Araxes?*" Mark asked. "One of the Eridani ships thought missing in that solar flare. One of the ships Vosa was asking about on Needle."

"The very same," Netty confirmed.

"Shit," he said, then grabbed his overlay and zoomed in as far as it would go. The image was grainy, but he could just make out the massive ship, and, on its side, painted in stylized print easily five times larger than the serial number, was the name *Cavu Lixl.*

"But now that you found this place, I guess I have no choice," the mercenary finished after talking to someone off-screen.

"Mark, I've got heat blooms all over the place. *Ships*. There are *ships* hiding in the debris field," Netty called.

"Perry—"

"I'm already tracking them, boss. No hostile actions yet. No shots fired, but there are a lot of them."

"We didn't come here to fight you, Mala," Mark said, turning back to the overlay. She twitched at the use of her given name, but the movement appeared to be more from shock than anger.

"We know about this place, what the Eridani did to your people.

If you stand down, we will help you."

"Help us? We Piraxians have sought help before, but no one would listen. Not even the Ixtan Cabal, long feuding with the Federation, would help. We sent emissaries to your Guild for help. They turned us away. Time and time again. How do you think your Master Gyl-Mareth elevated himself to his position? What do you think he was cooking up in that weapons facility?" Glass asked, her face twisting with fury at the casual repetition of war crimes.

Mark felt his face tighten at Gyl-Mareth's name but fought to hide the tell. Was she telling him that his Master had been the one to develop the weapon that killed her people?

"Yes. I think—no, I know you know," Glass said, a cold laugh rattling from her depths. "The Gyl and Cai have been perfecting mass-casualty weapons for generations as they kill each other in secret."

"I found his fuel-skimming scheme on Chevix. We have the greasy Ligurite connecting him and others in the Guild to those crimes. We can call special council and put him on trial…for all of it."

"The saddest part of my people's story is that they gave up. They returned to their new masters' homes and waited, hoping for justice. And what happened? Nothing." She snorted. "The worlds tried to forget us—about Decopolis and the mass murder of my people. We were an inconvenience, one they longed to brush aside so they could move on with their lives."

"That's wrong. Let us help you bring it to light. Given the right venue, we could make real, lasting change," Mark argued.

"How, Peacemaker Tudor? You and your three ships? Are you going to make the billions who didn't care about a small, independent people fifty years ago suddenly care about them now? Are you going to bring my grandparents, aunts, and cousins back from the ashes below? Generations of Piraxian bloodlines lost to the flames of an uncaring empire?"

"No. I can't bring them back," Mark said, using his peripheral vision to track the enemy ships on Perry's overlay. Almost two dozen shapes moved within the debris field, slowly converging on the *Fafnir*. That fact gave him pause, but only for a fugitive moment. His purpose bubbled back up, clear and hot. "We can—and *will*—fight to bring them justice."

"There's only one road to justice," Glass snarled, her face contorting. "There's only one way to ensure this doesn't happen again, and it's a path of blood and death. I'm sorry it came to this, Mark Tudor. I truly am. For what it's worth, Gyl-Mareth put me in your path with the hope that I would kill you. Just so you know."

"If you unleash this weapon, you'll be no better than the Eridani monsters who firebombed Decapolis," Mark said, realizing he'd run out of arguments.

"I know, but unlike those cowards, I accept both the burden and my fate. I'm sorry you were pulled into this, I truly am. But our time has come to an end. Goodbye, Mark Tudor."

The connection terminated a split second before a Christmas tree of warning lights appeared on the forward console.

"She didn't deny it," Perry said. "That means the weapon is on that—"

"That freighter," Mark confirmed and jammed the throttle forward. "Valint and Drogo, I'm going for the freighter. Stick to the debris field as long as you can; otherwise, that heavy cruiser is going to cause real trouble."

Directly to his left, the darkness peeled open as the *Stormshadow* launched a missile and its glitter caster. The weapon streaked right at a fighter as it emerged from its hiding place, only to hit the tumbling fuselage of a wrecked ship instead. The warhead ignited, but the secondary explosion billowed in a violent cloud, catching the mercenary ship in a vicious rain of shrapnel.

"Some of these ships are still carrying ordnance and fuel. Be careful," Perry offered.

"Noted," Mark grunted as he vectored down and around the tail section of a transport.

"Birds in the air. Birds in the air," Perry crowed a heartbeat later as more lights blossomed on the forward panel. "We've got ships moving in all around us, too. Are we only defending, or are we fighting back?"

"They made their choice. The line's been drawn. I don't want to kill them, but..."

"Copy that, boss. Save innocent lives," Perry shouted back over the roar of the PDC. "Weapons are hot. I'll keep the PDC in burst mode to conserve ammo. Maybe I can disable some of these fighters, but there's only so much I can do."

Mark rolled them right and down, the PDC chattering off three more short bursts. The first missile exploded instantly, but the second collided with debris and broke apart in a silent fury.

"Splash one missile—the other's gone too. Never got the chance to arm. Good flying, boss. Keep it up," Perry said.

Weapons launched in the chaos and hit debris before Mark could even register them on the overlay, his field of view filling with the fire and clouds of shrapnel. A wave hit the *Fafnir*, peppering the hull.

"I'm trying," Mark said, pushing the *Fafnir* for more speed.

The mercenary fighters pushed in, the three Peacemaker ships matching their firepower shot for shot. Unfortunately, neither could land clean hits. The debris field was just too chaotic.

"I'm registering heat blooms in the reactor and drive of that freighter, Mark," Netty said. "It looks like they're going to hightail it out of here."

He pulled the nose around until he was facing directly at the distant wreck of a space station and confirmed visually. The freighter was pulling away, and unfortunately, the heavy cruiser and several smaller attack boats were burning with it.

A missile abruptly streaked in from ahead of them, the weapon appearing too quickly for Mark, Netty, or Perry to react. The PDC tracked and fired but missed high as he wrenched the stick over, the bow thrusters firing hard. They rolled right and down in a desperate, last-second maneuver, then watched as the missile floated on by, as if it were out for a leisurely afternoon cruise.

"What, are we not good enough to blow up?" Perry stammered, then they turned to Tan at the same time. The Druzis sat in horrified shock, one hand held over one eye while the other clutched his console.

"Was that you?"

"I think so. Maybe. Actually, yes."

"The inner workings of the teenage Druzis mind, folks," Netty said.

"I flinched and covered the missile with the null field but didn't have time to inject a kill code. I-I-I froze."

"Well, it didn't appear to matter."

"The null field broke the target lock," Perry reasoned. "So, in a way, in the missile's eyes, we disappeared."

"Keep that up," Mark grunted as a larger ship bulled its way through the debris ahead.

"That's a frigate. Class eleven. Heavily armored," Netty said. "They've got a lock."

Missiles jumped from the attack boat before the AI could finish the sentence.

"Tan, give those birds the slip," Mark said.

"Smart. We'll need every round available for that cruiser," Perry agreed.

"Okay, I will—I will do so. Please cease yelling at me," the flustered Druzis yelled, manically typing at his screen.

"No one is yelling, princess," Perry muttered.

Mark rolled away from the bigger craft as the frigate's forward battery fired, a stream of laser blasts raking the side of the *Fafnir*. Tan yelped as half a dozen shots thudded against the hull, but the ablative armor held.

"I'm tired of people trying to put holes in my ship," Mark grated and rolled back toward the frigate.

"What are you doing? Fly away from them. Fly *away*," Tan gasped.

"Prey runs," he growled. Selecting the rotary cannon on his overlay, Mark grabbed the weapon's control stick, centered the reticle on the bigger boat, and squeezed the trigger.

The first shot boomed, with the second and third shots following suit. The big weapon picked up speed as its forty-five-millimeter Shatterstar rounds cycled through, spitting tracers into the dark. The first few shots missed low, but with his ears ringing, Mark walked the fire up and into the frigate.

The mercenary ship seemed to recognize the risk and banked away, only to take several rounds directly to its belly. Iridium shattered in a glittering shower, with the armor-piercing sabot rounds passing clean through its thick, plate armor. Half a dozen extra rounds walked up the hull, each leaving a glowing hole in its wake. The frigate was on the float, its marker lights and viewports dark, by the time the rotary cannon spooled down.

"Well, that works," Perry exclaimed, "but couldn't they make it louder? Why are my auditory input sensors buzzing?"

"You wanted teeth," Mark said. "Ja-Ra got us tusks instead."

"The freighter is running for it," Netty cut in. "It looks like there's a channel on the far side of the planet, below the ecliptic. That's their route out of here."

Mark jammed the throttle forward and turned the ship's nose to intercept. He navigated around another cloud of debris, leaving the frigate behind.

"Tell Valint and Drogo—"

"They drew the fighters to them, Mark. Right now, they're holding their own but are badly outnumbered and cut off."

"Then it's down to us. Hold on, you two."

"To take on a heavy cruiser by ourselves?" Perry asked, his voice rising an octave. "You must be sitting on some nice cards, Mark, or are you just feeling lucky?"

"We'll come up with something?"

"We will?" the bird asked.

Without pausing, Mark pushed the throttle forward again, painfully sucking in a breath as the pressure mounted on his chest. A moment later, the *Fafnir* broke from the debris cloud and rocketed out into the open. Decapolis loomed ahead, the massive fields of scorched ground now unmistakable. The burned, dead land bisected the largest continent, like a lasting scar.

Mark's overlay automatically zoomed in and locked onto the retreating ships, the cruiser and two frigates bracketing the freighter. Judging from the drive plumes, the heavily laden ship was pushing hard.

"Judging from their trajectory, I think they're going for a sling-shot. If they're successful, we will never catch them," Netty said.

"Then we can't let them get away."

Their PDC tracked and fired once, then twice, and hit a missile streaking in from the debris ring behind them. Another missile appeared, but his tactical map showed no pursuing ships.

"Netty, we've got missiles and the Invictus. See if you can't poke some holes in that freighter."

"You've got it, boss. Time to be a nuisance," Netty confirmed.

A single Firewing launched, with the laser humming its deadly tune. They scored a solid hit on the freighter before the escort ships could move to block them. Unfortunately, at their range, the laser shot was too dispersed to deal much damage. The frigates flipped and burned, launching missiles almost simultaneously.

"Tan, can you change those missiles' target data and have them target each other or the freighter?"

"Wouldn't that be nice?" He snorted. "But I doubt it. With them coming straight at us, and the emitter's limited range, I would never get the kill code uploaded in time. The best we can do is to hit them with the null field and promptly alter our course. That should send them flying right on by. But you'll need to be quick. Like really quick."

"Do it."

Mark burned after the freighter, the incoming missiles rocketing directly toward them.

"This feels counterintuitive, Tan—like I'm playing chicken with ship killers. Tell me when. Please."

"Yep."

"I feel like that request warranted more of a response than yep," Perry retorted.

"Yep," Tan echoed.

"Great. We're going to die with Wisconsin slang ringing in our ears," Mark said.

Perry leaned over. "We about ready, dontcha know?"

The cruiser came alive ahead, its PDCs looping strings of fire into the black, and with an almost inconsequential poof of light, their missile disappeared.

"Now," Tan shouted.

Mark nosed down and left, the incoming missiles burning by so close he could hear the rumble of their ion drives.

"*Damn* that was close. Think they scalded my feathers," Perry declared.

"And more coming in. Same thing, Tan," Mark said, watching the overlay. "Netty, please do something about those frigates."

"With pleasure."

The Invictus chattered and buzzed, sending potent bolts of energy ahead. The ship on the left launched countermeasures and tried to evade, but the first high intensity shot hit it squarely in the nose cone, blasting away the buffer shield. The next shot punched through, and the ship's atmosphere vented violently forward.

"We're lucky these Piraxians are trash pilots," Tan said. "Oh. Evade. Now!"

Mark jerked the stick right as Perry launched two missiles.

The second frigate rolled over, its PDC killing the first missile, only to have the second streak through unscathed. The gunship came apart in a cloud of expanding gas, fire, and debris.

"I'll give you credit, Tudor, there's no quit in you," Glass said, pushing in on comms. "But there's no way your little ship is going to stand up to the abuse. I have more armor and weapons. This is a battle of attrition, and we have more to sacrifice."

"You would be surprised. Sometimes quitting is the right move. Abandon the freighter, and I'll let you leave."

Glass's laughter was the only response, the sound fueling Mark's anger into a roaring inferno. He jammed the throttle all the way forward, the new drive slamming him back in the chair like a mountain had been dropped on top of him.

"They're dipping into the exosphere and gaining momentum. Even at full burn, we aren't going to be able to match pace for long. I hope you have a plan, Mark," Netty yelled.

"I have a plan, and I think you're going to hate it."

"Does it involve a high probability of our untimely and fiery deaths?" Perry asked. "Because if yes, then I would hate it."

"We're going to settle right into this big bastard's wake and ride on up under its belly. Then, if we're still alive, we'll hit that freighter with everything we've got and let the atmosphere do the rest."

"You're glossing over several small issues. Like first, they know we're here. These aren't complacent Salt Thieves, Mark."

"Then give me a clean avenue. Start picking off their point-defense weapons."

A laser blast hit the left, forward viewscreen, rocking the ship to the side and scorching the armored glass black. Tan screamed—the noise surprisingly high-pitched.

"It would seem Glass does not like that idea. We could not die and come back with an army," Perry spat.

"Keep Glass busy and use those teeth I finally got you."

"Yeah, she seems plenty busy slowly picking us apart."

The rotary cannon tracked and fired, the Invictus joining in, as a Firewing missile launched. Mark's ears were already ringing as a headache formed behind his eyes, but his goal was as clear as ever.

"Keep hitting it," Mark said, looping the *Fafnir* out and around a pair of streaking missiles. Tan didn't even have to tell him this time. He knew.

The Invictus fired as one missile launched, followed by another. Mark rolled left as the cruiser's PDCs opened up, their brain-rattling rotary cannon answering with fire of its own. Sabot rounds hit the larger ship, and a defensive placement disintegrated.

The ship started to vibrate as they dipped ever closer to the atmosphere, the planet's gravity adding surprising weight to the stick.

The *Fafnir* jumped and popped as several thirty-millimeter rounds skipped off the hull, followed by a blistering stream of laser shots. Fire seemed to come from every corner of the large ship, chasing every vector change he considered. The rotary cannon answered again, followed by the laser, their larger sabot rounds hitting the big ship and punching through another PDC.

"Tan, do you see that armored module on that fat tub's underside?" Perry asked.

"Yes."

"That's the primary sensor enclosure. Point our null field emitter right at that," the bird explained, then turned to Mark. "Don't hate me for saying this, but you're going to have to get even closer before that works."

"We just have to last long enough," he grunted, cursing as a full power laser blast hit somewhere on the top of the ship.

"Crap. I think that was our PDC. Closer, Mark. Closer! Now is not the time to be bashful about our ship's new reactor and drive. Don't spare the horses."

"Horses are just tractors with opinions," Netty recited.

"We're almost there," Tan whispered. "Just a little bit more."

Rounds hit the ship again and again, with smoke drifting lazily out to cloud the air, but Mark refused to flinch. And somehow, the *Fafnir* held together.

"Come on," he muttered.

"We might actually make it," Perry yelled. "Come on, little dragon."

The engine roared as he pushed it harder, and the gap shrunk ahead. And yet, the controls felt heavy and sluggish. Warning lights started to pop up on the forward control board a split second before a panel exploded in a shower of sparks. Half the cockpit lights went dark, and his overlay flickered.

A thruster malfunctioned, slewing the ship left, and the weapons abruptly stopped. The cruiser was still firing, spitting its bright, armor-piercing venom into space, only not at them. Mark looked left and found Tan clutching his console, his eyes wide.

"I got it. Holy shit. I *got* it."

The *Fafnir* slid into the cruiser's shadow, their velocity still increasing.

"What did you do, Tudor? What did you do?" Glass roared, her voice crackling over comms. Only half the speakers worked, and if the panel's flickering lights were any indication, it wasn't far behind them.

"Netty. You take the stick. You keep us here in their shadow, no matter what they do. Do not let them shake us loose," Mark said as the front of the ship appeared.

The freighter burned ahead, paint and bits of hull flaking off from the intense friction. The cruiser rolled, and Netty followed suit, the planet giving way to the black backdrop of space as his stomach flipped. Mark's hand flinched on the fire control stick, his index finger missing the button.

"Glass, have your freighter crew eject their cargo and we'll let them go."

"Never!"

"I'll turn that ship into plasma, you preening idiot. Do it *now*," Mark shouted into the comm, his hand shaking on the stick.

"You claim to serve justice and order but fire on us? I thought you fought for the innocent, the oppressed. You are false. False!" the mercenary hissed in return.

"Mark," Perry shouted.

"There is crew on that ship. People…"

"People prepared to kill hundreds of millions," Perry reminded him. "You can't save them, not in the way they need, but you can safeguard so many others. They won't hesitate with their finger on the trigger, and nor should you."

"Dammit to hell and back," Mark swore, as his finger hovered over the comms button. Then before he could stop himself, he mashed the trigger.

Their rocket pod erupted, and all sixty weapons streamed

forward. The first few hit the back of the freighter and popped, blowing chunks free from the drive cones.

"No! Stop it," Glass screamed.

The rocket barrage continued, the cloud of weapons pouring out and over the freighter and bathing it in fire. A transport container broke loose and tumbled free, before hitting the heavy cruiser with a terrifying boom. A large chunk of the ship broke free as it careened out of control.

Mark wasn't aware of grabbing the stick, but it was in his hand as the *Fafnir* fell out of the sky. He fought for control as the ship spun but only managed to slow the rotation. Above them, the freighter sagged in the atmosphere, and like a massive comet of ice and ore, broke apart and streaked down and around them in a thousand tendrils of fire.

A large chunk of burning debris appeared next to the ship, its surface surrounded in a halo of fire and heat. Mark fought for control as the hulk approached and finally managed to slow the *Fafnir*'s spin. He pulled the stick left and then right, the ship's limited aerodynamics taking over and helping him straighten out.

With the nose down, the rocky landscape loomed large in the scorched viewscreens, the fire-blackened mountains growing larger by the second. He fought the compulsion to look to his left, but after a long, heavy moment, he succumbed. The freighter rained toward the ground, the long, smokey trails like beautiful strokes of black paint against the blue canvas.

"We didn't have a choice," he muttered, trying to shake off the mounting grief pressing in all around him. "They didn't give us a choice."

EPILOGUE

MARK REMEMBERED MORE of the twist out to the Junkway than the first time, as their wounded ships struggled to twist the distance all in one shot. They'd left Decopolis behind, but unfortunately, he couldn't get the planet off his mind. Not even the low frequency effect would wash those recent events away.

"We will make it make sense, boss," Perry said, pulling his attention away from his overlay. The bird gave him a heavy nod and quietly returned to his work.

"How do you give needless death a semblance of—of purpose? Of meaning?" Mark asked, his voice soft and distant.

Perry shook his head but otherwise had no response.

Tan flitted erratically through three different emotions as he worked with Netty to repair battle damage to the ship. The Druzis slid effortlessly from disbelief to unguarded optimism, then seemed to plummet into inconsolable grief, and somehow, right back to the start again.

"I don't understand why they would do that. All they had to do was abandon their weapons, and we would have let them go. It doesn't make any sense. Why didn't they?" he asked, staring blankly at his wire crimpers.

Netty used reason and logic when she responded, showcasing an almost saintly level of patience and understanding. Mark gave them space as they worked, using the time and silence to sort out his own thoughts. The Guild was infected and shriveling into something unrecognizable, while colonized space fought to blind itself to anything of consequence. How was he supposed to clear his name and expose Gyl-Mareth? How could they shine light on the Piraxian massacre and enact necessary change? It all stacked up into an almost insurmountable mountain before him, and somehow, Mark had to scale it.

Valint and Drogo twisted in shortly after, the two powerful Peacemaker ships wearing their battle damage openly. The *Glorious Column of Benevolent Fire* was still venting atmosphere from micro-fissures in its hull, while the *Stormshadow* had dropped out of twist space four times during the trip.

Striker and Bunn did what they could en route but had taken several direct penetrating shots to the aft section, blowing out wiring relays and a reactor heat exchanger. Mark could see the damage from her comm video, as wires and smoke filled the background.

"We'll make it," Valint reassured him. "The *Stormshadow* has gotten me through worse."

They limped along, operating on the hope that Ja-Ra and his clan could put all the pieces back together in the right order. If there were enough pieces left to work with, that is.

"I want missiles spun up and ready. Netty, warm up all active scanners and keep them pinging. If there are Jackals lurking, I want to know about it," Mark said as the helix-shaped Junkway finally came into view.

They soared in close, carefully navigating the ships around the dangerous gravity and magnetic pockets. Fresh ice shards glittered in space all around them, hinting at a recent collision or asteroid strikes.

His overlay twitched and skewed as they approached the entrance to the underground tunnel system—the winding and twisting caves serving as the *Belle*'s hiding spot.

"How do we tell him? *Should* we tell him?" Mark asked.

"Ja-Ra told us everything he did because we were in a position to do something about it," Perry reasoned. "Forget about his connection to Mala, whether friendship or family. He knew she meant to hurt people and that bothered him."

"I was going to be straightforward and honest."

"I think that's the best option, boss. As usual, your instincts serve you well."

The *Fafnir*'s exterior floodlights clicked on as the tunnel turned, the space around them darkening. Then it opened into the large cavern, and Mark's stomach dropped. Floating chunks of detritus and ice hung in the space before them, and beyond. Where the *Belle of Antrades* should have been loomed a massive, jagged hole.

"Strange," Perry muttered, directing the ship's floodlights forward. "I distinctly remember leaving a relatively large spaceship filled with tiny aliens right here."

"Someone took out Tunis?" Tan asked.

Mark shook his head as he studied the debris, his gaze crawling to the exit on the other side of the chamber. Something large and round had departed recently, leaving a noticeable impression in the ice.

"It looks like Ja-Ra answered that question we were proposing, Perry. The *Belle of Antrades* is free."

"Why does that sound far more ominous than I think you intended, boss?"

"Because you're a cynical bird?"

"Good point."

"Um, not to interrupt your banter—because it's amazing to hear you two not moping for a change," Netty said, "but I'm picking up on an incredibly weak signal directly ahead."

"What kind of signal, Netty?"

"Unknown, but it is unrecognizable according to all registered languages and frequencies."

"Can you track its location and give me a visual cue on my overlay?"

"Done."

His screen updated, displaying a three-dimensional map of the large chamber. A pulsing red dot appeared in the far corner, ironically centered in the spot where the *Belle* previously sat, locked in the ice.

Mark pushed the throttle forward, easing the ship through the ice and debris. It clunked and banged off the hull, the *Fafnir* parting the flotsam to either side. He fired the bow thrusters as they entered the cavity, slowing their momentum, before bringing the ship to a halt barely two meters from the solid ice.

A large, perfectly round object projected from the gleaming surface, with several long, damaged antennas sticking out. Mark swiped at his overlay and shut off the floodlights, allowing darkness to sweep back in. Sure enough, strange greenish lights pulsed on the object, surging in time with the signal.

"What is it, bird?" he asked, unbuckling from his harness to stand. Perry fluttered to the ground and leapt up onto the forward instrument panel, eyes glowing with mischief.

"Nothing I've ever seen before," he said, turning to Mark. "You know, we really need to stop unearthing things we can't immediately explain."

"Unearthing? Are you suggesting we dig it the rest of the way out of the ice?"

"What a horrible idea," Perry said, hopping down. "But yes. Get your suit on. It's time for that most midwestern of hobbies."

"Physical labor?" Mark asked.

Perry spread his wings in apology. "Yes, boss. It's time to farm."

———

Amazon won't always tell you about the next release. To stay updated on this series, be sure to sign up for our spam-free email list at jnchaney.com.

Mark will return in FOUNDATIONS OF GLASS. Available on Amazon.

BACKYARD
STARSHIP
[WIKI]

CHARACTER PROFILES & ART
SETTING DESCRIPTIONS
ALIEN RACE DESCRIPTIONS
TERM DEFINITIONS
& MORE!

HEAD TO
BACKYARDSTARSHIP.WIKI

CONNECT WITH J.N. CHANEY

Don't miss out on these exclusive perks:

- Instant access to free short stories from series like *The Messenger*, *Starcaster*, and more.
- Receive email updates for new releases and other news.
- Get notified when we run special deals on books and audiobooks.

So, what are you waiting for? Enter your email address at the link below to stay in the loop.

https://www.jnchaney.com/peacemaker-wars-subscribe

CONNECT WITH TERRY MAGGERT

Check out his website

http://terrymaggert.com/

Connect on Facebook

https://www.facebook.com/terrymaggertbooks/

Follow him on Amazon

https://www.amazon.com/Terry-Maggert/e/B00EKN8RHG/

ABOUT THE AUTHORS

J. N. Chaney is a USA Today Bestselling author and has a Master's of Fine Arts in Creative Writing. He fancies himself quite the Super Mario Bros. fan. When he isn't writing or gaming, you can find him online at **www.jnchaney.com**.

He migrates often, but was last seen in Las Vegas, NV. Any sightings should be reported, as they are rare.

Terry Maggert is left-handed, likes dragons, coffee, waffles, running, and giraffes; order unimportant. He's also half of author Daniel Pierce, and half of the humor team at Cledus du Drizzle.

With thirty-one titles, he has something to thrill, entertain, or make you cringe in horror. Guaranteed.

Note: He doesn't sleep. But you sort of guessed that already.

Printed in Great Britain
by Amazon

36733357R00297